DEDIC

My debut novel is dedicated to my three sisters, Eilis, Jane and Marie, avid readers and writers themselves. And to my lovely brother, John—my childhood hero.

WITHDRAWN FROM STOCK

ACKNOWLEDGEMENTS

I am sincerely indebted to the following people and groups—

Jean Chapman: For your friendship, keen interest in my books and generosity with your time.

Margaret Kaine: Your constructive criticism and unfailing support, and above all your belief in me.

Lorraine Buckingham: Your invaluable guidance and friendship over many chats and cups of coffee.

Rosemary Hoggard: For your belief that I would one day become a published author.

Bead Roberts: For your help and constructive feedback.

Rosie Goodwin: You noticed the first spark and fanned the flame. Your unwavering slogan, 'You'll be next' so encouraging.

Lutterworth Writers' Group: Your guidance helped me to see my potential.

Just Write Group: For your invaluable support and feedback, that has helped me towards publication.

Romantic Novelists' Association: The New Writers' Scheme, and in particular the dedicated readers' who helped me to hone my craft and learn from my mistakes.
Leicester Writers' Club: Your diversity of opinions; and keen observations in spotting errors.

Peatling Magna Group: For your friendship and never failing interest and encouragement.

Tirgearr's Publisher, Kemberlee Shortland, super editor Christine McPherson and the Tirgearr Publishing team for making my dream come true.

My lovely husband Dennis for your quiet and uncomplaining patience, especially when meals are late. My children Samantha, Sharon and Jason for believing mum could do it. My wonderful grandchildren, especially my grandson James, for your insight and knowledge of football.

CHAPTER ONE

Dublin City, 25th March 1961

Sergeant McNally would never forget the pink icing sugar. It was the worst accident he had witnessed in the twenty years since he first joined the Garda Síochaná. If his doctor hadn't suggested walking as a healthy exercise, he would have taken the car and avoided Dock Road that day.

Most collisions just happen; usually during bad weather, when cars slide into one another. That wasn't the case here. It was dry, with a clear sky – ideal for a brisk walk. This was no accident. It appeared to him that the driver of the van, travelling from the docks at speed on the wrong side of the road, was intent on killing himself and anyone else he could take with him.

The van hit the black Morris Minor, the force sending the car spinning out of control into the path of oncoming traffic. Then all McNally could hear was the sound of crunching metal as the car collided with other vehicles causing a pile-up. The van overturned several times, while the car ended up on its side.

'Good God!' He was stunned at the magnitude of the scene as it unfolded before his eyes. Children cried; people screamed out for help.

***

McNally acted as fast as he could, alerting the ambulance services and relaying news of the crash to his colleagues at the station.

An eerie silence descended. Eyewitnesses looked at the pile-

1

up in horror, and the Dublin street came to a standstill. Car doors opened and those uninjured scrambled out. Some, bleeding from cuts and bruises, stood around in a daze.

'Help's on its way!' McNally shouted.

'Over here!' a man cried. 'The van driver's dead. Can someone check for injuries in the other cars?'

'I'm a doctor!' someone else called. 'This one's bad. The man at the wheel is dead.'

McNally climbed on top of what had once been a Morris Minor, but which now resembled a mound of compressed metal, and peered inside. Pink icing sugar splattered the shattered windscreen. 'God Almighty!' he cried. 'There's a child trapped in the back. I can see a tiny hand. *Glory be to God!*'

***

Oona and her sister laughed as they blew up coloured balloons for Jacqueline's fifth birthday party, placing them prettily around the room.

'This is hard work.' Sighing, Oona hooked her long dark hair behind her ears. 'I wish I'd asked Eamon to do all this and gone to fetch the birthday cake myself.'

'Oh, yes. Can you see our men making fairy cakes and arranging a table as pretty as this one?' Connie was perched at the top of the stepladder, tying pink balloons around the lampshade above the party table.

'Give over!' Oona handed her another balloon. 'Eamon wouldn't have a clue how to bake a cake.'

Oona Quinn was twenty-six, two years younger than her sister, and as dark as Connie was fair. A petite five feet two inches, with dark brown eyes and small slender hands, she worked part-time in a shipping office. Her husband had wanted her to be a stay-at-home mum, but she had won him round by telling him that it gave her a sense of importance to be contributing to the family income.

'Have you tried Mam's new teacake recipe yet?' Connie asked.

'Is it good?'

'Well, Dessie loves it. You soak the fruit overnight in cold tea. I'll bring you some over next time I bake one.'

'All this talk of food's making me hungry.' Oona clutched her stomach. 'Let's have a cup of tea and then we can finish blowing up the rest of the balloons.'

'I'd love a cup.' Connie stepped down from the ladder and followed her into the kitchen. 'Eamon's done a grand job on the extension.' She glanced around at the spacious kitchen with new Formica work surfaces and red cupboards.

Connie, a hairdresser, had been married to Dessie Flanagan for ten years, but they had no family. It made Oona realise how lucky she was to have two healthy children.

'It's made such a difference. Although it has taken up most of the back garden, I'd rather have the space inside. More room for the kids.' Marriage and children were all Oona had ever dreamt of, and after two years of being a single mother and all the heartache that came with it, she had married Eamon. He earned a good wage working for the Dublin Gas Company and, since the birth of Jacqueline five years ago, she'd felt complete.

'I wonder what Mam and Dad have bought Jacqueline this year.' Connie broke into her thoughts. 'They wouldn't tell me, no matter how hard I tried to worm it out of them.'

'I've no idea. But last year she ended up with three pushchairs and a doll.'

'I remember! By the way, is Sean playing football today?'

'Yes, he is. You'd never believe he was eleven years old, the fuss he kicked up this morning. And just because Eamon couldn't go with him.'

'Do you think he's a bit jealous of Jacqueline?'

'Don't know. But he'll be down later with Mam and Dad.' Oona placed some biscuits on a plate and poured the tea.

'I've got something for him that'll put a smile on his face,' said Connie. She would do anything for Oona's two children, and was always buying them treats.

'You spoil him.'

3

'Well,' Connie couldn't hide her sadness, 'who else can I spoil?'

'I'm sorry, Connie. Any luck yet?'

'It's not for the want of trying.' She picked up a biscuit. 'Oh, chocolate digestives; they're my favourite.'

'You're as bad as Jacqueline. She loves custard creams. I've made a strawberry jelly and Angel Delight, but I bet she won't eat anything, she'll be so excited.'

'The little pet. When does she start school?'

'We're not sure which one to enrol her in. We don't want her spirit broken.'

'Aren't you going to send her to St. Bridget's then?' Connie bit into her biscuit. 'I thought you'd already decided.'

'Well, Eamon thinks the nuns might be too harsh on her. She'd never sit still.' Oona sipped her tea. 'Remember how strict it was for us?'

'I do. But it didn't do us any harm.'

'Umm . . . I'm not so sure about that.' Oona recalled how Sister Catherine used to chase her around the classroom with a strap, for talking during prayers. 'Besides, if I put Jacqueline's name down for St. Mary's, I can drop them both off at the same time. What do you think?'

'Suppose it makes sense. Get plain biscuits next time; I can't leave these alone.'

After their brief break, the sisters went back to finish off the party room, singing along to Cliff Richard's 'Livin' Doll' on the radio.

'Well, that's that job done.' Oona released the last balloon and it whizzed noisily towards Connie, who playfully retaliated until they fell about laughing.

'What about records? What have you got?' Connie flicked through the labels. 'What about this one?' She plucked out 'Twenty Tiny Fingers' by Alma Cogan.

'She loves that. Oh, see if you can find the Happy Birthday one.' Oona danced a Highland fling to an Irish jig on the radio and Connie joined in. They linked arms and swung each other round until they were both dizzy. 'Will you look at the pair of us? We're worse than the kids are. Speaking of kids, have you thought any more about adoption?'

'Yeah, but Dessie wants to wait a bit longer. You know what he's like.' Connie sighed. 'But I wouldn't change him for the world.'

'I know what you mean. I can't imagine my life without Eamon.'

'Sure, he adores you and Jacqueline. And he's great with Sean.'

'That's true. Sean can be such a wilful child. Sometimes it can get me down, but Eamon has a way with him, and what's more, Sean listens to him.' Oona recalled the time Sean had run off into the crowds at the Royal Dublin Show. She had been frantic with worry until Eamon found him playing in the stables. Luckily, the animals had been on show at the time; she dreaded to think what might have happened otherwise. 'I don't know what Eamon's secret is but, of course, it helps that they both love football.'

'Don't talk to me about football. Dessie'd watch it all day if it were possible.'

'Bless us! Is that the time?' Oona glanced at the clock. 'The children will be here soon.' She wrapped coloured tissue paper around a small plastic doll for the game of pass the parcel. 'Don't forget to put a sweet between each wrapper.' She passed it to Connie, who stuck the final pieces of paper around the parcel, then hid it behind the sofa in the party room.

***

The sun had just come out, and McNally cursed the task ahead of him. The child's death had touched him deeply. At the station, he had seen tears in grown men's eyes. This was, by far, the hardest thing he had ever had to do.

He parked the car outside the house with the shiny green door and well-maintained garden, and walked slowly up the path. He hesitated. From inside he heard laughter and music, and it pained him to be the bearer of such shocking news. A

5

lump formed in his throat. He removed his hat and held it in front of him, before knocking on the door.

'Mrs.. Quinn?'

Oona stared at the uniformed man on her doorstep. 'That . . . that's me.' She clutched the door. 'Has . . . has something happened?'

'I'm Sergeant McNally. There's been an accident. May I come in?'

Connie joined her in the hall, the smile slipping from her face.

'Are you a relative?' he asked.

'We're sisters. What is it?'

He thought Oona was going to faint but her sister's hand guided her towards the living room. A moment later, the two women sat on the sofa clutching hands.

'May I sit down?'

Oona nodded. She was trembling. McNally could see a glimmer of hope in her big brown eyes.

'I'm afraid your husband's been in a serious accident, Mrs.. Quinn.' He saw all her fears encapsulated in that one terrible moment as he delivered the news.

'Please, tell me he's not dead.'

He swallowed, barely able to answer, and then he nodded.

'No. No. Please don't tell me that. Dear God! Eamon can't be dead. You've made some mistake. Are . . . are you . . . sure it's my husband?'

'We found his driving licence.' He gripped his hat. How could he tell her about the little girl?

'My little girl! What about Jacqueline?' she cried out. 'Where is she? She'll be frightened. I must go to her.'

'I'm afraid there was nothing we could do, Mrs.. Quinn. It all happened so fast.'

'God! No! Not my little girl! Not Jacqueline!' She was shaking hysterically. 'Connie! Tell him; tell the Sergeant he's got it wrong. Please, Connie.'

'They're not, not both of them,' Connie pleaded, her face distraught.

'Everything that could possibly be done was done at the scene. A drunk driver coming off the boat caused the crash. He's dead, too. I'm afraid I was a witness. I've spoken to a number of other eye witnesses who saw the white van veering erratically before hitting your husband's car.' He swallowed again. 'There was nothing your husband could have done, Mrs. Quinn. I'm so sorry. If it's any consolation at all, they were both killed instantly.'

'God Almighty! No! No!' Oona rocked back and forth. Her breath was coming in huge spasmodic lurches as if her chest was about to explode. He had seen people grieving before, but to lose a child . . . He wished this was all a dream and that he hadn't been a witness. He sat with his head bowed, turning his hat round and round in his hands.

Oona stood up, shaking uncontrollably. Before he could do anything, she collapsed onto the floor.

McNally rushed towards her. 'If you have any brandy in the house, bring it,' he told Connie.

When she came back, Oona was sitting up, supported by the Sergeant. Connie handed him the tumbler.

'Try and sip this.' He held the gold liquid to Oona's lips. 'You've had a terrible shock.'

She took a small amount and wrinkled her nose. It made her cough. She struggled to stand up. 'I, I should . . . I should be with them. We must hurry.'

Connie's face was full of concern. 'We're going now, Oona,' Connie said, scribbling a note for their parents and sealing it in an envelope. The note simply said:

Mam and Dad,
There has been an accident. We've gone to the City Hospital. Please hurry,
Dad! Don't bring Sean.
Connie

McNally shook his head. 'I'm so sorry, Mrs. Quinn. So sorry.' He helped her into her coat. He could see she was in shock and his heart went out to her. How could anyone come to terms with such a loss? Tears streaming down her face, Connie placed a supportive arm around her distraught sister's shoulders.

'I should never have let Jacqueline go, Connie. How can life be so cruel? Eamon! Jacqueline!' she wailed. 'Oh, Jacqueline, my baby!'

McNally, his face grave, led both women to the car and drove off towards the city.

CHAPTER TWO

In the weeks to follow, Oona suffered from severe panic attacks and had to be sedated. The tragedy of the deaths, especially that of a young child, had made headline news for days – the gruesome facts so detailed that her father, James O'Hara, refused to allow a newspaper anywhere near the house. More than once he had chased away a fresh-faced reporter looking for a story on how the widow was coping. At times Oona's mind was so fragile she had clung to Sean as though she would never let go, refusing to allow him out of her sight.

The medication numbed her pain, and in that zombie-like state she felt herself fading away into nothingness. Each time the fog cleared from her mind, the pain was so great she wanted to die. The last glimpse of her baby girl and her husband lying side by side in the morgue had given her nightmares, their bodies bruised and broken beyond recognition. Thoughts of never seeing them again caused her to cry out in agony.

On the day of the funeral everywhere was unnaturally quiet, and neighbours came to pay their respects to the family. A large crowd of sympathetic mourners lined the street to watch the funeral cortège as it passed over the bridge towards the church.

Dazed and bewildered, Oona and Sean were supported by their family. Sean's determination not to cry in public gave her strength as he sat next to her in the packed church. After the inevitable outpouring of compassion from the parish priest, neighbours and friends, Oona felt numb.

Throughout this terrible period, Connie rarely left her side. Although there were a few times when she witnessed her

9

parents' grief, they managed to stay amazingly strong in helping her through her terrible loss. They were there when nothing on earth, not even the fact that she still had a son who needed her, could entice her to get out of bed. It was thanks to them she had survived this far.

Each day she opened her eyes, red from crying, convinced her heart would never mend. Each day she told herself that if she was ever to get through this, she had to endure one day at a time.

Weeks passed before she even noticed Sean's sullen behaviour and, although she did her best to reassure him, she sensed him closing up and drifting away from her. It made her all the more mindful of how much they had both lost. She had to pull herself together for Sean's sake; no matter how difficult that might prove. But each time she considered returning to work, it brought on an attack of nerves. Sobs choked in her throat when she recalled how her husband had wanted her to give up working. Now her only choice was to hope that her miserly employer would take her on full time.

***

Stepping back inside the drab office did nothing to uplift her. The walls were stained with nicotine and covered in drawings, cobwebs clinging to the high ceiling. The tightly shut windows, thick with grime from years of neglect, blocked out the sunlight and made her feel claustrophobic.

The eccentric couple who ran the Dublin shipping office where Oona worked, readily agreed to her request to work full-time. Yet, even with her mother's help with Sean, she would have to work nine hours a day, making every penny count, until the boy was old enough to make his own way in the world.

'I think you're really brave, so I do,' said Brenda, the office junior. 'It must have been *awful* for you. My ma said she'd never ge' over it, if anything like that was to happen to our family.' An innocent remark, but nevertheless Oona felt again the terrible ache in the pit of her stomach. The last thing she wanted was to become emotional on her first day back at work. She closed her eyes in an attempt to block out the pain, silently praying she would find the strength to get through the day.

The door opened, and Mrs. Kovac hurried in. 'Vhen do you vant to commence your new hours, Mrs. Quinn?' It was a stark reminder to Oona that life must go on.

'Immediately, if that's all right.' With the house to pay for each month and mounting bills, the situation she now found herself in worried her more than she cared to admit.

'I'll sort it out straight avay.' She unlocked the filing cabinet as if it contained the crown jewels. Oona was grateful that the woman made no reference to her tragic loss. She had no idea if the Kovacs had a family; it wasn't the sort of thing they were likely to discuss with the staff. The woman's pink fluorescent dress, canary-yellow cardigan and red woollen stockings accentuated her peculiarity as she walked from the office clutching a buff-coloured folder.

'She must be colour blind,' Brenda said, when the middle-aged woman left.

Oona wondered the same thing. Although Olga Kovac's fashion sense was the last thing on her mind, it briefly transported her outside the turmoil going on inside her own head. The Kovacs had arrived in Ireland from Czechoslovakia as agents for Worldwide Shipping, operating from a shabby tenement block in the city. Although they spoke fairly good English, they reverted to their own language when disagreements erupted between them.

The humidity of the office made it impossible for Oona to concentrate and, after many mistakes, she wondered if she had been naive in assuming she was ready to return to work. Removing her cardigan, she blew out her lips.

'I like your dress,' Brenda said. 'Black's my favourite colour.'

'Is it?' Oona said, thinking that she would never wear a bright colour again. 'Has he said anything about getting a fan fitted?'

11

Brenda's eyes widened. 'Are you coddin'?'

'I can't work in this stuffy atmosphere.' She got up and propped open the door.

'Sure, I'll make you a cup of tea.'

'Thanks, Brenda. Don't go getting into trouble on my account, though. You know how strict he is about us making tea before elevenses.'

'Sure, he's been grand lately. Honest to God, he has, Oona.'

'That old grump knows which side his bread's buttered on.' Oona knew very well how contrary he could be; arrogant, without a shred of remorse for the way he treated his staff. She had stood up to him on many occasions, which was probably why she'd lasted longer than her predecessors. She had even told him on one occasion that, with her qualifications, she did not intend to put up with his foul temper. That seemed to work, because from then on he had been careful how he addressed her.

True to form, that afternoon Mr. Kovac reverted to his old familiar ways. Shuffling into the office, belly protruding above his trouser belt, grey hair sprouting from his ears and his spectacles perched on the end of his nose, he barked, 'Get me Mr. Frazer at the Dublin Steam Packet Company.' He stood over Brenda, irritatingly tapping his fat fingers on the back of her chair.

The young girl flushed and her hands trembled as she fumbled through the phone book.

'You stupid girl! It von't be in there! Vhat have you done vith it?' he yelled.

He snatched the directory from her and threw it to the floor, stamping his feet in a childish tantrum. Oona was on her feet, her pulse racing. But, before she could say anything, his wife hurried to his side.

'Careful, Josef, your blood pressure. Don't forget vhat the doctor said.' Taking her husband's arm, she led him, still grumbling, back to their office and closed the door behind them.

Brenda burst into tears. Oona mentally counted to ten and dialled directory enquiries. Using a biro and the back of her hand, she wrote down the new number. She ripped a page from her notebook and scribbled down Mr. Frazer's number. In a defiant mood, she marched into her employers' office and threw the piece of paper on the desk.

Surprised faces glared up at her. Smoke from a smouldering cigarette swirled upwards from an overflowing ashtray. It caught the back of her throat, making her cough. Without speaking, she went back to comfort the sobbing Brenda.

***

By the time Oona had finished work for the day, she was exhausted but her mind gave her no peace. It had been a glorious day for April and the sun cast a kaleidoscope of crimson and yellow across the evening sky. She paused briefly on the bridge, noisy with passing traffic, and untied her hair, letting it fall to her shoulders. Then she turned her face towards the cool breeze that blew up from the river. Eamon had proposed to her on this bridge; that, and wanting to be near to her parents, were the reasons they had decided to live here.

A row of houses faced onto the river, including the one where she now lived alone with her son. She felt overwhelmed with sadness. This evening, if the opportunity allowed, she would speak to her father about Sean's unsettling behaviour. The change in him startled her – after two weeks back at school, he was playing truant. She had tried being patient, to give him time to heal, as she'd heard it said that grief affects people in different ways. She recalled the moment she had told him the shocking news, when he had cried openly in her arms. They had clung to one another, as if their world had ended. After that, his gradual coolness puzzled her.

Now she could see him in the lane playing with his friends and she raised her hand in greeting; he did not respond. Even after his friend nudged him and gave her a friendly nod himself, Sean continued to dribble his football further down the lane. The snub shocked her deeply, making her feel quite trembly, and she needed to catch her breath before going into her parents' house.

James O'Hara came in from the back yard, unbuttoning the collar of his shirt. 'This nice weather will hardly last. Here, sit yourself down.' He pulled out a chair from underneath the kitchen table. Weary now, she collapsed into it.

'How did you get on, love? It can't have been easy having to work a full day on your first day back.'

'I have to get used to it, Dad,' she shrugged, her mind consumed with Sean's uncaring attitude moments earlier.

'Ah. Well, I'll just make you a cup o' me special brew.' He filled the kettle and switched it on.

She was conscious he was treading as if on thin ice around her, and at times she could hardly bear to see the pain that reflected in his eyes. After all he had done to support her over the years – her mother too – she felt guilty to be worrying them again. 'Where's Mam?'

'She's just nipped over to Connie's. Sure, she won't be long, so she won't.' He placed the tea on the table in front of her and sat down. 'It's got something to do with a new football for Sean. You know how your sister loves to spoil him.' He forced a smile.

James O'Hara worked at the local bakery, so the family never went short of bread except during a strike. And even then, he always managed to bring home a loaf or two. He ran his hand distractedly down one side of his thin face and glanced at his daughter.

'You look tired, love.'

'I'm *fine*,' she barked. 'I'm . . . I'm sorry, Dad. I didn't mean to snap. Sean deliberately ignored me outside just now. I can't work out what's eatin' him.'

'He's a kid. It's only been a few weeks; such a terrible blow to him.' A sad smile played on his lips.

Her dad was right. Four weeks and four days, to be precise. It did not excuse her son's behaviour. 'Oh, Dad,' she cried, covering her face with her hands. 'I can't *bear* it. I can't. Living without Eamon and little Jacqueline is—' she broke off. 'It's torture, without Sean being...'

Her father stood up and hugged her to him, stroking her long hair as he had often done when she was a child. Sobbing, she buried her head in his chest.

When she calmed down, he drew away and straightened his shoulders. 'It's hardly believable that such a thing could have happened.' His voice cracked.

'I wish I could . . . If only I'd—'

'Sure it was an accident, love! Nothing you could have done.' He shook his head.

She sipped her tea. No-one could make tea like her dad. She was grateful that she had her family to confide in. 'If only Sean would talk to me,' she said. 'You know, Dad, sometimes it feels like I'm going out of my mind. I keep asking myself if there's anything more I can do to make him feel secure again.'

'Don't torment yourself, love.' He patted her hand. 'You're doing a grand job, so you are.' He sucked in his breath, and pushed aside a strand of wiry grey hair. 'Have you heard from the insurance people yet? The money would pay for a change of scenery for you both.'

She shook her head. 'No. It could take months, Dad. I can't consider going away, though. I have to work,' she stressed. 'Anyway, a holiday wouldn't help, and without Eamon and Jac—' She stopped, recalling the holiday that Eamon had been planning for them at Butlin's holiday camp later in the year. Now it seemed like she had only dreamt it.

'Well, God knows, you could do with the money,' he sighed. 'If only they'd stop shilly-shallying. They know full well who's to blame for the deaths of two precious people.'

'Oh, Dad,' she choked back another sob. 'I miss them so much.'

'I know. We all feel for you, love. It's not easy.'

'Does Sean ever, you know,' she hesitated, 'talk about his daddy or Jacqueline?'

'No. However, he can be a bit surly at times. We make allowances. Give him a bit more time.' He winked. 'Now, try not to worry.' He leant over and hugged her.

'Thanks, Dad. I don't know what we'd have done without you both.' She forced a smile.

'That's what families are for. How about another brew?' he said, as Sean sauntered in. Clumsily kicking the leg of the table, he flopped down on one of the chairs. 'Hey, watch it, boy, you nearly had that jug over,' his grandfather joked.

'Didn't,' he scowled.

Oona glared at him. 'Watch your manners.' She felt like shaking him in the hope it would bring him to his senses. 'And why did you ignore me in front of your friends, Sean?'

'Don't know,' he shrugged sulkily.

'There must be a *reason*,' his grandfather said.

'It's nuttin', Grandad.' He clenched his fists on the table in front of him, showing white knuckles. 'I'm thirsty. Can I have a drink of milk?'

'What have I just told you about your manners, young man?' Oona glanced at her father and her insides tightened. The boy did not reply. 'Don't I get a kiss?' She reached out.

With a brazen look, he shook his head. 'I'm too old for all that stuff.'

'Since when?' He lowered his head. 'Well, how was school then?'

'Every day you ask me that. You weren't like this when me—' he broke off.

'And you never played truant when your dad was here.' In the silence that followed, Oona struggled to curb her frustration. She picked her words carefully. 'Why are you shutting me out, Sean? We were so close not that long ago. Talk to me!'

'No. I won't ever again,' he yelled, jumping up from the table and knocking over the glass of milk his grandfather had put down in front of him. 'It's all your fault!'

'*My fault?*' They were all on their feet now, the milk streaming from the table.

'No! My God, Sean. What are you saying?' Her face paled. It was the last thing she had expected to hear from her son, and she gripped the back of the chair to steady herself.

'*God's truth, Sean!* Have you taken leave of your senses?' His grandfather took him firmly by the shoulders. 'You'd better apologise straight away, or you and I are going to have a serious falling out.'

'*Won't.*' Averting his face, he clenched his hands in front of him. 'And I'm not going home with her either, Grandad. I'm staying here!'

Her heart hammered against her chest, and she could barely comprehend the scene unfolding in front of her. 'You're coming home with me, young man, and you and I are going to—'

He pushed past her, knocking her off-balance, and stomped his way upstairs like an elephant. The bang of the bedroom door made them both shudder.

Her father placed a comforting arm around her shoulder. 'I had no idea!'

CHAPTER THREE

Oona's mind churned with a mixture of emotions as she scribbled a note of apology to her boss. After the telephone call from her son's headmaster, she had been left with no option but to abandon her post. The Kovacs were at lunch and she dreaded what would happen once they returned to find her missing, but right now Sean was all she could think about. She could not get to the school quickly enough.

'What if Grumpy gets back before you? What will I tell 'im?' Brenda cried. It was their nickname for the boss when they were sure he was out of earshot.

'I'm sorry, Brenda. I have to go. I'll be as quick as I can.' She pulled on her coat and rushed from the office. The Kovacs would no doubt insist she should have waited for them to return. They would never understand her irrational behaviour where her son was concerned, and would be quite within their rights to treat her misdemeanour as a sacking offence. She felt guilty for leaving Brenda to Mr. Kovac's tyranny, but decided to face the consequences of her actions later.

The roar of the traffic made her head ache as she hurried along the pavement towards the bus stop. People hurried past and life went on, but Oona felt hers had truly ended.

Foolishly she had assumed that her love, together with constant reassurance from the family, would be enough to help heal Sean's pain. She had been shocked to discover that deep down he was struggling with his own demons. Sean playing truant, and his disruptive behaviour, was tearing her apart. She couldn't take much more. It was only a week since she had last been at the school to discuss him. Confusion scrambled her mind as she tried to work out what might have happened this time.

Pausing to catch her breath, she knocked on the headmaster's door. Her stomach tightened.

Mr. Mulvane glanced at her over his thick-rimmed spectacles. 'I'm sorry to have taken you away from your work *again*,' he said, 'but I'm afraid...' he cleared his throat, 'shall we say that Sean is heading for expulsion if he continues to misbehave. The cane has little effect on him, and it grieved me to have to use it.'

Her heart sank. 'What's happened? What's he done now?'

'I know this is distressing for you, Mrs. Quinn, but there's been another altercation in the playground. This time it has resulted in a bloody nose for the O'Neill boy.'

'Oh, dear God, no.' She sighed. 'What with the truancy and now this.'

'That is why I called you.' He paused. 'Your loss was a terrible shock to us here at St. Joseph's, and the school is very much aware of Sean's vulnerability. His behaviour is so out of character that I feel now might be the right time to consider letting him talk to someone; someone trained to deal with children suffering bereavement.' He clasped his hands in front of him. 'To lose a father and sister at Sean's tender age is as tragic as it gets.'

'Do you think it would help?' she asked. 'Sean's not the kind of child to open up to a stranger.' Tears collected in her eyes. 'He closes up, and it's difficult to know what's going on inside his head,' she confided.

'I can't begin to imagine the pain you're going through, and believe me...' He shook his head, 'if I could have spared you this, I would have, but the longer it goes on the harder the pattern will be to break. Exclusion from school would also mean that he would be ruled out of the football team.' Mr. Mulvane set his lips. 'From what I've heard, that's why the boys were fighting.'

'It doesn't make sense.' Oona twisted her hands nervously.

'Have you spoken to Sean? I'm sure—'

'Yes, I have,' Mr. Mulvane interjected. 'And he refused to explain his actions.'

'I'll talk to him. Please give him another chance. Playing on the team helps him to stay focused.'

'Don't misunderstand me, Mrs. Quinn. I'm not insensitive; indeed, quite the contrary.' He cleared his throat. 'The city of Dublin, and indeed the whole country, is becoming more volatile. Within our schools we are experiencing children traumatised in various ways. Some have benefited from talking to someone outside the family.'

'Well, to be honest, I'm at my wits' end.'

'If you like, I could have a word with Father Michael. He visits the school once a week, and he's good with the lads.' His suggestion gave her new hope.

'Anything would be better than the way things are at present.'

He stood up. 'Let's see how things develop when you've had a chance to speak to Sean.'

She nodded. 'I'm grateful for your patience, Mr. Mulvane. Can I see Sean for a few minutes?' Her insides were tight with worry.

'My advice would be to leave it until he comes home from school,' the headmaster said. 'Thank you for coming in, Mrs. Quinn.'

***

That evening Oona was relieved when Sean walked home with her without having to be asked twice. She had decided to wait until they were alone before confronting him about the trouble at school.

He threw his school satchel into the hall, while Oona went into the living room where she kicked off her shoes and sank down onto the sofa.

'When will tea be ready?' Sean called from the hall.

'Come in here. There's something we need to talk about

first.' He stood by the door. 'No, over here,' she said, patting the sofa.

He slouched down in a chair as far away from her as he could, and her sigh was audible.

'Firstly, you can tell me what happened at school today. Mr. Mulvane telephoned me at work again, and I narrowly missed getting the sack.' She paused, willing him to offer some explanation. He said nothing.

She stood up. 'Sean, do you realise what it would mean if I were to lose my job? This has got to stop. I can't take much more.' Exasperated, she sat down again.

He hung his head. 'I, I'm sorry, Mam.'

'Talk to me. What happened?'

'O'Neill's been takin' digs at me for days.'

'It's just one thing after another. Why didn't you walk away?'

'Because, he said I wouldn't get into the leagues because I didn't have a dad to coach me. I just got mad and hit him.' Instinctively she wanted to hug him, tell him that everything would be all right. Before she got the chance, he jumped up.

'Now can I get something to eat? I'm hungry.'

'Sit down, Sean. Okay, so it was a cruel thing to say. You know what O'Neill's like. That's why he's never picked to play. Can't you see, son? All this bad behaviour is putting your own chances in jeopardy.'

'So? Why should I care?' He snivelled, dashing a tear away with the back of his hand.

Oona felt his pain as intensely as her own. She placed her arms around him. He shrugged her away.

'You should care,' she snapped. 'You're good, one of the school's best players. What would your daddy say if you were to give up the game you love? If you won't do it for me, then do it for Daddy and Jacqueline.' Mentioning their names like that brought a lump to her throat. And she saw a tear glisten in Sean's eyes too, before he turned his head away.

She wanted to tell him again how much she loved him, had

done from the day he was born, but she couldn't trust herself not to explode into tears that might never stop. 'Mr. Mulvane suggested it might help if you were to talk to Father Michael, you know, about what happened. How would you feel about that?'

'Don't know,' he muttered and slunk from the room, leaving Oona feeling empty and wondering if she had said the wrong thing once again.

***

Sean could not get to his room fast enough. No longer hungry, he turned up the volume on his radio to full blast. It helped him to cope with the horrible feelings inside him. He threw himself across the bed and pounded his pillow, letting his anger spill out in heaving sobs. All he could think about was that he would never see his dad again. One day he was here and the next . . . Now he didn't care about school or anything. This is all her fault, he sniffed. If his dad had been at the football field that morning, he would still be alive.

Why did my dad and sister have to die? He never expected to have an awful feeling in his stomach every time he thought about them. O'Neill still had his dad. It wasn't fair. Sean loved his grandad, but it was not the same. He couldn't do the things his dad could, like heading the ball, playing rough and tumble, and tackling him to the ground. His dad had been fun and Sean remembered how happy he had been when they'd come home after a game, caked in mud. Mam had complained at first, but when Dad told her what had happened, the three of them laughed. Now, everything was different.

O'Neill was right. You were nobody without a dad. Now he was sure he would never laugh again. He cried some more, wondering when it would stop hurting.

He could hear his mother calling him for tea. He blew his nose and dried his eyes. He would never let her see he had been crying like a baby. Rolling off his bed, he sauntered downstairs.

***

The following day, as Oona returned home with Sean, she lingered on the garden path to catch the last remnants of the summer evening. It was the first time in ages that she had bothered to look closely at the flowers. The heat of the day's sun had brought out their scent and the smell was intoxicating.

'Look at the roses, Sean. They smell wonderful.' She paused to press her nose close to the delicate pink petals.

Sean gave the garden a cursory glance. 'They were like that when Dad entered them in the horticultural show.'

'That's right, they were,' she said, surprised that he had remembered. Suddenly she felt the urge to do some gardening. 'Would you like to help me tidy it up a bit, Sean?'

'I've homework to finish,' he said, going inside the house.

At one time he would have jumped at the chance to trim the hedge; he had loved helping Eamon to plant flowers and shrubs in the wide borders on either side of the lawn.

She walked into the centre of the lawn to examine the small apple tree that Eamon had planted when Jacqueline was born. She reached out, gently touching the soft green foliage. There was no reason to assume that this young tree would not flourish and grow to its full size. It was what she had dreamed of for her young daughter – to grow up, fall in love as she had done, get married and have a family.

After working her way around the garden, pulling up weeds and tidying the borders, Oona went inside. She used to love this time of the day when Eamon was here to greet her and take her in his arms. She climbed the stairs wearily and was about to look in on Sean when she heard him sobbing. The beat of her heart quickened. She rushed into his room. He was sitting in his blue stripey pyjamas with his back towards her, his head bent over a photograph, his shoulders shaking.

'Sean, what's the matter?' It was the first time she had seen him cry since just before the funeral.

Startled, he turned round. 'Nuttin'.' His eyes were red, and he wiped his nose with the back of his hand. He pushed the photo into his drawer and jumped into bed.

'Sean, sweetheart, I, can I..?'

He lay half on top of the blue silky eiderdown and, turning onto his side, hid his face with his hands. 'Go away,' he mumbled.

'It's okay, sweetheart. It's all right to cry.' She sat down on the bed, and his textbooks slid off onto the floor. She smoothed the hair sticking up on the back of his head. 'You know, grown-ups cry, too. I know how much you miss your dad and Jacqueline. So do I.' He didn't speak. Swallowing a lump that kept forming in her throat, she stayed motionless, looking down at her only remaining child. He had Vinnie Kelly's sandy hair and she prayed God that that was all he had inherited.

If he were to discover that Eamon was not his real father, it would destroy him – and her, too. If only she had gone along with her husband's suggestion to tell him the truth. Instead, she had followed her mother's advice and left well alone.

When she was sure he was asleep, she gently lifted his legs and placed them beneath the bed covers. Flexing her tired shoulders, she opened the drawer and drew out the photo of Eamon, with Sean, aged three, on his shoulders; both of them smiling happily. A sob caught in her throat.

Sean had only been two when she had met Eamon. He had been such a good father to him, treating him no differently than he did Jacqueline. Tears overwhelmed her. She put the photo back, switched off the lamp and quietly left the room.

CHAPTER FOUR

On Saturday, there was only one thing on Oona's mind as she hurried towards Bewley's café, where she had arranged to meet Connie. Her sister had been a constant source of comfort and support in the days following the accident, when she could barely distinguish night from day. Connie had cried with her for days over the enormity of their loss.

As Oona approached the café, the aroma of freshly ground coffee wafted through the door. The delicious smell of freshly filled sandwiches and cream buns, displayed along the counter, revived her waning appetite.

It was midday and excited chatter reverberated around the establishment's stained-glass windows and high ceiling. Connie stood up and beckoned her to a table near the back.

'I need to talk to you, Connie.' Oona removed her jacket and sat down.

'What's wrong? Is it Sean?'

'Yes, I'm afraid so.'

The server placed the coffee and iced buns down in front of them.

Oona took a sip of her coffee. 'I'm trying to stay positive, Connie. But things are going from bad to worse.'

Connie arched her eyebrows. 'What's he been up to this time?'

'He gave the O'Neill boy a bloody nose.'

'Did you ask him why?'

'He was poking fun at Sean, about his dad not being around to coach him for next season's matches.'

'Oh, the poor kid! Children can be cruel.' Connie bit into her bun, licking the cream from the corner of her mouth. 'It can't be easy for him.'

Oona picked at the icing on her cake. 'If only he'd talk to me. I feel so isolated when he shuts me out.' Leaning her head to one side, she cupped her face in her hand. 'Do you think it might help if I got him to see someone?'

'With none of my own, who am I to advise?' Connie sighed. 'But if he were mine, then, yes, I would consider it.' She touched her new hairdo. 'Who did you have in mind? Do you mean a priest, or someone like that?'

'Mr. Mulvane suggested the school chaplain.'

'What harm can it do, if Sean's willing? There's a new American priest, Father Gabriel at Sandymount Church. I've heard he's quite liberal and easy to talk to.' She bit her lip. 'Maybe you . . . I mean, it wouldn't hurt to have a word with him yourself.'

'Well, one thing's for sure, Connie, I can't leave things the way they are. I'll talk to Mam and Dad, see what they think.'

'You know what Mam's like. She thinks troubles are best kept within the family. You must do what you feel is right for Sean. And if there's anything that Dessie and I can do, you've only to ask.'

'You've both done so much already.' Oona pulled on a strand of her long hair. 'I should have protected him. I thought he was coping, but now . . .' She sipped her coffee, relieving a lump in her throat. 'I feel such a failure.'

'You're no such thing. In fact, you're a wonderful mother.' Connie reached across the table. 'Why don't you let Dessie and me have Sean for a few days? It's a while now since he stayed, and you know we love having him.'

Oona pushed her plate to one side. 'With everything that's going on, I'm not sure it would be a good idea right now. Besides, what would I do?'

'Sure, you have enough to do concentrating on that job of yours. And there's the garden to do. Mam said you enjoyed it the other day.'

'I'll think about it.'

Disappointed, Connie sat back in her chair.

Sean and Jacqueline had spent many a night with Connie and Dessie when Eamon had taken her out for the evening. Now, thoughts of losing Sean's affections to anyone else, even to her own sister, filled Oona with fear. Refusing Connie's simple request left her feeling selfish and miserable, but she needed to keep Sean close; it was the only way she could stop herself from going insane.

'I understand,' Connie said kindly. 'Do you think you went back to the house too soon? It's bound to make you sad. And who knows what's going on inside Sean's head? He's too young to understand such a big loss.'

'Yes. You're probably right.' She twisted her wedding ring. 'I'm beginning to realise that now more than ever.'

'But it'll get easier, and we're here for you, no matter how long it takes.' Connie smiled.

'Thanks, Connie. I feel better now we've had a chat.'

'Oh good, because Dessie's taking us dancing at the Olympia Ballroom tonight and I don't want any excuses, Oona Quinn. We haven't been out for ages.'

Oona sighed. This was not the first time her sister had tried to cajole her into going out, but she didn't feel ready for anything yet. Anyway, she would feel like a gooseberry without Eamon.

'Go on, Sis, you need to get out and meet people. You don't have to put on a brave face with us.' With Oona showing no enthusiasm, Connie's smile faded.

'Maybe another time.' How could she consider leaving Sean the way things were? She glanced at her watch. 'Have you any shopping to do, Connie?'

'No, have you?'

'Just some flowers for the graves tomorrow.'

They went outside and moved along the busy street to the florist's.

'Does Sean still go with you?'

'Sometimes, although I doubt he'll want to come with me tomorrow.' She bought two neat sprays of Spring flowers, and then continued towards the bus stop.

'It can't be healthy, you know. The number of times you go up there.' Immediately regretting her choice of words, Connie clapped her hand over her mouth. 'I'm sorry. I shouldn't have said that.'

'I know you mean well,' Oona climbed onto the bus ahead of her sister.

How could she tell Connie that each evening as darkness fell, she could hardly contain the strong urge to rush off to the cemetery and cover the newly-dug pile of earth with a blanket to keep her little girl warm?

CHAPTER FIVE

After a weekend fraught with anxiety, Oona changed her mind and Sean went to stay with Connie and Dessie without giving his mother so much as a backward glance. Her mother said it was because he was growing up and did not want fussing over. Oona wasn't convinced though; her son's nonchalant attitude cut her to the core and had kept her awake for most of the night.

On Monday morning, Brenda's face brightened when Oona walked into the office.

'What kind of mood's he in?' she asked, slipping off her coat.

'Orrible! 'e's been givin' out since he arrived. I'm keeping out of his way,' Brenda pouted as she opened the mail. There was a stack of letters, advice notes and documents on Oona's desk and, with a heavy sigh, she uncovered her typewriter. She was not looking forward to being cooped up in a stuffy office all day, but right now she had no choice.

She inserted a letterhead and began to type. Each time the phone rang out, she closed her eyes and crossed her fingers. Any repeat of Friday and she would be out on her ear, and no mistake.

'I could murder a cup o' tea,' Brenda sighed.

'Go ahead and make one. Bring theirs in first – it might soften him up a bit.'

'What if he comes out and catches me? He'll go berserk. Look how he treated you the other day.'

A loud thud and then an ear-splitting scream echoed through the building.

'My God, what was that?' Oona said, just as Mrs. Kovac rushed into their office. Her dyed auburn hair was set in big ringlets around her face.

'Quick. Ring for an ambulance – my husband's having some kind of attack!'

Totally unprepared for the sight of her boss slumped on the floor by his desk, his breath coming in loud gasps frightened Oona. 'Good God! What happened?'

'He . . . he just . . .' Mrs. Kovac waved her arms. 'Oh, stop asking questions and do something!' She paced the floor, wringing her hands. Brenda stood in the doorway, her mouth open.

Oona snatched up the phone. Fingers shaking, she dialled 999 and asked for the ambulance service. As she waited to be connected, Mrs. Kovac's tedious ramblings distracted her while she noted a few pertinent details about her boss. They were bound to ask her his age and, although she did not know for sure, she guaged him to be in his late fifties. She noticed how his eyes flickered like a faulty light bulb, his face deathly pale; it caused her to panic inwardly. Blood trickled from a cut on his head into the thin grey carpet. Brenda, as if coming out of a trance, disappeared to answer a telephone in the other office.

In spite of the chaos surrounding her, Oona made a note of the instructions relayed to her over the telephone. Swallowing her fear and trying to appear calm, she said, 'The ambulance will be here shortly, Mrs. Kovac. Help me to turn your husband onto his side.'

Wide-eyed, the woman rushed to her aid. 'Are... are you sure you know vhat you're doing? Is, is that vhat they said you should do?'

'Just *do it*. There's no time to lose.'

Both women knelt down beside him – one besotted with him, the other dependent on him for her living – and swiftly rolled him over. 'This will help drain any fluid from his mouth and throat.'

Brenda stood watching, a terrified expression on her young face. Oona grabbed his coat and placed it over him. His mouth sagged in a way that she had never seen before, his eyes glazed. It felt strange for her to be administering help to this pompous, pot-bellied old man, now incapable of speech, who just days ago had bawled at her for leaving the office.

It was the first time she had ever been this close to him; close enough to notice his bald patch. And when his wife loosened his shirt collar, Oona was more than surprised to see a tattoo of a bird on his neck.

'Do they know it's *urgent*? Did you tell them to hurry? Vhy aren't they here?'

'Yes, yes, I did. They're on their way.' She did not know what else to say, and the recognition of fear in the woman's eyes brought a lump to her throat. 'What happened? How did he fall? Can you remember, Mrs. Kovac? The ambulance men might want to know.'

'A dizzy spell. I don't know. He stood up, and the next minute . . . Oh, Josef, Josef,' she cried. Oona turned away, unable to watch him struggle to speak, pouring out a string of incoherent syllables that neither of them understood. Stubby fingers gripped his chest, his face the colour of ash and his lips now blue.

'Try to stay calm. It won't be long now.' From his reactions, Oona felt sure that he could hear her. As much as she disliked the man, she prayed that help would arrive in time to save his life.

'*Vhere* are those stupid people? Ring them again, Mrs. Quinn.'

Oona did, and she was assured that they were on their way. She went back to her office, her heart racing, and almost collided with Brenda.

'What's the matter with him? Can I do anything?' the girl asked miserably.

'Where in God's name is the ambulance?' Oona asked,

oblivious to Brenda's question. 'She's becoming more anxious by the minute and I don't know what else to do. Go outside, Brenda, and make sure they know where to come.' Pleased to have something to do, the girl rushed outside into the street.

When Oona returned, Mrs. Kovac was stroking her husband's brow. '*My Miláček! My Láska!*' she murmured. When she glanced up, Oona saw tears in her eyes.

'Brenda's watching for the ambulance.' If it didn't come soon, Oona could see herself having to attend to Mrs. Kovac as well. She could only imagine what the old man was feeling as he lay on the floor of his office, powerless to make demands on behalf of his clients' cargo waiting for clearance at the docks.

When at last the ambulance bell echoed through the building, Oona felt a rush of relief. She hurried outside to where Brenda was standing, biting her nails. A small group of passers-by had gathered on the pavement.

Two male attendants in navy uniforms with white armbands appeared, carrying a stretcher. 'Stand back, please,' one called.

'He's in here,' Oona led the way.

Mrs. Kovac, kneeling on the floor next to her husband, glared up at the men. 'If my husband dies . . .' Her voice cracked.

'We'll take over now, Madam. Take the lady into the other office, please, Miss.'

As Oona helped Mrs. Kovac to her feet, the older woman offered no resistance. Tears of frustration ran down her hot face, and Oona pitied her. She glanced at her watch. It was only nine-thirty and yet she felt as if she had done a day's work.

'He's in good hands now,' she tried to reassure Mrs. Kovac.

Brenda brought in some tea, and offered them both a cup.

A few moments later, Mr. Kovac was carried out, an oxygen mask placed over his face. 'I'm coming too,' his wife called, and she followed them outside where she was helped into the back of the ambulance, onlookers pushing forward and craning their necks for a better view. Bells blaring, the ambulance sped off towards City Hospital.

Back inside, both girls were silent. Oona sat at her desk, staring into space as if it had all been a dream. Then, without warning, tears ran down her face.

'Sure, look at you. That's upset you all over again.' Brenda placed an arm around her colleague. 'You did great in there. I couldn't have done it. It made my skin go all creepy, so it did.'

'I'm fine now, Brenda. We'd better clean the blood off the floor in there,' she said, relieved when Brenda offered to do it.

For the remainder of the day, Oona could not concentrate on anything. Her mind was full of regrets. If only she had been there to comfort her loved ones like she had her boss, a man who had done nothing to make her life easier. Her own little girl – a sob choked her – and her beloved husband had died surrounded by strangers.

CHAPTER SIX

Oona's parents persuaded her to stay the night with them. She sat on the settee in her dressing gown. The small sitting room was homely and the rug felt soft beneath her bare feet. Her mother was watching television but Oona had no interest in what was on. The evening sun splashed into the room, settling on her wedding picture, hanging side-by-side with Connie's. The terrible ache in the pit of her stomach increased. It was like being inside a giant vacuum from which she could not break free.

The fact that Sean had not called to see her after school only added to her turmoil. She wondered what he was doing, and felt jealous that Connie might replace her in his affections. Without him to care for, she dreaded to think what she would be like by the end of the week.

'My word, that Enid Sharples is a one,' her mother said, cutting across her thoughts.

Her father shook out his newspaper. The constant clicking of her mother's knitting pins was having an irritating effect upon him. 'God's truth, Annie! How much longer are you going to keep that up? Can't a man read his paper in peace? I can't hear meself t'ink.'

'Typical man,' her mother said. 'You won't say that when it's your winter jersey I'm knitting.'

Her father rolled his eyes and winked at Oona. She was used to their banter. It was harmless and never amounted to anything serious. Thirty years they had been married; something she would never experience. She was twisting her wedding ring on her finger when she heard the latch click on the back door and Connie and Dessie walked in. 'Hello, everyone!'

Oona jumped up. 'Where's Sean?'

'He'll be here in a minute,' said Connie. 'He wants to go to the zoo with Tommy on Saturday. We thought we should ask you first.'

Oona had been counting the days to Saturday when she would have Sean to herself again. Providing there had been no more trouble at school, she was planning a cinema trip for them both. With a sigh, she sat back down. 'The zoo! I don't know about that. How's he been?'

'He's been fine, hasn't he, Dessie?'

'Not a bother,' Dessie replied, loosening his shirt collar. 'He's worn me out kicking a football.'

'You love it, Dessie Flanagan, so stop complaining.'

'Will you sit down, the pair of you.' Annie placed her knitting down the side of her chair.

'Sorry, Mam, we can't stay. You look like you're ready for bed, Oona.' Connie was concerned. 'Bad day at work?'

'Yes, it was. The boss had some kind of stroke.'

'Good God!' Connie sat down next to her. 'What will happen now?'

'I don't know.' She shrugged. 'I haven't thought about it.'

'I'm sorry to hear that,' Dessie said. 'I'm not surprised, though, the way the man carries on.'

She was in no mood to continue the conversation about her boss. 'What's keeping Sean?' She glanced towards the door.

'I'll go and get him,' Dessie said.

Just then Sean ran in, his breath coming in short bursts as if he had just run a marathon.

'Whoa there, Sean lad,' his grandfather said. Annie ruffled his sandy hair. He was tall for his age and athletic in build.

Oona's face brightened and she placed her arms around him. 'I've missed you.'

'Oh, Mam,' he said dismissively. 'Tommy's dad wants to take me to the zoo! Can I go?'

'I didn't know Tommy's dad was home.'

'Can I, Mam?' he pleaded. 'His dad's got one o' them new Mini cars.'

Oona felt her chest tighten and it almost took her breath away.

'We didn't know about the car,' Dessie said.

'Oh, I don't know.' Panic gripped her and her voice cracked. 'I'll . . . I'll let you know in a day or so, Sean. There's no rush.'

'Ah, come on, Mam! Tommy's waiting outside.' Annie smiled towards Oona, urging a response.

'Okay! But I need to know—' She never got to finish her sentence before Sean rushed off again. She immediately regretted her decision.

Dessie touched her shoulder 'You did the right thing. Tommy is a nice kid. And we'll make sure we know what time he'll be home.'

Fighting a rising irritation, she eased herself down onto the settee. She wasn't at all certain that she shared Dessie's opinion, or that she had made the right decision. But she knew if she had refused, she would have been seen as the ogre. Why had she allowed herself to be pushed into letting him go? It was too late now, the moment was lost.

'Sorry, but we have to dash,' Connie stood up.

'Why, where are you going?'

'We're taking Sean to see *Lawrence of Arabia*, and there's a bus in five minutes.'

'You know he's been in trouble at school, and he shouldn't be going anywhere.'

'I'm sorry, Oona. I promised him ages ago. I can't break a promise now, can I? Try not to worry.'

'Well, of course I bloody worry. You're spoiling him, as per usual.'

Her parents glanced towards each other.

Dessie glanced apologetically towards her and hurried out after Connie.

How could she help it? Sean was the only reality left in her world. He was the reason she wanted to go on living.

'Well, how about that?' her father tried for a light hearted tone 'One day, God willing, those two will make smashing parents. And that rascal of a grandson, he dashed in and out without a by-your-leave.'

'They're spoiling him, Dad. He shouldn't be going to the cinema.' A sob caught the back of her throat.

Her mother rushed to her side, a worried expression on her face. 'You can't tie him to your apron strings, love. He'll resent it.'

Her father folded his newspaper. 'He needs the distraction, love.' Like Oona, he found it difficult to talk about painful issues.

Her eyes clouded. 'He thinks he can do what he likes and get rewarded.'

'Course he doesn't!' Annie glared. 'Whatever gives you that idea?'

'Sean's changed, Mam. You refuse to see it. Dad witnessed his behaviour last week. He's growing away from me. I can see it in his eyes. He'd rather be anywhere but with me.'

'You're talking a load of baloney. Sure, the lad loves the bones of you, so he does.' Annie was determined.

'Have you given any more thought to what the headmaster suggested?'

'Do you think I should, Dad?'

'I don't know, love,' he sighed. 'I've never had any cotter with that sort of thing myself but, sure, if you think it'll help.'

'Well, I don't like it,' Annie said. 'You don't know what sort of things they'll be delving into. There's nothing wrong with the lad, after what he's been through.'

'You didn't see him the other day, Annie. He'd calmed down by the time you got back from Connie's.'

'And he didn't deserve that football either,' Oona stated.

'Someone has to encourage him, now that Eamon . . .' Annie paused. 'That lad's going to be a footballer one day, you'll see.'

'Come to think of it,' her father sat forward, 'Gerry at the bakery had a problem with one of his lads some time ago. You remember me telling you about that, Annie?'

'That was a different matter altogether,' she snapped, picking up her knitting. 'And you know full well why I'm against it. Talk to someone, my eye!'

CHAPTER SEVEN

Rain fell during the night and a hazy mist moved swiftly over the river as Oona crossed the bridge to the bus stop. Each morning she glanced over at Connie's house with its polished brass knocker, and it took all of her willpower not to call in. She was desperate for a glimpse of her son. Tidying up after him in the morning was what she missed most. She wanted to apologise to her sister for the way she had spoken to her the other night.

The responsibility of running a busy shipping office with only a junior to help was stressful, and her boss's illness was of little consequence to clients waiting for merchandise. Without the forwarding agent's say-so, containers of shipments waiting for clearance at the dockside were put into temporary storage at a cost. Her only consolation was that Mr. Kovac did not deal in perishable goods.

Outside the shabby office block, she looked up at the pale blue sky before taking a deep intake of breath and going inside.

Brenda, who had just finished painting her nails, rose to greet her. 'There's a really nice man in Grumpy's office. He was here when I arrived.'

'What do you mean? Who is he? Have you spoken to him, asked him why he's here?'

'He didn't say, but he wants to see you, Oona.' Brenda blew across her crimson fingernails.

Oona bunched her hair into her fist and tied it up into a ponytail. 'Well, I'd better go and see what he wants then.' She knocked on the office door.

'Please come in.' Unaccustomed to such pleasantries, she

took heart and went in. The man was holding the phone to his ear and doodling on the blotting paper with Mr. Kovac's black fountain pen. The smelly ashtrays were gone and Oona noticed his fingers bore no sign of nicotine. The drawers of the filing cabinet were open, with brown folders lying across the top. A man of about thirty swivelled to face her. 'Sorry about that. You must be Miss Quinn.'

'Mrs.!'

'I'm sorry, Mrs. Quinn.' He stood up and buttoned the jacket of his suit. 'Jack Walsh,' he said. His hand closed gently over hers and she noticed his gold signet ring, engraved with initials. He smiled. His eyes were as dark as his slicked-back hair. 'I work for Universal Shipping in Dun Laoghaire. My boss, Mr. Mountjoy, is a good friend of Mr. Kovac and has sent me to take over until your employer recovers.' He smiled again. 'I hope this won't be a problem for you, Mrs. Quinn.'

'Oh, no. Not at all. I'm pleased you're here. It's been, well, hectic really,' she said.

'Yes, I'm sure. Terrible business.' He shook his head. 'A stroke, I believe. It must have been a shock.'

'Well, yes. How is he, do you know? I've heard nothing, apart from a brief telephone call from his wife.'

'I believe he's having tests.'

'I see. So you don't know any more?'

'I don't believe the doctors know anything yet.'

Jack Walsh had a calming effect on her, unlike the frenzied Mr. Kovac, and she began to relax. When she glanced up, he was staring at her and her hand went immediately to the buttons on her white blouse. Averting his eyes, he cleared his throat. 'But I'll keep you informed, should I hear anything more.'

'Thank you. Well, I'd better be getting on,' she rolled her eyes towards the outer office.

'In the meantime, I hope you'll assist me until I find my way around this jungle of paperwork,' he said. 'Mrs. Kovac has spoken highly of you.'

The remark surprised her. The Kovacs never praised the staff, no matter how hard they worked. 'I'll do what I can, although Mr. Kovac dealt with the majority of our clients himself. But you know where I am, if you need me.'

His unexpected arrival was a huge relief. She could barely believe that someone with perfectly good manners was working in the same office that the miserable Kovacs had occupied just a week ago.

'Does that mean Grumpy won't be back for a while?' Brenda asked when Oona explained.

'I've no idea. It depends on how badly the stroke's affected him.'

'I'll go and make the tea. Do you think I should make yer man one? And should I bring it in on a tray with a china cup and saucer, like I do for the Kovacs?' Brenda asked, wide-eyed.

'A mug with two sugars would be lovely, Miss Byrne.' They both turned round to find Jack Walsh standing in the doorway of his office.

'Yes, Mr. Walsh. I'll get you one straight away.' Brenda blushed, highlighting her rosy complexion, as she hurried away on lopsided high heels.

A smile washed over his face. 'As a matter of interest, Mrs. Quinn, do you know who uses the upstairs?'

'Mr. Kovac and some of the market traders use it for storage,' she told him, 'but we never see anyone during the day.'

'I see. So, are these the only offices operating from these premises?'

'I believe so. Excuse me a moment.' She picked up the phone ringing out on her desk. 'I'll check that, Mr. King.' She quickly thumbed through the paperwork. 'It states two containers of cut paper and one bale of pulp. Yes, I'm sure, Mr. King. The estimated time of arrival is next Tuesday.' Sighing, she replaced the receiver.

When she glanced up, Jack Walsh was still leaning against

Brenda's desk, his arms folded.

'Is there anything else I can help you with, Mr. Walsh?'

His hand moved across his brow, hiding his rugged looks. 'I'm finding it rather difficult to understand the way in which Mr. Kovac operates. There are so many bills of lading missing and, as you know, Mrs. Quinn, the bills act as a contract between the shipper and the agent, without which we cannot operate efficiently. You must get complaints.'

'Of course, it's an everyday occurrence. If it doesn't arrive on time, the packages can't be shipped or delivered. Mr. Kovac gets extremely upset, but his wife usually manages to pacify them until the paperwork arrives, although sometimes it's too late for that week's shipment,' she told him. 'Most days he collects the documentation from the ship himself, but very often he refuses the bill of lading if the cargo is defective.'

'What about insurance?'

'I don't know about that, Mr. Walsh.'

'Well, thanks. You've been very helpful.' Brenda handed him his tea. 'That looks a good cup,' he smiled. 'If you find any late advice notes, could you let me have them straight away, Miss Byrne?'

Brenda nodded, and with new interest, she scanned every piece of paperwork diligently in the hopes of finding one, and pleasing her new boss.

'What's in this filing cabinet?' He attempted to open it.

'Personal files, that kind of thing.'

'Why is it locked? Do you have a key?'

'Mrs. Kovac keeps the key,' Oona told him, turning back to her work.

Jack exhaled deeply. 'Well, in that case, I'll have to wait.' There was a note of irritation in his voice and Oona could hardly blame him. As he walked away, he called over his shoulder, 'Feel free to put awkward callers through to me, Mrs. Quinn.'

'Thank you, Mr. Walsh.' She did not envy him the task. He

had no idea just how infuriated Mr. Kovac's clients could get.

**

It was mid-morning before he came out to talk to them again. He placed some hand-written letters and envelopes on Oona's desk. 'It's stifling in there.' He loosened the knot of his tie. 'Don't you find it humid in here?' He opened the top button of his white shirt, revealing a glimpse of dark hair.

'We prop the door open, but when the traffic gets too noisy, we have to close it again.'

'What about this window?' He gestured. 'Won't that open either?'

'I'm afraid not. The windows have never been opened.'

'That's ridiculous!'

He cleared a space on the table underneath the window, where Oona spread out her paperwork, and climbed up on it. Brenda nudged Oona and she glanced up. His long legs reminded her of Eamon and her heart flipped. The sash window made a rattling sound but the catch was stuck to the frame with paint, making it impossible to budge.

He got down and brushed dust from his hands. Then he picked up the letters, extracting two manila envelopes, before handing them back to her. 'Type these letters, Mrs. Quinn. Can you do an extra copy for my file, please, and get them off in tonight's post? Miss Byrne, would you take these letters to the post office? They're very important. And bring back a dozen stamps.'

Brenda stood up, fingering the hem of her mini-skirt. 'Yes, Mr. Walsh. I'll go straight away.' She fluttered her eyelashes, showing a thick layer of mascara.

'Give her ten bob from petty cash.'

'I'm afraid we don't keep petty cash in the office.'

'Why doesn't that surprise me?' He flicked open his wallet and handed Brenda a ten-shilling note. 'Bring back a packet of Jacob's Creams, too.' He went into the hall. 'I'll be out the back if you need me, Mrs. Quinn.'

'Have we *died* and gone to heaven?' Brenda whispered. 'He's just gorgeous, isn't he, Oona?' She bit her lip, freshly painted with red lipstick.

'It's early days, Brenda,' Oona smiled. 'You'd better get off then. Enjoy the fresh air.'

Glad to have an extra pair of hands to help with the running of the office, Oona dared to hope that it would continue. Nothing good ever does, she thought pessimistically, as she pounded her Olivetti. All the same, she could not help wondering what changes Jack Walsh was about to make to Worldwide Shipping.

CHAPTER EIGHT

'What's going on?' Oona glanced over at the ladder leaning up against the office window.

'Yer man doesn't waste much time,' Brenda said. 'The winders have been cleaned, and a workman's trying to get them to open.'

'Really?' Oona looked out at the sky now visible through sparkling windowpanes. 'How extraordinary!'

'Oh, isn't it grand?' Brenda smiled.

'Is Mr. Walsh in the office?'

'Yes, and so is Mrs. Kovac.'

'How's her husband?'

'Don't know, but she must be worried, 'cause she's forgotten to put on her red stockings,' Brenda giggled. 'You should see 'er legs!'

'Brenda Byrne! One of these days.'

The workman returned. He was wearing white dungarees, stained with green and red paint, and carrying a kerosene blowlamp. 'Sure, I'll have this window open in a jiffy, ladies,' he said, climbing the ladder. 'How ye ever stuck the heat these past few days, is beyond me.'

'We didn't have a choice.'

'Aye, I can see that.'

The heat, along with the smell of burning oil, made Oona feel faint. Then, just as Jack Walsh walked in, the window opened and fresh air filled the room.

'Good man,' he said. 'That's grand. Will it close easy enough?'

'Aye, it will indeed. You might need the stepladder. I found this one out the back.'

'Well done. There's another window in there,' he gestured.

As the man picked up his ladder, Mrs. Kovac bustled out carrying a bulging brown folder. 'My husband von't be happy about this.'

'Not my problem, Missus. I'm only doing me job.' He went inside followed by Jack, who closed the door behind them.

There was no mistaking the disapproval etched on Mrs. Kovac's face as she unlocked the filing cabinet and replaced the fat folder. She was wearing the same dress and canary-yellow cardigan; her varicose veins snaked around her legs like thick pieces of wool. The two girls, their heads bent over their work, glanced towards each other. Oona was in no mood to get into a dispute about the office windows. After all, she only worked there. Besides, it was a rare treat to see the blue sky on such a warm day.

'How's your husband, Mrs. Kovac?'

She glared at Oona as if she had no right to ask, then her face softened. 'Well . . . erm . . . the doctors are optimistic he'll make a full recovery,' she said pointedly.

'Oh, that's good news.'

'He vorries about this place all the time, and all these changes won't do his health much good,' she sighed. 'Have you been keeping things up to date, Mrs. Quinn?'

Her sweet sickly perfume caught the back of Oona's throat. 'I'm doing my . . . ' she coughed to clear her throat, ' . . .best, Mrs. Kovac.'

'And *you*, Miss Byrne!' she said. 'You're hardly run off your feet, are you?'

'I . . . I . . . got in early to catch up with the filing,' Brenda stammered.

'Yes, vell, don't expect to be paid extra. You, Mrs. Quinn, see that she keeps busy.' Before Oona could reply, she continued, 'Mr. Valsh will have enough to do without vorrying about the staff.'

Oona stiffened. 'There's no reason for Mr. Walsh to worry about us.'

'Good! It vas kind of him to step in at such short notice. But even so, I shall be calling in from time to time and on Friday to do the wages.' She leaned across Oona's desk to examine an invoice and, if it had not been for the light breeze coming in through the open window, Oona felt she would be sick. 'I vant you, Mrs. Quinn, to see that there are no major changes made to the running of this office vhile my husband's recuperating.'

'But... but Mrs. Kovac, surely . . . well, that's up to Mr. Walsh, isn't it?'

'My husband trusts you to follow his instructions, Mrs. Quinn.' And as Oona caught her breath, the woman walked out of the building.

'Can you believe that? Well, of all the . . . if she thinks . . .' Oona pounded the keys of her typewriter so hard it hurt her fingertips.

'She's a fecking *bitch* that one,' Brenda said. 'I reckon she'll be worse than him. No wonder she covers those legs of hers.'

'I've told you about your language before, Brenda,' Oona said. 'If you're overheard, it'll be instant dismissal.'

'Sorry.'

Oona rolled her eyes. While inwardly she agreed that the woman would make a goose swear, she had things more pressing on her mind than Olga Kovac's ropey legs. She strongly objected to the woman's suggestion. The very idea of her interfering in the way Jack Walsh chose to run the shipping office made her heart race and her anxieties return. The more she thought about it, the more irritated she became.

'Have you found that missing document yet, Brenda?' she stressed.

Just then Jack came out of the office, followed by the worker. He looked just about as fed up as she did. 'I've paid Mr. McGuire. Can you get a receipt, Mrs. Quinn?' he said, before returning to his office.

Towards the end of the day, when the phones were ringing non-stop and Oona's fingers were sore from typing, Jack Walsh casually threw his trench coat over his shoulder and walked out into the street.

***

He was starting to regret agreeing to cover for Mr. Kovac. Nevertheless, he did not like to refuse his boss, who ran Universal Shipping in Liverpool, where Jack had worked for five years before coming to live in Ireland. After two years assisting Mr. Mountjoy at the fast-growing subsidiary in Dun Laoghaire, the picturesque seaport where fresh breezes blew in across the bay, Jack was finding it hard to adjust to working in the stuffy confines of an old tenement block.

To have that old dragon breathing down his neck was more than he could stand. She was an eccentric, stuck – he was sure – in the last century. The woman did her best to undermine everything he did. Well, he was in charge now and she could either agree or disagree, but he would stand his ground.

His train to Dun Laoghaire was not due for another half hour, so he called into a pub close to the railway station. He paid for a pint of Guinness and took it to an empty table, then ran his hands over his face, rubbing his tired eyes. He had no idea how long he would have to work at Worldwide Shipping. From what he had heard of stroke victims, the amount of time taken to recover varied enormously from one person to another. He found the place claustrophobic already. If McGuire had not arrived when he did to unleash the window catch, Jack would have had to make an excuse to get away earlier.

As the drink relaxed him, he thought about the dizzy junior who was always making tea and painting her nails, and it made him smile. This was obviously her first job, and ideas of encouraging her to improve her skills came to mind. The pretty older girl, Oona, puzzled him. Why would someone as bright as that want to work for the Kovacs? She was married, so why did she need to work? She looked like she had the world's worries on her shoulders. He had liked her instantly. There was something about her that made him want to know more about her; find out what went on in that pretty head of hers.

CHAPTER NINE

The weather at the weekend was glorious and Oona felt optimistic as she prepared her father's breakfast. The headmaster had reported an improvement in Sean's behaviour and the news had eased her mind. While things were going well, she agreed with Mr. Mulvane that a one-to-one would be set up with the school's chaplain. She was looking forward to seeing Sean later that evening, after his visit to the zoo.

Her father returned from his shift at the bakery. 'That smells good, but is it good enough to eat?' he joked.

'Right!' She lifted the plate as if to take it away. 'Next time you can wait till Mam gets back.' James O'Hara was known to make some remark when anyone else, other than his wife, cooked his food.

'Put that back; I'll take me chances.' Laughing, he pulled off his overalls, rolled them up and placed them by the sink. Then he washed the flour from his hands and tucked in.

'I wanted a word with you, Dad.'

He stopped eating and egg yolk dripped from his fried bread. 'Is something wrong?'

'Not really.' She sat opposite him and poured two mugs of tea from the aluminium teapot with its blue knitted tea cosy. 'I wondered if you had managed to talk to Gerry – you know, we talked about it the other night?'

'Well, yes I did, love.' He continued to mop up the rest of his breakfast. 'Although, I'm not sure it'll be any help where Sean's concerned but, from what Gerry was telling me, his lad, who's grown up now, talked about all kinds of stuff to some doctor at the hospital.'

'What kind of "stuff"?'

'He didn't say. People are cagey about family matters. But when the lad was the same age as our Sean is now, he was having nightmares and wetting the bed.'

'It's hardly the same thing, is it, Dad?'

'No, I'll grant you that. According to Gerry, opening up to a stranger did the trick, so it did. I could find out the name of the doctor. But Gerry's not on my shift next week.'

'Thanks anyway, Dad.' She got up and went round the table to hug him. A smell of yeast from the bakery lingered on her father's clothes and, at times, felt comforting. 'Oh, Dad, I wish I didn't have to put Sean through this. But Mr. Mulvane is arranging a meeting with the school's priest.'

'Are you going to be there with him?' He pushed his plate to the side and stood up. He warmed the pot, scooped in tea from the caddy, and made another brew.

'I don't think he'll want me there. Do you?'

'Suppose not. I'm sure the headmaster will keep you informed.'

'Yes, perhaps you're right. I really miss Eamon and Jacqueline.'

'I know, love. Sure, they're a terrible loss to us all, especially the boy.'

'Well, I hope the priest will be able to get through to him.'

'It can't do any harm to try. But say nothing of this to your mother, Oona. There's no point in getting her worked up.' He poured himself more tea. 'Have you time for another?'

'Sorry, I'm meeting Connie at one o'clock, after she's had her hair done. You know what she's like.' Oona smiled.

'It's good to see you smile again, love, so it is. And I know you've missed Sean these last few days, but it's not the first time he's stayed at Connie's now, is it? It'll have done him good. He'll be all over you when he gets back.'

'I hope you're right. It's been hard, especially as our Connie's only a stone's throw away,' she sighed. 'I'd better be off. You'll want to catch some shut-eye, and I want to go down and check on things at the house.'

'Is that a good idea, love? Are you sure you're ready for that? You know if you want me to come with you . . .?'

'Thanks, Dad, but I'll be fine. It's not the first time I've been back.'

***

That morning as Oona approached the house, the bright sunlight wrapped itself over the white pebble-dashed walls, set against the green foliage that had grown like wildfire these past three months. She had loved the house from the moment she and Eamon had moved in. Each time she turned the key in the lock now, a strange empty feeling engulfed her and produced knots in her stomach. Today that feeling had lessened and, in spite of everything, she was determined to overcome her despair for Sean's sake.

Every room in the house held special memories. In the kitchen she switched on the radio before going upstairs. In the bathroom she snipped the corner of a Silvikrin sachet and shampooed her hair, ignoring the clatter of the letterbox. Domestic bills were all she got in the post these days, and she was in no hurry to open them.

As if it were only yesterday, she could picture Jacqueline, splashing about in the bath, submerged in bubbles, her squeals of glee echoing around the house. 'Oh, Jacqueline baby, how I miss you.' She choked back a sob. Turning away, she picked up a towel and wrapped it round her head, turban style, then went into the bedroom. Connie and Dessie had spent a whole weekend re-decorating it, but nothing could ever take away the sting of loss. They had done the same with Jacqueline's room; taken away her toys and put them in the attic, because Oona could not bear to part with them. She had even kept back a few special toys bought for Jacqueline's birthday.

After drying her hair, she brushed it until it shone and

noted how it had grown. She had not been inside a salon for months. These days she needed every penny for more important things.

She pulled on a floral skirt and a white lacy blouse, spread a light coating of red lipstick across her full lips, checked her purse for change, then went downstairs. She scooped up the post and placed it on the hall table, before going to catch the bus.

**

Connie came out of the salon to a light wind that lifted wisps of her fair hair. She wished now that she had not declined a spray of hair lacquer. Placing a summer scarf over her hairdo, she tied it loosely under her chin and cut through the buzz of shoppers.

At one time the sisters had regularly shopped in the centre of town, enjoying the hawkers down Henry Street and the delights of O'Connell Street. Since the accident, they just didn't have the heart for it.

Connie admired her sister for the way she was coping with such sadness. The tragedy had rocked everyone who knew them. Whenever she had felt like giving way to her emotions, she had done so by crying herself to sleep in Dessie's arms. Some days she found it hard to stay brave in front of Oona and Sean, but it was the only way to help them come to terms with their huge loss.

Thoughts of Jacqueline, the little girl with the blonde curls and mischievous grin, still brought a lump to her throat. It made her realise how lucky she was to have Dessie, even though they had no children of their own. She had looked after her sister's children on many occasions, and Dessie had loved having them. If she felt such a void in her life, God only knew how her sister contemplated each day. It made her a unique human being in Connie's eyes.

As she approached the park, she saw Oona sitting on one of the park benches, and hurried towards her.

'I've had to fight my way up Grafton Street. Would you look at the crowds? You'd think it was Christmas,' Connie said, hugging her.

'It's this lovely weather. You look hot, Connie. Let's see if we can find somewhere quiet for a snack.' They left the park and turned into Wexford Street. 'I can't wait to hear how you got on with Sean. I've missed him so much. It was a penance keeping away.'

'Yes, but I'm glad you let him stay. We've enjoyed having him around the place, although he spent more time playing outside with Tommy than he did with us.' She peered through the window of a bistro. 'Let's go in here. I can see a couple of seats in the corner.'

When they sat down, Connie said, 'He'll be back from the zoo about six, and I reminded him to go straight home and let you know he was back safely.'

'Thanks, Sis. I do appreciate what you do, even if I don't say it sometimes. And I'm sorry I was in a mood the other evening. It's just—'

'Don't worry about it,' Connie said good-humouredly, removing her headscarf and patting her hair.

'Is that one of the new soft perms?'

'Yes! I was fed up with it straight. Do you like it?'

'Umm . . . but knowing you, it'll be different the next time I see you. By the way,' Oona leant in close, 'did Sean behave himself?'

'Ah, sure he was grand. What do you want to eat?' Connie glanced at the menu.

Smiling, Oona realised that she would get nothing more out of Connie until she had food in front of her. 'I'll have a ham sandwich and one of those scrumptious-looking cakes, please.'

'Oh, go on. I'll have the same.' Connie watched the server jot down their order. 'Oh, and tea for two as well, please. It's all right for you, Oona Quinn. I only have to look at a cake and I put on weight.'

'You'll dance it off tonight.'

'Well, I hope so. But we might end up at the cinema if Dessie feigns tiredness, on the grounds that Sean has worn him out playing football.'

Their food arrived and they began to eat the freshly-made sandwiches. 'This place is doing a roaring trade. Look, it's packed already.' Oona glanced around at the other diners, all engrossed in conversation against a background of clinking cutlery.

'What was Sean like in the mornings? Did he get up for school okay? And he didn't give you any cheek?'

'I only called him once. I think he's settling down again.'

'Oh, that's good. And he's back in the headmaster's good books.'

'Well, there you are then.' Connie sipped her tea. 'But, according to Dessie, Sean can't wait to grow up so he can go and live in England.'

'I wonder what made him say that.'

'He thinks he'll have a chance to play for Manchester United, or work for one of the clubs there.' Connie leaned back in her chair. 'Now, you have to laugh. It's just the kind of thing kids say. Remember when you and I dreamed of marrying a prince and living in a fairy castle?'

'That *was* a fairytale, our Connie. Sean's dreams could well become reality.'

'Yes, maybe. But not for a long time yet.'

Oona placed the half-eaten cake back onto the plate. She was aware how over-protective she had become, but she couldn't help how she felt. Thoughts of losing him, however far down the line, worried her deeply.

'Come on,' Connie said. 'Let's do some shopping. It's been ages. They've got those new three-tiered skirts in Dunnes Stores.'

***

The two sisters flopped down on the sofa in Oona's lounge,

dropping the bags of shopping at their feet. It was a beautiful room – light and airy, comfortably furnished with the latest G-plan furniture. Connie glanced at the walls decorated with photos of Oona's lost loved ones. The glass cabinet displayed some of Jacqueline's toys, including her favourite doll. 'It must be lonely, with all the memories. I couldn't stand it if... you know?' Connie said.

'Well, yes... it is.' Oona sighed. 'I... I wouldn't recommend it. I've never been aware of the clock ticking before and now, sometimes, I feel like throwing it in the river, but then the silence would be unbearable.'

Connie leaned across and hugged her. 'You don't have to be on your own, you know.'

'I have to get used to it, Connie. Come on, let's look at what you've bought.' She picked up one of the bags, lifting out a white skirt. 'I don't know, our Connie, you must have more money than sense.' Oona stood up and held it against her.

'You keep it,' Connie offered. 'You'll have to exchange it for a smaller size, or get Mam to put a few tucks in it.'

'No, I can't do that. You're wearing it tonight!' Folding it, she placed the skirt back inside the bag.

'It's *yours*,' Connie insisted, pushing the bag towards her. 'I can always wear something else.'

'It is *lovely*. Thanks, Connie. It'll go with my sapphire blouse. I hope Sean likes his new shirt. He's growing so fast I can't keep him in trousers, never mind shirts.'

'I know you missed Sean these last few days, Oona. Having him to stay has made me broody again. I'm beginning to wonder if I'll ever conceive.'

'You mustn't say that, Connie. It will happen when you're least expecting it. Look at Mrs. Kelly. She's expecting again. And she waited years for her first.'

'I know. Life's so unfair.' Connie bit her lip. 'Oh, God! I'm sorry. Look at me, feeling sorry for myself.'

'Oh, don't be silly. It's natural that you should want a baby.

You'll make a wonderful mother.' She got up and went towards the kitchen. 'I'll put the kettle on.'

'Not for me.' Connie gathered up her bags. 'Dessie won't think of taking the washing in once he's watching the football. Besides, Sean will be home soon and you need time alone with him.'

'Thanks, Connie – you know, for everything.' She watched her sister waddle down the garden path, balancing her shopping on both arms, and closed the door.

Oona was busy in the kitchen when Sean ran in. 'Hi! I'm back.'

'Hello, Sean.' She wiped her hands on the tea towel. 'Oh, it's good to have you home. Did you have a nice time?'

'Yes. I like being with Tommy. He's not like the kids at school.'

'Oh, how's that?'

'He's fourteen. He knows everything.'

'Does he now?'

Oona, unable to bear the distance between them any longer, pulled him to her like a monkey clinging to its young. 'Are you glad to be home?'

'Yes. Give over, Mam.' He pulled away. 'Can I go upstairs?'

'Don't you want something to eat? It'll be ready in a minute.'

'I'm not hungry. We had chips.'

'Oh, okay. I thought we could talk.' She pulled out a chair.

'What have I done now?' he scowled.

'Nothing… just . . . we need to clear the air, Sean.'

He lowered his eyes. 'I'll try not to get into any more trouble. Promise.'

'Well, that's good. But we need to talk… you know, like we used to.'

'Erm…What about?'

'Well, sometimes there are things that need to be said, no matter how painful.' She swallowed. 'Do you know what I'm saying, Sean?'

He pondered a moment then glanced up. 'Is this about me having a talk with Father Michael?'

'Well, yes, but—'

'It won't bring me dad back,' he snapped.

'I know that, love, but it helps to talk about it. And, if you have something on your mind,' she moved closer, 'like, what you said to me at Grandad's.'

He traced his finger along the edge of the table then eased himself from the chair. She touched his arm, forcing him to sit back down. 'I do understand... I know how confused you must be.'

'Don't want to talk about it. Can I go now?'

Every nerve in her body tightened, until she felt like shaking him. 'No, you can't. Now *sit down.* You've got to stop this nonsense, Sean, and talk to me. Life's hard enough without you shutting me out. Whatever it is you think I've done, talk to me, and we can sort it out.'

His jaw moved from side to side, and he sucked in his cheeks. 'It's nothin'!'

'Why is it my fault? How in *God's* name am I to blame for what happened?'

'You sent me dad and Jacqueline for the *stupid* birthday cake,' he yelled. 'You promised *you'd* pick it up. And if... if you had, me dad would have been at the football club with me,' he jumped up. 'So it's your fault he's dead!' he cried. Oona pulled him into her arms. She could taste the salt from his tears.

'It was an accident, Sean.' A sob caught in her throat. 'I've blamed myself for weeks over not being able to collect the cake. I'm so sorry, love. My heart's broken, just like yours is.' She sighed. His blaming her was understandable to her now. He was only a child: who else could he blame?

'I could have gone with them,' he sniffed. 'Dad asked me to.'

'Thank God, you didn't. I'd have lost you too!'

'So? I wish I were dead,' he snapped.

'No, love. You don't mean that. In time you'll see there was nothing either of us could have done.' And for the few moments he stayed in her arms, she calmly reassured him. 'I love you. We have each other and a good family to be grateful for. I'll never let you down again, I promise.'

Later, as they sat together watching television, she managed to get him to smile. When she handed him his new shirt, his eyes brightened and he rushed upstairs to try it on.

That night, when Sean kissed her goodnight, she felt the gap between them gradually closing.

CHAPTER TEN

After her talk with Sean, Oona slowly emerged from the dark place that had occupied her mind for weeks. She became less anxious and Sean less wilful; her life started to have some kind of meaning again.

The following Saturday she came home to find her post lying on the hall floor as usual; mostly unpaid bills. She took it through to the kitchen and opened it without much interest. A brown envelope slipped to the floor and she picked it up. It was posted in Leicester five days before and redirected from her old address, Oona's Christian name printed in spaced capital letters across the front of the envelope.

Her heart raced: there was only one person she knew who printed her name that way, with two dots on top of the letter 'Ö'. A cold shiver ran through her body. Her past was catching up with her, and a surge of anger and resentment swept over her. She brushed a tear from her cheek with the back of her hand. Why now, after all these years? She fingered the envelope, turning it over several times in her hand, then pushed it, unopened, into her bag. Sean would be home any minute and the last thing she wanted was for him to find her upset.

It was late when Oona went to bed. She took the letter from her bag and fingered it nervously. From its size and weight, she could tell that there was just a scribbled note inside.

There was a time when she had longed for an envelope such as this one to drop through her letterbox, but now it filled her with dread. Her instinct was to tear it to shreds. Maybe, just maybe, she thought, it might contain good news. By the law of averages, she was due some. With a sigh, she ripped open the envelope and slipped out the folded piece of lined paper that read like a telegram.

Hi Gorgeous,
Sorry to hear about your loss. I read about you in the newspaper. I'd have been in touch sooner only I'm just out of the nick. Roly stitched me up – the bastard. He'll pay. You remember Roly, the nice family man.
He's a grand boy you've got there. What's his name? I'm looking forward to meeting him. A boy needs his own father.
I'll be in touch.
Vinnie x

She felt sick at the thought of seeing Vinnie again. News of the accident must have been carried in the English newspapers; how else would he have known? But why now, when she was just getting body and soul together? Would he try to take Sean away? Then she remembered that bringing up a child was not his style. He had walked out of her life, leaving her numb with shock.

Her father had been furious at the time. He had made it clear from the outset that he had no liking for the man. 'If he shows his face round here again,' he'd said, 'I'll swing for him.' Her brother-in-law had an equal dislike for Vinnie and had warned her off him, but Oona had been convinced she was in love.

Being an unmarried mother had not exactly made her popular on the estate where she lived with her parents. One neighbour – once a good friend – had called her a cheeky hussy. 'You ought to be ashamed of yourself, Oona O'Hara,' the woman had said. They had been hard times; some memories, even now, were too painful to recall. Her parents had moved house to be closer to her father's work, but she knew they really did it to give her and Sean a new start.

She had been only fifteen when she first met Vinnie Kelly. She and a school friend had gone dancing and he'd walked towards her, his hand extended. 'Shall we?' She had never danced with an older man before, and had felt nervous when he led her onto the crowded dance floor. His fair hair slicked back, he'd slipped his arm around her waist, the cuffs of his blue silk shirt shifted upwards, revealing an expensive-looking watch and colourful tattoos. He did not speak during their first dance, except to exchange names, but she had been aware he was observing her. When he returned her to her friend, she had thanked him. With each dance that followed, he had talked a bit more.

'You look like a girl who's had a pretty normal upbringing,' he smiled.

'How can you tell that?'

'You have social graces.'

'What do you mean?'

'You've got style. Most of the women I've dated don't look like you.' He smiled again. 'You have a nice name. Can I call you Oona?'

She nodded. 'Kelly. You're Irish then?'

'I suppose so . . . I was brought up,' he shrugged, 'in Poland, but my old man must have been Irish.'

'Don't you know?'

'I've no memory of my parents. I only remember being moved from one foster home to another.'

'How terrible.' She had been sympathetic.

'Why don't we sit over here? Let me get you a drink. Babycham okay?' Before she could reply, he had gone to the bar. The sophisticated drink with a cherry on a stick made her feel quite grown up. She was enjoying herself too much to tell him she was under age. When the dance finished, he slipped a note into her hand with his phone number.

'Are you going to see him again?' her friend had asked on the way home.

'Don't be silly.'

Her parents had been shocked when she took him home to

meet them. 'I know his type. Why settle for someone like that?' her father had said

Her mother had been upset and warned her Vinnie was too old for her.

Ten years difference meant very little to Oona. She was infatuated. He took her to fancy restaurants and to race meetings. He gave her money to bet on a horse. 'How did you know it would win?' she asked, delighted with her winnings. He had laughed and tapped the side of his nose.

As the months passed, she stopped listening to her parents when they gave her advice. Vinnie gave her expensive jewellery and treated her as if she was special. None of the boys her own age had treated her like that. Oona thought she could change Vinnie – show him what real family life was all about. But, by the time she saw the flaws in his nature, it was too late. She was already pregnant.

Now, looking back, she regretted everything about their relationship. Telling herself that she had been young and gullible at the time was her only defence.

She glanced again at the letter lying on her bed. A shiver ran through her body. Vinnie had been in prison. She shouldn't be surprised. Back then, he had mixed with some shady characters.

Fearful of his intentions, she couldn't sleep. For the remainder of the night all she could think about was protecting her son from the father who had deserted him at birth.

On Sunday morning, she developed a bad migraine and Connie took Sean with her to church. Oona said nothing about the letter. If her father knew that Vinnie had contacted her, there was no telling what he might do. She needed time to think how best to deal with it. Twelve years was a long time. Time in which she had found true happiness – something she would hold close for the rest of her life. She was no longer the naive pupil that Vinnie could influence, but a mature, strong-willed woman who was ready to fight for what was hers. Her mind made up, she put the letter out of her mind and kept herself busy baking apple pies for Sunday dinner. Later, Sean helped her to carry them round to her mother's.

CHAPTER ELEVEN

Oona's mind swung like a pendulum from the problems at work to her worries over Vinnie. If he harboured any notions of them getting back together, she would soon put him straight. He may have been able to use his powers of persuasion once, but not any more. Being married to a good man had taught her the true meaning of love.

Brenda, who was busy checking invoices, looked up. 'Are you all right? Only you don't look it. Would you like some tea?'

'Yes, that would be nice. Thanks, Brenda.'

And for the third time in an hour, Oona reached for the Tippex. Annoyed with herself, she placed a piece of paper between each copy and waited for it to dry.

Jack Walsh had been an inspiration since her boss's stroke. Each morning when Oona arrived, he was in his office and still there when she left in the evening. He had given her a timetable enabling her to keep track of consignments and their destinations, and had involved her in the day-to-day running of the shipping business. While he dealt with discrepancies over damaged goods at the dockside, he had given her leeway to make decisions on consignments that were ready for release. Hoping he would not regret it, she pulled yet another smudged letter from her typewriter. Crushing it in her hands, she threw it into the wastepaper basket.

'Damn you, Vinnie Kelly!' she muttered. By now she was convinced that he would try to take her son away from her. Why else would he have got back in touch?

Brenda was coming out of Jack's office carrying an empty tray, when the sudden appearance of Mrs. Kovac startled her.

'Have you nothing better to do, Miss Byrne? I don't pay you to make tea.' She glared at Oona. 'I thought I told you to keep her busy, Mrs. Quinn?'

'She's . . .' Oona was about to say, 'She's entitled to a break,' but as usual the woman turned on her heel and marched off, closing the door behind her. 'I wish she wouldn't do that.'

'Do what?'

'Never listen to reason.'

'What's she come in for?' Brenda sat down at her desk and studied her fingernails, absent of polish for once. 'I thought you said she was only coming in on Fridays?'

'Her husband's still legally the boss, Brenda. She can come and go as she pleases.' Even so, Oona hoped that the woman would not make a habit of popping in unexpectedly. It wouldn't be so bad if she didn't upset the smooth running of the office.

Mrs. Kovac swept back in. 'Can you find the bill of lading for DeLaMars, Mrs. Quinn? Quickly!' she demanded. 'They're on the phone.'

'That bill hasn't arrived yet.'

'But it must be here somewhere.' She began to search, flinging documents into the air and turning the place upside down.

'It won't be delivered for a couple of days yet,' Oona said through gritted teeth. It was on days like this that she wished she could walk out and never come back. Having created a mess, Mrs. Kovac calmly walked away, leaving Oona furious.

'Why can't Mr. Walsh tell her to go away?'

'I wouldn't underestimate him.' Oona rubbed her hand over her brow. She was beginning to run out of patience herself, so God knows how Jack must be feeling. 'When you've drunk your tea, can you find this invoice, please?' She wrote the number down on a piece of paper for Brenda. 'I need it as soon as possible.'

The phone rang and the girl picked it up. 'Just a moment, I'll put her on.' Then she placed her hand over the mouthpiece. 'It's some man asking for you.'

'Did he say his name?'

Shrugging, Brenda passed her the phone.

Vinnie immediately sprang into Oona's mind. Could he have found out where she worked? She stood up. Her hand shook as she lifted the receiver to her ear.

'Yes, this is Mrs. Quinn.' As she recognised the voice, she felt her shoulders relax. 'Hello, Mr. Mulvane. There's nothing wrong, is there? Sean's not . . . I mean . . .' There was a pause and then a gradual smile lifted her face. 'It's so good to hear you say that.'

Brenda glanced up, a curious look on her face.

'Oh, that's wonderful news, Mr. Mulvane. Does Sean know yet? Yes, yes, of course, I understand. Thanks for phoning. Goodbye.'

'Who was that then?'

'It was Sean's headmaster. He's recommending him to the new football coach. The trials are coming up soon.'

'What's that mean then?'

'If Sean's picked out in the trials, he'll play on the school's football team again.' Oona could hardly hide her excitement. 'I can't wait to see him tonight.'

'Oh, that's grand news for a change.' Brenda swung round in her chair. 'Here's that invoice you wanted. Can I go for lunch now?' She glanced towards the boss's office. 'What's she doing in there?'

'God knows! No doubt she'll be looking for something to complain about.'

After Brenda left, Oona had lots of catching up to do. Her careless mistakes that morning, not to mention the unnecessary interruptions, meant that she was behind with the letters Jack had asked her to type for the afternoon post.

She was pounding her typewriter when she heard voices. Jack strolled out of his office, followed by Mrs. Kovac. 'Very well then,' he said, his tone stroppy. 'If you won't co-operate with the changes I feel are necessary to the smooth running of this office, I can't do my job.' He let out an exasperated sigh. 'I'm going for lunch before I say something I might regret.' He almost ran from the building.

'Did you know about this, Mrs. Quinn?' Mrs. Kovac waved a folder in front of Oona's face.

'Know about what?'

'My filing system; it's been changed. It's taken me ages to find things this morning. Mr. Valsh says it vill be easier, but I don't agree,' she rattled on. 'You typed these labels. Do you agree vith vhat he's doing?'

Oona wasn't sure how much more of the woman she could take. Nothing was ever right, no matter how hard she worked. She had seen the strain on Jack's face just now, and she was prepared to back him all the way.

'Yes, I do.' In fact she was pleased that Jack had revised the outdated system. Not only would it save time, but they now had a filing method that worked. 'What's the matter with it?'

'Vhat's the matter with it? My method worked very vell for the past five years.'

'For you, maybe,' Oona muttered, continuing to thump the keys of her typewriter.

'My husband vill find it hard to cope vith all these changes vhen he comes back.' She unlocked the filing cabinet and put the folder inside.

'Oh,' Oona remarked. 'When is he coming back?'

'The sooner the better, by the looks of things,' was the sharp reply.

Why was she being so awkward? Although she asked herself the question, Oona knew what the woman was like. Her life remained private. Well, as far as Oona was concerned, she could get on with it. She would not ask again. Jack received updates from his boss, Mr. Mountjoy, and only last week he had told her that Mr. Kovac was still very ill.

'By the vay, Mrs. Quinn, how long has Miss Byrne been at lunch?'

'She's only just gone.'

'Keep her busy vhen she comes back,' she said, and swept out of the office.

There was no satisfying the woman, and there must surely be a limit to how much interference Jack Walsh was prepared to take. Oona guessed it was only a matter of time before there was a serious bust-up between them.

***

That evening Sean ran to meet Oona from the bus. 'Where's Tommy?' she asked.

'He's gone on an errand for his ma.' She could tell he was bursting to tell her his news. He hopped from foot to foot. 'Guess what? Mr. Mulvane's putting my name forward for the trials!'

'That's wonderful, Sean. Wait until your grandad hears about this.'

'He knows already. I told him and Grandma earlier, before he left for the bakery.'

'What else did Mr. Mulvane say?'

'"Over the past year, there's been a marked improvement in your studies, Sean Quinn",' he mimicked. '"Your education comes first, young man, and we mustn't forget that".'

Oona smiled. 'Isn't that what I've been telling you? Oh, well done, Sean. I'm so proud of you.'

'He also said that I am an important member of the team and that me dad did a lot for the club. But . . .' He frowned and kicked a stone in front of him. 'It'll be up to the new trainer.'

'Happen it will, love.'

They were crossing the bridge when she spotted a shady-looking character leaning against the river wall facing her house. He was not a local. Could it be? Now she was getting paranoid. Vinnie had no idea where they lived. The beat of her heart returned to normal.

'Mam! Are you listening?'

'Sorry, Sean. I was miles away. What did you say?'

'Do you think I'll get picked?'

'Well, you have as good a chance as anyone else. But be prepared, Sean, new trainers do drop people. I don't want you to get disappointed.'

When she glanced up again, the man was gone. She placed her arm around Sean's shoulders and they walked towards the house. 'Let's wait and see what happens, eh?'

CHAPTER TWELVE

Just weeks before the school holidays, Sean was finishing his cornflakes when the post dropped through the letterbox. Oona picked up two letters, smiling when she spotted one was from her friend. Monica had moved to Swords, an area north of the city, but still kept in touch. She pushed it into the pocket of her jeans to read later. Sean glanced up expectantly as Oona walked into the kitchen.

'Is there anything there about the trials?' He had been asking the same question every morning for the past week or so.

'This might be it, Sean.' She pulled out a white envelope, slit it open, and quickly scanned the letter. 'It's from the football club.'

'I've not been picked, have I?'

'Here, read it yourself.' Smiling, she passed it to him.

Dear Mrs. Quinn,

I am the new trainer for St. Joseph's football club. I'd be obliged if you can arrange for your son, Sean, to be at the school's playing fields this Saturday at 10am for the trials. I shall be putting together a team to represent the school.

At this point, I am only interested in enthusiastic players who show potential and flair.

Yours sincerely,
John Dunmore

Sean's eyes brightened and a slow smile spread across his face. 'Oh, isn't it great? I can't wait to tell Tommy.' He grabbed his school satchel and made for the door.

'Hang on, I'll come with you.'

'You don't need to walk me to school. I'll be fine.'

'Okay.' The last thing she wanted was for him to think that she did not trust him. 'I'll see you tonight.' She kissed the top of his head and watched him sprint down the path. When he reached the gate, he turned round.

'I'll make me dad proud.'

It brought a lump to her throat. Forcing a smile, she waved him off. All she could do now was to hope that Mr. Dunmore would pick him. It was what Sean needed now, more than ever.

Left alone, she sat down to read Monica's letter. Her friend's updates always made her smile, but this one seemed rather serious.

Dear Oona,

I'm sorry I've not been in touch for a while. Hope you, Sean and the family are okay. I think about you often and wonder if things are any easier at work with your new boss.

You'll never believe this. I've met someone and I can honestly say that this is the real thing. His name's Chris Mulligan. We met at a ceilidh on Parnell Street. Now, have you ever known me to go ceilidh dancing? It was strange and we hit it off straight away. We've been going out for a month now. So I want you to come and meet him at Mammy's some Sunday. Let me know when you're coming. I've told Chris all about you and he's looking forward to meeting you.

Your forever friend,

Monica xx

A smile crept across Oona's face. She was pleased for Monica. Fate was a strange thing and she looked forward to meeting Chris. She opened the drawer, took out some notepaper and wrote a quick reply.

***

On Saturday morning Sean stood in the kitchen, his duffle bag on his back, his socks stuffed inside the football boots hanging around his neck. 'I'm scared. What if I'm not good enough?'

'You'll be fine. I know you will,' she reassured him.

'But . . . I don't want you there.'

'Why not?'

'All the other kids will have their dads . . . and . . . ' He looked down at the floor.

'It'll be okay, you'll see. Sure, Grandad and Uncle Dessie are going.'

'Won't me grandad be at work?'

'No, he'll be watching you. Is that all right?'

'Yes, that's great. Can we go and get Grandad now?'

Her father and brother-in-law were waiting when they arrived.

'Thanks,' she said, glancing at them both. 'It means so much to me having you both there supporting Sean.'

'Well, what are we waiting for?' James O'Hara said.

They arrived at the playing fields. 'Gosh, Dad, I never expected to see so many here.' Oona glanced around her as boys and their parents turned up in scores.

'Lots of them will be supporters, Oona,' Dessie said. 'But all these lads are not from St. Joseph's, are they, Sean?'

Sean didn't hear, he was intent on making sure his boot laces were tied correctly and limbering up in readiness.

At ten o'clock sharp, Mr. Dunmore arrived. He ran onto the pitch, blew his whistle and gathered the boys together. There were enough of them to make up two teams. When the trainer walked down the line, some of the lads were impatient to let him know what position they played. But he stopped in front of Sean. 'What position do you play, boy?'

'Midfield, sir.'

'Okay.' He placed his hand on Sean's shoulder. 'You, you and you, over here.' When he had finished his selection, the boys he'd chosen lined up in something that resembled a football team. 'Don't worry,' he called to the disappointed faces lining the pitch, twitching impatiently, each boy eager for his opportunity to impress the new trainer. 'You'll all get your chance.'

On the trainer's say-so, the centre forward tipped the ball to his inside boy and, like bats out of hell, they chased the ball. As spectators cheered on their favourite, Oona jumped up and down excitedly when Sean dribbled the ball down the pitch before kicking it to O'Neill, who missed it. Sean's mouth dropped open and he threw up his hands. 'You bloody eejit!' he yelled at the top of his voice.

Oona's hand rushed to her face.

'Let's hope the new trainer didn't hear that,' her father said.

'He'd be hard pressed not to, Dad.'

'He's just letting off steam,' Dessie said, his eyes fixed on the players.

'Come on, Sean. Keep with it, lad. It's your ball,' James O'Hara called, as Sean again took possession. After another five minutes, the whistle blew and two more teams were picked to play. At the end of the trials, when Mr. Dunmore had assembled his prize team, Sean was one of them.

'Oh, Dad,' she cried. 'I thought he'd ruined his chances.'

'His excitement spilled over, that's all.' He placed an arm around her shoulders.

'Look, Dad. Mr. Dunmore's called Sean out of the line.'

'What's your name, young man?'

'Sean Quinn, sir.'

'Right, Sean Quinn. There'll be no swearing on my team. Is that understood?'

'Yes, sir. Sorry, sir, Mr. Dunmore.'

'Be here at the same time next week.'

CHAPTER THIRTEEN

On Friday, Olga Kovac lumbered into the office. 'Vhere's that stupid girl?' she barked. 'Making tea again, is she? I'll have to speak to Mr. Valsh about this time vasting.'

'Brenda's on an errand for Mr. Walsh!' Oona said, placing her wages into her handbag. She was feeling a lot more positive since Sean's exciting news. With important shipping bills to prepare, she was determined not to let Olga unnerve her today. The phone rang out and she picked it up, glad of the interruption. When she replaced the receiver, the woman was rummaging through the filing cabinet.

Just then, Brenda returned, her face flushed. 'Mornin', Mrs. Kovac,' she said breathlessly.

Olga did not respond. She turned round and handed Brenda her wages as though it pained her to part with them. 'I only vish you vere vorth vhat we pay you,' she glared. Then she picked up her heavy, dog-eared folder and walked away.

'Oh, I 'ate her, so I do. I wish Mr. Walsh did the wages,' Brenda said, opening the brown packet. 'Good Lord! This can't be right.' Her eyes widened. 'I've not been paid any overtime!'

'Let's have a look.' Oona was aware that Brenda had worked late at Jack's request when she had been unable to. 'How many extra hours did you do?'

'Two hours altogether. It's me ma's birthday, so 'tis.'

'She's left you three shillings short.' Oona shook her head. 'In that case, I'd better check mine. She's left me short before now. I complained to Mr. Kovac and even then it was weeks before she paid up.' She emptied her wages onto the desk and checked the amount carefully. 'Mine's all right,' she said, placing it back inside the packet.

Disappointment was etched on Brenda's face. 'What shall I do?'

'I'll go and have a word with her for you.' Oona got up and knocked before entering the adjoining office. When she came back, Brenda was recounting her money. 'She'll be out in a minute.'

'Will she sort it today?' Brenda frowned.

'I don't see why not. It's her mistake.'

When Mrs. Kovac finally came through, she looked agitated and became annoyed when Brenda tackled her about her wage shortage.

'This office has never given overtime to juniors, Miss Byrne. Who gave you permission?'

'Brenda stayed behind at my request, Mrs. Kovac.'

At the mention of her name, Brenda blushed.

Olga turned her head sharply. 'You asked a junior to stay behind after normal vorking hours, Mr. Valsh? Vhat for?'

'You have no right to question my motives,' he stated calmly.

'Mr. Valsh, while you work here, you'll comply with company policy.'

'Well, I'm afraid your policy conflicts with mine.' Jack picked up Brenda's payslip. 'My instructions were clear enough. This young lady put in thirty-seven hours last week.'

'How dare you question my competence in front of the staff, Mr. Valsh!' Her eyes protruded through her heavily made-up face, until it looked like she would collapse there and then. 'Ve'll discuss this in private another time,' she snapped.

'We'll discuss it now, Mrs. Kovac.' Jack walked ahead of her into the office and closed the door behind them. Oona and Brenda could hear muffled voices for a few minutes before Mrs.. Kovac stormed out, a look of disdain on her red face. She did not say a word when she placed Brenda's money down on the desk next to her. Then, with her coat swinging open and

76

a shopping bag in each hand, she left the building.

***

After witnessing Jack's dealings with Mrs.. Kovac, Oona felt a surge of admiration for him. Her first impressions of him had proved right; he was a man who knew his own mind, and she liked that in a man.

That evening, she was surprised to see that Sean wasn't waiting for her at her mother's house.

'He's taken himself off to the park with Tommy. That old busybody at number ten was complaining about them playing football in the street. You know what she's like. She's got a voice like a foghorn. Sean was kicking his ball against her wall.'

'Oh, dear! Anyway, what's wrong with our wall?'

'It's not smooth enough. Bless 'im. He's that excited about being back on the team.' She reached for the teapot.

'I'm so relieved. His football will keep him focused.'

'He's got talent. I think he has the makings of a good footballer, so I do.'

'Oh, Mam! What do you know about football?'

'I've picked up a few tips from the television. And don't forget, I watch it most Saturdays with your dad.' Annie placed the tea and digestives in front of Oona.

She lifted the cup to her lips and took a sip. 'I needed that.'

'Bad day, was it, love?'

'Same as usual. Mrs.. Kovac had a run-in with Jack Walsh, but he was wonderful, the way he stood up to her.'

'Good for him,' Annie laughed.

'You'd never believe what she's like,' Oona sighed. 'She's far worse than her husband ever was.'

'How is the old devil anyway?'

'She never tells me anything, but according to Jack, his recovery is very slow.'

'Surely she's enough to do without coming in to work?'

Oona shrugged. 'I'd have thought so.'

'And you're still getting on well with the new man, Jack, is that his name?'

'Yes. He's really nice.'

'Well, what's he planning to do about the old woman's interference?'

'After today's episode, I feel she's been put well and truly in her place.'

Oona took her cup to the sink and rinsed it. 'The summer holidays are almost here, Mam, and I've been meaning to ask you. Do you think..?'

'Will you give over,' Annie said. 'I'll keep my eye on Sean for you.'

'Thanks, Mam. Money's a bit tight.'

'Sure, I know that. If you need help, sure your dad could—'

'Thanks, but I'll manage.'

'Any word yet about the compensation?'

She shook her head. 'Dessie thinks it might take months.'

'I can't see why. They know whose fault it was, and God knows you could do with the money.'

Her mother was right. With Sean growing so fast, she was forever buying him new clothes. 'Thanks for the tea.' She kissed her mother's cheek. 'I'd better be off. I'll pick Sean up on the way.'

Outside, Sean and Tommy came running towards her, dribbling a football between them. Tommy offered to carry her heavy shopping bag. He was wearing one of his dad's shabby peaked caps that came down over his eyes. He looked thinner.

'Would you like to stay for tea, Tommy? It's only beans on toast.'

'Ah sure, that would be grand, Mrs. Quinn. But only if you're sure it's no trouble, like.'

'No trouble at all, Tommy.' She shook her head as the two boys walked in front of her towards the house. Tommy was quite a character, and she was beginning to see why Sean enjoyed his company. According to Sean, Tommy was leaving school after the summer holidays. Oona wanted more than that for Sean when he finished at St. Joseph's. She had plans to send him to a training college, where he could learn a trade. Whatever the future held for him, she did not want Vinnie Kelly to have any part in it.

CHAPTER FOURTEEN

Oona was working underneath the open window and a light breeze lifted her hair from her shoulders. She was aware of Jack's closeness as he hovered by her desk.

'Have you anything special to do over lunch, Oona?' They had dispensed with formality except when Mrs. Kovac was around.

'Not especially.'

'I wondered if you'd have lunch with me. There's something urgent I need to discuss with you.'

'What is it?'

'Can we talk later?'

'Yes, okay then.'

For the remainder of the morning, Oona was curious. Why couldn't he discuss whatever it was in front of Brenda? Was he planning more changes to the office? The staff, maybe?

'What's up?' Brenda frowned.

Oona shrugged. 'I'll let you know later.'

'And why's Mr. Walsh taking you out?'

'It's only lunch, Brenda.' Oona smiled, glad that she had decided to wear her new sapphire blouse, flattering the slim lines of her navy skirt, and matching summer sandals.

A short time later, Jack escorted her into a nearby city café.

'It'll be more private in here,' he said, ushering her across to one of the chequered tables in the corner. The lunchtime rush had not yet started, and the place was quiet apart from the clatter of crockery behind the counter and the intermittent roar of traffic. 'What would you like to eat, Oona?'

'Just coffee, thanks.'

He removed his jacket and hung it over the back of the chair. She watched him walk to the counter in confident strides. Men like him were hard to come by; handsome, kind and self-assured. It was the first time she had let herself think about him in that way. Then, feeling disloyal to Eamon, she quickly dismissed any more thoughts of that kind and wondered what he wanted to discuss with her.

Had he come to the end of his patience with Mrs. Kovac? If that was the case, she didn't mind admitting that she felt the same way at times. If he resigned, the office would be unbearable without him. She had come to rely on him.

He returned with two coffees and a selection of neatly-cut sandwiches. 'You must eat. I hope you like ham or cheese. I'm afraid there wasn't much choice.' He placed them on the table and sat down opposite her.

She had no appetite, and there was enough to feed four people. Not wanting to offend him, she reached out and took one. 'Umm . . . This ham's nice,' she savoured the taste then sipped her coffee. 'What's on your mind, Jack?'

He cleared his throat. 'I didn't want to say anything to embarrass you at the office.'

'Sounds ominous. Have I done something wrong?'

He paused to finish his cheese sandwich. 'Well . . . Do you remember, about a week ago, there was a large consignment of paper for delivery to DeLaMars, North of Dublin?'

'Yes, I certainly do.'

'You sent it to the wrong place. It ended up in Northern Ireland.'

'What? I don't believe it!' she laughed out loud. 'I didn't send it.'

'You didn't? I don't understand. Who..? You don't mean..?'

'Mrs. Kovac insisted on dealing with it. She turned the office upside down looking for a bill. It was for DeLaMars.'

'Well, I never.' Now Jack was laughing. 'Oh, I wish I'd known. I'm sorry, Oona. The old dragon was in the office when the customer rang, and I purposely kept the details from her.' He paused to eat another cheese sandwich and drink his coffee.

'So that's why you invited me to lunch?'

He wiped his fingers on his serviette. 'Well, yes. Besides,' he placed both elbows on the table, fingering his signet ring, 'it was an opportunity to get you away from that drab office.' Their eyes met across the table. Her heart skipped and she quickly lowered her eyes. Then, straightening her shoulders, she tried to ignore what had just happened between them.

'Well, I won't argue with that.' She swallowed. 'What are you going to do about the mistake?'

'They're sending the consignment back down at our expense. And I'm going to make sure she knows about it.'

'I'd love to see her face when you tell her. Can you imagine how she would have reacted had it been one of us?'

'Yes, indeed. But it was worth it, to hear you laugh like that.'

Laughing was something she had thought she would never do again, and it felt good. 'I'm sorry. I'm not miserable by nature.'

'I'm sure you're not.' He smiled and picked up the bill.

'Thanks for lunch,' she said. 'I'd better be getting back. Brenda's on an urgent cosmetic shopping spree.' Smiling, she stood up and picked up her jacket.

Jack put his hand on her arm and gently pressed her back down. 'Tell me to mind my own business if you like, but I can't understand why a girl like you would choose to work for such an ill-tempered employer.'

A silence fell between them.

She fingered the silver locket around her neck, containing pictures of her loved ones. He was not the first person to ask her that.

'Forgive me, I didn't mean to pry.'

'It's all right, Jack,' she said, finally. 'I guess, after what happened . . .' She swallowed, feeling a host of emotions. 'At that time, I didn't think I could cope with changing jobs, you know . . . Then, when the Kovacs agreed to increase my hours, I just went along with it. I didn't really have a choice.'

People brushed past with trays of food. Suddenly the café was quite noisy.

'Why? I don't understand. What does your husband do then?' Jack asked, draining his cup.

Didn't he know? It had been in all the newspapers. She started to feel hot.

'Eamon . . . Eamon and . . .' Gripped by anxiety and as if rooted to the spot, her chest hurt and she fought for breath.

'What's the matter?' Concerned, he jumped up. 'I'll get some water.' He returned with a jug and poured her a glass. 'Sip this, you'll be fine.'

Instead, she took some deep breaths and tried to stay calm. Just when she'd thought she'd got these attacks under control, this one had taken her by surprise. It was a while before she could breathe normally. 'I'm sorry. This is embarrassing.'

'Have I said something to upset you?'

She shook her head.

He reached across the table and covered her hand with his. For a brief moment, their eyes met again. She looked away. 'We should be getting back.'

'Are you sure you're okay?'

'I'm fine, thanks.'

He searched his pockets for change and left a tip. Then he picked up his jacket and followed her out of the café.

CHAPTER FIFTEEN

In the middle of the week, Connie and Dessie went on holiday to Galway, after failing to persuade Oona to take Sean and go with them. It had been a spur of the moment trip; Dessie had seen the holiday cottage advertised in the *Evening Herald* for that particular week and booked it. She didn't blame them, but it would happen just when she had decided to confide in her sister about Vinnie's letter. Now she could not wait for her to get back.

Saturday morning shopping with her mother was not as much fun without Connie.

'This rain's down for the day,' Annie said. 'I think we'll make for home.' Oona agreed, as drops ran down her mackintosh and into her boots. They had managed to get most of what they wanted and there was no joy in walking around getting soaked.

'Is something worrying you?' her mother asked as they sat on the bus. 'It's not the first time this week I've caught you staring into space.'

'No, I'm fine, Mam. I just never thought I'd miss Connie so much.'

Hiding her worries from her mother had always been difficult and Oona hoped her answer was enough to satisfy her. If Annie knew that Vinnie had been in touch, there was no telling what it might do to her. She had already suffered enough stress over her daughter's past association with him, and his name had not been mentioned from the day Oona had married Eamon.

'Ah, of course you miss her. Sure, she'll be back soon, so

84

she will, her bag full of presents for Sean. The lad's precious to us all, so he is.'

'Connie will have a child of her own one day.'

'Please, God. I hope you're right, Oona. Has she said any more to you about adopting a baby?'

'Not for a while. Perhaps they're still considering it.'

A blustery wind blew and the rain had swelled the river by the time they arrived outside her mother's. 'Here's your shopping, Mam.' Oona untangled a string of bags hanging over her arm, while at the same time making an earnest attempt to keep her umbrella upright.

'Aren't you coming in then?' Annie looked disappointed.

'You don't mind, do you, Mam? I want to do a bit of cleaning and cook a meal for Sean. Working full time, it's amazing how the housework piles up.'

'Oh, all right, then. As long as you promise to make yourself a hot drink, and that you'll come down later with Sean.'

'I promise. Now stop worrying about me, and get yourself inside.' Oona kissed her mother's cheek before hurrying home. She picked up the post and rushed through to the kitchen with her umbrella, letting it drip into the sink, and threw her damp coat over the back of a chair. While she waited for the kettle to boil, she unpacked her shopping. She had cut down on groceries this week in a desperate effort to get ahead of the bills. It seemed that no sooner had she paid the gas and electricity than another bill arrived. She made tea, crunched a ginger snap and sat down.

There was a scenic view 'Wish you were here' postcard from Connie and Dessie. They were having sunny weather and had been for a picnic on the pebbled beach. She felt a slight regret now, not to have gone with them. Despondent, she flicked through the remaining post, mostly bills, and one from Cavendish the furniture shop about an overdue payment. Sighing, she pushed it aside and only then noticed a thin envelope in familiar handwriting. It made her gasp and her

Cathy Mansell

stomach churned. This time it had not been re-directed. Anger surged through her and she ripped it open. It began in much the same way as the previous letter.

Hi Gorgeous,

As you haven't bothered to answer my first letter, I decided to come over and find out if you're okay. I'll be in McCarthy's at 8 o'clock on Sunday night. Surely you haven't forgotten the good times. We've lots of catching up to do. I can't wait to see you. Don't disappoint me, babe. I know where you live now. You wouldn't want me showing up unannounced now, would you?

How's the boy? Does he know I'm his real dad?

I'll be waiting.

Vinnie

There was no date on the letter, but the postmark was dated three days ago. That meant he would be expecting her to meet him tomorrow. The very thought threw her into a panic. She covered her face with her hands. He was pushing her into a corner, giving her no option but to find out what it was he wanted. She was furious. How dare he assume that just because she was a widow he could wheedle his way back into their lives? Dear God! What was she going to do? If only Connie were here. She trusted her not to say anything, and two heads were better than one at a time like this.

She read the letter again. He hadn't changed; still confident that she'd come running. Well, she would show him. She was not going to give in to his demands. Thirteen years ago, maybe, blinded by what she mistook for love, but she did not intend to go down that road again.

She had never been frightened of him, but then he hadn't stayed around long enough. She recalled her father once saying that he believed Vinnie could be dangerous if things did not go his way. She feared for her son if Vinnie were to be allowed anywhere near him. She wrapped her arms around herself and

86

shuddered. Closing her eyes, she wondered what Eamon would have done. He had been decisive in everything.

'You made the right decision. Don't ever regret it,' he had said, when she first told him about Sean. If only he could tell her what she should do now. She thought about Jack, so kind and understanding, but she was too ashamed to divulge anything about this part of her past life to anyone outside the family.

If she sat much longer, she would drive herself crazy. She pushed the letter into her handbag and vowed not to let it spoil her afternoon with her son. She got up and vacuumed every room in the house, then set about making a meal for Sean.

That evening the rain stopped, but Oona could not rise above her dampened spirits. She struggled through an evening at her parents', grateful that they, as well as Sean, were too engrossed in their favourite television programme, *Double Your Money*, to notice her.

That night she couldn't sleep. Creaking sounds from the roof unnerved her. It was foolhardy of her to consider going alone to meet Vinnie. It was a mad, impulsive idea. Finally she convinced herself that if she continued to ignore his letters, he would give up and return to Leicester. With that thought, she drifted into an uneasy sleep.

The following morning she woke with a headache, and her mind swirled with assumptions about why Vinnie was so keen to see her. Her decision not to meet him seemed wrong in the cold light of day. Would he see it as an invitation to come calling? That would be far more difficult to handle. She took a couple of tablets to ease her head and went to the usual Sunday church service, but she might as well not have been there. Afterwards, she walked with Sean to her mother's for Sunday dinner.

As she helped to prepare the meal, she thought about Connie; she did not really want to involve her, but who else could she tell? She made excuses each time her mother glanced worriedly towards her. At the dinner table, she played with her food while Sean enjoyed every mouthful of beef, gravy dripping from his chin.

Her mind elsewhere, she was hardly aware of what her father was saying. 'What's the matter with you, love? You haven't a word to throw to a dog.'

'Sorry, Dad! I was miles away. Just thinking . . . you know?'

'Well, I wouldn't do too much of that. It won't do you any good, so it won't. Look, if you're worried about money, I've got a bit saved. You could take Sean and catch a train down to Connie and Dessie,' he suggested. 'Sure, they'd be over the moon to see you.'

'Thanks, but I can't, Dad.'

'Oh, go on, Mam. Can we?' Excitedly, Sean got up from the table.

'I'm sorry, love. I can't go away right now. We're busy at work.' If only he knew how much she would love to do just that. But a few days away wouldn't solve anything; Vinnie would still be waiting for her when she got back.

'Oh,' Sean scowled. 'Can I go and call for Tommy then?'

'Okay. But don't go far.'

The boy gave her a quizzical look as he sped from the room. James O'Hara sighed and glanced at his wife. For a few moments they were all silent. Her father shook out his newspaper and buried his face behind it, and her mother gathered up the dishes and took them into the kitchen.

Sensing their unease, she wished there was something she could say that wouldn't seem contrived. To Oona, her father was like a big soft cuddly bear, loving and generous. But she also knew that he had old scores to settle with Sean's father and wouldn't think twice about squaring up to him if he knew he'd come anywhere near his daughter again. He was in his mid-fifties now and she did not want him involved. This was her problem and somehow or other she would sort it. But she'd no idea where to begin.

If she stayed at her parents' for a while, she could not stop Sean from playing out in the street. Vinnie could recognise him and there was no telling what he might say to him. She could take Sean to the Sunday matinee for a few hours, but what about later? If she didn't turn up to meet Vinnie, she risked him calling at the house. The way she saw it, she had no choice but to meet him.

She thought about Monica, whom she had not seen in ages, and her alibi began to form in her head.

'Dad?' Her father glanced up from his newspaper. 'Would it be all right if Sean sleeps here tonight? He was asking me the other day if he could.'

Her mother came back into the room carrying a tray of tea and biscuits. 'Well, you know the answer to that, love,' she said.

'What about you?' her father asked. 'Are you staying too?'

'Well, I wasn't going to, but if you don't mind?'

'There's nothing wrong at the house, is there?'

'No, of course not, Dad.' She smiled. 'I bumped into Monica the other day, and we decided to meet up in town. It's been a long while, and—'

'Well, why didn't you say?' her father said. 'You have to start going out some time, love.'

'I'm glad,' her mother said. 'I've always liked Monica. Did she ever marry?'

'She's going steady now. Are you sure you don't mind? I won't be late.'

'Have a nice time.'

Oona quickly shrugged on her coat, and hurried out before incriminating herself further. She hated herself for the lie, but if her father had any idea where she was really going, he'd want to come with her and then there'd be hell to pay.

CHAPTER SIXTEEN

Oona arrived outside McCarthy's at eight-thirty, half an hour late. Queues were forming outside cinemas on both sides of the street. She had forgotten how exciting the city looked at night; the traffic was lighter apart from taxis and buses. Courting couples, arms entwined, reinforced her feelings of loneliness. She glimpsed her reflection in the glass door of the public house. It was exactly the look she intended: flat shoes, her old trench coat, hair scraped back in a ponytail and no make-up. She couldn't afford to give him the wrong impression.

Being here was the last thing she wanted; she felt the muscles in her stomach tighten. Taking a deep breath, she pushed open the door, pausing inside as her eyes became accustomed to the smoke-filled room. The place was packed. Men crowded the bar. She scanned the room, hoping he had not turned up or he'd become tired of waiting and gone away.

A band of fiddlers played jigs in a corner of the room, and the smell of spilt beer assailed her nose. As she moved through the crowd, Irish music filled her head.

Would he have changed much after all this time?

A man she didn't immediately recognise stood up and beckoned her to his table.

Vinnie!

He looked older than thirty-seven. Feeling faint, she gripped a table. It was wet and sticky. She turned to leave, but it was too late.

'Oona, over here,' he called.

Determined to hide her fear, she straightened her shoulders

and made her way across to his table.

He crushed his unfinished cigarette into the ashtray. 'Here, gi's some privacy, mate,' he said to the shifty-looking character sitting opposite him.

The man picked up his pint and glared at Oona. 'Hey, aren't you that woman who—'

Some people had long memories, she thought, and felt the blood drain from her face.

'Get lost, will yeh?' Vinnie flapped his hand, and the man slithered towards the bar. 'Here, sit down.'

He smiled, revealing a broken front tooth. A shudder ran through her body. How could she ever have found him attractive? He was unshaven, but his stubble didn't hide the scar that ran the length of his left jaw. She remembered the expensive jewellery he once wore – gold chains and diamond rings. What had he done with them? She was aware of him staring at her.

'God, it's great to see yeh. I'd forgotten how lovely you are. What d'yeh want to drink?'

'I'm not here to socialise. What is it you want?'

'Don't be like that. I missed yeh.' He reached for her hand.

She drew back. His hands, once tanned and smooth, were as rough as sandpaper. 'What do you want?' She struggled to keep a steady voice. 'Why . . . why the sudden interest after all this time?'

'Oh, my little Oona's developed a fighting spirit, I see.' He laughed aloud.

'I'm not your little Oona. And how did you know where I lived?'

'I have my ways.'

'The only person who knows is old Mrs. Malloy, and she wouldn't...you...you didn't hurt her, did you, Vinnie?'

'Naw! Didn't have to. I told the old biddy I was your cousin from England and she coughed up the information I needed.' He grinned.

91

'You stay away from us, Vinnie Kelly. We don't need you. Sean knows who his real father was.'

'I'm his real father and don't you forget it.' He glared.

'You walked out on him. You can never make up for that.'

'I know. Can't have been easy for 'im; you neither, Oona. And that terrible accident. But, look, I'm back now and I want to see 'im.'

He certainly wasn't the kind of father she wanted influencing Sean. 'Well, it's too late. Stay away from my son.'

'Okay, Oona, my love. If that's how yeh want t' play it.' He leaned in close. 'I know me rights, honey. The law's on my side. And yeh can't stop me seeing him.' He banged his fist down hard on the table, spilling over his drink. She jumped up.

The anger in his eyes frightened her.

People were starting to glance towards them and she didn't want to cause a scene. She turned to leave.

He gripped her wrist, forcing her back down.

'Let go of me! You're hurting me.'

'Don't go, Oona. You've only just got here. Don't you want to hear how I've been all these years? What I've been thinking and planning? How I've never stopped wondering about you and the boy?'

Oona felt her blood boil. How dare he look to her for sympathy? 'No, no I don't. I'm not interested.' She rubbed her wrist. 'We were never married, and when you walked away, you ended our relationship.'

'Let me make it up to you both,' he wheedled. 'Gi's another chance.'

She looked at him aghast. His charm might have worked on her once, but then it had been easy for him to manipulate a fifteen-year-old. Now she felt nauseated by him. Her nerves tight, she ran clammy hands down the length of her skirt. Why in God's name had she come here?

'You and me, we were good together once. We could be a family now.'

Horrified, she glared at him. 'Look. Get this straight. We don't want you in our lives. Stay away from my family. I never want to see you again.'

'I think we should talk about this. I know what's best for you and the boy.' He ran his tongue over his lips. 'I need another drink. Don't go anywhere.' He got up and nudged his way to the front of the bar.

He was not going to take no for an answer. She had to get away. The musicians played faster. Feet tapped to the beat on the wooden floor. A hand reached out and grasped her arm, then swung her round and round until she felt dizzy. Breaking away, her head pounding, she pushed through the crowd, knocking drinks over in her haste. Angry voices called out behind her as she fled from the pub.

Outside, she sucked in the air. The city was bustling. Groups of young people stood around chatting and smoking cigarettes. She sidled into a long queue outside a nightclub and out the other side. Frightened he would follow, she hid in a shop doorway and glanced back towards McCarthy's.

Vinnie was in the doorway of the pub.

She held her breath.

He came outside, pacing up and down the pavement, before going back inside.

When she saw her bus approach, relief washed over her and she ran towards the stop. As the bus moved away and her heartbeat returned to normal, suppressed tears ran down her face.

CHAPTER SEVENTEEN

The following morning Oona went to work, continually looking over her shoulder, and again on her way home.

'Where's Sean? Where is he, Mam?' she panicked as soon as she got in the house. 'I don't see him outside.'

Her mother looked up from what she was doing. 'What's the matter, Oona? For God's sake, give the lad some slack. He's playing in Tommy's back yard.'

She couldn't go on like this. 'I'm sorry, Mam. I was looking forward to seeing him, that's all.' But she really meant she wouldn't be happy until she could see for herself that he was all right. If Vinnie got to him before she could figure out what to do, she would never forgive herself.

'What do you think is going to happen to him?' Annie asked, spooning tea into the pot. 'You're worrying over nothing.'

If only it were that simple. Oona slipped off her coat, opened the cupboard and took down two mugs. She couldn't confide in her mother. The truth would horrify her.

'Look, love. You're probably run down.' Annie poured the tea and sat down next to her. 'Why don't you go and see the doctor?' She took the top off the biscuit barrel. 'He'll understand and give you something to help you relax.'

'I said I was all right, Mam. It's been a rough day at work, that's all.'

Sighing, her mother went back to the cooker. 'I had hoped your night out with Monica would have cheered you up, but it seems to have had the opposite effect.' She lifted the saucepan lid and the smell of Irish stew with mutton and dumplings

94

wafted around the kitchen. 'Nothing's happened that you're not telling me, has it?'

'Like what?'

'I don't know. But something's the matter with you.'

'I told you, I'm fine.'

Annie narrowed her eyes.

Her mother could read her like a book, but there was nothing she could say to ease Oona's mind.

'Well, I hope you're hungry. You need to keep your strength up.'

'Yes, I am. It smells wonderful.' Although she didn't feel much like eating, she hoped her mother's cooking would revive her appetite.

'Good! Your dad'll be home soon and it'll be nice to sit down together.'

She set the table and forced herself to keep cheerful while her mother harped on at her about her eating habits. She recalled Annie's disappointment when she'd first started going out with Vinnie. 'He's not your type at all, Oona.' After he had left, her parents had stood by her when others less fortunate had been shipped off to homes for unmarried mothers. Now she felt as if she was letting them down all over again.

When the table was set, she said, 'I'll go and get Sean.'

'He's had no trouble finding his way home before.' Sighing, her mother put the plates to warm in the rack above the cooker.

'You know what he's like. He'll forget all about the time when he's with Tommy.'

'Well, it'll be a first,' Annie said as Oona shot out of the back door. She ran up the lane shrugging on her coat. She crossed the bridge and hurried past her sister's house until she reached Tommy's. There were no children playing nearby and the quietness unnerved her. She hurried round the back and peered over the fence. The boys were not in the yard. Her heart skipped a beat. She went to the front door and knocked. A woman in her thirties opened it, two small children tugging at her skirt.

'Where are the boys?' From the woman's expression, Oona realised she must have a crazed look about her.

'Why? What's wrong?'

'When did you last see them?'

'About an hour ago. Sure, do you want to come in?'

'No thanks. I have to find Sean.' She ran back towards the bridge. At that point, she could have sat on the pavement and wept. Instead she leaned on the bridge. When she glanced up, she saw Sean and Tommy coming towards her from the direction of the park. Oona let out a huge sigh; they were both laughing and tricking. Straightening her shoulders, she took a deep breath and then acted as though she did not have a care in the world.

Later that evening as they watched television, Sean said, 'Can I go and see if Aunty Connie's back yet?'

'No . . . No, love, she won't be. Will she, Mam?'

'I doubt it. You know what the country buses can be like. Besides, she'd come over if she was back.'

'You'll just have to be patient,' his grandfather said.

'Well, can I have a glass of milk, Grandma?'

'It's a cow I'd be wantin' to keep you, Sean Quinn.' His grandmother ruffled his hair and followed him into the kitchen.

'Make us a cuppa while you're out there, Annie love,' James O'Hara called. He folded his newspaper and pushed it down the side of his chair, then went and sat next to Oona.

'I'd have made you one, Dad, if you'd said.'

'I just wanted a quick word on our own, love. I've been thinking. Would you consider renting the house and moving back here? Sure, there's plenty of room. That way we can keep an eye on Sean, and you can go out whenever you like.' He stood up, pulled her to her feet and hugged her. 'I'm proud of the way you've coped, love, these past months. You need to start making a new life for yourself. It's what Eamon would want, so he would.'

'Oh, Dad!' His thoughtfulness was all she needed for her

emotions to spill. She placed her head against his soft, round shoulder, hoping he had not seen the fear in her eyes.

'You're too young to bury yourself in work and worry. Sean will be fine.'

'But, what else is there, Dad?' She sniffed. 'I know I'm being over-protective but—'

'All you need to remember, love, is that Sean's doing okay. He's back to normal, almost.' He took her by the shoulders. 'Think about what I said, eh?'

'Thanks, Dad. I will.' Normal was all she wanted. Now, with Vinnie in Dublin, how could their lives ever be normal again? She had composed herself when Sean bounded in, followed by Annie carrying a tray of tea and homemade scones with strawberry jam.

Oona wanted to return home for a change of clothes and a toothbrush, but she felt nervous about going alone. What if Vinnie was out there? If he really meant what he'd said about wanting to see his son, she wouldn't put anything past him, and she was worried he'd try and kidnap Sean.

Eamon had wanted Sean to know the truth, but the family had thought it was best to leave well alone. Now her fear was heightened by the fact that Vinnie would not be as sensitive, especially if he thought he could win the boy's trust. The thought made her feel sick.

'I'm going home to get some of my stuff, Sean. Is there anything that you want?' But she could see he wasn't bothered. His eyes were fixed on the strawberry jam.

'I'll come with you,' her father said. 'I could do with the fresh air.'

'What about your tea?'

'Sorry, Annie, I'll have it later.'

'Typical,' she said, folding her arms.

***

Oona couldn't concentrate at work; she felt exhausted, debilitated, and had no appetite. For once it had nothing at all to do with Mrs. Kovac, who had not put in an appearance since her bust-up with Jack. Oona had forgotten to phone a couple of clients about late shipments, and when a regular client phoned claiming he had not received an urgent consignment due two days earlier, Oona was near to tears.

At five-thirty she was about to leave for home when Jack called her into his office.

'I'm sorry about the late deliveries,' she said, before he could speak. 'I've sorted it now.'

He swung round to face her. 'You're not infallible, Oona, none of us are. Please, sit down. You look stressed. Is there anything I can help you with?' His voice was soft, caring. 'If you want to talk, I'm a good listener.' He smiled.

'Thanks, Jack. It's family stuff and I'm sorry to have let it interfere with my work. It won't happen again.' Her life with Vinnie was the last thing she wanted to discuss with anyone, least of all Jack. 'I really must be getting home. I'll see you tomorrow.'

'Look, just answer me this. Has it anything to do with the other day? I'm sorry if I offended or upset you. I—'

'No! Of course not.'

'What your husband does is no concern of mine, and I'd no right to ask.' He shifted in his chair.

She did not want to go over this now, but she owed him an explanation. 'You really don't know, do you, Jack?'

He frowned.

'My husband's dead.'

A brief silence followed. 'Dear Lord! I'm so sorry, Oona. Had I known, I'd never have . . .' He looked away, as if trying to find the right words.

'Mrs. Kovac never mentioned it to you? Why doesn't that surprise me? She never raised it with me, nor did she offer me condolences at the time.'

'No, she never said a word. How, when..?'

'Five months . . . on my little girl's birthday – the 25th of

March.' Everything crowded in on Oona and she could not hold back the tears.

He moved his chair closer and handed her a handkerchief. 'That was when I was abroad.'

'Both Eamon and Jacqueline were killed by a drunk driver.' She paused to dry her tears.

'My God! Was that you? I remember my brother talking about it. I'm so sorry, Oona. You never said.'

'It's not something I like to talk about. It takes . . . some getting used to, you know . . . being a widow with a lad to bring up.' She forced a smile.

'It must do.' He reached for her hand. 'Come on. You need a drink and so do I. Then, I promise, I'll walk you to the bus, and I won't take no for an answer.'

CHAPTER EIGHTEEN

By the time Oona reached her mother's, a mixture of strange emotions were buzzing around in her head. Jack Walsh had been kind. He was someone she felt comfortable talking about Eamon and Jacqueline with. On the way to the bus, he had asked her about Sean, and as they conversed freely, he'd said, 'You're an absolute brick, Oona. I don't know anyone so brave.'

'I'm not brave, Jack. I'm just trying to survive, with a son to bring up.' Would he still think so, if he knew how reckless she had been in the past?

That night her father lit a fire in the lounge. Oona's eyes drooped and she could hardly wait to get to bed. But when she lay down, her mind began to race. The mattress was uneven; a relic of happier times when she and Connie used their bed as a trampoline. The memory made her smile, but even so, it took her ages to get settled, and she dozed uneasily. At 4.30am, she got up, dressed and went downstairs.

Her father was already up, scooping tea from the caddy into the big brown teapot. When he saw her in the kitchen doorway, he put out an extra cup. 'Couldn't you sleep, love?' He sat down to finish his porridge.

'On that lumpy mattress, Dad?' she joked.

'Ah, sure, if you decide to stay, I'll invest in a new one, so I will.' He picked up his lunchbox, and kissed her forehead. 'I have to go. Will you take your mother up a cuppa before you leave?'

Her father's suggestion to live at home would certainly be a temporary solution to her problem. Her concern for Sean's safety, and what Vinnie was capable of, consumed her thoughts. Not knowing when he would make his next move left her feeling powerless to get on with her life. He would be planning something, she was sure of it. It was as though she was on permanent vigil, and close to slipping into a deep depression she felt she would not be able to shake. Her stomach rumbled but she couldn't eat, and it left her feeling lethargic.

How could she possibly go to work feeling like this? Having lied to her parents about meeting Monica, she was about to do the same to her employer.

She was on her third cup of coffee when she heard Sean moving about upstairs. She got up and began to cook his breakfast.

A short time later, he sauntered into the kitchen, still in his pyjamas. 'Why didn't you call me?'

'I thought I'd let you sleep in.'

'Why, what's up?'

'Nothing's up,' she said casually. 'I'm having a day off work and I thought we might do something together.'

'Like what?'

'I don't know. We'll think of something.' Something as far away from the house as possible was what she had in mind.

'But, me and Tommy, we . . . we're going swimming in Bray.'

'It's not very warm today, Sean. Won't the sea be cold?'

'Course not. Anyway, some of the lads from the football team will be there. I can't wait for the football season to start again, Mam.' He yawned and flopped down at the table.

Oona was disappointed that he preferred to spend time with Tommy, just when she needed his company. She placed his breakfast of beans on toast, topped with a poached egg, in front of him. 'How long are you planning to stay in Bray?'

'All day. We're going to the cinema afterwards.'

School holidays were proving expensive but it was worth it,

knowing that Sean would be out of the area.

'I want you to come straight back to Grandma's afterwards.'

'Why? Can't I go to Tommy's house? And why are we staying at Grandma's?'

Trying to keep the anxiety out of her voice, she said, 'Please, Sean, just do as you're told. Grandad needs help in the garden. The holidays will be over soon, and you've hardly spent any time with him.' She glanced towards the clock. 'When you've finished your breakfast, get dressed. I'm just nipping to the phone box. I won't be long.'

***

That evening, Oona crossed the bridge towards her sister's house. She was a bundle of nerves. Connie threw open the door and welcomed her into the plush-carpeted, narrow hallway. A pretty chandelier, hanging from the high ceiling, was the main feature.

'It's great to see you, Connie. How was your holiday?'

'Oh, it was grand. You'd have loved it, Oona. But the coach was delayed on the way back and we didn't get home until after midnight. Anyway, come on through. Dessie's gone to the newsagent's for cigarettes. He won't be long.'

Finding Connie alone was a relief for Oona. Dessie had strongly disapproved of Vinnie from the start and she was dreading his reaction. The last thing she wanted was for him to think she had encouraged Vinnie by going to meet him.

The living room was tidy, and the chandelier hanging from the ceiling was new. Connie was always spending money on the house, but tonight Oona barely noticed as she settled herself in the beige leather sofa under the window.

'How's Sean? I've brought him back a present.' Connie sat down next to Oona, curling her legs underneath her.

'He's fine. He wanted to come over with me, but I need to talk to you alone.'

'Why? What's up?' Connie gave her a worried look. It was a

loaded question – one Oona was desperate to answer.

'Vinnie Kelly's in Dublin.' She blurted it out before she could change her mind. Her head felt like it was about to explode.

'What?' Connie cried. 'How do you know that? I don't know how he has the gall to come back here after what he's done.'

'He wants to see Sean.'

'Don't tell me. You've not been to see him – have you?'

'I went to meet him in McCarthy's on Sunday night. Now I'm worried that he'll try to see Sean behind my back.'

'You did what? Are you mad, Oona Quinn? You know what he's like. Does Dad know?'

'Of course not! Look, Connie, what else could I do? He threatened to call at the house. I was worried sick about Sean.'

'We can't keep this to ourselves. Dessie will hit the roof, but we have to tell him.'

'I don't believe this,' Dessie said when he heard. 'I thought you'd burnt your bridges as far as Vinnie Kelly's concerned. What in God's name possessed you? Haven't you learnt anything from the past?'

His harsh tone upset her, and she sniffed into her handkerchief.

'Don't be so hard on her,' Connie said. 'She did what she thought was best.'

Dessie lit a cigarette, and smoke swirled round the room. 'Let me get this straight. Tell me exactly what happened when you went to McCarthy's.'

Once she began talking, she could not stop herself, pouring out everything including her worry over Sean's safety.

Neither of them interrupted. Then, stubbing out his half-smoked cigarette, Dessie sat down. He leaned forward in his armchair and rubbed his hands over his face several times. 'Do you really believe he's here to see Sean, Oona?'

'Why? Don't you?'

Dessie shook his head. 'I know one thing: that scoundrel

has more than Sean on his mind.'

'What do you mean?' Connie asked.

'This is Vinnie Kelly we're talking about. He's never been one for domestic bliss now, has he? Emotional blackmail, that's what it is. Am I the only one that can see through the blighter? Couldn't you have waited until we got back?' he said. 'You acted foolishly. What were you thinking of?'

'I . . . thought I could . . . I just wanted him to go away and leave us alone.' When Oona could no longer hold back her tears, she sobbed bitterly. 'This is entirely my fault. I should never have gone to see him.'

Sighing, Dessie stood up and began pacing the room.

'Don't get upset,' Connie placed her arm around her sister. 'You're not to blame,' she said kindly, glaring at her husband. 'He could have come back at any time.'

Dessie walked over to the small cabinet in the corner of the room and took out a bottle of wine and some glasses. He poured them each a glass.

'I'm sorry, Oona. Try this. You're trembling. You mustn't let him scare you like this.'

She wasn't scared of Vinnie; more upset by the fact that her brother-in-law thought she'd gone there without any thought whatsoever. She sipped her drink, and would have downed the lot, if it would take away the pain and the shame she was again bringing to her family. She had never seen her brother-in-law so angry and was beginning to wish she hadn't involved him.

'He won't have changed, you know.'

'I know that, Dessie. Do you really think I want him in our lives?'

'Well, you took a risk.'

'I . . . I'd no choice?'

'Of course you had.'

'For the love o' God, Dessie, will you stop going on at her!' Connie was on her feet. 'What are we to do?'

'Well, I'm not going to stand by and let that villain upset this family again.' He clenched and unclenched his hands.

'But you could end up getting hurt,' Connie said.

'I'll be fine, but others might get hurt if this is allowed to get out of hand. Your father mustn't get wind of this. And there's your mother to consider.'

'Do you think I want to hurt them again?'

He placed both hands on his head. 'Let me think.'

The room fell silent, apart from the ticking of the mantel clock. 'Do you have any idea where he's staying, Oona?'

'I don't know,' she sniffed. 'He looked as if he hadn't two pennies to rub together.'

'In that case, he'll be staying in a hostel. Leave it to me now,' he said, and poured more wine into her empty glass.

CHAPTER NINETEEN

The following morning, on her way to work, Oona felt a modicum of relief since her talk with Connie and Dessie, but guilty at upsetting them. Involving Dessie only compounded her misery, and if anything happened to him, she would never forgive herself.

At the office, Brenda, usually as chirpy as a sparrow first thing in the morning, greeted her sullenly.

'What's the matter?'

'Mrs. Kovac's back. She's in with Mr. Walsh.'

Oona removed her coat and hung it up. 'That's all I need.'

'If looks could kill,' Brenda said, tears glistening in her eyes. 'She's going to gimme me cards, I know she is.'

'Don't be silly, Brenda. Jack is in charge now.'

The door to the office opened and Mrs. Kovac stepped out.

'Mrs. Quinn,' she said, by way of greeting, and glanced at her watch. 'Mr. Valsh vill explain everything to you. He knows vhat needs to be done.'

Oona hadn't a clue what she was talking about, and began to wonder if what Brenda said could also apply to her.

'Is something wrong, Mrs. Kovac?'

'Nothing you should vorry about, Mrs. Quinn. I've important things to see to,' she snapped and hurried out.

'Jesus!' Oona cried. 'Give me patience!'

Brenda burst into tears. 'It's not fair, so it's not!'

A polite cough made Oona turn round. Jack was in the doorway. 'What's not fair, Miss Byrne?'

Brenda's face reddened. Embarrassed, she rushed from the office.

He spread his arms. 'What's going on?'

'I wish someone would tell me. Brenda's under the impression Mrs. Kovac's going to sack her.'

'Olga's got a lot on her mind right now.'

She's not the only one, Oona thought. It was the first time she had heard him call Mrs. Kovac by her first name. Now, more than ever, she wanted to know what was going on. 'Why? Has something happened to her husband?'

'See if young Brenda's okay, will you? Then, can you both come into the office?'

***

'Sit down,' he said, removing files from a chair. 'There's no need to look worried, Miss Byrne.' He smiled at Brenda.

'This sounds ominous, Jack. What's it all about?' Oona asked.

'Mr. Kovac's coming out of the private nursing home today. Apparently, he's not completely recovered yet.' He linked his fingers.

'Will she employ a nurse?'

He raised his eyebrows. 'She's planning to take care of him herself.'

'She'll find it demanding. Anyway, I'm pleased he's coming home at last,' Oona said. 'It can't have been easy for him.'

'Won't . . . she?' Brenda hesitated. 'I mean, won't Mrs. Kovac be able to come to work then, Mr. Walsh?' She fluttered her eyelashes.

'Not for the time being, Miss Byrne, but,' he added, 'I think we'll manage, don't you?'

Brenda's face flushed a deep red. She lowered her head and picked at the chipped varnish on her nails.

'Is there anything else worrying you, Miss Byrne?'

Brenda glanced up, her eyes smudged with blue eye shadow. 'I'm . . . not . . . being . . . sacked then, Mr. Walsh?'

'What gave you that idea?'

She played with the hem of her red mini-skirt. 'I thought . .'

'I've no complaints about your work, Miss Byrne. And, if you have any concerns, you come to me.'

She glanced sideways at Oona, who gave her a reassuring smile. 'Thanks . . . Mr. Walsh.'

Oona smiled. She felt sure Jack had no idea the girl had a crush on him.

The telephone rang in the outer office. Brenda jumped up. 'I'll get it,' she said, making a hasty exit.

'I'd better be getting on with some work,' Oona said, opening the filing cabinet and plucking out a folder.

'Hang on a minute, Oona.' He placed his hand on her arm. 'Please, sit down.' He looked grave. 'There's something else.' He straightened his shoulders.

'What is it, Jack?'

'Mrs. Kovac believes her husband will be fit to return to work before Christmas.'

She was speechless for a second. Keeping disappointment from her voice, she asked, 'Have the doctors said so?'

'I'm not sure. They want to see him again in a month's time.' He leaned back in his chair.

'I see.' She paused, trying to imagine what this extra piece of news would mean to both herself and Brenda. Would Jack have to leave? If so, the thought upset her more than she cared to admit. Working alongside him had seemed so natural. He had made her job more interesting and, as far as was humanly possible, he'd improved their working conditions. How could she go back to the way things were? She was certainly no longer prepared to put up with Mr. Kovac's temper tantrums. She would look for another job rather than resort to that.

'I thought you should know,' he said, cutting across her thoughts.

'Does it mean you'll be leaving, Jack?'

'I guess so.' A sad expression crossed his face.

'You'll be going back to your own office then?'

He glanced around him. 'I'll hardly miss this place. But, I'll miss you, Oona Quinn. The truth is . . .' He swivelled round in his chair so he was facing her. His next words stunned her. 'You're the reason I've put up with the old dragon for so long.' He smiled. 'I think I'm falling in love with you.'

Taken aback, she gripped the folder to her. His statement, so unexpected, sent her heart racing. She wanted to reciprocate, but her eyes stung and a tear rolled down her face. 'Jack, I . . . I'm . . .'

He leaned over and gently wiped her tear away with his finger. She longed to confide in him about her past, but was frightened he would think badly of her.

'Don't worry. I understand. I would never have said anything before . . . but now . . .' He reached out and took her hand. 'I don't want to lose touch with you, Oona.'

Smiling through her tears, she said, 'Me neither.'

'Perhaps we could go to a movie sometime?'

'Yes, that would be nice.' It was all she could think of to say. A host of emotions filled her mind; joy one minute, guilt the next. She could hardly comprehend how she felt about Jack. Not to see him again was something she could not contemplate right now. She would miss his cheerful greeting when she arrived at the office each morning. The knock on the office door gave her the breathing space she needed.

Brenda popped her head round the door and, with a cheery smile, said, 'Mr. Frazer's on the phone, Oona, something about a shipment from Germany. Shall I put it through?'

'No!' she replied quickly. 'I'll take it at my desk.'

***

That evening, she thought about Jack until visions of Vinnie Kelly loomed in her mind, driving her mad. She would never close her eyes until she knew the outcome of her brother-in-law's meeting with him.

Once Sean and her mother had left for the early showing at the local cinema, she hurried across to see Connie. When she opened the door, Oona tried to read her expression. She didn't

109

look happy. 'I'm glad you're here,' she said. 'Come in.'

Elvis Presley's *A Fool Such As I* drifted down the hall. Oona did not need reminding. 'Has something happened?'

'Not really. Come into the kitchen.'

She followed Connie down the hall into the galley kitchen, which was just big enough to hold a small Formica table and four chairs. The smell of cooked fish and cauliflower cheese wafted around. Connie turned off the radio, then she placed her husband's dinner over a pot of boiling water. 'Dessie's going to be late home. I'm afraid we'll have to sit in here and talk, otherwise the pot will boil dry.' She looked dejected.

'What is it, Connie?' Oona's pulse quickened. 'Where is he?'

'Just before I left the salon, he rang to say he was calling in to McCarthy's after work.' Connie sighed.

'Oh, Connie, I'm sorry. I . . . wish we hadn't involved him.'

'We had to tell him, Oona. It wouldn't have been right to keep it from him. Oh, I do hope he's all right.'

'So do I. You don't think he . . .' Oona closed her eyes. 'Oh, God, Connie, if anything . . . happens to him . . .' She couldn't stand still.

'Sit down, you're making me nervous. He'll probably be home by the time we've drunk our tea.' Connie poured them both a cup. 'Besides,' she said, 'Dessie can take care of himself. I know him, and he won't do anything silly.'

'Oh, I hope you're right, Connie. You don't think we should go and find him, do you?'

'That would really please him,' Connie snapped.

After that, they sat in silence, each with their own private thoughts. Fear and uncertainty scrambled Oona's mind.

Connie stood up. 'Keep your eye on that saucepan. I'll just look out and see if there's any sign of him.' Worry wrinkled her brow.

An hour later, still sipping tea, they heard the key turn in the lock and Dessie made a hasty entrance.

Connie hurried down the hall, followed by Oona. 'Are you all right?'

'Just give us a minute.' He took the stairs two at a time.

Oona looked puzzled, but Connie smiled. 'He's probably had one Guiness too many.'

The sight of her brother-in-law brought tears of relief, and Oona brushed them away with the back of her hand.

'He's okay,' Connie said, slipping her arm around Oona's shoulder. 'He's okay.'

'Sorry about that. Guinness goes straight through me.' He was smiling when he came back down.

Connie's face brightened. 'Here, sit down, love. I'll put your dinner out. So, what happened then? Did you go to McCarthy's?'

'Yes, I did. And you two ladies can stop biting your nails.'

'Really,' Oona said. 'Did you speak to Vinnie?'

He lifted a forkful of fish and started to eat. 'This is lovely. I'm absolutely famished.'

'Do you realise how worried we've been, Dessie Flanagan?' Connie lifted his plate off the table. 'Did you talk to Vinnie?' she demanded, the plate held high.

'Look, gimme me dinner back.' He was smiling. 'We can all relax. He's gone.'What do you mean, gone?' Connie sat down next to him.

'I spoke to one or two of the regulars, who saw someone fitting Vinnie's description buying farewell drinks two nights ago. So, it looks like he's gone back to Leicester.'

Oona, who was still standing, gripped the back of the chair. 'Oh, I can't believe it. Has he really gone?' she asked. On the night she had gone to McCarthy's, she had seen more than one odd-looking character hanging around the bar. 'Do you really think it was him, Dessie?'

'More than likely. He probably won on the gee-gees, the lucky blighter! You haven't heard from him, have you?'

'No. But . . .' she paused.

'Put him out of your mind.' He looked up at her and smiled. 'I'm sorry if I was hard on you last night, you know . . . I was only looking out for you,' he said, between gulps of tea. 'It looks like Kelly took you at your word, Oona. Well done!'

'That's a relief.' Connie blew out her breath.

'You're not joking. Why don't you two go into the room and make yourselves comfortable. I'll finish up here.' He sighed. 'Then we can go across to your Mam and Dad's.'

Pleased to be back in her brother-in-law's good books, Oona smiled. Perhaps she had not been such a fool after all.

CHAPTER TWENTY

With Vinnie gone, Oona was a different person; she smiled more and her eyes were brighter.

'Sure, it's grand to see you smiling again, love,' her mother remarked. 'It gladdens my heart, so it does. I'm going to the pork butcher's. Is there anything special you'd like for your tea, now your appetite's back?'

'Whatever you decide will be fine, Mam.'

Her mother was standing in front of the mirror wearing a headscarf, a present from Connie. 'I'll be a walking advertisement for holidays in Galway.' She chuckled again.

'It's a souvenir, Mam. I don't expect Connie meant for you to wear it.'

'What else would you do with it?'

'I don't know, Mam.' She smiled. 'We're off to town. Sean needs a new pair of shoes.'

'He needs trousers more, God bless him,' Annie smiled back. 'The ones he's wearing are half-mast. Sure, buy him a new pair from me.' She took three pounds from her purse.

'Thanks, Mam. I can manage, honest. You've done enough already.'

Sean called from the hall. 'There's a bus in five minutes.' He and Tommy had spent hours sitting by the bridge watching the buses going to and coming from the city, and writing the times down in his little notebook.

Both women exchanged a glance then picked up their bags and followed him outside. Oona was glad to be doing normal things again without looking over her shoulder. Simple things like going to the city with Sean made her happy. In fact, she was working up to telling her parents that she felt ready to return home. She could not wait to make the house into a home again for herself and Sean. Now that Christmas was close, she was determined to make it a happy time for her son.

After trudging up and down Henry Street, in and out of every shoe shop in Dublin, finding shoes to fit Sean proved a problem. Finally, she asked the assistant to measure his feet and was amazed that he had grown so much over the holidays.

'Ah, sure, children grow fast these days,' the woman told her. 'He's got a very broad foot. Footballers' feet, I'd say. You'd be better off trying the men's department. You'll get a better fit there.'

Men's shoes would cost more, so Oona decided to try Clery's department store. When Sean was duly fitted with broad fitting shoes, she wondered why she hadn't gone there in the first place. She bought him a pair of trousers at the same time. It had cost her a week's wages but, after refusing her mother's help, she had no choice. He looked so grown up. Raising one foot at a time, he shook the bottoms of his trousers over the tops of his shoes and glanced sideways at himself in the mirror.

Oona recalled how, months ago, he had wanted her to buy him a new jacket. Her refusal had sent him skulking to his room. He was learning that things were different now, and that he could not have everything he wanted. It was her responsibility to see he grew up to be a well-rounded person with none of Vinnie Kelly's traits.

Later, as they boarded the bus for home, he said, 'I'm going over to Tommy's when we get back.'

'Okay,' she said as they sat down. 'How's he getting on? Is he happier now he's working?'

'Yeah, he likes it well enough, but Mr. Mulligan's only taking him on until Christmas. He'll be delivering the Christmas turkeys and hams. He takes fish and meat to those posh houses on Anglesey Road. He smells fishy when he comes home.' Sean wrinkled his nose.

'Isn't it well for some people, having their messages delivered? I'm sure his mother's glad of the extra money though.'

'Suppose so.' Sean lifted a shoe from the box and ran his hand over the smooth leather soles. 'Tommy has holes in his shoes, and has to scrounge back money from his ma.' He placed the shoe back in the box and covered it with the white tissue paper.

'Poor boy! There's a big family to feed as well as clothe. Would your old ones fit him, Sean?'

'I need them for kicking around in.'

She felt disappointed by his response, and wished that he hadn't told her about Tommy. 'But, surely you have another old pair that might fit him, Sean?'

'I have, Mam, but they're too small for him.'

'That's a pity.'

She had enjoyed their day together and didn't want anything to spoil it.

'What would you like to do, Sean, when you leave school?'

'I'm not going to college, Mam.'

She frowned. 'What do you mean?'

'I'm going to apply to the Manager, Matt Busby, at Old Trafford. George Best got a job there when he was fifteen. I read it in the newspaper.'

Hearing the excitement in his voice, she was reluctant to dampen his hopes. 'George Best has the backing of the club manager, but it's still only part-time. Anyway, there are some good clubs in Ireland.'

'Manchester United's the best. I wish I was as good as George Best. I'm going to look for work there, Mam.'

His determination to leave home surprised her and reminded her of what Connie had told her a while back. She felt strange. It was as if someone had just walked over her grave.

Forcing a smile, she said, 'You're not George Best, Sean. One day, you could be as good. But first you need to finish your studies and get a good job.' She glanced down at her hands. 'Otherwise, you'll finish up in a dead end job, like Tommy.'

He shrugged and turned his head away, but not before she saw the frustrated expression on his face.

'I'm sorry, Sean. My wage won't always be enough.'

'But I don't want to stay in Ireland. I want to go to England and see other places.'

Oona was astounded. He'd only just turned thirteen. 'Travelling takes money, and to get it you need a good job,' she told him. 'Sure, there's plenty of time to be thinking like that.'

As the bus approached Baggot Street, it was getting dark and the street lamps were coming on. Shopkeepers were arranging fairy lights around the inside of their windows. One was decorating the window with artificial snow. She doubted that Sean still believed in Father Christmas. Whatever happened, she would give him a Christmas to remember.

***

That evening, as Oona sat chatting with her parents, telling them about the changes due to take place at the office, she said, 'I could end up looking for another job, Dad. If you hear of anything, will you let me know?'

'To tell the truth, love, there's not much going. It might change nearer to Christmas.'

'Well,' her mother said, 'something will turn up. You've got your scholarship in book-keeping and commerce.'

Oona lifted her hair and dropped it down her back again. 'That will depend on the type of job, Mam.'

'What'll happen to that nice Mr. Walsh?' Annie asked.

'He'll go back to his office in Dun Laoghaire.'

'Oh, that's a shame.' She counted the rows of her knitting.

'Why don't you try the Irish Hospitals' Sweepstakes?' her father said. 'It's on the doorstep and you'd save a packet on bus fares.'

'Monica was telling me that they never advertise and that any vacancies, few that there are, get snapped up quickly through word of mouth.'

'Well, that may be so, Oona. But they do employ a lot of women. What's the harm in tryin', eh?'

'You're right. I'll call in and pick up an application form.' She reached for one of her mother's knitting patterns and began thumbing through it. Now might be a good time to tell them of her plans to move back home. They had been so good to her, bending over backwards to accommodate her and Sean. And she loved them dearly. Now that Vinnie had disappeared out of their lives again, she'd found a new inner strength and determination to get on with her life. She had plans to make the house a joyful place again and give Sean no reason to want to leave home.

'Mam, Dad. I hope you won't be upset, but . . .'

Her father dropped his newspaper onto his lap; a worried frown creased his brow. But her mother, who continued to knit, said, 'You're ready to move back home, aren't you?'

Her face brightened. It shocked her at times the way her mother had this uncanny way of reading her thoughts. 'Well . . . yes . . . I feel it's time. How did you know?'

'Ah, sure, I'm a woman. I know these things.'

She glanced from one parent to the other. 'I can't rent the house, Dad. It means too much to me. You understand, don't you?'

'We guessed as much,' her mother said.

'I'm grateful for everything, but . . . well . . .'

'I thought you'd wait, at least until Christmas was over,' her father said, drawing his lips into a tight line.

Oona went and sat by him. 'I'll be fine, Dad.' She kissed his cheek and smiled over at her mother. 'I want Sean to have a good Christmas with a proper Christmas tree and decorations like we've always had. Connie will help me.' The idea filled her with happy thoughts.

Okay! You know best, love.'

'As long as you pop in to see us and not stay on your own too much,' her mother said.

'I will. I'll go down tomorrow and make a start on the cleaning. There's bound to be dust everywhere,' she said brightly.

'In that case I'll come with you. I can check the place over for you, make sure everything's in working order.'

'Thanks, Dad.'

He folded his newspaper and leaned forward in his chair. 'I pruned Eamon's roses the other day and dug in a bit of manure around Jacqueline's apple tree.' Yawning, he stood up. 'Well, anyone with a bed is in it.' He glanced across at his wife, seriously counting stitches and studying her knitting pattern.

'I'll just finish a couple more rows, James, otherwise I won't know where I've got to.' She continued to knit.

As he muttered under his breath and made for the stairs, Annie folded her knitting and dropped it into her knitting bag. 'I'll say goodnight, too, love. You ought to think about getting to bed yourself.'

'I will.'

She knew they were still anxious for her welfare, but things would be different from now on. Yet, as she lay awake, Oona couldn't help wondering how they'd react if they knew she was developing feelings for another man.

CHAPTER TWENTY-ONE

Each morning Oona pondered how it would feel to walk into the office and find Jack gone and Mr. Kovac sitting at his desk barking orders. And each day, her heart lifted to find that he was still around.

Just before lunch, he walked across to her desk and placed his hand on the back of her chair. Her heartbeat quickened. She had just finished typing an urgent letter and whipped it from the roller of her typewriter for him to sign. Whenever he stood close to her, she felt a frisson of excitement. She watched the way he held his pen between his fingers as he signed the letter; the way he straightened up and clipped his pen back inside his top pocket.

Oona chewed the top of her pencil. 'Is there any news on Mr. Kovac, Jack?'

'Mr. Mountjoy has doubts about him coming back to work. Apparently, he's not coherent enough on the telephone.'

Brenda flicked them both a glance, and a smile swept across her face.

'I see.' Oona looked thoughtful.

'We'll just have to wait and see.' He smiled.

***

A couple of days later, while Oona was in Jack's office sorting through the files, she could feel his eyes on her. When she turned round, he was looking intently serious.

'Can you sit down for a minute, Oona?'

'What is it?'

'I hope you won't think me insensitive.' He began to circle something on his newspaper.

She did not like the sound of this and wondered what he was going to say.

'There's a car I'd like to view after work, and I was hoping you'd come with me.' He placed both elbows on the desk and fiddled with his watchstrap.

'You're buying a car?' Eamon was the only one in her family who had owned one, and cars were still taboo to her.

'It's just what I've been looking for,' he said excitedly.

'I know nothing at all about cars, Jack,' she couldn't help sounding dismissive, 'except the heartache they can bring into people's lives.'

'I'm sorry . . .' He pressed his fingers to his forehead. 'If you'd rather not . . .'

Already she was failing in her promise to herself. This would be a real test that she'd put the past behind her. Was this his way of helping her to overcome her fears? How could she be party to him buying a car? It could end up killing him. She wished he hadn't asked her. She wished it was a pushbike, or a musical instrument. But a car!

'I don't see how I can help,' she said.

'I'm probably sticking my neck out here, Oona.' He put a paperclip on some dockets and put them to one side. 'When my aunt's husband died, she felt isolated because he did all the driving, but she solved her problem by learning to drive at the age of forty.'

'Are you suggesting I should learn to drive?'

'It's just a thought.'

She could see where this was leading, and she guessed he was trying to help her overcome her phobia.

Not wanting to seem ungrateful, she said, 'You're very kind, Jack, but I'm not ready. Not yet anyway.'

'Ok, then I'd like a woman's perspective. You can let me know if you like the colour.'

She couldn't help but smile. 'I'm good with colours. I might be of some help in that department. Is it very far?'

'Leeson Street. That's on your way home, isn't it?' The phone rang out on his desk. He picked it up, placing his hand over the receiver. 'You'll come then?'

'Okay,' she replied.

***

The 1956 Hillman Minx was in mint condition. Oona stood on the pavement as Jack walked around it, looking it over admiringly.

A man in a well-tailored suit ran down the steps to meet them. Smiling, he unlocked the car. 'I've driven this one over from England,' he said, glancing at Oona. 'But I'm a sucker for cars and I've seen another one I want to take back with me.'

Jack opened the door and looked inside. 'What do you think, Oona?'

'Well, it's up to you, Jack. I like the colour.' It was two-tone, painted in pale blue with a white top. At least it wasn't black, she thought.

'Sit inside,' the man said. 'Do you drive, Miss?'

'No, I'm afraid not,' was all she said. It was a lovely car, but she didn't want to give her opinion on it one way or the other. She sat down with her legs out of the car. It was in pristine condition, and she could smell the blue leatherette interior. She stood up and ran her hand along the shiny chrome trim. Jack lifted the bonnet and the man turned on the ignition. The engine was so quiet she could hardly hear it.

'Well, what do you think, Miss?' he said.

Puzzled, she glanced at Jack.

'Look, I'll give the two of you five minutes to talk it over,' the man said.

A rueful smile crossed Jack's face. 'I told the owner that I wouldn't buy it unless you approved,' Jack admitted, and buried his head underneath the bonnet.

'That's not fair, Jack. I won't be held responsible if it breaks down.'

He thought he had offended her, but then saw a glint of

laughter in her eyes.

'But, you do like it?'

'Yes, it's lovely. Why buy a car now? You won't need it if you move back to Universal Shipping.'

'You've got a point, but I'd prefer to stay hopeful. Besides, I've always wanted one and I'd like to take it on the ferry to Liverpool to visit my parents.' He smiled down at her.

'Perhaps you'll come with me, Oona?'

She felt his hand brush against hers, and was surprised by the strange sensation she felt. She glanced up at him. 'Do you miss Liverpool?'

'Not at all.' He smiled. 'I get to go home twice a year. Have you any relatives in England, Oona?'

'Distant cousins in Birmingham, but we haven't been in touch for a long time.'

He closed the bonnet and ran his hand over the shiny paintwork. 'You definitely like the colour?'

She nodded. 'Yes, it's lovely.'

The man returned. Jack passed him a cheque, and the two men shook hands. Then he threw the keys into the air and caught them, before jumping into the driver's seat. 'Get in, Oona. Trust me.'

Just thinking about it made her feel queasy. She shook her head. 'I can't, Jack. I'll see you tomorrow.'

'Oona, wait.' He jumped from the car. 'I'm driving past the bridge. It seems silly for you to catch the bus.'

'I'd love to, Jack. But I can't do it, not yet. Drive carefully,' she called, walking away.

He caught up with her, placing his arm around her waist. 'In that case, I'll see you to the bus and come back for the car.'

CHAPTER TWENTY-TWO

Dessie took Sean to see *Hell Bent for Leather*, starring Audie Murphy, and Connie went to Oona's house. The two sisters settled down in front of the cosy gas fire with a tray of tea and an assortment of biscuits.

'You know,' Connie said, when Oona told her about her plans for Christmas, 'I was dreading talking about it in case it upset you. Dessie and I were thinking that we might all go away somewhere.'

'Oh no, Connie.' Oona shook her head and passed the sugar. 'Mam and Dad would never go for that. It's taken me ages to persuade them that I'm quite capable of cooking a turkey this year.'

'We were thinking of you and Sean.'

'I know you were.' She reached over and touched her sister's arm. 'Besides, wherever I am, Eamon and Jacqueline won't be far from my thoughts,' she said, stirring milk into her tea.

'Same here,' Connie said sadly. 'Are you sure it's what you really want?'

'Sure. I'm determined to do this for Sean. He's my incentive.' But she knew she had other reasons now, too. She gave a little smile. 'It'll be fine.' She was feeling extremely positive since moving back home. Sean was happy, she had heard nothing more from Vinnie, and she was working hard to get her life back on track.

'I do admire you, you know.'

'I still cry over them, Connie, but there comes a time when you know you've got to move on.'

'I wish I could be like you,' Connie said, draining her cup.

'But, if you change your mind . . .'

'I won't. It'll be grand, you'll see.' She lifted the teapot. 'More tea?'

'No thanks. We can start Christmas shopping this weekend,' she said. 'Are you having a Christmas tree?'

'Yes. Sean's helped me pick one out, and Tommy's bringing it round on his bike. I'm not sure he'll want to decorate it though, but he seems happy to be home. Has he told you he's playing against the Donnycarney boys' club at Fairview Park at the weekend?'

'He's asked Dessie to go with him.'

'He doesn't want me there.' Oona glanced down at her hands. 'I have to remind myself that he's not a little boy anymore.'

'He's growing up, and very strong willed, but at least he's happy.'

'His school reports are getting better, too. Last night he helped me to make coloured paper chains. Then he surprised me by fetching the stepladder and stringing one from each corner of the dining room, like he was the man of the house.'

'Well, I suppose he is.' Connie smiled.

'But I'm still concerned about what he said on the bus. It's not so much what he said, but the certainty with which he said it.'

'It's just Sean talking. He's a kid, dreaming of being a famous footballer, that's all.'

'You didn't hear him.'

Shifting her position, Connie said, 'The world's changing. By the time he's older, it's inevitable he'll want to spread his wings.'

'What worries me is that you hear about kids as young as fourteen and fifteen years old catching the ferry to England.' Thoughts of children going away alone, and maybe falling prey to undesirables, sent a cold shiver through her body. Life had not offered her any guarantees so far, and she knew how stubborn Sean could be once his mind was made up.

'Don't think about it. Besides, you can't hold on to him

forever.'

Oona sighed. Connie was right. She was turning into a clingy mother and that wasn't at all what she wanted. If she carried on like this, she would drive him away.

'Look,' Connie broke her reverie. 'You're still young, Sis, and you're bound to make a new life for yourself. Jack Walsh sounds perfect.' She cocked her eyebrow. 'He's good looking, and you get on well with him.'

'Stop that, Connie.' She felt her colour rising.

'He's already told you how he feels about you. And you're no plain Jane,' she added.

'Can we change the subject?'

But Connie persisted. 'He must pass the bridge on his way home. Has he offered you a lift?'

'Every day! And Brenda's disappointed he hasn't asked her.' Oona smiled. 'You know she has a thing for Jack.'

'Poor cow! Couldn't you give him a hint?'

'I'm sure he knows. He can't help but notice, but he doesn't want to encourage her.' She curled her feet up under her.

'Has he got money?'

'I've no idea.' The question threw her slightly. 'Why do you ask?'

'How many people do you know who own a car?'

'None, come to think of it.' Oona didn't want to talk about cars, and wished the wretched things hadn't been invented. 'It doesn't mean he's well off, Connie. Remember, we owned one once.' She glanced down at her wedding ring.

'I'm sorry, Oona, I know it can't be easy. But, if you trust he's a good driver, it won't do any harm to let him give you a lift home once or twice,' Connie suggested. 'It might help you overcome your fear of cars. Otherwise, you'll never get over it.'

'I know. I'm genuinely nervous. I hate cars. Why do you think I refused a lift the other day in the pouring rain?'

Connie placed her hand on her shoulder. 'You've overcome worse.'

Yes, she had, and one day she would overcome this too. Then, straightening her shoulders, she reached for her handbag and took out a pencil and notebook. 'What about this Christmas shopping list we're supposed to be doing?'

***

On Saturday morning, a heavy fog lingered over the river. Sean insisted that his team would still find their way to Fairview Park. Just the same, she was relieved when the mist lifted half an hour before Dessie arrived.

When they left, she pulled her red woollen beret down over her ears and, with matching scarf and gloves, crossed the bridge to her sister's. Connie greeted her in a warm hooded coat, edged with fake fur. Both girls were sporting brown, furry ankle boots to keep out the cold.

As the bus crossed over the Liffey into O'Connell Street, the trees that lined the street were festooned with fairy lights and some of the larger stores had Christmas trees in their windows. The town was unusually busy and the streets thronged with shoppers.

'Look at all these people, Connie. I haven't seen a crowd this big for a while.'

'Dessie said there's a match on in Croke Park. That will bring people up from the country. It's an opportunity for the women to do a spot of Christmas shopping.'

'I dare say,' Oona said, as they made their way down Henry Street. 'Shall we take a look in Woolworths? I want to get a few bits for Sean's Christmas stocking.'

Once inside, Connie made straight for the big red weighing machine just inside the door and was about to push a coin into the slot, when Oona stopped her.

'You know it'll upset you, come on,' she pulled her further inside. The shop was heaving with customers and they were literally carried along the aisles; it was impossible to get near the counter. Each time Oona waved her hand at the assistant, the girl turned to the other side of the counter. Eventually they were served, then they had to fight their way out again with only half of what they wanted to buy.

Outside, the streets were full of festive cheer. Musicians played Christmas songs and a group of carol singers collected for the Catholic Children's Society. Both girls opened their purses and dropped some loose coins into the box.

They couldn't resist a walk down Moore Street, where the shrill cries from the street vendors was deafening. Stalls bedecked with tinsel and a variety of Christmassy aromas rushed at them. Soon Oona and her sister were caught up in the happy atmosphere as they passed along the line of jolly stallholders laughing and joking with Christmas shoppers.

'We haven't been down here for a while.' Connie found herself shouting above the banter of the traders selling their wares.

'This is what I love about Dublin,' Oona said, and scooped up a bunch of holly. 'Look at the red berries, Connie.'

'It's very Christmassy. I'll have to buy some.' Connie leant down and selected hers from the large cardboard box.

'Sixpence a bunch, love. You won't get nicer.' The stallholder tied it together with string for easy carrying.

After that, they stopped to look at the wind-up mechanical toys for sale.

'Do you think Sean would like one of these monkeys in his stocking, or is he too old for that?' Connie was unsure.

Oona shrugged. 'Now that he's behaving like a teenager, it seems silly to buy him toys, Connie. I think football socks, or gloves, would be best.'

'I know what he'd like.' Connie shifted her bag from one shoulder to the other.

'I'll get him a new pair of football boots from me and Dessie.'

'But they're too expensive.'

'Well, it's Christmas,' Connie insisted, and led the way to one of the larger department stores. Neither woman stopped to look at the stylish children's clothes hanging on the rails but, as they passed the baby counter, Connie admitted, 'I always get broody at this time of the year.'

'Is Dessie still against adoption?'

'I'm working on him,' Connie said, picking up a pair of size five football boots. 'Will these fit?'

'Try a size seven, Connie.'

'Really? What are you feeding him on? Dessie only takes a size nine.' Laughing, Connie found the larger size and handed the boots to the assistant, who boxed and wrapped them.

'Thanks, Connie. He'll be delighted with them.'

Oona bought a Meccano set that she felt sure would keep Sean occupied for hours. He loved making things and spent a lot of time doing jigsaw puzzles. By the time they had finished, she was ready for a sit down and a cup of coffee, but Connie insisted on traipsing round Bulgers, and then Dunnes Stores, where she bought a pair of fleece-lined slippers for her mother. Oona selected a brightly coloured wrapover apron and a slab of her mother's favourite toffee.

'Have a look at these,' Connie chuckled, holding up a pair of long johns. 'Shall I get these for Dad?'

'You wouldn't *dare*, Connie?' The two burst into fits of laughter and had to run outside because they were causing such a stir. They were still giggling as they made their way towards a cafe at the far end of O'Connell Street.

CHAPTER TWENTY-THREE

At 8am, two weeks before Christmas, Jack pulled up outside Worldwide Shipping. Having heard of property being vandalised in the area, he parked his car directly underneath the window where he could keep an eye on it.

He wanted to clear the remaining backlog of assignments waiting for release at the dockside before the women arrived and the phones started buzzing. The office files were up to date, thanks to Oona, and he wanted to double check everything before he had to leave. The last thing he wanted was for her to take the blame for anything he might have overlooked.

His position was still unclear; in fact, he was more than surprised to find that Mr. Kovac hadn't returned to work as his wife had predicted. If he was honest, he was reluctant to pursue the matter; he still couldn't bring himself to precipitate any change that would mean not seeing Oona every day.

He removed his dark woollen coat and scarf, and threw them across the back of a chair. Sitting down, he swivelled round to face his desk and flicked open his diary, found the number he wanted, and reached for the telephone. It rang out before he could make the call. Surprised, he glanced at his watch. It was still only 8.10am.

'Hello. Worldwide Shipping. Jack Walsh speaking. What can I do for you? Ah, Mrs. Kovac.' He leaned back in his chair. 'I'm glad you rang, I . . .' He paused to listen. 'I see! I presume you've thought this through carefully.' He picked up his pen and began to doodle on the large pad that stretched across his desk. 'What would you like me to do?' He cleared his throat.

129

'Okay, if you feel that would be best. We'll talk later. Goodbye for now,' he said and replaced the receiver.

For a few seconds, Jack pondered the consequences of the phone call, then he picked up the receiver and made the necessary calls to the docks. He had just finished a lengthy conversation on the phone to his old boss, Mr. Mountjoy, when he heard Brenda answer the phone in the other office.

***

Later, when Oona arrived, she was surprised to find Jack sitting on the corner of her desk absent-mindedly twisting his pen between his fingers. She couldn't quite make out whether his expression was one of worry or displeasure.

'Good morning, Jack. I'm not late, am I?'

'Umm . . .' he said distractedly. 'Sorry. I was miles away. Good morning, Oona.'

It was unusual to find him so preoccupied. 'Is there . . . something I can help you with?' She removed her coat and scarf, and sat down.

'No. Sorry,' he said again, removing himself from her desk.

'Hasn't Brenda turned in then?' she asked, lifting her hair and tying it up in a ponytail.

'We've run out of tea.' He half-smiled.

She uncovered her typewriter then began to write a list of urgent things to deal with, matters that had been delayed waiting for the appropriate paperwork.

Jack was still hovering. He appeared to be working something out in his head and she wondered what it could be. Before she could find out, he said, 'When Brenda comes back, could you pop into my office?'

***

'Sit down, please. I'm sorry about earlier, Oona. I'd better explain.'

She perched on the edge of a chair. 'Is something wrong?'

'Mrs. Kovac phoned me earlier.'

'Oh,' she said, and eased back in her seat. 'What did she

have to say for herself?'

'She and her husband have decided to return to Czechoslovakia. It's taken me totally by surprise.'

'But why? I thought her husband was coming back to work.'

'His doctor doesn't feel he's fit enough, nor that he will be in the near future. That's the reason they've decided to retire back to their own country.'

'Goodness me!' Her hand rushed to her face. 'Will this office close? What will happen to the business, Jack? Did she say?'

He got to his feet and adjusted the knot of his tie. 'I don't know the answer to any of your questions, Oona. But she's coming in this afternoon to talk to me. I've already discussed it with Mr. Mountjoy but, until I know whether Mr. Kovac plans to dissolve the agency, my hands are tied. I'll certainly keep you posted.'

For the rest of the morning Oona was subdued.

Brenda, on the other hand, thought it was wonderful news and walked around with a permanent smile on her face. 'Sure, Mr. Walsh won't have to leave now, will he?'

Oona smiled back in spite of the doubts that crowded her mind. Would the Kovacs suggest that Jack should continue to run the agency? Knowing them as she did, she felt it unlikely they would hand the business over just like that. Her mind whirled with all kinds of possibilities – some good, some not so good. She was glad she had already begun her search for another job; perhaps she ought to advise her young colleague to do the same. Brenda needed a job as much as Oona did, in order to support her mother's large family. For the first time ever, they both waited eagerly for the arrival of the woman who would determine their fate.

An hour before they were due to go home, Jack glanced up from his paperwork just as Mrs. Kovac lumbered her way into the outer office, dressed like she'd come from the North Pole. In spite of the cold weather, a trickle of sweat moistened her brow. A heavy red shopping bag, filled with fruit and vegetables, hung from her arm and she was carrying a large brown briefcase. Putting her shopping down, she unlocked the filing cabinet and thrust two large buff folders, marked "Immigration Papers" and "Contract", into her briefcase. Then she plodded into Jack's office.

Despite straining to hear, the muffled voices revealed nothing to Brenda and Oona. Brenda grimaced, huddled into her coat and picked up the post. 'Tell me everything in the morning.'

Oona glanced at her watch. 'I'll stay and catch a later bus, but if they're not done by then, I'll have to go.'

It turned out she had to wait until morning to talk to Jack. When she arrived, he was at his desk, his face buried in his hands.

'Is it that bad, Jack? What did Mrs. Kovac have to say yesterday?'

He glanced up, his expression sombre. 'First of all, to answer the questions you asked me yesterday, I don't think the agency will close so there's no need for you or Brenda to worry about your jobs,' he said. 'According to Mrs. K, my replacement will be sent soon. So it doesn't look like I'll be here for much longer.'

Oona felt numb. Jack had been treated shabbily and she couldn't find the right words to alleviate the humiliation he obviously felt at being passed over. He had done so much to build up and establish new clients.

'Didn't . . . she . . . even suggest that you should take over the agency?'

He shook his head. 'No. I'm afraid not.'

'I can't believe it,' she couldn't disguise her amazement.

He sighed. 'She was more concerned about terminating their agreement. Apparently, after five years they're legally bound to give three months' notice. But, in view of her husband's illness, she's hoping to have it waived.'

'I see. Did she thank you for the work you've done?'

He raised an eyebrow.

'I'm sorry, Jack. The company knows you've been running the agency successfully for eight months, don't they?'

'I suppose they must, although I've never had confirmation from Head Office.'

'Well, I suppose after this madhouse, you'll be pleased to be back working for Mr. Mountjoy.'

'I don't know about that. I've enjoyed making decisions and being my own boss. With the Kovacs out of the picture, I think I could make a success of this agency.'

Hearing him say that gave her hope. 'Did you let her know you were interested?'

He nodded. 'I made enough references to the fact, but she didn't appear interested in my plans.' He gave a little laugh. 'She said things had a way of working themselves out. What she meant, I've no idea.'

'If it's what you want, Jack, you shouldn't give up without a fight. What have you got to lose?'

Folding his arms, he leaned back in his chair. 'Exactly my thoughts, Oona. I'll give it some serious thought.'

'Good, and if there's any new developments, you'll let me know?'

'Of course.'

She stood up. 'By the way, Jack, did you know that Mrs. Kovac kept her immigration papers in the office?'

'Where?'

'In the filing cabinet. Why would she do that?'

'I've no idea. Why would she risk important documents being stolen?' Jack ran his fingers through his hair.

'It's probably a duplicate.' Oona laughed. 'Mr. Kovac was always sending me to Getstetners to have things photocopied. I never thought much about it at the time. She probably has the originals in a safe at home.'

Jack drew his lips together. 'Very odd behaviour, if you ask me.'

Smiling, she walked towards the door.

'One other thing before you go, Oona. A delivery van will arrive here tomorrow morning to take away furniture that's been stored upstairs.'

'Furniture!'

'Yes, apparently Mr. Kovac collects antique furniture as a hobby, so they're having it shipped to Czechoslovakia. You might find it noisy, as they have to pack it all before carrying it down.' He turned round and picked up a piece of paper. 'You'll need these details to prepare the necessary documentation. I'll get on to the shipper this morning.' He sighed. 'When it'll be shipped, I really couldn't say.'

This was going to take her most of the morning, on top of her already busy day. The whole business left her feeling unsettled and undecided in her plans to find other employment.

She told Brenda what she needed to know and left her to her opinion that Jack would automatically become the new agent for Worldwide Shipping. Ideally, that is what should happen, Oona thought, but life was never that straightforward. Even if Jack sent off his application tomorrow, it would be New Year before he knew the outcome. If he did get the job, she certainly wouldn't want to leave. She loved working with him. He had a calming influence on her.

She couldn't deny that she enjoyed the unpredictability of the shipping business, and found the movement of cargo to and from Poland, Hungary and Russia interesting. Destinations such as Sweden and Norway were places she could only dream about visiting one day. Working in a typing pool all day, with earplugs in her ears, seemed boring in comparison.

All she could do for now was wait and see what changes the months ahead had in store for her.

CHAPTER TWENTY-FOUR

It was mid-afternoon when Jack returned from lunch and handed the girls a box of Cadbury's milk chocolates each, with a silky red ribbon tied in a bow at the front. Attached to each box was a Christmas card.

Brenda's eyes widened. 'Oh, they're lovely! Thanks, Mr. Walsh. I've never been given chocolates before.' She brushed her hand over the box, as though she was stroking a new kitten.

'Well,' he said. 'In that case, Brenda, I've chosen well.'

She hooded her eyes.

Embarrassed, Oona felt a flush to her face. 'I'm sorry, Jack, I . . . haven't . . .' She played with her wedding ring. She had not so much as given him a Christmas card.

'Please . . .' He smiled. 'It's just a token of my thanks to you both for all your hard work over the past months.'

'Thanks. It's very kind of you,' she said.

'I'm closing the office early. You're both free to go whenever you want.'

'Really?' Brenda couldn't believe her luck. 'That's great. I've got some bits to pick up for me ma, in Henry Street. Are there any more letters for the post?'

'This is the last one.' Oona sealed an envelope and handed it to Brenda. 'Unless you have anything, Jack?'

'No, I'm about done,' he said.

Brenda gave her a hug. 'Merry Christmas, Oona.'

'Thanks, Brenda. Have a lovely time. See you after the holiday.'

'Happy Christmas, Mr. Walsh,' she said, boldly planting a kiss on his cheek. At her unexpected gesture, Jack gave a little

135

cough and straightened his shoulders; Oona had to stifle a giggle.

'Oh, I'm sorry. Am I sacked?' The young girl blushed and her hand covered her face.

'Not in the least. I'm flattered. Merry Christmas, Brenda.' His smile broadened.

Mumbling apologies, she picked up the post and her belongings and hurried from the office.

Oona glanced at Jack and they both laughed.

'I don't know what came over her,' Oona said.

'Well, it is Christmas. Which reminds me.' He reached inside his pocket and took out a neatly packaged present. 'This is for you. I hope you like it.'

'Jack. You shouldn't have. I haven't . . ..' She felt embarrassed not to have something to give him in return.

'Don't give it another thought.'

'Thank you.'

'Aren't you going to open it?'

Smiling, she opened the box to reveal a gold watch with a linked bracelet. She placed it round her wrist and Jack helped her to fasten the clasp. His touch awakened in her sensations she so missed, and she circled the face of the watch with her finger. 'It's lovely, thank you.'

'I'm glad you like it, and I hope you'll think of me whenever you check the time.' He sighed. 'I know I'm going to miss you every minute I'm away.'

'Away?' Her face clouded. She would miss him too; more than she cared to admit.

'Oh, just to my parents for Christmas. My brother and I are taking the ferry to Liverpool.'

'Won't the sea be rough at this time of year? I heard England's having a cold snap.' She couldn't keep the concern out of her voice.

'It won't bother me. I've sailed through bad weather before.'

Oona placed the small empty package inside her bag, picked

up the chocolates and followed him into the hall. Jack locked the door behind them.

'When do you go?'

'I'm catching the boat tonight.' Their voices echoed in the stark hallway.

'What are you doing for Christmas?' he asked, and looped the length of her red scarf around her neck.

'I'm cooking Christmas dinner. With Sean and the family, it's bound to be eventful,' she smiled.

'You have a beguiling smile, Oona Quinn.' He moved close and she thought he was going to kiss her. Then he glanced at his watch, folded the lapels of his coat across his chest and smiled down at her. 'Look, I've a couple of things to pick up in town before I go. I'll walk with you as far as O'Connell Street.'

***

On Christmas Eve, Oona found herself distracted with thoughts of Jack and the gold watch he had given her. She was preparing food for the big day, and wanted everything to be perfect. The ham had been simmering for hours, and all manner of appetizing smells emerged from the kitchen. While she prepared vegetables, spices and herbs to make soup, Sean poured boiling water over the chestnuts and helped his mother to blanch them, ready to make his favourite stuffing. Finally, the turkey was prepared and placed on top of the cooker, ready to go into the oven early on Christmas morning. Then she made batches of mince pies, and fairy cakes – Jacqueline's favourites. It was a habit she found hard to break. As soon as she took them out of the hot oven, Sean couldn't resist swiping one.

Laughing, she slapped his hand. 'If you keep eating them, there'll be none for tomorrow.' She placed the remainder onto a cooling rack out of his reach.

Oona and Connie had made their Christmas cakes weeks before, and Oona was delighted that hers hadn't sunk in the middle this time. Neither of them was prepared to tackle making a Christmas pudding, because it never tasted anything like their mother's. It was left to Annie to bring one of hers, already cooked, on Christmas Day. According to her proud husband, she made the best puddings south of Dublin.

Finally, Sean helped his mother to wrap up the remaining small gifts to place beneath the tree. His presents were hidden underneath her bed, where she hoped he wouldn't think of looking.

Later that night, too excited to sleep, Sean went to Mass with his mother, and his aunt and uncle. Oona had not been to Midnight Mass on Christmas Eve since Jacqueline was born, and she enjoyed catching up with the neighbours and parishioners who greeted her and her family warmly, wishing them all a happy Christmas and a better New Year. The church was decorated with ivy and she could smell the polished pews. Holly highlighted each station of the cross. An abundance of flowers adorned the altar, and the smell of candle wax was quite strong. The voices of the choir singing carols moved her to tears.

Lately, whenever she went inside a church, she became emotional. And the Star of the Sea held special meaning for her; it was the church where she and Eamon had been married. Tonight she felt its ambience wrap around her like a glove as she joined in the celebrations of Christ's birth with the rest of the congregation.

As they all knelt in front of the crib, her prayers were for her baby girl and her husband. And Sean helped her light candles in honour of the loved ones they would miss the next day and for the remainder of their lives.

Outside, the air had turned bitter as they walked home. The early morning was still, apart from the sound of their shoes slapping the pavement. The stars seemed brighter than usual and light spilt out from every window.

Sean, who was walking next to Dessie, broke the silence. 'I miss me dad and Jacqueline.'

'I know you do, lad.' Dessie placed his arm round his

shoulders. 'We all do.'

Oona glanced at Connie and they linked arms. 'They should be here,' she said.

'Perhaps they are,' Connie replied.

CHAPTER TWENTY-FIVE

On Christmas morning, Oona woke early and drew back the curtains. The street lamp was still on and she gazed down the garden, shimmering with frost, to the sleepy river beyond. How could she not remember? In her loneliness, she could hear Jacqueline's laughter ringing in her ears; the patter of her little feet, and Sean's protests when she pulled at his blankets. A tear rolled slowly down Oona's face and she wiped it away with a stroke of her hand.

She heard Sean's bedroom door open and jerked her head round. He plodded across the landing and stood in the doorway. His face held a sad expression. She guessed he too was remembering.

'It's all right, Sean,' she said, pulling on her dressing gown. 'We'll open our presents downstairs.' She walked towards him and placed her arm across his shoulders, unsure how he might react to the gesture. Now that he considered himself grown up, he had objected to any overt displays of affection. And although she wanted to hug him to her, she refrained, saying instead, 'Happy Christmas, son.'

He didn't reply, but just glanced down at his slippers, and she could see he was fighting back tears.

'Come on, love. Let's open our presents. The day will get better, I promise you. Aunty Connie will be here soon, and Grandad has bought tickets for us all to go to the pantomime tomorrow, at The Father Matthew Hall.'

A little smile brightened his face. 'Can Tommy come too?'

'I'm sure Grandad won't have forgotten him; if he has, Tommy can have my ticket.'

140

Downstairs it was dark, and she switched on the lamp and the gas fire. Sean turned on the Christmas tree lights and the room came to life. He looked down at the brightly wrapped Christmas presents on the floor by the tree. Jack's present was in the drawer of her dressing room table. She couldn't risk Sean or the family asking awkward questions she wasn't yet ready to answer.

'Are they all for me?' he asked excitedly.

In no time at all the room was littered with discarded wrapping paper and they found themselves surrounded by Meccano pieces and jigsaw puzzles.

Later, Sean settled down to watch television, while she busied herself in the kitchen. She wondered where Connie was. It was not like her to promise to help then not turn up.

By the time her sister did arrive, Oona's face was flushed, and a strand of her hair had come loose and hung down over her face. 'What happened? Where have you been?'

Connie stepped into the hall. 'My, that turkey smells good.'

'No help from you.'

'Sorry, Oona. I'm sworn to secrecy. You can blame Dessie. There's no buses running today, and we had to walk there and back.'

'What are you talking about? Walk where?'

'I can't tell you. But it's the reason I'm late.'

'Where's Dessie?'

'He had to go home to pick up a few bits. Is Sean in his room?' She glanced towards the stairs.

Oona smiled. 'He's trying on his new shirt.'

Connie walked across the hall to the dining room, which was only used on special occasions. The table was set for six, and Oona had made pretty serviettes from red crepe paper to compliment the white tablecloth. Red and green Christmas crackers decorated the table, and the glasses sparkled against the polished cutlery. A red candle in a silver holder centred the table. Behind every picture, a generous sprig of holly completed the room.

'Oh, it all looks lovely. You've left me nothing to do.'

'Don't you believe it,' Oona said, pulling her into the kitchen. 'If we're lucky, we might have time for a gossip and a glass of sherry.'

***

Oona was upstairs freshening up before serving dinner, when she heard squeals and whoops of laughter. She finished brushing her hair and hurried down stairs.

Sean was hunkered down, stroking the cutest crossbreed collie Oona had ever seen. Mainly black, it had a white apron down its front and two white paws.

Sean straightened up and threw his arms awkwardly around his uncle. 'Thanks, Uncle Dessie. Is he really mine? Isn't he lovely, Mam?'

Her eyes widened. '*A dog!*' She leaned and stroked it. The animal looked up at her with brown soulful eyes, wagged its tail and gave a little yelp. 'Does it come with instructions?'

'I hope you don't mind, Oona? It's only six months old, and lovely natured,' Dessie said.

'And it's house-trained,' Connie added quickly.

'Look, he likes me,' Sean was almost bursting with excitement. 'He's licking my hand.' He patted its head and the dog glanced up expectantly.

Perhaps it was just what Sean needed, and the twinkle in his eyes proved her right.

'Well, what can I say?'

'Sorry I didn't warn you,' her brother-in-law added. 'I wasn't sure until last night. Besides, it would have spoiled the surprise.'

It would have been better if they had consulted her first, but then, she might have said no. Now that she could see first hand how Sean had taken to the dog, how could she refuse?

'Where did you get him?'

'I bought him from a lady in Booterstown. Her husband's

away a lot and she doesn't have the time to take it for walks. She seemed pleased when I told her it was for a young lad. We'll help out with walks and stuff.' Dessie clipped the lead to the dog's red collar. 'Here, take him a run, Sean. He needs to get used to his new surroundings.'

'What are you going to call him?' asked Connie.

'Shep! I'm going to call him Shep.'

'What's wrong with Patch?' Connie offered. 'He's got a brown patch over both eyes.'

'Sorry, Aunty Connie. Come on, Shep,' Sean called, then bounded from the house.

Oona closed the door behind them. 'I can see he's bonded with the dog already. Thanks, Dessie.'

'I'm forgiven then?'

'What do you think?' She laughed. 'Help yourself to a drink. Dinner won't be long.'

When Oona's parents arrived, their arms were filled with bags and brightly packaged parcels. Her father was carrying his melodeon strapped across his front.

'Where's Sean?' he asked, as soon as he came through the door.

'Dessie's given him a dog for Christmas and he's taken it for a walk,' Connie explained, removing their coats, while Oona relieved her mother of the Christmas pudding and took it into the kitchen.

'I've got Sean's present outside,' James O'Hara said. 'I've hidden it behind Eamon's shed.'

'What is it?' Connie asked. 'You've never gone and got him a . . .?'

'Stop, Connie. It's a surprise. I'm going to leave it until later.'

'What, another one?' Oona cried, coming out from the kitchen. 'This is turning out to be an exciting day for Sean.'

'That's how it should be.' Her father followed his wife into the room.

'Can you switch on your television, Oona?' Annie settled herself in the comfy armchair. '*The Kennedy's of Castle Ross* will be on in a minute. You know how I hate to miss it.'

Oona laughed. 'It won't be on today, Mam, not on Christmas Day. You'll have to wait until next week.'

'Oh, that's a shame,' she tutted. 'I was looking forward to it an all.'

When Sean returned with the collie, his grandma made a fuss. 'Where did you come from?' She bent to pat the dog's head.'

'He's mine now, Granny, and I'm calling him Shep. Do you like him?'

'Of course I do, pet. He has eyes I couldn't say no to, and I'll save him all the scraps,' she chuckled. 'But wait until you see what I've bought you, Sean,' she said, searching her bag, and finally pulling out a football magazine. 'Although, I don't think Georgie Best will be featured in it yet,' she smiled.

'Oh, thanks, Granny. I love it.'

'And, look at this. I've knitted you an Aran sweater. It goes perfectly with your hair.' She held it up against him.'

And so the unwrapping of Christmas gifts went on. Shep sat between Sean's legs and watched him unwrap the rest of his presents.

Dessie passed round boxed nylons to the women. Connie, Oona and Annie had saved shillings on hosiery since Dessie got them at the factory for little or nothing. Some were imperfect, but the flaws rarely showed.

'I'm afraid they're all the same shade,' he said. 'I hope you all like American Tan.'

'They're my favourite. I keep snagging mine on that old desk at work. They are very welcome. Thanks, Dessie.'

When Oona's dad stood up, everyone stopped talking. 'I want you all to come to the door for a minute, especially you, Sean.'

'What for, Grandad?' He clambered to his feet, the collie

144

at his heels. His granddad disappeared behind the shed and emerged with a shiny, black racing bike.

'Cor, blimey! Who's that for, Grandad?'

'It looks about your size, lad,' James O'Hara said. 'I reckon you're old enough.'

Sean's eyes grew wider. 'It's smashing. I've always wanted a racer. Can I ride it now? Can I, please?'

'Come on, wrap up warmly and I'll take you up as far as the bridge.'

'Mam, will you look after Shep until I get back?' he called.

Smiling, they all watched him wobble a few times as he rode down the garden path, his grandad running to keep up with him.

When they got back, the smell of turkey and chestnut stuffing, roast potatoes and parsnips wafted down the hall as Oona and Connie carried the dinner to the table. It was a great success and, apart from the turkey having to be returned to the oven twice because it wasn't cooked enough – and finally ending up with its legs burnt to a crisp – everyone said how much they had enjoyed it. Annie's pudding went down a treat, covered with lashings of Bird's Custard, made by Annie herself.

Later, when they played Snakes & Ladders, Ludo and party games, Annie fell asleep. But when James played Christmas tunes on his melodeon, Annie was singing along with the rest.

Everyone had gone out of their way to make Sean's Christmas a happy one. He was the only child in the family now, Oona thought sadly, and it was understandable that they all wanted to indulge him.

That night, Sean made a bed in the corner of his room for Shep. They were already inseparable. Oona knew that he would be up at dawn to ride his new bike over to Tommy's, and she was happy for him. They had all got through the day exceptionally well but, as she got ready for bed, she thanked

God that Vinnie had decided to leave Ireland when he did. And she prayed that she would never set eyes on him again. When she heard Sean switch off his bedroom light, Oona, exhausted after the day's events, fell asleep as soon as her head hit the pillow.

CHAPTER TWENTY-SIX

While Oona enjoyed Christmas with her family, Vinnie Kelly was having a miserable time in Leicester. The weather had taken a turn for the worse and he couldn't ever remember feeling so cold. Snow and ice gripped the country and the newspapers referred to it as the Big Freeze.

He wished he hadn't been so hasty; he should have stayed in Dublin at least until after Christmas and enjoyed some festive fare from the hospitable Irish. Instead, he was holed up here with a woman whose cooking skills did not match her physical attributes. He had picked her up soon after arriving in the city. She lived close to the railway station, which suited him for now; easy access to the city and the dole queue.

His own room, at best, felt warmer, but he'd left owing a month's rent and couldn't go back. He blew into his cupped hands and peered out through the grimy curtained window, cursing the incessant snow. Without a shilling to heat the place, the cold seeped through his overcoat. He kicked a chair across the room. It made a crashing noise against the wall and splintered, doing nothing to relieve his frustration. Why couldn't he have gone for a woman with a bit of cash, instead of one who drank and smoked most of what she earned? Her jewellery was junk, she'd nothing he could sell. He flung open the fridge. It was empty apart from a couple of bottles of cider. He drank one and dropped the other into his coat pocket.

After weeks of trying to track down Roly, who had committed the robbery with him, he was desperate to get his hands on his share of the money. According to a trusted source, there had been sightings of him in Leicester. And eventually, he wouldn't be able to resist a visit to his family. Roly was a sucker like that. When that happened, Vinnie would be waiting.

At the time he'd agreed to drive the getaway van, he had known the gang members were intent on armed robbery. It had made no difference to him; he wanted the money as much as they did. Roly had managed to give the police the slip, while Vinnie had paid with two years of his life. It wasn't supposed to happen like that, and he still harboured resentment towards Roly and the accomplice who'd helped him.

He clenched and unclenched his hands, anger burning through him. One way or another, he would not return to Dublin empty-handed. The snow was still falling. If he stayed here much longer, he would freeze to death. The only way he could keep warm was to mope around the shops until lunchtime. Then he would pay her a visit at the cafe where she worked, near the market. She might take pity on him, slip him a free dinner as she usually did.

His stomach rumbled as he closed the door behind him and trudged through the snow and treacherous conditions. He could barely feel his feet. As he walked, his mind drifted back. He hated to admit Oona was out of his league; it only made him want her more. But there was a time when he felt sure she had loved him.

How easy it had been to win her trust back then. He hadn't been truthful with her about his past – he didn't want to lose her. The first Christmas after they had met, she had invited him to her house for dinner. Just thinking about the food made his mouth water and he imagined himself sinking his teeth into one of her mother's pastries.

He lingered outside the window of the pork butcher's. People hurrying past out of the snow stared at him. He realised how desperate he must look. The wonderful smell of the pork pies made him drool and his hunger pains came back stronger than ever.

Being broke was all due to other people letting him down. Things might have turned out differently had he waited until he was financially secure before contacting Oona. But, once he knew she had been widowed, he hadn't been able to wait to see her again. Her rejection had bruised him badly.

Next time, his approach would be different. Next time, he wouldn't fail. Once he arrived in Dublin, he'd rent a nice flat, surround himself with expensive ornaments and tasteful art; buy some fashionable clothes, a gold ring, or two. She was bound to be impressed and realise he was serious about winning her back, and the boy too.

He'd often wondered how they were but he'd never done anything about it, then time passed. He felt a pang of regret. He could have had it all – Oona, the boy, a nice home to come back to at night.

She had parents who cared about her, a family and friends as he remembered. No doubt she still had. Who did he have? *The kid!* The kid was his, all right. All he could lay claim to for now. He'd never known his own parents. As far back as he could remember he'd been fostered, and discovered early on he'd been put into care soon after birth. No-one ever came looking for him. Why should he care about anyone? He'd take what he could from life, wherever he could, and think no more of it.

At sixteen, the authorities had disowned him and sent him out onto the streets of Dublin to fend for himself. He'd tried working for a while, but then he'd turned to petty crime to make ends meet. One thing had led to another, and before long he had found himself in trouble with the Gardí. Even now, he had to watch his step, because he was known to the police on both sides of the Irish Sea.

He arrived at the Town Hall Square, his stomach rumbling. He shook the snow from his shoulders and sat down by the fountain to smoke his last cigarette, drawing the smoke around his numbed fingers. He glanced at the clock, willing the hands to move. She'd told him not to turn up at the cafe before twelve, and he had to keep her sweet.

If Roly didn't show soon, he thought, it would be a pleasure to pay his family another visit. The weekend might be a good time to make his move. Sure as hell, he wasn't leaving Leicester until he'd been paid, and paid in full. Right now, he wasn't particular what he'd have to do to get it.

CHAPTER TWENTY-SEVEN

The New Year arrived with no word from head office regarding Jack's status at Worldwide Shipping, and Oona did her best to relieve his flagging spirits.

'If you weren't being considered, wouldn't they have sent a replacement by now?'

A few mornings later, a letter arrived with an English stamp. Brenda crossed her fingers before taking it to Jack. Moments later, Oona went into his office to get his signature on a missing consignment. The letter lay open on his desk.

'Good news, I hope, Jack?' She passed him the paperwork.

'Well, it depends.' He signed her document and handed it back.

'Why?' She sat down and crossed her ankles. 'What do you mean?'

'One of the directors, Mr. Peterson, is flying over from London on Friday to see the Kovacs before they leave, and he's coming here first to interview me. He wants to see how the agency's run and talk over some of the finer details.'

'What time does he arrive?'

'His flight gets in at noon. I'll pick him up. Show some Irish hospitality.'

'Will you take him for lunch?'

'I guess his priority will be the interview, don't you?' Smiling, he said, 'I'll offer to take him for a Guinness later.'

'This run-down tenement won't impress him.'

'*Hardly!*' He raised an eyebrow. 'The first day I arrived, I couldn't wait to get outside again in the fresh air.' He folded his arms.

Oona smiled. 'I remember.' She stood up. 'I hope he realises how much we need you at the helm.'

'You're very kind, Oona. If the worst happens, you'll cope admirably.'

'Now you're being kind,' she said. All she could do was to pray that Mr. Peterson would see Jack's potential.

Brenda walked in with an invoice Jack had asked for the previous day. She leaned across his desk, showing more thigh than usual in a white mini-skirt.

'Thanks. Just about to come and ask you for that.'

The girl blushed and fluttered her eyelashes.

Oona shook her head slowly from side to side. She was beginning to weary of Brenda's constant flirting with Jack. And that skirt was definitely a couple of inches shorter than the last time she'd worn it.

'Is there anything else you want, Mr. Walsh?' Brenda asked, lowering her gaze.

'No. That'll be all thanks, Brenda.' He stood up and ran his hand through his hair. For the first time, Oona heard the tension in his voice and noticed a frown wrinkle his brow. Friday's meeting meant a lot to him – and not just him.

'Well, good luck with the interview, Jack,' she said.

Nodding, he smiled and lowered his head over a stack of documents.

'What interview?' Brenda asked, when she came out. 'Is someone taking over from Jack?' Her eyes widened.

'No, Mr. Peterson is coming over from London to interview him for the job.'

'Well, in that case, I'm definitely going to St. Jude's tonight. Do you ever go?'

'No. I'm usually too tired when I get home from work. Connie and Dessie go every week. They're praying for a baby.'

'Sure, my ma was married two years before she conceived with me, so she was. She prayed to Him and now she's got six of us.' Brenda giggled.

Oona forced a smile. Strange how people's lives turn out.

Connie believed in the power of the saint of hopeless causes but, since the accident, Oona found it hard to believe in prayer.

'Sure, why don't you come and see for yourself? You might enjoy it.'

'Thanks, but no thanks, Brenda. I don't think St. Jude can do anything for me.'

***

That afternoon, Brenda picked her nails and stared into space. Oona bit her lip in an attempt to remain calm in spite of a growing mountain of paperwork. The girl was beginning to irritate her, continually talking about Jack. 'How many girlfriends do you suppose Jack's had?' she asked dreamily.

'Oh, for heaven's sake, Brenda! There's all this work to get through and I'm still waiting for these invoices.' She threw a list of numbers across the desk.

'What's eatin' you?'

'*You are!* And if you choose to do nothing but ask stupid questions, you might as

well not be here.'

Brenda rustled a few papers and mumbled, '*feck off*' under her breath.

Oona stared stonily. It wasn't the first time she'd heard her use bad language, and by now despaired of her ever changing. 'I've warned you before about using that word in the office.'

Brenda lowered her head and a tear trickled down her face. In a short time her desk was tidy, her paperwork in neat piles. 'I'll make the tea now, if it's all right with you!'

Left alone, Oona wondered if she had been too harsh. After all, Brenda was young and, at times, a bit naive. She could not help noticing the growing confidence in her recently, acting as if she was the boss's girlfriend. It crossed Oona's mind to speak to Jack, but he had enough on his plate right now. To Brenda, Jack was becoming more than just a fantasy that could soon get out of hand. Anyone other than Jack might have taken advantage of her by now, but she'd hate to see the girl get hurt.

Brenda carried the tea in on a tray and for the next hour concentrated on the filing. When Oona noticed the amount of work they had done without chatting, she gave Brenda an encouraging smile.

***

On Friday morning, Oona found Jack poring over the accounts.

'Morning, Jack.'

He glanced up. 'Morning, Oona.'

'Is there anything I can do?'

'Everything appears to be up to date,' he said, closing the books.

'Do you think Mr. Peterson will make his decision today?'

'I don't see why not. He's a director and I'm hoping for some clear indication afterwards. Between you and me, if he turns me down it'll leave me no choice but to return to Universal Shipping.' He paused to glance at his watch.

She imagined him counting the hours to Mr. Peterson's arrival.

'At least Mr. Mountjoy has guaranteed me my job if . . .'

'I'm sure that won't happen. Stay positive, Jack. Brenda's done the Novena to St. Jude.'

'Really! I'm touched. I hope he listened.'

'Well,' she said, 'if you think of anything I can help with . . . although, I've not been very successful lately with job interviews.' She hadn't meant to say that. It had just slipped out.

'I didn't know you were looking, Oona.'

'I thought Mr. Kovac was coming back.'

'I see,' he said. 'Are you still looking?'

'That depends,' she said, awkwardly.

'On today's outcome, you mean?' He sighed. 'That makes two of us, then.'

She felt awful now. 'Well . . . I suppose . . . it would make my decision easier.'

'Have you been offered another job?'

'No.'

'Good! Well, hang on, and wish me luck.'

'Oh, I do. I'm keeping my fingers crossed.'

He glanced at his watch again, leaving Oona in no doubt how anxious he was not to be late arriving at the airport.

***

When Jack returned with the director, Oona was busy on the phone and Brenda dashed about looking for paperwork. Mr. Peterson paused inside the door and glanced around. His navy overcoat swung open to reveal a dark grey suit with matching waistcoat. His black, quality shoes shone as if for inspection. In spite of sporting a dark moustache, his grey wispy hair showed signs of thinning.

Oona replaced the receiver and scribbled numbers onto a notepad.

'This is Mrs. Quinn, and our junior, Miss Byrne,' Jack said.

'How do you do, Mrs. Quinn? I trust you're well.'

'Very well thanks, Mr. Peterson,' she said and shook his outstretched hand.

'Good, good.' He smiled warmly. Her phone rang again and she had to answer it. Jack steered him towards his office.

For the next hour the women worked diligently side by side, both with their own private thoughts, aware that the important interview taking place next door could well change their lives.

When the men finally emerged, Jack was smiling. He informed Oona that he would be out for a while and Mr. Peterson smiled and nodded. After they left, the phones rang continuously. With no time to dwell on what the two men had discussed, Oona could only trust the interview had gone well. She was desperate for Jack to return and put them out of their misery.

At four thirty, Brenda reluctantly gathered up the post. 'Oh, do I have to go?'

'I'm afraid so, Brenda. Jack might not come in again today.'

'Do you think he's got the job?'

'I hope so. Mr. Peterson didn't look like a man who'd just delivered bad news.' Just the same, she hoped her observations proved right.

CHAPTER TWENTY-EIGHT

Jack rushed into the office just as Oona was about to leave. 'Shake hands with your new boss.'

'Oh, that's wonderful. Congratulations, Jack.' His hand felt soft as he held hers in a warm handshake. 'What did Mr. Peterson say?'

'Quite a lot, Oona. After he'd offered me the job and I'd accepted, he went on to discuss the lease of this property. It runs out at the end of February.'

'Mrs. Kovac hasn't renewed it then?'

'Apparently not!' He was still smiling. 'Can we discuss it over a drink?'

'You mean now?' She glanced at her watch.

'Well, it's not every day one becomes manager of a shipping agency.' He laughed.

She would have to get word to her mother, otherwise she'd assume all sorts had befallen her. 'I'll just phone our Connie before she leaves the hair salon.' A few minutes later, they were on their way.

'How old is Sean?' Jack asked, as they left the building.

'He's almost a teenager, would you believe? And he's never home now he's got the dog.'

'You've got a dog?'

'Yes. A Christmas present from my sister and her husband.' Keeping pace with his long strides, she continued a breathless commentary as they crossed O'Connell Bridge. Gulls squawked and circled over the Liffey, and passing buses – full to standing – belched out chemical exhaust fumes.

'As a boy, I wanted a dog, but my mother wasn't keen.'

'Not sure I am.' A cold wind rushed at her face and blew wildly at her hair. Her high heeled shoes started to pinch. 'Can you slow down a bit?' She stopped to catch her breath. She was carrying a small amount of groceries in a string bag.

'I'm sorry. Here, let me carry that.'

'Is it much further?'

'It's just off Grafton Street. Davy Byrnes. Have you heard of it?' He placed his hand lightly on her elbow as they stopped for traffic.

'Can't say I have, but if it's anywhere near Grafton Street I've probably passed it a dozen times.'

A street photographer flashed his camera, handing Jack a ticket. Without stopping, he pressed it into his breast pocket.

'Can't tell you the number of times Connie and I've been caught by a street photographer. We never collect the pictures.'

'I suppose they have to make a living,' Jack said as they headed up Grafton Street, still busy in spite of the fact it was almost closing time. 'My brother, Michael, talks about this place all the time so I thought I'd give it a go.'

'Well, here we are.'

It was nothing like she had expected, and she was not surprised that she and Connie had passed it by. From outside, the large plate glass window resembled a posh sweet shop minus the sweets, while the doorway had the markings of a well-used pub entrance.

Jack held the door open. 'I hope I've made the right choice.' He noticed her curious expression.

She hurried in, delighted to be out of the bitter cold. The pub's cosy atmosphere drew her further inside. McCarthy's pub flashed fleetingly into her mind, but this place was different. She felt safe here. Men and women shared space at the bar. The mood was friendly and women sat on high stools sipping cocktails.

'The pub's quite old, but you'd never think it, would you?' he said. 'Some of Ireland's literary greats are known to have visited at some time and James Joyce was a regular.'

'Really! I'll just check out the ladies.' She couldn't wait to tidy her windswept hair, check the seams of her stockings and smear a light coating of lipstick across her lips.

When she came out, Jack, perched on a stool by the bar, was looking up at the Art Deco stained glass windows in the ceiling, the colours reflecting the light.

She followed his gaze. 'The bold colours are remarkable.'

'Yes, I think so too,' he said, turning towards her. 'What would you like to drink, Oona?'

'As we're celebrating,' she said smiling, 'I'll try a Cherry-B, please.' All along the bar she could hear the noise of pleasant conversation.

'Will you have something to eat with it, only I'm famished?' He laughed. 'Now that I can relax, I could eat a horse, and I hate eating alone.'

She remembered Connie saying similar to her on occasions to get her to eat. But her appetite had improved since then. 'Anything with cheese will be grand,' she said. It was almost teatime and she was feeling peckish.

'You sit down and I'll join you in a moment,' he said, turning to the bartender.

Surprised to see so many people in the pub at this time of the evening, she walked towards the empty seating underneath the window, stopping on the way to admire the murals of Joyce's Dublin and other priceless paintings of the 1940s by Brendan Behan's father-in-law.

'It's very nice, Jack,' she said, as he slid into the curved seating next to her.

'I was hoping you'd like it. Are you all right here?'

'Fine.' She slipped off her coat. 'So, what's this story about the lease?'

'Mr. Peterson was appalled at the conditions we operate from, especially the outside privy. He suggested looking around for somewhere else.'

'When will you do that?'

'It'll have to be soon.'

'You must have impressed him.'

'I hope so. He wants to see trade doubled by next year. The business is out there, Oona. I've just got to bring it in.'

'That's great. You must be pleased.'

'Yes, I am.'

The barman arrived and placed their drinks on the table with a selection of sandwiches, along with two cream slices.

'If there's anything else you'd prefer . . . I can . . .'

'Oh, no. This is fine.' As she spoke, she was trying to work out the best way to tackle the thick sandwiches.

She picked up her drink. 'Well, here's to you, Jack.' Their glasses touched, making a clinking sound. Then they tucked in, enjoying the food and the pleasant surroundings while Moore's melodies played softly in the background.

'Is it too soon to ask if you're still looking for another job?'

She had no intention of leaving and missing the fun of moving to new premises. Besides, where else would she find such a handsome boss she felt comfortable working with? And, if she was honest with herself, she was growing to like him more with each passing week. 'To be truthful, Jack, I was dreading Mr. Kovac coming back. I wouldn't have stayed.'

She bit into the cheese and tomato sandwich. The bread was crisp and fresh and the full flavour of the cheese melted in her mouth. She hadn't expected to enjoy it so much. The juicy bits of the tomato ran down her chin and he gently wiped it away with his napkin. She felt the colour rise on her cheeks.

'So, you'll stay?'

Smiling, she nodded, munching her bread.

'Is that a yes, then?'

'I think so.'

'Great.' He polished off a ham and mustard sandwich and supped his pint. 'I can promise you, as business increases your job will become more interesting. I'd like to start viewing some leasehold properties straight away. Are you free tomorrow morning, Oona?'

'Tomorrow morning! Yes, I think so.' At least she would be, once Sean left for football practice. 'Do you have somewhere in mind?'

'No. Not really. Somewhere along the quay would be great. I'll have to see what's on offer.'

'Okay!' She pressed her serviette to her lips, leaving a red imprint.

'Can you meet me outside Harry Lisney's on Stephen's Green? Ten o'clock. Would that suit you?'

'Great! I've never viewed business premises before.'

'Me neither. Two rooms would suffice. Anywhere would be better than where we are at present. Indoor facilities are a must.'

'Can we afford such luxury?' They both laughed.

'Old buildings can be dusty, Oona. So, don't wear anything good.'

'Thanks for the warning. I'll wear flat heels too.' She licked cream from the tips of her fingers. 'Umm . . . that was delicious.'

He smiled. 'Well, I've taken up enough of your time. Sean will be wondering where you are.' He stood up and helped her on with her coat.

'I doubt that. He spends more time with his friend, Tommy, than he does with me.' She glanced at her gold watch.

'Is it keeping good time?'

'Accurate to the second.' She had hardly noticed how quickly an hour had passed. 'Thanks for the drink and the lovely food, Jack.' She tied the belt of her coat around her waist, and wrapped her scarf around her neck.

He grabbed his coat and picked up her shopping. 'We can catch the same bus.'

'What about your car?'

'I've had a few pints today, Oona. Although I'm sure my

body's absorbed the earlier ones, I'll pick it up tomorrow.' He nodded towards the barman and, with his hand on the small of her back, guided her from the premises.

CHAPTER TWENTY-NINE

Just when Oona thought that the weather couldn't get any colder, a coating of heavy frost covered the pavements. Dressed in jeans and a white sloppy Joe, she pulled on the fleece-lined jacket she had borrowed from Connie and zipped it up. Wearing the black, knee-high leather boots her parents had bought her for Christmas, she made her way to the bus.

In the city, trees in and around the park appeared twiggy with a dusting of white. It was still early and Saturday shoppers had yet to descend on Grafton Street.

She didn't recognise Jack huddled in the estate agent's doorway, until he turned and faced her. The hood of his duffle coat completely covered his head and his chequered scarf flapped in the breeze.

'Have I kept you waiting?'

'Not at all. My train was early.' He rubbed his gloved hands together. 'I thought it best to pick the car up later.'

'Very wise.' Oona was quite happy to walk, even in this Arctic weather.

'Thanks for coming,' he said. 'Shall we make tracks?'

She glanced down at his brown boots and dark green corduroys and smiled.

He looked so unlike the impeccably suited Jack she worked with.

'Where're we going?'

'All four premises are in the centre,' he told her.

The pavements were treacherous and they walked carefully; at least she didn't have to keep up with his long strides today. When she almost slipped, Jack reached out to steady her. 'Here, take my arm, Oona.'

Frightened she'd fall her length, she linked her arm through his. It reminded her just how much she missed the physical contact of a man. To onlookers, they were no different to any other happy couple strolling through town on a Saturday morning.

'Trust me to drag you out on the coldest day of the year.'

'That's okay! Really, I don't mind.'

They viewed luxury offices above the bank in O'Connell Street that were way over their budget, but they couldn't resist looking at them anyway. The next was a damp warehouse with leaking windows, along the quay, with an outside convenience that didn't work.

'Who'd want to rent this dump?' Jack's face creased with disappointment.

'You'll just have to keep looking.'

'There's a couple more to see, but I'll understand if you've had enough.'

'No. I'm fine. Where's the next one?'

They paused on O'Connell Bridge and Jack scanned his piece of paper. 'It's further down towards City Quay,' he pointed across to the other side of the bridge. 'But after what we've just seen, I'm not holding out much hope.'

'No harm taking a look,' she said brightly.

They walked for a while before they heard the sound of men's voices and cargo being loaded. Large cranes lifted heavy bulk on and off the ships. It was the first time she'd come this close to the docks and she stopped to watch the activity. Hungry gulls screeched overhead and one swooped down.

'Watch out, Oona. Seagulls have no respect for ladies.' He waved it off, but not before it deposited a streak of sticky white mess down her long hair.

'It's not the first time I've been christened,' she said, good humouredly searching her bag for a tissue.

'Here, let me.' Lifting her hair, he placed it over his hand and wiped it clean with his handkerchief. 'That's got most of it.'

'Thanks. My mam says it's lucky.'

'Isn't that when it falls on the washing?'

'Oh, you've spoilt it now, Jack,' she said.

'Sorry. Can I take that back?' He smiled, then paused outside what looked like a lock-up garage.

'Do you think we've walked too far up, Jack?'

'Umm . . . I was expecting units of some sort. There's a path down the side. I wonder if it's down there?' Jack walked in front of her along the entrance, where they discovered a grey pebble-dashed building with a flat roof. It looked nothing like an office from the outside. The key turned in the lock, but the door wouldn't budge. Turning sideways, Jack pushed his shoulder up against it and it opened. A stack of mail, leaflets and advertisements were piled up on the other side. Jack went behind the door and shifted them into a corner of the small vestibule. It was dark inside, apart from a small skylight.

Oona popped her head round the door, pulled on a string and a light came on. There was a musty smell and she wrinkled her nose.

'What was it used for, Jack?'

He looked around. 'I don't know. It doesn't look like it's been occupied for some time. But why leave the electricity on?'

Oona placed her handbag on the wooden draining board, where a plant resembling a geranium in a terracotta pot withered on the window sill. The tap dripped into a cracked ceramic sink.

'The water's not been turned off either.'

Jack turned on the single tap. The water gurgled in the pipes and splattered out in a burst. He lifted the plant, barely alive, and placed it under the running water.

Oona looked on amazed. 'Do you think that will revive it, Jack?'

'Who knows? Stranger things have happened.' He glanced up at the ceiling and then down at the floor. 'See if you can find anything interesting this end, Oona. And watch out for loose wiring. Can't have you tripping up again,' he said, smiling. 'I'll have a gander down here.' He wandered off down the narrow passage towards the back of the building.

When Oona rejoined him, he was hunkered down at floor level, the mottled lino rolled back. He'd removed his coat, revealing a yellow crew-neck sweater over a checked shirt, the tail of which hung down below his jumper. He straightened up and ran his hand up and down the green painted wall. 'There's no sign of any damp.'

'Good, and there's a toilet and a wash basin at the far end.'

'Such luxury,' he joked, and turned to face her. 'Could you pass me that tape measure on the window ledge please, Oona?' And as she handed it to him, he said, 'Grab one end, will you? I want to measure the floor space.'

As she watched him scribble down dimensions onto a piece of paper, she was beginning to realise there was much more to Jack Walsh than she'd first thought.

The windows looked out onto a concrete yard and a few dead flowers in pots. There was a build-up of mildew along the window. When he saw her looking at the mould, he walked over to join her. 'That'll disappear once air is circulated.' He undid the window catch. 'Have you looked in the other room yet, Oona?' Jack went with her down the passage, their footsteps echoing in the empty building.

'It looks okay to me,' she said. 'Do you think the radiators work?' She ran her hand along the top.

'It's hard to say. I can always find out. What do you think of it so far?'

'It's great. I don't think you'll better it, Jack.' She liked it a lot, but it wasn't really up to her. Despite it being further away from the centre of town, her imagination was running away with her as she pictured what it could look like if they moved up here. 'Will it be noisy so close to the docks?' she asked.

'It could be, but if we're working at the back it might be

okay. And with vacant possession, we could be up and running within weeks.' He was gesticulating with his hands. 'I'll get Mr. McGuire to check everything out before I do anything else. The move shouldn't be too difficult. I can take a lot of the files across by car,' he said. 'Carry down a few boxes if I have to. Of course, I'll hire a van to take the bigger stuff.'

She heard the excitement in his voice and struggled to keep her own emotions in check.

As they walked back toward the front of the building, Oona slipped a silk Paisley headscarf from her bag and tied it underneath her chin. 'I'm not taking any chances,' she explained.

Laughing, Jack gave the door a sharp tug. The handle came off in his hand.

Oona giggled. 'Another job for McGuire.'

Outside, the frost had disappeared and hazy sunshine struggled to come out from behind the clouds.

'If we hurry, I'll catch the estate agent before he closes.' He placed his hand on her elbow. 'Then you must let me buy you a sherry to warm you up, Oona.'

'Oh, I can't, Jack. I'm meeting Connie. It's a sisterly thing, you know; a weekly catch-up.'

'That's a shame.' He sounded disappointed. 'But thanks a million for coming.'

They walked together as far as O'Connell Bridge then parted company. And for the first time ever, she wished she hadn't made arrangements with Connie.

***

At the coffee house, Connie beckoned her towards a table. Oona unzipped her jacket and sat down. 'Did you see the frost earlier?'

'Can't say I noticed.' Connie smiled impishly and Oona gave her a curious look.

'I know that look, Connie Flanagan! You're up to something. What've you bought now?'

'Nothing!'

The server carried in their food and as she left, Oona said, 'You've not been to work this morning, have you?'

'How can you tell?'

'You smell different.'

'Oh, you mean I don't stink of setting lotion.'

Oona laughed. 'Well, I wouldn't put it quite like that. I prefer the smell of lavender.'

'Nice, isn't it?' Connie sniffed her wrist.

'So, why'd you stay off work, Connie? You're not sick, are you?'

'No, but I said I was.' She giggled. 'Well, it's a little white lie, but I am sick; sick with excitement, Oona.' Connie hugged herself as if to contain her glee.

'Why, what's happened?'

'Dessie's agreed to adopt. I could hardly sleep for thinking about it.'

Oona leaned across the table and squeezed her hand. 'That's brilliant news, Connie. I'm thrilled for you. About time Dessie saw sense. You don't want to be too old when you adopt.'

'*Too old!* I've just turned thirty, for heaven's sake. You don't think..?'

'No. Of course, I don't.'

'I rang one of the adoption societies this morning and they're sending me details. I want to strike while the iron's hot, before Dessie has a chance to change his mind.'

'He won't, will he?'

Connie's eyebrows shot upwards. 'I'm not taking any chances.' She laughed.

'Have you thought about the sleepless nights? For Dessie, I mean. And you'd have to give up work.'

'Oh, I don't mind that, but you're right, he might find it hard to adjust. He likes routine and you can almost set your watch by him. But he'll be fine once he holds a new baby in his arms.'

'So, what do you have to do now?'

'I've no idea. There's bound to be forms to fill in. Then I suppose we can go to the orphanage and pick out a baby. I'm not bothered if it's a boy or a girl,' she beamed. Connie looked radiant, as if she'd already conceived her own baby.

Oona had never doubted Connie's sincerity about wanting to adopt. But her brother-in-law concerned her. His idea of adoption could well mean a child he could interact with, take to the park and do boy things with. It could be the reason he had held off making his decision for so long. But these were only her assumptions; as close as she was to her sister, Oona didn't know everything about their marriage. She knew even less about adoption procedure. Her instinct told her that there was more to it than just filling in a form. Adopting a baby could take a long time. What if they were asked to foster an older child with problems? One like Vinnie!

It was early days, and she did not intend to dampen Connie's expectations. She and Dessie would discover these things for themselves.

'Anyway!' Connie broke her reverie. 'How did you get on this morning?'

'Oh, it was great, Connie. You'll never believe . . .' And, once she got started, she hardly stopped for breath, relating all that had happened at the office since Thursday. She was surprised to hear the excitement in her own voice.

Connie pushed her empty coffee cup aside and placed her elbows on the table.

'It sounds to me as if you enjoyed being with him.'

'Yes, I did.' When she'd linked her arm through his that morning she realised he meant more to her than she had first thought. 'He's a real gentleman, Connie. He understands how I feel, and he's always asking after Sean.'

'He sounds nice. I'd like to meet him.'

'We'll have to wait and see, Connie.' She laughed.

'You won't be looking for another job then?'

'I don't think so. Can you imagine Mr. Kovac involving

me in the business?'

'He's an old fuddy-duddy. And I dare say that Jack Walsh appreciates a woman's point of view.'

Oona finished her drink and Connie, looking lively again, pulled on her coat.

'You've not finished your cake.'

'I'm too excited to eat,' Connie said. 'Come on. Let's go round the shops. I can't wait to start looking at baby clothes.'

***

The following Wednesday Oona crossed the bridge to her sister's, a bitter wind swirling round her ankles. She wanted to hear more about the adoption and tell Connie all about the changes at the office.

Connie opened the door, her eyeliner smudged. 'Oh, Oona!' Her expression downcast, she said, 'Come in.'

'What's wrong?'

'Oh, it's nothing.'

Oona knew her sister better than that. She also detected a whiff of cigarette smoke; a clear indication that her brother-in-law had something on his mind. She followed Connie into the kitchen.

'Hi, Dessie,' she said.

Nodding, he crushed his half-smoked cigarette and pressed it forcibly into the ashtray. He looked as tense as a coil ready to spring at any moment. Connie bit her bottom lip then hung the shirt she had finished ironing on a hanger.

'Not interrupting anything, am I?' Oona felt she'd walked right into the middle of something important.

'Course not.' Dessie folded his newspaper. 'I need more ciggies,' he said, giving his wife a peck on the cheek before leaving the room.

Connie removed the ashtray from the table.

'What's the matter with Dessie?' Oona sat down. 'Have you two fallen out?'

Connie looked troubled. 'No! Nothing like that.' She

unplugged the iron and wrapped the cord around the handle. 'I'm being silly.'

Oona got to her feet, folded the ironing board and placed it inside the cupboard.

'Oh, Oona. I . . . I don't know what to think?' She sat down and ran her fingers distractedly through her short hair.

'What is it, Connie? You're not having second thoughts about the adoption?'

Connie shook her head.

'The other day you were so happy. What's changed?'

'It's Dessie.' She paused. 'I thought he'd be more enthusiastic, that's all. I'm frightened he's going to change his mind.'

'Surely not!'

'It wouldn't take much to put him off.'

'Why? What's he said?'

'He's worried about the change it will make to our lives. He . . . wants more time to think about it. Can you believe that?' Connie sniffed. 'I don't want to wait, Oona. What would you do?'

'Don't get disheartened, Connie. He'll come round when he's had time to get used to the idea.' Oona stood up and hugged her. 'Come on, Connie. I hate seeing you like this.'

'I'm sorry. I thought we'd settled on it.' She played with the corner of her handkerchief, damp from her tears.

'Well, that's men for you.' Oona smiled at her. 'You've got to be together on this before you take things any further, Connie.'

'I know. That's what's worrying me.'

'He agreed to it, didn't he? Now stop fretting.'

'This might be my only chance, Oona.' She sniffed into her handkerchief. 'I'm getting older and I might never have a child of my own.'

'Course you will.' Oona smiled at her. 'There's a baby out there somewhere for you. I'm sure of it. And you, Connie, need to stop worrying, otherwise Dessie may start to wonder if it's worth it. And don't let's forget how long it's taken for him to agree. Would you like me to have a word with him?'

'Thanks anyway, Oona. I'll have another chat with him when he gets back.'

'That's more like it. Stay positive.'

'What about you?' She forced a watery smile. 'When is the big upheaval taking place?'

'Oh, it's already underway, Connie.' Her own concerns regarding the office move and the missing files seemed unimportant now. 'Do you want me to hang on until Dessie gets back?'

'No. I'll be fine. You get yourself home. I'll let you know how things go.'

Outside, the wind was lighter and it was starting to rain. As she went past the bakery, the smell of the newly-baked loaves made her hungry. Her father was on the night shift, churning out bread for the early morning delivery.

On her side of the bridge, she glanced down the avenue. The lamp outside her house had gone out and a mist hung over the river. In the darkness, she could just make out the figure of a man, his shoulders hunched, sitting on the river wall opposite her house.

Her hand flew to her mouth and her heart began to pound. Vinnie. Please, God, not him. She gripped the wall, wet and slippery from the rain. She was about to turn back towards her sister's, when he stood up and limped away in the opposite direction. Could it be the same man she'd seen weeks before Vinnie's letters started arriving? She'd thought it was him that time too, and hoped it wasn't an omen!

CHAPTER THIRTY

It was a sunny day; but to Oona, March would always be a miserable month. Her mind seemed to be swirling with depressing thoughts as she walked with Brenda to the new offices. Both were dressed in clothes fitting the work that lay ahead. Oona's jeans flattered her slim figure, while Brenda's white plastic jacket and red trousers only accentuated her large thighs.

'You make me feel fat. I'm not, am I?'

'Don't be daft, Brenda. It's not a fashion parade.'

'My trouble is I've a sweet tooth,' she groaned.

The sweet tooth reminded Oona of Connie, and she wondered if she'd spoken to Dessie when he got home last night.

'Is it much further?' Brenda moaned. 'My heels are blistered.' She paused, lifted her leg and removed her shoe. The galvanized bucket she carried made a clattering noise as she dropped it down on the pavement. The sound of a wolf whistle from the nearby barge made them glance out across the Liffey. Two young men unloading barrels stopped to wave.

'Hey, Oona. Have a gander at those muscles,' said Brenda, lingering.

'Come on, you.' Oona shook her head. 'Let's get inside before you cause a riot.'

The two pots of early flowering narcissus and a couple of trailing plants were awkward to juggle as she pushed the key into the lock. She expected a struggle, but the door opened at the first attempt. The earlier fustiness of the empty building now smelled of freshly painted walls. 'A few days ago these walls were dark green,' she said, surprised at the effect.

'I love creamy-yellow, don't you?' Brenda was impressed. 'It's so fresh.' She stood with her back to the sink, her mouth open. 'It's lovely. I can't believe we'll be working here.' She rushed around opening doors and cupboards, pointing out where she intended to put the cutlery and the provisions, as if she was moving into her own house. 'Isn't Jack wonderful, finding this place for us?'

Oona nodded. 'Wait until you see the size of the offices.' She walked ahead, followed by Brenda, who marvelled at everything that caught her eye, especially the large radiators switched on to dry out the paint.

'Which office is ours?'

'They're both of similar size, but I guess this one.'

'Oh, yes, I can see us working in here.' Brenda shifted her gaze to the windows. 'They could do with a good clean. Where do you want me to start?'

While Oona cleaned the windows, Brenda scrubbed the kitchen floor, cupboards and the sink until it shone. Oona was amazed by her energy. 'You've done a grand job, Brenda.'

'I do it every week for me ma.'

If only she'd show the same dedication to her filing, Oona smiled to herself. She glanced at her watch. 'Look at the time. We'd better be getting back.'

On their return, they hardly recognised their old office. Desks were piled one on top of the other, boxes clearly labelled and filled with bills of lading. Other important records lay on the floor, and old carpets were rolled up ready to go.

Jack came out of his office when he heard them. He was wearing an old sweater, denims and a donkey jacket. 'Can you and Brenda fill all the empty boxes? If you need more, the corner shop might oblige. I want this place cleared today. Mr. McGuire will be here any minute to help me move the heavy stuff.'

'You should have said. We'd have come back sooner.' Oona

handed him the keys, which he dropped into his pocket.

'That's okay!' He winked at Oona. 'As you can see, there's still plenty to do.'

Brenda, zipped into her plastic jacket, busied herself packing the provisions. She wrapped newspaper around each piece of crockery as though it was precious china.

'When I get back, I'll take what's remaining across by car,' Jack added. 'Don't forget the kettle and, if there's any post, Brenda, I'll drop you off at the post office.' His voice echoed in the almost empty building.

Brenda's eyes widened. Oona knew only too well how long the teenager had waited for a ride in Jack's car. Luckily, there was one large package and a few letters to go.

'If all goes to plan,' he said, turning to Oona, 'we should be operating from the new premises tomorrow. I've informed most of the clients, but if I've missed anyone, could you let them know? There's still one phone connected.'

'Okay. I'll get stuck in.'

'Top of the morning to you, ladies.' Mr. McGuire paused just outside the door. He was covered in dust and smelling of putty. 'The devil woman's not here, is she?'

'Don't mention her, please, Mr. McGuire. You'll put a jinx on the day,' Oona said.

'Woe betide me. Now, I wouldn't want to do that, miss.' Smiling, he rubbed his dusty palms together. 'You'll be warm as toast over at the new place.'

'Thanks, Mr. McGuire. We've just come from there. It's looking great.'

'Ah, sure, it would do, after this place, miss.' He glanced round. 'Ye deserve a bit of comfort.'

He popped his head around Jack's door. 'Are ye ready then, Mr. Walsh, sir? Shouldn't take us long once we get started.'

'Good man. What're we waiting for?'

After they left, Oona kept busy and time flew by. Brenda was less than useless. Like a child waiting for Christmas, she glanced out of the window every five minutes for Jack's return.

'I've never been in a car before, except for one of me uncle's tractors, but you can't count that, can you?'

Oona nodded, hoping the girl would not read too much into it. When Jack finally returned, he placed the remaining bits and pieces and the kettle into the boot. Brenda ran outside, excitement brightening her face. She sat in the passenger seat waiting for him, the post perched on her knee.

He turned to Oona. 'I hope you don't mind being the last one here. Can you finish off and push the keys through the letterbox?'

Alone in the deserted building, the cold grimy walls appeared to close in around her. She was glad to be saying goodbye to the old tenement block; it was a reminder of too much sadness in her life. With the anniversary so close, she was not surprised she felt jittery. But it wasn't just that. Something else was bothering her. She didn't believe in ghosts, but the quiet, desolate office gave her the creeps. With one last look around, she gathered up her belongings and the few remaining folders. Pulling the heavy door shut behind her, she posted the keys through the letterbox and made her way home.

***

When she got off the bus, Sean ran up behind her, Shep at his side. There was a smell of wet dog as she bent to stroke its ears. The collie nuzzled her hand.

'Has he been swimming in the river, Sean?' she said, as they walked towards the house.

'Shep jumped into the pond. I couldn't stop him. The ducks made such a racket. They flew up, skimming the top of the water and fluttering their feathers.' Laughing, he shook his head. 'It was great fun. You should've heard the park keeper, Mam. He called Shep a mongrel, amongst other things, but we managed to pull him to safety.' Sean laughed again and patted the dog. 'You're a good swimmer, aren't you, Shep?'

Oona shook her head, too tired to argue. Sean's happy

laughter brought a smile to her face. 'You know you should keep him on his lead around the duck pond, Sean. You never learn, do you?'

'I'm sorry, Mam.'

'Take him round the back and dry him off before bringing him inside. Have you seen Gran?' She had to ask, because he had a habit of collecting Shep from his kennel and scooting off without a word, leaving her mother to worry where he was.

'Yes. I called in after school. She walked me home and peeled some potatoes for you.'

Her mother was like that, and Oona was grateful for all the thoughtful things she did. Tonight she wanted to forget about everything, put her feet up and relax.

'I've got good news, Mam,' Sean called from the back door, where he was attending to the dog.

'What's that, love?' She flicked through her post.

'It's in my school satchel on the kitchen chair. Have a look.'

The gas and electric were due – both for large amounts – making her sigh. With the recent cold snap, the gas fires had been on full. She despaired of ever getting on top of the bills that kept mounting each week.

'Mam, have you seen it?' Sean came back in, Shep's coat dry and fluffed up again.

'Sorry, love. What did you say?'

He opened his bag, pulled out the form and handed it to her. 'I need you to sign this.'

'What is it?'

'We're playing away next month.'

'Oh, so soon?' Her heart gave a little tug. She still worried that something might happen to him once he was away from her; something else she would have to get used to.

'It's only Limerick,' he said, noting her expression. 'Mr. Dunmore's taking us by coach. We've got to pay the money in by next week. I can't wait.' He clipped Shep's lead back on. 'Can I go and tell Uncle Dessie?'

177

'Yes . . . of course. Dinner in half an hour,' she called after him. She sat down and closed her eyes. Sean's trip to Limerick was another expense to add to her mounting debt.

She put on the dinner and sat down again to work out which bill she could afford to leave unpaid – electric, gas, or the instalment on the furniture. No matter how many hours she worked, it would take her weeks to clear this lot. She hadn't had a pay rise in well over a year and she hoped Jack, unlike the Kovacs, would appreciate the extra responsibility she'd taken on.

The vegetables boiled over and she jumped to her feet. Food was the last thing on her mind, but Sean would be back any minute with the hunger of an ever-growing boy. At least she didn't have to worry about him not eating properly. Most weeks he ate everything she could afford to put on the table, and more. She lit the grill, placed the small chops underneath and quickly set the table.

A lonely feeling settled around her. She could not put her finger on what ailed her. And for the second time that day, she felt a shudder run through her body as if someone had just walked over her grave.

CHAPTER THIRTY-ONE

South of the city, two miles from Oona's, Vinnie Kelly settled into a cosy flat. Since arriving in Dublin, he had kept to himself, speaking politely to the property owner only when he had to. Time enough for friendly chats with the neighbours when he had his girl on his arm. Just thinking about her got him excited. He wasn't sure how he felt about the boy, but he supposed he was part of the package. Perhaps he could learn to be a father to him. They would be like a real family.

He thought about Roly's family and felt only a modicum of regret at having threatened the woman and the kid. He hadn't killed anyone, but he'd have had no qualms about slitting her throat if she hadn't paid over the money. Roly was to blame. He could have spared them the anguish by paying up in the first place. The man's greed had almost cost him his wife and kid.

Roly was bound to come after him, so he figured the best way to keep him off his back would be to cut off contact with his old cronies. Any one of them would grass him up for a few quid.

He liked the flat; glad of the comfort he could now afford. He'd picked up a reliable second hand car. Old habits die hard, he grinned, remembering how easy it was. Once he had a new identity, he could relax. Until then, he'd keep his head down. He thought of the stuff he'd done in the past, the things he'd learned in prison, and how he'd survived. Existing on the outside had to be easier.

The property owner already knew him by his new name; it was on his rent book. Money had gained him respect in certain

179

quarters, and he intended to keep it that way. Only this morning, a neighbour had tipped his hat as he walked back from the shop, his newspaper rolled up under his arm, and the woman across the way smiled at him as she picked up her milk from the doorstep. All he had to do now was act like any respectable man privileged to live in Dublin 4, and no-one would be any wiser.

His hurried escape from Leicester had left him no time to buy a made-to-measure suit, so he'd settled for an off-the-peg, stylish, pin stripe from Burtons. A bad fit. Although it was similar to one he'd worn the first time he'd met Oona, he wasn't happy with it. He looked at himself in his bedroom mirror and pulled in his beer belly. He'd put on a few pounds here and there, but a couple of trips to the gym and he'd soon lose that. He ran his hands through his thinning hair, once the colour of sand and his pride and joy. Now the tint barely covered the grey. But it made him feel younger.

He wasn't old. Not that bad looking either, if it wasn't for this damn scar. He would have been a dead man if it hadn't been for the prison security guard. Maybe he should re-grow his stubble; disguise it somehow. He flashed a gold tooth. He had gone through a lot of pain to have that done, but it was impressive, even if he said so himself. Winning Oona back had been his incentive.

That afternoon, casually dressed in a black jumper, brown corduroy trousers, a black leather jacket and carrying a bag with his workout clothes, he went to the gym. Afterwards he had his hands and nails treated before going to the barber's. It was ages since he'd pampered himself and it felt good, even though his hands still felt rough.

Later that evening, he went to a secret address in the city to pick up his new identity papers. The guy wouldn't give his name and kept his face covered during the transaction. When Vinnie complained of being overcharged, he was reminded of the risk the man was taking on his behalf, and paid up without further objection. With his new identity, there was nothing to link him to Vinnie Kelly. He was home and dry.

That night he slept soundly. But a few nights later, he woke in a cold sweat, his arms and legs lashing out as if fighting off a monster. He dreamt Roly's fat face was bearing down on him, his enormous body suffocating. Vinnie couldn't breathe and thought he was going to die. For the first time he felt fear. It was not until he forced his eyes open and they became accustomed to the light, that he realised he had been having a nightmare. Was his conscience pricking him after all? He'd never believed in all that stuff, nor confessing to the priest that Oona used to talk about. He did what he had to and that was it, as far as he was concerned.

As soon as he was happy with his appearance, he'd call. He knew where she lived and he was desperate to see her again. But he couldn't afford to mess up this time.

A few nights later, a loud buzzing sound woke him. Thinking it was his alarm, he reached out to silence it. It was five in the morning. Once he'd focused, he realised it was the door.

'Who the hell?' he muttered. Roly immediately came into his mind and his heart raced. He crawled from the bed, pulled on his silk dressing gown and peered through the curtains. A car belonging to the Gardá was parked outside under the lamp. He grinned. The police had nothing on him. He wasn't Vinnie Kelly. Gathering his thoughts, he walked across the room and threw open the door.

Two police officers stood on his doorstep. 'Sorry to disturb you, sir. This is highly unusual, but we're calling on a number of houses in the area, investigating a car theft. The car belongs to a foreign diplomat and we are anxious to trace it as quickly as possible. Would you mind telling us how long you've lived here?'

'A few weeks.'

'And you've not noticed anyone acting suspiciously in that time, sir?'

'Can't say I have.' He shook his head. 'Sure, you can't trust anyone these days.'

'Can we see some form of identification, sir? A bill or a rent book, please?'

'Sure.' And as he turned back into the room, a slow grin spread across his face.

Moments later, the officers were tipping their hats. 'Sorry to have disturbed you, Mr. Dempsey.'

Nodding, he closed the door. A decent citizen like himself would never be under suspicion for car theft now, would he? The vehicle was in a lock-up garage a few miles away and, in view of this incident, that is where it would stay until he changed the number plate.

He switched on the kettle, sat on the bed and smoked a cigarette all the way down. Then he lay back on the pillow, hands behind his head, his mind preoccupied with Oona and plans to sweep her off her feet.

The kettle clicked off and he made himself a strong coffee. He opened the curtain and gazed out at the empty street. Soon, very soon now, he would be ready to execute his perfect plan.

CHAPTER THIRTY-TWO

On the long walk from the bus to City Quay, Oona always found she had too much time to dwell on her money worries. Each morning her intention to ask Jack for a pay increase got pushed aside, as one problem followed another at the office. The settling-in period was proving difficult. Parcels and packages continued to arrive late due to mislaid paperwork. Irate customers refused to listen to her explanations, demanding to speak to the manager.

'Give it time,' Jack said. 'Things will settle down.'

Although Oona agreed with him, she ended up staying late most evenings in an attempt to find missing documents and shift the backlog that seemed to mount with each passing day.

One afternoon, she arrived back from lunch to see a man carrying a rolled-up carpet into Jack's office. So when she found Brenda perched over her typewriter, boldly hammering the keys, her desk littered with documents, and the phones ringing, she felt perplexed.

'What are you doing, Brenda?'

'I'm practising! Jack's sending me to night school for typing lessons.'

'He said that?'

'Yes.' Engrossed in what she was doing, Brenda continued her efforts, oblivious to the mayhem around her.

'Did he also say you weren't to answer the phones, Brenda?'

Giggling, the girl moved across to her desk and picked up her phone. When she replaced it, she said, 'Isn't it grand? I can't believe it. Me ma'll be that chuffed.'

A weak smile was all Oona could muster. She was pleased

for Brenda, but felt disappointed Jack had not mentioned it to her, nor had he said anything about the new carpet. There was only one machine in the office, and she had grown quite attached to her reliable Olivetti. Surely he didn't expect her to share it with Brenda? With important documents to be typed each day, she would never get anything done. She didn't know what to think.

Sighing, she placed a sheet of paper between the roller and found a gummed label stuck to it. She picked irritably at the sticky pieces.

'Jesus! This could take ages.' She glared at Brenda.

'Sorry.' Brenda looked contrite, her face flushed. 'It must've got stuck to the back of the paper.'

'Don't make me answer that.' Oona sighed aloud. The last time she'd felt this angry was when Sean had played truant. She knew if she said any more they would end up having a row. It wasn't Brenda's fault that her bills were overdue, she hadn't asked Jack for a pay rise or that he'd stopped confiding in her. She took a deep breath and hit the return carriage with such force it almost flew off the machine, making Brenda jump.

'Holy Mary . . . Oona! What's up with yeh?'

'Sorry, Brenda, I didn't mean for that to happen.' The situation was ridiculous. She needed a word with Jack, and the typewriter was added to her list of grievances. She would do it now before anything else stopped her.

Jack was on his hands and knees in the corner of his office, the carpet almost fitted. She could smell the newness of the green pile. Was there no end to his talents? He made no attempt to get up. 'Does that need signing, Oona? Pop it on the desk and I'll do it in a moment.'

Irritated, she watched him expertly push the carpet up to the wall so that it fitted perfectly. Clearly he no longer needed her help or advice. The carpet was his choice, just as it was to send Brenda to night school. If he hadn't felt it necessary to tell her himself, she decided not to raise the subject. If he noticed her sullen mood, he didn't comment.

She was desperate to speak to him about her money worries, otherwise she would go home miserable again. Trying to keep the annoyance out of her voice, she said, 'Can I have a word please, Jack?'

Smiling, he got to his feet. 'I'm sorry, Oona. Can it wait 'til morning? I'll sign these then I have to dash. I'm meeting Mr. Flynn and I can't be late.' He shrugged into his coat and hurried from the office.

Flummoxed and confused, she didn't care if Jack Walsh never confided in her again.

***

The following morning, Brenda was in the kitchen watering the plants when Oona arrived. 'Jack asked me not to put any calls through. What's going on?'

'I've no idea, Brenda.' Without bothering to remove her coat, she went down the corridor to his office. Jack closed the file he was working on and glanced up. 'Morning, Oona. Are you staying?' He was glancing at her green coat, still buttoned, and her scarf still wrapped snugly around her neck. Frightened she'd say something she might later regret, she took a deep intake of breath but remained standing. 'I thought I'd catch you before you disappeared again.' She unbuttoned her coat. Noting an edge to her voice, he sat forward.

'Please, Oona, sit down. You're making me nervous.'

Feeling silly now, she sat.

'What's on your mind?'

She felt hot, and colour flushed her face as she loosened her scarf and pulled it from around her neck. If only he would mention her wages and save her the indignity of having to ask. What she said next totally surprised her.

'If you want me to continue doing a professional job, Jack, I can't allow Brenda to use my Olivetti.'

'I'm sorry.' He touched his forehead. 'I've been so busy I forgot to tell you that your new machine will arrive in a few days.'

185

Cathy Mansell

What could she say, except to wish he had mentioned it before and that she had been more patient? 'Thank you. I hear you're sending Brenda for typing lessons?'

'I told her not to say anything until I'd spoken to you, but she couldn't keep it to herself, the little minx. Don't you think it's a good idea?' He folded his arms.

'It's a great idea . . . but what . . . what I . . . really . . .' she paused.

'I'm sensing a but, Oona. What is it?'

'I'd like to discuss my wages, Jack.' There, she'd said it.

'I'm glad you brought that up. I've been waiting for the right moment to discuss it with you. You know how it's been this past few days. Have lunch with me?' He stood up from behind his desk. 'We can talk about it then.'

She nodded, a smile lifting her face. The phone rang out and within seconds, he was pulling on his overcoat. 'Trouble at the docks, and Oona, if I'm not back by twelve, meet me in O'Keefe's in Abbey Street.'

***

When she arrived, Jack was sitting in a window seat glancing down the menu. She stood for a second looking across at him. How handsome he was. Soothing, classical music played in the background. They both ordered the leek and potato soup. It was cold outside and the soup was just what she needed.

As they tucked into the tasty soup and crusty homemade bread, Jack asked, 'When is Sean off to Limerick?'

'Next weekend, and I can't say I'm looking forward to him going.'

'I've no children, so I don't know what it's like. I'm sure he'll have a great time, though. I was in a boys' rugby team when I was ten, but I outgrew it, I'm afraid. Sean seems more dedicated.'

'Yes, he is. It keeps him out of trouble.' And, just as she was hoping Jack wouldn't keep her hanging on for a decision about her wages, he said, 'Oona, about what you asked me earlier. I'd

186

like to offer you promotion.'

Stunned, she frowned.

'I could do with an assistant manager. Your salary would be considerably more, of course.' Smiling, he continued, 'We make a good team. I'm thinking of advertising your position.' He leaned forward in his chair. 'That is, if you're happy to share my workspace? It makes sense with an office so big. I suppose you noticed I've been trying to make it girl-friendly. Not sure it doesn't still need a woman's touch.'

She could have cried, and ended up biting her lip in an attempt to stave off tears.

'What do you say?'

She swallowed to relieve the lump in her throat and, in spite of everything and the fact that they were in such a public place, tears filled her eyes.

'I never intended to make you cry.' He frowned. 'Wasn't it what you wanted?'

She lowered her head and her dark hair fell across her face, hiding the tears.

'Do you need time to consider?'

'No. No, I don't.' She brushed back her hair and looked up at him. 'Thank you, Jack, that's wonderful.' He had no idea how much it meant to her. Her money worries had turned her into someone she hardly recognised, and tonight she'd go and see Connie to tell her the good news. She stood up, a smile lifting her face. 'I'll be back in a second,' she said and made her way towards the powder room.

CHAPTER THIRTY-THREE

As Sean watched Z Cars with Tommy, Oona was in the kitchen ironing, and thinking about Jack. Talking things over with him had been easier than expected and she'd been wrong to doubt him. The positive way he got things done impressed her, and she found herself looking forward.

Having worked for Jack for nearly a year now, she admired him greatly; not just as her boss. He had the qualities she liked in a man – decisive, considerate and caring. Even so, he must have another side, just as she had.

The ironing done, she flicked through the bills on the table before pushing them into a drawer. She couldn't bear to look at them right now. Out of sight and out of mind. At least now they would get paid sooner, rather than later. With a contented sigh, she sat down to open Monica's letter which she'd saved to read in peace.

Dear Oona,

It's taken me days to pluck up the courage to write this letter. Chris is going to live in Canada, you know, on the assisted passage. He's always loved Ontario. Now, after a lot of soul searching, I've decided to go with him.

It's been bedlam at home. You know what Daddy's like and Mammy's been in bits. I feel bad about leaving them all, but it's not as if I'm an only one, is it? I've never felt this way about anyone before. You understand, don't you, Oona? Please write back with your support. All I can hope for is their blessing before I leave in April.

Forever friends,
Monica xx

April! Only a few weeks away. A lump caught in her throat. She'd known Monica since they were four years old; had gone to school with her. She'd miss her dearly. All she could do now was reply, show her support, wish her all the luck and happiness in the world and arrange to meet up before she went.

The click of the door made her glance up. 'Goodnight, Mrs. Quinn.'

'Oh, are you off, Tommy? I guess Sean's told you he's going to Limerick?'

'Ah, sure he'll have a grand time, so he will.'

Smiling, she nodded. 'Well, goodnight, Tommy.' As he turned to go, she couldn't help noticing he was wearing one of the new skinny polo shirts in dark brown with a yellow stripe across the back. The colour did nothing for his sallow complexion, but Oona felt pleased to see him in something new for a change.

After Tommy left, Sean talked non-stop about his weekend trip while she compiled a list of things he would need to take with him. He was growing fast. Most of his clothes were too small. Even the stripey pyjamas her mother had bought him in the January sales didn't fit any more.

He made a point of showing her his football kit. He was hard on clothes, and his shirt looked the worse for wear, yet he'd only had it a couple of months.

'Can't I have a new one, Mam?' he moaned.

'Where do you think the money comes from, Sean? You'll have to manage and make do with your boots too.'

'But they're pinching,' he scowled.

'Take them off and hand them here a minute.' She spread an old newspaper on the table. 'Your grandad loaned me these.' She held up a pair of wooden shoe stretchers.

'What are you going to do with them?'

Removing the laces, she pushed a shoe stretcher into the boots, tightening each peg as much as she could. 'Now leave

189

them like that until tomorrow and we'll see what happens. Your grandad swears by these.'

It would have been nice to be able to buy him new ones, but it would be a month before she felt the benefit of her increase in salary. Life was never easy. She'd have to borrow money from her dad to tide her over, otherwise she'd never manage. 'Now, go and get ready for bed, Sean. I'm going over to see Aunty Connie. Will you be okay?'

'I'm not five, you know.' He poured himself a glass of milk from the jug on the dresser, spilling some in the process.

'Go easy with that Sean or there won't be enough for breakfast.'

'We never have enough of anything. I thought you got promoted.'

'I did, but being on a salary means I'll get paid monthly. I'm sorry, love. Money is tight at the moment, but we're better off than most.'

***

Dessie opened the door with a bottle of wine in his hand, making her wonder if they'd had news from the adoption society.

'Come on in, Oona. You're just in time for a glass.'

'Are you celebrating?'

'No, not yet, but if you've got time, we'd appreciate your opinion on this adoption thing.'

'Okay,' she said and smiled. Her own news could wait. A new baby was much more exciting and she was delighted to see a smile on Dessie's face.

'Hi, Sis!' Connie called, as she entered the room. 'Here, sit down.' Lifting her feet from the sofa, she patted the cushion next to her.

Slipping off her coat, Oona settled on the comfortable couch. Dessie handed her a drink. 'Is red okay, only we're out of white?'

'Red is fine.' It was just what she needed to help her relax.

190

The coffee table was covered with literature on adoption.

'What's all this?'

'I'll give you one guess,' Connie laughed.

The atmosphere seemed relaxed, unlike the last time she'd called.

'Well,' Dessie said, picking up a few of the leaflets. 'We've read through all this lot and Connie's made a list of questions we might get asked at the interview.'

'You've got one then?' Oona's eyes widened.

'Yes, next week.' He sipped his wine.

'Can you think of anything we might have overlooked?' Connie passed her the notebook.

Oona ran her eyes down the page. 'You've covered quite a lot here, Connie, but they won't be interested in the fact that you have a comfortable home and two spare bedrooms, one you plan to turn into a nursery. They'll want to know how you'll cope as parents. Their concern will be for the baby or child they will be releasing into your care.'

'What'd you mean?' Dessie asked.

'Well. It's clear that Connie wants a baby. Are you prepared to be flexible? How would you react if they asked you to take on a difficult child, or one with a disability, for instance? I'm sure your home will be inspected later.'

She leant back, relaxed by the wine. 'You could mention you've looked after my kids.' And in the brief silence that followed, Oona knew they were all thinking of Jacqueline.

'Yes . . . of course. You're right, Oona,' he said. 'And there's the question of fostering.'

'I don't know about that, love,' Connie said. 'I'd want the child to have stability. There's nothing permanent with fostering.'

'Then we must agree not to foster,' he said. 'Surely there's dozens of babies and children in Dublin no-one wants?' He turned to Connie. 'I know you have your heart set on a baby, love. But does it really matter how old the child is?'

'I suppose not. But we need to be accepted first.'

'You will be. You'll be perfect. Any idea what the age is for adoption these days?'

'It says here,' Dessie quoted, '"Couples must be married and living together, and must have the same religion as the child they adopt." And, this is the important bit, "they must both have attained 30 years of age".'

'No problem there then.' Oona smiled.

'I'm both excited and nervous at the same time,' Connie admitted. 'And I can't wait to get things moving.'

'Well, good luck.'

'More wine?' Dessie lifted the bottle and began to fill their glasses.

'Not for me.' Oona held her hand over hers. 'I've had enough already. I'll never get up for work.'

'How are things at work, then?' Connie asked.

'Jack's promoted me to assistant manager, starting next week.'

'But, aren't you that already?' Dessie frowned.

'Not really. Not officially. Jack's getting someone in to do my job. I'll be working alongside him in his office.'

'Oh.' Connie giggled. 'You'll be like . . . his partner.'

'Not quite! I guess I'll be more involved in what goes on in the agency, though.' Smiling, she stood up. 'I'd better be getting back. I've left Sean.'

'Well done.' Connie got to her feet and hugged her. 'I'm pleased things are working out for you.'

'I suppose Sean's excited about Limerick, then?' Dessie said. 'Are you feeling better about him going?'

She shook her head. 'It's just so close to the anniversary.'

'Aye, that'll be tough.'

'The sooner the better you two adopt some children,' she said, moving towards the door.

'Hey, hang on a minute,' Dessie chortled. 'One step at a time.'

CHAPTER THIRTY-FOUR

The next few days slipped by and Oona spent an hour each morning talking with Jack, being instructed in her new duties. When he said he would be happy for her to make decisions in his absence, she'd smiled. Worldwide Shipping held more meaning for her now, and she was determined not to let him down.

It seemed her luck was changing. Only yesterday he'd talked about her accompanying him to the docks. It would be nice to put faces to some of the characters she had only spoken to on the telephone.

Brenda, on the other hand, wasn't pleased when she heard about the changes.

'Who'll I be working with then?'

'I don't know yet, Brenda. An older girl with experience, I guess.'

'But I like working with *you*,' she stressed. 'Anyway, why can't you work in here?'

'The agency's expanding, and we need extra staff. But, don't worry. You'll be fine.' Then she added. 'Now you're having typing lessons, it'll give you more scope.'

'Yeah, maybe, but it won't be the same.'

Oona smiled. 'It'll be better. And if there's anything worrying you, you can always pop in and see me whenever you want.'

Jack had been out for most of the morning and on his return, Oona took an extended lunch hour. She had a few things to pick up for Sean. Towards the end of the afternoon, Oona glanced over at Jack. He was chewing the end of his pen, his mood pensive.

'Penny for them,' she said.

193

He looked up. 'Sorry, I was away with the fairies then. Have you phoned the recruitment agency yet, Oona?'

'No, I'll do it now.' She reached for the phone.

'Hold on.' He stood up and walked around the desk. 'I want to talk to you about that.'

She leaned back and gave him a quizzical look.

'Mr. Mountjoy's recommended someone.' He perched on the corner of her desk. 'His name's Tim Riley. He's twenty and has worked for a short time in shipping.'

Oona's lips parted in a smile. 'You're taking on a man? Can he type?'

'Has a real flair for it, apparently, and he can start straight away. What do you think?'

'Well, I'm surprised. Does Brenda know?'

'Are you kidding? I've not seen him yet.' Then he winked. 'Brenda can flutter her eyelashes at him for a change.'

'Oh! I see. Very crafty! I never knew you could be so devious, Jack Walsh.'

'Devious, never! Just forward thinking.' He was smiling now. 'Would you prefer we employed a lady?'

She stood up and passed him a bundle of letters to sign. 'I'm looking forward to meeting him.'

He walked back to his desk and began signing the letters. 'That might be sooner than you think. I'm meeting him in O'Brien's at six and I want you to join us.'

'Oh . . . I can't Jack.' She slipped on her coat. This was one interview she didn't want to miss, but she couldn't be late home. She gathered up her bags. 'Sean's leaving tonight.'

'Of course.' He clapped his hand across his forehead. 'Sorry, I completely forgot.'

'Never mind. You can tell me how it went later.'

'Don't forget to wish Sean good luck from me.' He smiled but she saw disappointment on his face.

***

That night the house seemed strangely quiet without Sean's

loud music, and at bedtime she kept the radio on for most of the night. On Saturday, Oona spent time with her sister. It was Connie's 12th wedding anniversary and Dessie had tickets to see the Royal Show Band that everyone was talking about.

'Why don't you come with us?' Connie asked for the umpteenth time. 'It'll take your mind off Sean.'

As much as she would have loved to say yes, she did not intend to intrude on their special time together. 'Not tonight, Connie. I don't fancy it. Working so many hours in the week, leaves me little energy for dancing at the weekends,' she lied. 'Look, I'll be fine, honest. You two go and enjoy yourselves.'

'Well, if you change your mind,' Connie said, kissing her cheek.

As she approached the house, a cold March wind blew across the river, making her shiver. It was then she noticed an unfamiliar black car parked at the far end of the avenue. Her neighbour, Mr. Murphy, usually parked there, but on closer inspection she realised it wasn't his car. The rustle of leaves along the garden path made her pause but she dismissed it as the neighbour's cat. Then she heard something snap, like someone stepping on a twig. Nervously, she pushed her key into the lock and hurried inside. Strange how little things frighten you when you're on your own, she thought, and went through to the kitchen. Shep barked and came towards her wagging his tail.

'Good boy. Are you hungry?' She bent down and stroked him, then switched the kettle on and fed the dog, before making herself scrambled egg on toast.

Shortly afterwards, curled up on the settee watching television, she thought she heard the letterbox rattle. Unfolding her legs, she got up and turned down the volume on the television. Shep, who was lying at her feet, gave a little yelp.

'It's all right, boy. Just the wind,' she said, and settled back down. When she heard it again, she recognised the rat-a-tat-tat. Shaking her head, she smiled. That'd be Connie and Dessie making a last attempt to get her to go dancing. She hurried down the hallway and threw open the door.

'Don't you two ever..?' The words froze on her lips. In the darkness, Vinnie Kelly stood on the doorstep, holding a large bunch of flowers.

'Hello, Oona.'

Horror filled her, robbing her of speech. She tried to close the door, but he forced it open with his foot. Shep appeared at her side. He growled and Vinnie quickly took his foot away.

'Please listen, Oona? I'm sorry I frightened you. I just want to apologize for my past behaviour . . .'

'What . . . what do you want?' She felt herself tremble.

'It was stupid of me to think we could pick up where we left off.' He pushed the flowers towards her. 'Look, I'm sorry. Say you'll forgive me for the past . . . for everything. Do you think you..?'

'Go away!' she screamed. 'Just go away . . . and . . . leave . . . me . . . alone!'

The dog barked a few times until Vinnie held up his hands in a defeated gesture. He turned away, but not before Oona saw something in his body language, that same arrogance she'd seen in McCarthy's, and a shiver ran through her body.

Her pulse racing, she quickly shut and bolted the door. Then she stood with her back pressed against it, unable to comprehend what had just taken place. How dare he come to her home like that!

Realising that she was still holding the flowers, she hurried through to the back, lifted the lid from the rubbish bin and dumped them inside. Then she locked and bolted the back door. Thank God Sean was away. What if? No, she couldn't bear to think about it. And to stop her shaking limbs, she reached up to the top shelf of the dresser for a bottle of brandy belonging to Eamon, splashed some into a tumbler and took a mouthful. It made her cough and splutter, but after a few sips she felt the amber liquid burn its way through and calm her.

What was she going to do? He could ruin everything. Tears of anger ran down her face. What was he up to? There was something different about him – his suit. Unlike the Vinnie who'd tried to manipulate her at McCarthy's, he'd smiled, as if to deliberately show off a gold tooth. That must have cost plenty. She wondered where he had got his money from, but then decided she'd rather not know. Could he be working in Dublin? Was that his car, the one she had seen outside earlier? How could she relax, knowing he could be living nearby?

That night, every sound inside and outside the house set her nerves on edge and she lay awake, frightened to let herself sleep. Shep, as if sensing her fear, padded upstairs and curled up at the end of her bed. About to doze off, she heard someone shuffling around in the garden. Shep barked. Her heart pounding, she climbed from the bed and carefully peered through the curtains. Even with the full moon, she saw no-one. Now she wondered if, in her nervous state, she'd imagined it. Leaving the light on, she got back into bed and the long night dragged on until morning.

CHAPTER THIRTY-FIVE

On Sunday morning, Oona gave church a miss. Her head ached and her eyes showed dark circles from lack of sleep. She decided to say nothing to her family about Vinnie, and she did not intend to go running to her brother-in-law again. After all, Vinnie had shown no menace; but experience had taught her not to trust him. Why had he turned up now when she was just starting to find some happiness with Jack?

She took a couple of tablets to relieve her thumping head before making apple pies to take to her mother's later. Rolling out the pastry, she placed it over the sliced apples, pinched around the edges and gently prodded the pies with a fork, before slipping them onto the oven shelf. Then she made herself a strong coffee and sat down. She tried to work out what might be going on inside Vinnie's head and how to stay one step ahead of him. How could she make sure Sean was safe without involving the police?

Unaware how long she'd sat there, the smell of the pies brought her to her feet. She clicked her tongue, disappointed to find them slightly overcooked. With a heavy sigh, she placed them on the kitchen windowsill to cool while she got ready.

Later she walked into her mother's kitchen to find her wrapped in a bear hug with Connie.

'Isn't it wonderful news, Oona?' their mother turned round to greet her. 'Let's hope it

won't be long before we have another babby in the family. Of course, it won't replace Jacqueline.'

'I know that, Mam,' Oona reached for Conie's hand. 'As far as I'm concerned, it can't come soon enough.'

'Haven't you brought the apple pies, love?'

'Sorry, Mam!' Her hand rushed to her face. 'I'd forget my head if it wasn't tied to me. I'll nip back. It won't take me a jiffy.'

'Here, give me the back door key. I'll get them,' Connie offered. 'You go in and chat to Dad. He's been asking after you.'

After handing over the key, Oona popped her head around the door of the dining room, where the table was set for their usual Sunday meal.

'Hi, girl. How are you?'

'Fine thanks, Dad,' she sat down, thankful he knew nothing about Vinnie's visit. The mere mention of his name would be enough to give her father a heart attack, and she did not intend to let that happen.

'I'm just telling Dessie here that he'll make a great dad when the time comes.'

Oona smiled. 'I agree, Dad.'

'I doubt anything will be happening for a while, Mr. O'Hara. We'll know more once we've been to see the woman next week. But, if Connie insists on wanting to adopt a baby, we might have a long wait on our hands.'

'Oh, well,' her father said. 'You've started the ball rolling. That's what matters.'

Excited voices coming from the kitchen stopped their chatter, and Connie rushed in holding a bunch of flowers that filled her arms. 'Look what I found sticking out of your rubbish bin, Oona. Aren't they exquisite?'

The sight of her sister holding Vinnie's flowers shocked her, and she struggled to hide her frustration.

'Who are they from, Oona?' Annie asked, following her in.

Oona shook her head. 'I've no idea, Mam. They're *not mine*.' She felt her colour rise with the lie. It was the last thing she'd expected Connie to return with.

'Have you a secret admirer?' her father asked with a chuckle.

'Will you stop that, Dad,' she replied, feeling a flush to her face.

'Ah, it'll be someone with more money than sense, if you ask me.' Her mother shrugged and returned to the kitchen.

'There're not from Jack Walsh, are they?' Connie asked, smelling the orchids.

'Oh, shut up, will you, Connie. He'd hardly leave them in the bin now, would he?' She pulled at her hair to hide her awkwardness, wishing the ground would open to consume her. If she'd known this would happen, she'd have stamped on the stupid flowers and buried them.

'They look expensive,' Dessie said. 'Shame to waste them.'

Oona swallowed. Never in a million years had she imagined this would happen, especially when Connie, gazing lovingly at the flowers, said, 'I'll put them in water. Whoever's thrown them away, it's their loss.'

Oona closed her eyes. Her heart raced. To have them in her mother's house was too much and she bit down on her lip to stop the angry tears forming. Then, trying to keep her voice steady, she said, 'I wonder how Sean's getting on in Limerick.'

'He'll be absolutely full of it when he gets back,' her father picked up his knife and fork and glanced towards the open door. 'Annie, will you stop gabbing out there and give us our dinners.'

Relieved that conversation about the flowers was over, Oona smiled. 'God, Dad, anyone would think you were starving.'

'Well, at this rate . . .' He chuckled.

Annie's Sunday roast was something they all looked forward to, and she only had to put a loaf of her freshly-baked soda bread on the table for it to turn into a feast. When at last Connie helped her mother carry in trays of piping hot food, the smell of roast beef and cabbage, crispy potatoes and Bisto gravy helped to revive Oona's appetite.

'That smells good, so it does,' James said. Silence descended, and they tucked in.

Connie's adoption was the focus of attention, but it wasn't

long before the conversation got round to Eamon and Jacqueline's anniversary. It had been a difficult year for Oona, and at times it still seemed surreal. Now she felt vulnerable again, her mind consumed with fear.

Just when she thought she'd got away with hiding her anxieties, Annie said, 'You're looking tired, Oona.'

She sighed. 'I'm not sleeping well, Mam.'

'It'll be the anniversary. But we'll get through it together, love.'

'Aye, we will that.' Her father patted her hand.

If only they knew. Anxiety over Vinnie Kelly exceeded any worries she might have had about the anniversary service.

'When are we going to get our apple pie, Annie?' James asked.

Smiling, Annie shook her head and stood up, while Oona collected the dirty plates.

'I can't wait to hear if Sean's team scored,' Dessie said.

'There'll be hell to pay if they've lost.' Oona followed her mother out. But, just the same, she couldn't wait to have him home.

The smell of the flowers, now taking pride of place on her mother's dresser, made her sick to her stomach. Diverting her eyes, she sliced into the apple pies, placing individual portions into desert bowls while her mother poured the custard.

Later, as she walked back home to wait Sean's return, she found it impossible to rise above her flagging spirits.

***

On Monday morning, Oona contrived enough excuses to keep Sean from school but, after his team's victory, he couldn't wait to get there. So by the time she arrived at the office, she couldn't shake her mind clear of the fact that Vinnie was back and it left her feeling vulnerable again.

Jack was coming from the kitchen as she walked in. He greeted her warmly, then fell into step with her as they walked towards the office. 'How did Sean get on at the weekend?'

'Sorry. What was that?'

'Sean. How did he do at the weekend?'

'They won 3-2.'

'Fantastic. He must be thrilled.'

'He's not stopped talking about it.' She slipped off her coat.

'I have to nip out, but before I go, I'd better introduce you to Tim.'

Until that moment, she had forgotten all about the new recruit, and hoped her wide-eyed expression hadn't made it obvious. How could she have forgotten? 'Yes . . . yes, of course. How's he settling in?'

'Fine, I think. Not so sure about Brenda, though. Shall we go in?' He held open the door.

The young man stood up and shook her hand as if he was pumping water. 'It's nice to meet you, Mrs. Quinn.'

Jack slipped away, leaving them to become acquainted.

'It's nice to meet you too, Tim.' Oona glanced down at the cycle clips still attached to the ends of his trousers. When he saw her looking, he reached down and pulled them free. He had the appearance of someone who needed feeding up. As her mother would say, there wasn't a pick on him. 'How long have you been typing, Tim?'

'About three years. Once I got the hang of the QWERTY keyboard, I was fine.' He laughed. 'Some of my friends think I'm a sissy.'

'You're not joking!' Brenda muttered.

'I'm earning my living and it doesn't bother me what people think, Mrs. Quinn.'

'Good for you, Tim. And you can call me Oona. I hope you enjoy working here.'

'Thank you. I'm sure I will.'

'Well, any problems, you know where I am,' she said, before returning to her office.

She wasn't sure what to make of Tim. Brenda was already building up a hate relationship with him, and she would not have it all her own way with Tim. What a contrasting pair they made. Just the same, she hoped they would eventually work well together. She could see why Jack had taken him on. He was clever, bordering on eccentric. She glanced over his reference on her desk, before filing it away. Meeting the new member of staff had transported her, if only for a short time, away from her morbid thoughts on what Vinnie might do next.

For the remainder of the day, she found it hard to concentrate. And each time the phones went quiet, she pondered on ways of getting the dreaded flowers out of her mother's house. If she was to replace them with a fresh bunch on the way home, would her mother be suspicious? Alternatively, she could pour weedkiller over them and get them to die quicker.

Her distraction hadn't gone unnoticed, and she felt bad about not confiding in Jack. Eventually, she would have to tell him about her past, but now was not the time.

CHAPTER THIRTY-SIX

March had been a dreary month, not least because of the anniversary. Oona and Sean, together with the rest of the family, attended a special mass and a church service to remember their loved ones. Although her mother assured her that the pain would lessen with each passing year, all she could think about was Jacqueline. When she saw the First Holy Communion children – the little girls looking so angelic in their white dresses and veils – tears of deprivation welled up in her eyes.

On top of that, her anxiety over Vinnie was mounting. He had not fooled her with the flowers and she knew he'd be back. Not knowing when was turning her into a gibbering wreck.

As the month of March ended, she attended a farewell party for her friend, Monica. The parting saddened her; there was little likelihood of them ever seeing each other again.

However, Sean was happy. His school football team, St. Joseph's, had moved up the league table and they were playing away again – this time in Kilkenny. Once he'd left, Shep followed Oona around the kitchen like a lost sheep.

'You're missing him too, aren't you, boy?' After she'd fed him, he slunk back to his blanket in the corner of the kitchen, his head on his paws, whimpering softly.

On Saturday evening, Jack and Oona arranged to go to the cinema and they caught the number 7 bus into the city. She had forgotten what Saturday nights could be like; she hadn't been to the movies since Eamon had taken her to see *Some Like It Hot*. It felt good to be going out again. The town bustled, and excitement murmured around every corner. Young people, intent on getting into dance halls and cinemas, tagged onto the end of queues that snaked along O'Connell Street.

Oona enjoyed romantic comedy and wondered about Jack. She needn't have worried; he let her choose. After they had queued outside the Capital for twenty minutes to see Elvis in *Viva Las Vegas*, the door attendant waved his arms in criss-cross fashion to let everyone know the house was full.

'Sorry. We should have got here earlier.'

'Don't worry, Jack. It'll be showing for a while yet.'

'Well, there are plenty of other films to choose from. What do you think?'

Natalie Wood was a favourite of hers, and she was tempted to suggest going to see *West Side Story* showing at the Carlton, but she felt too emotional to watch a tragic romantic musical so she opted for *One Hundred and One Dalmatians* at the Savoy. It also had a shorter queue. 'Do you mind, Jack?'

'Of course not. You've made a wise choice.'

'Are you sure . . . I mean if you'd rather . . .'

'Not at all! I love Walt Disney.' Smiling, he bought the tickets and guided her inside. Even though they sat on the back row, not once did he attempt to slip his arm around her shoulder. Instead, they sat comfortably together and munched their way through a bag of fruit jellies, tossing for the last one. Jack won and then popped it into her mouth.

Later, as he walked her home, he said, 'I've had a great time. I hope you did, too.'

Nodding, she smiled. She couldn't believe how much she'd enjoyed the evening. When he reached for her hand, it felt wonderful. They paused opposite her house, by the river wall. The water was dark and murky in spite of the full moon, and she gazed up at a clear sky dotted with stars. Two seemed to shine brighter than the rest. What would Eamon think of her now? She already knew the answer. He would want her to be happy.

'What are you thinking?' Jack placed his arm around her

shoulders.

'Oh, just what a lovely evening it's been.'

'Does that mean we can do this again soon?' He turned to face her.

She nodded. 'I'd like that.' Then on impulse, she reached up and kissed his cheek. 'Goodnight, Jack.'

'Hold on.' He gripped her hand again. 'I'll walk you to your door.'

'There's no need, really.'

'I insist. That way I get to hold your hand for longer.'

'You'll have the neighbours gossiping.'

He glanced at his watch. 'Surely they're asleep. Do you mind if I kiss you goodnight?'

She didn't mind one bit. As the light of the moon settled on them like the central characters on stage, she hoped he hadn't seen the flush that coloured her cheeks.

Drawing her close, his kiss was gentle, but she knew just as he did that this was the beginning of something more. Oona knew she was falling in love again, and if they stood here for much longer who knows what might happen.

Reluctantly she unfurled herself from the warmth of his arms and pressed her key into the lock. 'Goodnight, Jack. Thanks for a lovely evening.'

'A pleasure. Goodnight, Oona.'

She watched him walk down the path towards his car, then turn to wave. Once inside the house, she stood with her back to the door, overwhelmed by her emotions.

***

Halfway through the following week, on her way home from work, Oona crossed over the Liffey towards her bus stop when Vinnie Kelly sidled up to her.

'Hello, Oona.' Startled, she glared at him. He looked like he was dressed for an evening out. Ignoring him, she turned her back and hurried on.

'Oona, wait!' He was close behind her. She increased her

pace. Glancing over her shoulder, she accidentally bumped into people. Apologizing, she didn't stop. He was gaining on her. She ran, her heart beating loudly. Dicing with death, she criss-crossed fast-moving traffic, frantic to put distance between them, only stopping on the corner to relieve a stitch in her side. He was still following her, calling out her name. She ran faster. Dear God, why won't he leave me alone?

He was close behind her now. 'Hang on, sweetheart. I just want a chat.'

'Don't you dare call me that?'

'Sorry. Just listen, will you?'

People were staring. 'I've got nothing . . . nothing to say to you.' Hiding her fear, she continued towards the bus stop. The bus should be along any minute and she prayed she hadn't missed it.

He was at her side again. 'Have a drink with me before I go.'

Oona glared at him. 'You're the last person I'd drink with. Now, go away! Leave me alone . . . or I'll . . . I'll scream.' People looked on in astonishment, but no-one offered to help her.

He grabbed her arm. His eyes flashed angrily.

'Let go of me.' She had nowhere left to run.

'I might never see you again. I'm going away to work in Saudi Arabia. Surely, one drink . . .'

'Going away!' If only she could believe him.

Smiling, he released her. 'At last, I've got your attention.'

She could still feel the pressure of his fingers on her arm. She hated every second she was in his company and willed her bus to appear.

'Come on, Oona. Just one drink,' he drawled. 'Then I can go with a clear conscience knowing we parted friends.'

She knew he wouldn't try anything with so many people about and it gave her the confidence to say. 'I don't want to have a drink with you now, or ever. Is that clear?'

'Gee . . . Just one drink . . . just one . . .'

The bus approached. It looked full to standing. It was

obvious that the driver had no intention of stopping. She just had to get on it. She ran towards it, waving her arms in desperation.

Vinnie ran after her, caught her by the arm and swung her round. 'You walk away from me now and you'll regret it.'

'Get off me!'

The bus slowed in traffic and she jumped onto the platform. The conductor, who had observed the scene, barred Vinnie with his arm and rang the bell.

***

Back at his flat, Vinnie Kelly threw his coat over a chair and, balling his fist, thumped the wall, leaving it blood-stained. His plan to bring Oona back there for a drink had backfired. He'd wanted to see the look on her face once she realised how he'd turned his life around. His yarn about Saudi should have at least won him a drink with her, but she couldn't get away from him quickly enough. He must be losing his touch!

At the drinks cabinet, he unscrewed the cap of Johnnie Walker, poured himself a large measure, and gulped it down. He poured another and took it to the table, where he sat brooding. Everything he had done had been to win her back. She had no idea of the risks he had taken by coming into the city. If one of Roly's lowlife friends were to spot him, he'd be beaten to a pulp.

Who does she think she is? He had a good mind to go after her, give her what for. He had seen the way she had looked down her nose at him. In spite of all he had done to clean himself up, she hadn't shown the slightest interest. He'd tried being nice; expected a little respect. All he wanted was a sign, a glimmer, something to tell him she still had feelings for him.

Bored waiting for his luck to change, he stood and paced up and down in the confined space, trying to think. Suddenly it came to him. If he couldn't have her, he'd make sure no-one else would. He'd make her pay one way or another.

He slopped another drink into his glass. The tick of the

ornate mantle clock appeared louder in the silent room. Irritated, he picked it up and flung it against the wall. His patience was running out. He had spent a lot of money on his appearance already. So, Miss High and Mighty thought she was too good for him, did she? Well, he'd see about that! She wouldn't get away with treating him like dirt.

All was not lost. He grinned. It would be such a shame for Oona if she didn't change her mind and see things his way. He had his ace to play; one he had been keeping till now. If nothing else, that would force her into submission.

CHAPTER THIRTY-SEVEN

Over the next few days, Oona felt stressed, constantly looking over her shoulder; every knock on her door sent her heart racing. Her past life with Vinnie seemed like a lifetime ago, yet he continued to cause huge problems for her. Would she ever be free of him? If she involved the police, Sean would get hurt and her life history would be open to all and sundry. Would Jack still want her? What would he think once he knew Sean wasn't Eamon's son? Perhaps she'd have no choice but to put him to the test. She couldn't bear to lose his respect now, just when she was discovering that it was possible to love again.

At work, she put on a brave face and Worldwide Shipping was as busy as ever, showing a profits increase on the previous year.

'If we can maintain these figures, the turnover for this year will more than meet our given target,' Jack announced cheerfully. 'I've sent the data to Mr. Peterson. I'm sure he'll be pleased.'

'That's wonderful, Jack.'

He walked round the desk and placed a file on her desk. 'That's it for this week.' He perched on the corner of his desk. 'Oona.'

She glanced up.

'Are you . . . I mean . . . are you doing anything tomorrow night?'

'No . . . no, why?'

'How about I take you out for a celebratory meal? After all, you've done most of the work.'

'That's not entirely true, Jack. But, thanks, I'd like that.' After their cinema trip, she had hoped he would ask her out again soon.

On Saturday evening, Sean went to stay overnight with Connie, taking the dog with him. Oona spent longer than usual getting ready, finally deciding on a green velvet cocktail dress with a princess neckline and figure-hugging hemline, which she hadn't worn for some time. With her dark hair swept up in a French knot and secured with a diamante slide, she slipped her feet into a pair of black, suede high-heeled shoes then glanced at her reflection.

Satisfied, she picked up her coat, bag and gloves and left the house. Jack was waiting on the corner close to the bridge, where he had parked his car, and they caught the bus into town.

Later, when they walked along the pavement bustling with pedestrians, Jack took her hand. It looked unusually small against his. Smiling down at her, he placed it in the crook of his arm. His suit was light grey, one she hadn't seen before. He was tieless, in a black open-necked shirt. Tonight his brow was wrinkle free and he looked relaxed. 'How do you feel about Chinese food, Oona?'

'It's okay. I've yet to master the chopsticks. But it'll be fun trying.'

'Ching Changs it is, then.'

As the waiter took them across the room to a table for two, Chinese music played in the background, and little red lanterns glowed on each table. Once they were seated, Oona left her worries behind. Sitting with such an attractive man, she couldn't help the smile that lit up her face and made her eyes sparkle.

The food came in small, willow patterned bowls, and it was fun trying each dish. The sweet and sour textures made her pull a face, but mostly she enjoyed it. Laughing and joking, they fed each other noodles and rice.

'Have I told you how lovely you look tonight? '

'Only three times.'

'The glow from the lantern has changed your green eyes to hazel. Isn't that strange?'

She lowered her eyes, aware that he was staring at her. It had been a long time since anyone had paid her a compliment like that.

He reached for her hand, glancing down at her wedding ring, turning it round easily on her finger. 'Has it always been this loose?'

'Not really.'

'You should have a jeweller look at it. You don't want to lose it.'

'Yes, perhaps I should.' He released her hand and only then did she notice she'd forgotten to put on her engagement ring. But that had also become loose, so she'd taken to leaving it safely at home. 'I seem to recall you wearing a ring, Jack? You haven't lost it, have you?' She had wondered what had happened to it and now was the perfect time to ask.

'I removed it a while back. It no longer meant anything to me.'

'I see.' She picked up her Cinzano and lemonade.

Jack leaned across the table, picking up her hand again. 'There's something different about you tonight. I can't think what it is.'

'Oh,' she said. She was in love and it must be showing, but she wasn't going to tell him that, at least not yet. 'It could have something to do with the fact that I'm turning into a woman of means.' Thanks to him, she now had a little more money in her purse.

'Well, then, a woman of means shouldn't have to travel by bus when there's a perfectly good limo waiting to whisk her off at the drop of a hat.' He swallowed his drink.

She turned away. She hadn't thought about that for some time.

He placed his finger under her chin and turned her head

212

towards him, looking into her eyes. 'Are you happy, Oona . . . I mean . . . now, here . . . with me?'

She smiled. 'Yes . . . yes, and I'm very happy being with you, Jack.'

Much later, as they sat in Jack's stationary car listening to the Beatles' *Ain't She Sweet* playing on Radio Luxemburg, he said, 'This evening's been fun, hasn't it?'

'Yes, it has. If I'm honest, I'd almost forgotten what it was like.' She felt safe with his arms wrapped around her, his body close, the musky smell of his aftershave, the faint whiff of Brylcreem. Reluctantly she removed his arm from around her shoulder. 'But, as much as I'd love to stay, I'd better be getting home.'

'Is that the time?' He glanced at his watch. 'I suppose all good things have to end.' She wished he hadn't said that; she'd hoped that good times were just beginning.

'I'll walk back with you.'

'I'll be fine, really.'

'I insist.' He got out of the car and held the door for her.

They paused outside Oona's gate. He turned and drew her close. His kiss was long and passionate. When they drew apart, he said, 'I love you, Oona, and I hope one day you'll feel the same way about me.'

'Oh, Jack.' She wanted to tell him then; to get everything out in the open. But after such a wonderful evening, she couldn't bear to spoil it by seeing disappointment in his eyes once he knew the truth.

'So, do you think Sean will get used to us going out?'

'I really hope so. Now go, before you start the neighbours gossiping.'

***

As soon as Oona slipped off her coat, she realised she'd left her silk scarf in Jack's car, but she couldn't help smiling. Knowing he loved her made her feel warm and happy inside. She had switched off the lights and was heading for the stairs when the knock came. Thinking it was Jack returning her scarf, she couldn't help the feeling of excitement that bubbled inside her and she hurried to open the door. The smile slipped from her face when she saw the burly figure of Vinnie Kelly on her doorstep.

'Well, aren't you going to invite me in?'

'What do you..?' But the words died on her lips. Panic gripped her. She pushed the door, wishing Shep was there to protect her again, but his foot caught it, forcing it open.

'You'll let me in if you know what's good for you.' He gripped her arm roughly.

'Let go of me!' She pulled away. It was no use. He was in the hall, kicking the door shut with his foot.

'Get out! Get out of my house.' A mixture of anger and fear made her tremble.

Completely ignoring her distress, he stood, his back to the door, smirking. 'You've done all right for yourself.'

She swallowed but didn't speak, knowing the quiver in her voice would give him satisfaction. Gripping her wrist, he pulled her behind him, opened the lounge door and pushed her inside.

She cried out, rubbing her wrist.

He ran his hand over the furniture and looked round at the family photos, taking particular interest in a recent photograph of Sean. 'Where is he?'

She didn't answer.

'Where's the kid?' he yelled.

'He's . . . he's not here.'

'That's a shame.' He stood next to her. The smell of whisky made her want to retch. 'I was looking forward to telling him whose son he really is.' Leering, he pushed her onto the sofa.

'You . . . you wouldn't dare?' She eyed him with contempt.

'Wouldn't I?'

'Go on then, tell Sean. Tell him you're his father. I'll tell him myself.'

'Maybe I want more than that.' His eyes narrowed.

'You're despicable.'

'Nowhere to run now, have we?' He laughed mockingly. 'I saw you tonight, my darling Oona. Why didn't you tell me you had a fancy man? Very cosy, I must say.' His eyes flicked over her figure, making her shudder. 'You used to dress up for me once. But you've no time for me now, have you? Who is he?'

'He's a friend. How . . . how dare you question me? Now get . . .' She stood up and waved her arms. 'Get out. Get out!'

'You could at least offer me a drink. Where do you keep it?' Grabbing her arm, he pushed her ahead of him. 'In here?' He threw open another door, peering inside, then forced her along the hall until he came to the kitchen, switched on the light and pushed her into a chair. He leant down and pressed his face close. She edged away. 'Everything I've done was for you. And you throw me aside.'

'You're mad.'

He straightened up, pulling everything out of the cupboards. 'Don't you have any whisky in this place?' Then he caught sight of the brandy on the top shelf. Lifting it down, he poured a generous helping.

She blinked, hoping she'd wake up any minute from her nightmare. With a sense of foreboding, she watched him down the brandy. Try as she might, she couldn't stop herself shaking.

He dragged a chair across the floor and sat down. Oona looked away from the anger she saw in his eyes. 'I've given up my life for you. *All for you!* Are you listening?' he railed.

'You're fuddled with drink. You're talking a load of rubbish.'

He glanced around. 'I could have given yeh all this. I still can, Babe, if we can be together again.' He pulled his chair closer and took both her hands in his. She pulled away, swallowing to relieve the horror and revulsion she felt, then closed her eyes in an attempt to block the smell of his aftershave mingled with alcohol.

'Can't you see I've changed? I'd do anything for you, anything to win you back. We can be a proper family.' He

215

shifted slightly, tapping his fingers on the table.

She swallowed the bile rising at the back of her throat. She'd die first. She could see a knife lying on the worktop. If only she could get to it. But he was watching her every move. 'I told you before, it's too late. I . . . I have a new life now.'

'So, I'm still not good enough, eh?' He threw back his head, laughing loudly. Then he stood up, picked up a chair and crashed it to the floor.

She flinched.

'What about him then..? Mr. Nice Guy? You didn't mind snuggling up to him. Did you?' he bellowed. 'But you couldn't be bothered to have one measly drink with me?'

Her mind swirled. And she said the first thing that came into her mind.

'I couldn't . . . I can't trust you,' she cried. 'You've . . . you've lied about going away.'

'You stupid bitch. I did it for you. To impress you. To make you look at me again. You forget, I'm the boy's father.'

She stood up and faced him. 'I've . . . I've never forgotten that. He's a wonderful kid and I don't want him sullied by you.'

He grabbed her hair, making her cry out, then pulled her to him. She turned her face away but he forced her head round. 'I can have any woman, but I want you.' He pressed his mouth over hers. She punched his chest until he released her and ran screaming for the door, hoping her elderly neighbour would hear her. It was her only hope.

'You won't escape me, Oona. I've waited too long.' He grasped her arm and twisted it behind her back, picked up the brandy bottle in his other hand and marched her back into the lounge. She lashed out at him with her free arm until he slapped her hard across the face and pushed her to the floor. She lay there, curled into the foetal position. He switched the radio on and Oona feared the worst. Doris Day's *The Deadwood Stage* came gustily through the airwaves. He paused as if something had crossed his mind. Then he picked up the radio, smashing it against the wall. Turning his back, he paced the room, dragging his fingers through his hair. 'You're forcing my hand, Oona.'

She wasn't going to let him away with doing anything to her. An ornamental black poker lay near the hearth. She moved to grab it, but he noticed and kicked it across the room. She sat up and backed herself into the corner of the room. As he advanced towards her, she let out an enormous scream.

'Shut up! Shut up, I can't think.'

'Look, if it's money you're after, you can have it, if you'll just go.'

'How much? How much have you got?'

'Twenty . . . twenty pounds.' It was all she had. 'It's in the drawer, over there!' She pointed.

He rummaged, throwing everything out onto the floor. 'Call that money? It's a pittance.' He took it anyway. 'It's you I want.'

Gripping the wall, she dragged herself upright. Then, as a wave of dizziness passed over her, she felt a trickle of blood run down her face from just above her eyebrow. She wiped the sticky mess away with her hand.

'Sit down. You refused to drink with me once before. Maybe now you'll be a little more friendly.' Taking a large swig from the bottle, he passed it to her. Determined that one way or another she wasn't taking any more of this, she was about to swing the bottle above her head when a loud knock on the door made her stop.

Vinnie stiffened. 'Who's that?'

'I . . . I . . . don't know.' She prayed inwardly that whoever it was wouldn't go away.

'Well, think! Do you usually have callers at this time of night?' His eyes widened and he shuffled to his feet.

'It . . . it might be . . . my dad . . . or my brother-in-law.' Detecting the nervous twitch in his face, she added, 'They often call over to . . . check I'm alright.' Sure, he'd think twice about tackling Dessie. The knock came again. Oona swallowed

217

the bile that again rose in her throat.

His eyes flashed wildly.

She was about to try and reach the door, when he surprised her by rushing for the back door and disappearing into the night.

Pulling strands of her long hair across her face, her legs like jelly, she flung open the door. She couldn't believe her eyes when she saw Jack standing there.

***

Oona was so relieved to see him that she burst into tears.

'What's—? Oona, what's the matter?'

Suddenly, her legs buckled and she gripped the doorjamb to stop herself from falling.

'Are you ill?' He scooped her up, carried her inside, and placed her down on the sofa. His hand gently pushed aside strands of her hair. 'My God! Who's done this to you?'

She felt dazed, shaking so much she could hardly speak. 'He's . . . he's gone now.'

Jack ran through to the back of the house to check. When he returned, he asked, 'Where's Sean? Is he still at your sister's?'

Shivering uncontrollably, she nodded.

'You're in shock. Where can I find a blanket?'

'There's . . . a . . . cupboard on the landing.'

Jack rushed upstairs and came down carrying a blue blanket and a damp pink face flannel. Placing the cover over her, he gently dabbed the cut above her eye. She was still trembling and Jack took her into his arms. 'You're safe now.' He was looking round at the dishevelled room. 'Oh, honey . . . he didn't?'

'No . . . he . . . he took money, that's all.' She shuddered when she realised how close she'd come to being raped. If Jack hadn't arrived when he did . . .

'Did you get a good look at him?'

'No. It . . . it happened so fast.'

'Swear to God, if I get my hands on him . . .' He was on his feet pacing the room. 'I wish I'd come back sooner. The car broke down by the bridge and I've spent the past half hour trying to get it going again. I wouldn't have knocked, only I saw your light.'

'I'm so glad you did.'

'I'll make you some sweet tea. Then we must inform the Gardá. I won't be long.'

She knew it was the right thing to do, but her family knew nothing of Vinnie's return, and there was Sean to think about. She had let Jack believe she had been burgled and, although she hated deceiving him, she couldn't face seeing the love die in his eyes once he knew the truth.

They were sipping their tea when Jack said, 'That animal mustn't be allowed to get away with doing this to you. You can have him for burglary and assault. I'll go and phone them.'

'No, Jack, please. I . . . I couldn't . . . go . . . through all that. I can't . . .'

He sat down and stroked her hair. 'Don't worry, I'll be here with you when the police come. I won't leave you.'

'No . . . don't go, Jack . . . please.'

He gave her a quizzical look. 'Oona, love. Why? This isn't like you. Are you sure about this? Do you want me to let your family know?'

'No . . . I don't want them worried.' She knew he wouldn't go against her wishes.

'I'll go to the Gardaí tomorrow morning and file a complaint,' she said.

'God knows where he'll be by then. He needs locking up.' He frowned. 'Are you sure about this? Is there something . . .?'

She shook her head. 'I'll be grand, really.' She reached for him and he held her close for a long time. In his arms, she felt safe and she stayed like that until daybreak when he slipped from the house, instructing her to lock the door behind him. After he'd left, Oona placed her face in her hands and wept as if her heart would break.

CHAPTER THIRTY-EIGHT

Pulling herself together, she tidied the room and cleaned everywhere that Vinnie Kelly had touched, until the smell of him had gone. She despised him. She picked up the radio – splintered and broken beyond repair – and placed it into the bin. *How I hate you, Vinnie Kelly. And I won't let you destroy my family.*

Her feelings were so intense that if he'd dared to walk back in at that moment, she'd surely lunge at him with any weapon she could find and not regret it. He had wreaked havoc on her life for too long, and he wasn't going to get away with doing this to her.

Her normal Sunday duties forgotten, she knew it would not be long before she'd have to face questions and accusations. And once she opened the floodgates, there'd be no going back.

She took a long soak in the bath then sat in front of her dressing table mirror, trying to conceal the bruise above her eyebrow with panstick, but the make-up had little effect. It was ridiculous to think she could hide this from her family; things had gone too far for that.

Connie called straight after church. Oona let her in, turning away quickly, pulling strands of her hair across her face.

'Someone's had a late night?' Connie closed the door and followed her through to the kitchen.

'Where's Sean?' Oona asked, trying to keep the anxiety from her voice.

'Dessie's taken him for a kickabout before dinner. You sit down, I'll make the coffee. And I want to hear all about last night.' Connie had turned her back, spooning coffee into mugs, but any moment now, Oona would have to explain her injury.

'Glory be t'God! What's happened to you?' Connie faced her, placing the hot drinks on the table.

'It's all right . . . I . . .'

'Don't tell me. Has Jack Walsh done this?'

'Of course not. Don't be daft, Connie!'

'Who then? For, God's sake, tell me, Oona.'

All the excuses she had made up in her head seemed ridiculous now, as her sister held her gaze.

'Tell me!' Pulling out a chair, Connie sat down next to her.

Taking a deep breath, Oona told her everything, holding nothing back. When she'd finished, a tear rolled down Connie's cheek.

'Thank God Jack came back.' She stood up and straightened her shoulders. 'Have you reported him? He'll try it again if you don't.'

Oona got up and walked towards the window, then turned. 'I've no intention of letting him away with it, Connie. I'm mad as hell and I'd have done it last night when Jack suggested it, but I was thinking of Sean.'

'Listen to me, Sean's in danger once he's around. And you know I can't keep this from Dessie. You need him.'

'I'll deal with it. I don't want to involve him. It could affect your case for adoption.' She raked her fingers through her hair.

'Let me worry about that.' Connie lifted the mugs and poured the untouched drinks into the sink. 'You both need protecting from that maniac. Who knows when he'll be back?' Sighing, she placed her arm around Oona. 'At some point, Mam and Dad are going to find out.'

Oona nodded. 'I know, but not yet. I can't let them see me like this.'

'I'll think of an excuse, and I'll be back later with some healing ointment.'

***

Jack called by to see how Oona was and only left when she

221

promised to report the attack to the Gardá.

That night, Connie stayed at Oona's. And, while Sean accepted that his mother had carelessly walked into the doorjamb, that night when she went in to say goodnight to him, he said, 'You're not getting married again, are you, Mam?'

Her mouth dropped and she placed the glass of milk she was holding down next to him. 'Wh . . .whatever gave you that idea, love?'

'I don't want a new dad,' he said. 'I want my own dad.'

The irony made her cringe. She sat down on his bed. 'I know that Sean. But . . . all I'm saying is . . . do you think you might get to like Jack? He's a nice . . .'

'Don't know. I thought you loved me dad?'

'I'll always love Eamon. He's in my heart, always will be.' She bent down and kissed Sean goodnight.

On Monday, Connie and Dessie had an appointment with the adoption agency but before that, Dessie insisted on walking Sean to school, in spite of his protests. When he returned, he spent an hour discussing the best course of action to take regarding Vinnie Kelly.

'He's a lowlife, and if you won't report him, Oona, I will, and make no bones about it.'

'Do you think I don't want to? I can't wait to get it over and done with.' She crashed the crockery into the sink, breaking the handle off her favourite mug.

'If you go now, I'll come with you.'

'No, Dessie. Thanks, but I'll do this alone. Besides, you mustn't miss your appointment. I'll be fine.'

'Are you sure?' Connie said. 'I think they'll understand if he's not there this time.'

'I'm sure.' With hindsight, she should have gone to the Gardaí weeks ago.

'Until he's caught and locked up, we'll take it in turns to pick Sean up,' Dessie said kindly.

***

The young Gardá glanced up from where he was scribbling onto a pad. She knew she looked a mess, but she didn't care. She lowered her head to hide her bruise.

'Erm . . . can I help you?'

'I'd like to speak to Sergeant McNally, please.'

'Take a seat; I'll see if he's available.'

In a short time the door clicked open and McNally was ushering Oona into his office. 'Please sit down, Mrs. Quinn. What can I do for you?' He closed the folder he'd been working on.

'I want to report an assault that happened on Saturday night.' She pushed back her hair.

McNally stiffened. 'Dear Lord. Who? Why? I mean . . . why didn't you report this sooner, Mrs. Quinn?'

'I'm here now and I want Vinnie Kelly locked up.'

'You know who did this to you?'

'Yes.'

'You better start at the beginning, Mrs. Quinn.'

McNally took her statement and, when she had finished, asked, 'Why didn't you mention any of this before, Mrs. Quinn?'

'I was concerned for Sean.'

'I don't understand.'

She trusted McNally, he was more like a family friend. She swallowed the lump forming in her throat and explained who Vinnie really was. It was the first time she had admitted it to anyone outside the family. 'Sean doesn't know.'

'I see. Well, it won't go any further, if that's what you want.' His smile reassured her. 'You don't happen to have a snapshot of this Vinnie, do you?'

'I'm afraid I don't.'

'Any idea where he's living?'

She shook her head. 'I guess he's somewhere in the vicinity. Will he be charged?'

'Once we track him down, we'll take him in for questioning.

223

But, with only a name and a sketchy description, it might take time.'

'But,' she knew she sounded stressed, 'how long will that take?'

'Let's see what we can come up with. You did right to report him. And,' he stood up 'here's my number. Ring me any time, day or night. It might be advisable for you to return to your parents' home until we've questioned Mr. Kelly.'

Mumbling her thanks, she shook the proffered hand. She felt no better after her confession. What good would it be to question someone like Vinnie Kelly? Tears of frustration rolled down her cheeks.

On the way home, she phoned Jack at the office as she had promised. She explained as much as she could about her statement to the police, and asked for a few days leave of absence.

'Take as long as you need. I'll come over and see you. I just want to make sure you're okay.'

'I'm fine, Jack. Give me a day or two.' She felt a catch in her voice.

'Oona. Just ring me, please.'

'I will.' The phone clicked off. He deserved to know the truth, and Sean's hostility wasn't the only reason she couldn't face him. Once she confessed her past, it could well mean the end of their relationship.

CHAPTER THIRTY-NINE

As soon as Oona popped her head around the door, her mother's hand flew to her mouth. 'God in Heaven, what's happened to your face?'

'Now don't go fretting, Mam. I'm fine, honest.'

'What do you mean, fine? Is that why we've not seen hide nor hair of you for days?' A frown wrinkling her forehead, she removed her apron and sat down.

'I'm sorry about this, Mam, but . . . but . . . Vinnie Kelly's back.' She swallowed. 'I need to speak to you both.'

'Holy Mother! This is serious.' Annie played nervously with her wedding ring. She was on her feet. 'Has something happened to Sean?'

'No, no, he's fine.'

'Go in the room then and I'll call your dad down.' She hurried upstairs, mumbling that he wouldn't be pleased to be woken up at this time of the day. While she waited, Oona picked at her red nail varnish. A short while later her mother returned with her father, rubbing the sleep from his eyes.

Her mother tensed.

'Well. What is it?' James O'Hara pulled his dressing gown across his chest.

'Couldn't it have waited until I'd had me sleep?'

'I'm afraid not, Dad.' At times during the telling, Oona choked back tears. But she held nothing back. 'I'm sorry to have brought this on you both.'

Her father rested his head in his hands. When he glanced up, she saw the colour rising up his neck and, thinking he was about to explode, she braced herself.

'And you thought you could cope with that despicable man alone, did you? I'm disappointed in you, Oona. Why in God's name didn't you say something before it got to this?'

'I think you know why, Dad. I'll . . . I'll make it up to you both, I promise.' But when her mother burst into tears, she didn't see how she could ever do that.

'And those flowers, Oona. Why . . . why didn't you say something then?'

'I couldn't, Mam. Look, don't upset yourself. Sergeant McNally's dealing with it.'

'So,' her father said, 'that scoundrel's back, is he? He dared do this to you. I'll have him.' He stood up, clenching and unclenching his fists. 'Did Dessie know about any of this?'

She shook her head. God knows what he'd say if he knew she'd confided in Dessie first.

James O'Hara ran his fingers through strands of thinning hair and sat down again. Her mother choked back tears and Oona felt like the worst daughter in the world.

'What else could I do?'

'Apart from tell me, I suppose you did your best. But it's out now.'

'I'm so sorry, Dad.'

'Look, love. You've no need to protect us.' He placed his arm around her shoulder. 'You should have come to us first, as soon as he got in touch with you.'

'I was trying to . . .'

'We know.'

'But . . . but what about Sean?' her mother sniffled. 'We can't have him finding out the truth.'

'We can't shield him forever.'

'We have to,' Annie said. 'The truth will destroy him.'

'It might not be necessary,' James patted his wife's hand.

'What do you mean, Dad?'

'Well, I've every confidence in McNally and once he catches up with that rogue, he'll see justice is done.'

'I hope you're right, James.'

'Well,' he said, glancing across at Oona, 'the sooner the better you move back here where I can keep an eye on things.'

The chat with her parents had gone better than she had hoped. At least now, if McNally called on them, the shock would be less. Her father was right. She couldn't keep this from Sean for much longer.

***

Sean's father had been a well-kept secret for so long. And although opening up to Jack wouldn't be easy, Vinnie had left her no choice. If things went badly, not only would she lose a friend and confidant, but the man she had grown to love, even maybe her job. The person she had hoped to be her salvation might be lost to her forever. That thought brought an unsettling feeling to her stomach as she went to meet him.

She suggested early evening, knowing that the bistro would be quiet and private enough for what she had to tell him. As Jack ushered her through the door, she saw only one other couple sitting at the far end of the cafe.

'This sounds ominous, Oona. Have you changed your mind . . . about us?'

'No. No, it's not that.'

'I'm relieved to hear it.' He selected a table in the corner. 'Sit here. I'll get the drinks.'

Oona removed her blue jacket to reveal a white silk blouse. Her hair fell to just below her shoulders – held in place by a red headband. The bruise to her face was hardly noticeable, carefully concealed with make-up. She glanced across at Jack, his warm personality spilling forth as he chatted with the girl behind the counter. How easy it would be to say nothing, let things continue as they were. But her conscience was causing her discomfort. If their roles were reversed, she would want him to be honest with her.

Jack came back with tea and two plates of egg and chips.

'You must have read my mind,' she said. Her stomach

rumbled, but it was unlikely she'd be able to eat anything until she'd unburdened herself.

'I know you better than you think, Oona Quinn. I bet you've not eaten all day. And I'm guessing it's not work you want to talk about?' He pushed the plate towards her. 'In view of the serious expression on your face, it might be wise for us to eat first.'

Pleased to postpone the inevitable a while longer, she forced a smile to her face. They ate in silence, each engrossed in their own private thoughts. When they had eaten, Jack asked,

'Have the Gardaí got back to you yet?'

'No, I've heard nothing. I . . .' She paused as tears welled up in her eyes.

Jack reached across and touched her hand. 'Whatever you have to say, Oona, I can't stop loving you.' He leaned in closer. 'If you're not going to tell me it's over, then . . .'

'No, no, Jack. You don't understand.' She lowered her eyes.

He cupped her hands. 'Well, then, nothing you say will change how I feel about you.'

She glanced up. 'The other night . . . I wasn't entirely honest with you. I let you believe I'd been burgled.'

He frowned. 'And you hadn't? But how..? I don't understand.'

'I know the man who forced his way into my house.' And she told him everything, stopping only occasionally to dry her tears.

Jack, his face showing a range of emotions, listened without interruption until she had finished. The bistro remained quiet and the couple at the far end had left, so there was no-one to overhear them.

Jack rested his elbows on the table, a faraway look in his eyes. He didn't speak. She saw the pain in his eyes, and couldn't bear the silence that settled between them.

'Now you see, I'm not the woman you believe me to be.' She stood up. 'I'll go now, save us both any more embarrassment.'

'You're not going anywhere.' He pressed his hand lightly on her arm and she sat back down.

'You want me to stay?'

'I want to marry you, when you're ready.' He reached for her hand. 'I love you and, if you'd let me, I'd see that you never went through anything like that again.'

Her eyes brightened. 'Oh, Jack. You really don't mind?'

'Only that I didn't get back sooner that night. Oona, honey, I guessed about Sean.'

'How?'

'It wasn't that hard to work out.' He shook his head. 'So, my love, you've worried for nothing. As regards this Vinnie, if the Gardaí don't sort him out, I will. He won't hurt you again, nor will he stop us being together, if that's what you want.'

She beamed him a watery smile. 'It is.'

'And, another thing, I can understand how Sean might feel.'

'You can?'

'Yes, and I don't blame him. My father died suddenly when I was four and Michael was eight. My mother remarried a man called Tom Brennan and, although I missed my own father, I was young enough to accept things. But my brother was hostile to Tom for some time.'

'You never said.'

'No. Tom's been a good father, and it didn't affect me in that way. But Sean is at a vulnerable age. It's bound to be difficult for him.' He paused and looked into her eyes. 'Give him time. It'll work out.'

As if by magic, Oona felt the weight of the world lifting from her shoulders. Meeting his gaze, she said, 'You're a good man, Jack Walsh.'

CHAPTER FORTY

The following evening, after a busy but pleasant day at the office, she went to the house to collect her post. A long white envelope caught her eye. It looked important and she turned it over in her hand. Taking a knife from the kitchen drawer, she slit it open. The letter was dated April 1962.

Dear Mrs. Quinn,
In the High Court of Justice. DSC No. 642
*   Oona Quinn and the Estate of Redmond & Rigby.*
*   I am pleased to advise you that the Court has now reached a settlement in respect of the above. A copy of the Court Order is enclosed and the terms of the same are as follows:*
*   1. That Mrs. Oona Quinn shall receive the sum of £10,000 (Ten Thousand Pounds) in full and final settlement of all or any claims against the estate of Richmond & Rigby;*
*   2. That a sum of £100 annually is also awarded to Sean Quinn until he reaches the age of majority and to be invested by the Court in a high interest bearing account. No monies will be payable until the age of majority, with the exception that Mrs. Quinn may apply for payment out in the event that Sean attends Technical College or University;*
*   3. That Mrs. Oona Quinn shall sign a Note of Acceptance and lodge the same in Court to enable the Lump Sum Payment to be made;*
*   4. The Court Costs are awarded to the Plaintiff (yourself).*
*   Now that the Court proceedings are completed, I can release a copy of the Police Report to you upon request. However, the salient points are that Richmond & Rigby's driver was aged 16, and had consumed a large amount of alcohol at the time of the fatal accident on 25th March 1961.*
*   In conclusion, may I and the staff who have worked on your case*

express the hope that this settlement will give you and your son financial stability, and may in some small way assist your happiness.
Please return the Note of Acceptance in the envelope provided.
Yours sincerely
Thomas Finley (Senior Partner)
Finley and Son

Oona's eyes filled with tears. The letter, no matter how kindly worded, was a stark reminder of what she had lost. And a sob caught in her throat. She had no idea the driver had been so young. Why should she? She had hated him for so long; found it hard to forgive him. Dear God! He was only a child; some mother's son. Another family had suffered, too.

She put the letter back into its envelope and pushed it into her bag. She wasn't sure how she felt, except she couldn't deal with it now.

Her father was forever asking if she had heard anything about the compensation, but he was on the evening shift, so she would have to wait until morning to tell him. She felt dazed. This was more money than she had ever dreamt of having. Her father would think she was mad not to delight in it.

She could not begin to comprehend the changes it would make to their lives. Not to be permanently broke. No more would she have to worry about paying the bills on time. Now there was a chance Sean could go to university. The last year had been tough on them all. With that kind of money in her bank account, she could afford to take things a little easier. But that wasn't what she wanted. She loved her job and her relationship with Jack had become closer.

That evening, as she sat watching television with Sean and her mother, she found it difficult to contain her news from them. But so many things stopped her. She wanted to let it sink in first, and talking of the accident was sure to bring back painful memories. She had planned to tell Sean about Vinnie, but when she glanced across to where he sat side by side with

231

his granny – both of them laughing at the film, *Up in the World*, with Norman Wisdom – she wondered if she should perhaps take her mother's advice. Telling Sean the devastating truth was bound to have serious consequences. Besides, McNally was looking for Vinnie right now and, with a bit of luck, he would be taken in and cautioned never to come near them again.

***

The following morning, Oona took a few hours off work and, with Sean safely inside the school gates, returned to her parents' house. She wanted to catch her father before he went to bed after his shift. Her head felt muddled as if she had drunk too much wine.

Her mother was scrubbing clothes at the sink, rubbing Sunlight soap over the collar of her husband's shirts. She turned as Oona walked in. 'What's brought you back, love? Is everything all right at work?'

'Everything's grand, Mam.'

'Are you sure? *He's* not come back, has he?' A worried expression creased her face.

'No, Mam. It's good news this time. I've heard from the solicitor, but I'm just not sure how I feel about it, that's all.' She placed an arm around her mother's shoulder. 'Where's Dad?'

Just then, her father came in from the back, his braces hanging loose by his side.

'Weather, I ask you! Who'd believe it was April? Outside lavvy's a killer.' He sat down next to Oona. 'What's wrong? Are you okay, love?'

'Yes. How about you, Dad?'

'Sure, I'm game ball. At least, I was before I knew that Vinnie feller was back making trouble.'

'Let's leave that to Sergeant McNally now, Dad.'

'Shouldn't you be at work?'

'I'm going in later. I've had a letter from the solicitor,' she said opening her bag and handing it to him.

Annie dried her hands and sat with them at the table. She

linked her fingers, red and puffy from the hot water, and watched her husband's face as he read the letter. 'What is it, James?'

Clearing his throat, he passed it to his wife. Oona wiped away a tear.

After her mother read it, tears welled up in her eyes. 'It's too sad for words.' She turned towards her husband. 'What do you think, James? That company's responsible for that young feller's death, too.'

Her husband stood up and stared out of the window.

Oona found it difficult to hide her distress, and her mother reached over and patted her hand.

'There now, love. This is bound to bring it all back.'

James O'Hara blew into his handkerchief and sat down again. He glanced at his wife, then his daughter. 'We can't change what's happened, love. But it still takes my breath away. It's taken long enough and I'm glad it's all sorted now.'

'It might seem like a lot of money,' her mother sniffed. 'But it's not much for the taking of innocent lives.'

'My advice is to return the note of acceptance. And do so quickly.'

'I'm not sure how I feel about it, Dad.'

'Ah, love. That's silly talk,' her mother remonstrated. 'You'll feel differently in a few days.'

'What's the matter with you, Oona? Have you forgotten you've a son to bring up? Sean doesn't need the money? You don't need the money, is that it?' Her father's raised voice startled her. How could she blame him? Her reaction was weird and the whole thing made her come out in goosebumps.

'I'm sorry, love, that's the tiredness talking. But I meant it just the same.'

'I know, Dad.'

Her parents glanced towards each other.

'Look, Oona.' Her father covered her slender hands with his. 'I know you, and you can forget about sentiment. What went through your head went through mine for a split second. This money will change your life. You'll have the opportunity to pay off that mortgage of yours. It's like a millstone round your neck. That's the first thing you should be thinking of.'

'I haven't had time to think, Dad. What with all this business with Vinnie Kelly.'

'I know. But we've sorted that for now, haven't we? And you've promised not to keep things to yourself again.'

She nodded.

'Well, you listen to your old dad. Give Finley a ring, tell him to go ahead with the cheque transfer then, if you like, have a chat with Dessie. He'll tell you much the same thing. That's my advice.'

'Your father is right, Oona.'

He kissed the top of her head. 'I'm bushed, love. I'm off to me bed. We'll talk again later.'

***

At the office, Jack, curious about Oona's urgent need to see her father, hoped it had nothing to do with this Vinnie character. Just thinking about what he had done to her aroused a growing anger he had never experienced before.

He wanted to put the smile back on Oona's face and hopefully help Sean too, if he'd let him. They had both suffered enough, and once McNally organised a court order to stop Kelly coming within a mile of Oona and Sean, Jack hoped to take their relationship a step further. He was crazy about Oona and, if anything, his love and admiration for her had grown. Working full time and bringing up her son alone could not be easy. He wanted to spend the rest of his life with her and, if she would let him, devote his future to making her happy.

The business was doing well and he was making good money; enough to put a decent deposit down on a house.

Brenda interrupted his thoughts when she poked her head round the door. 'Where's Oona? Isn't she coming in today?'

234

'She'll be in later. Give this folder to Tim, will you? Tell him it's urgent. Thanks, Brenda.'

'Sure,' she said, without lingering.

The more mature Brenda impressed Jack. The increased responsibility and typing lessons were proving to be worthwhile and Tim seemed less of a threat to her now. Although she still dressed in her dolly-bird fashions, her make-up overdone, he guessed she waited until she was at work to apply most of it. But that was Brenda; at eighteen, she still had a lot of growing up to do.

***

Oona didn't go straight back to work. She spent the rest of the morning at the graveside. The wind whipped wildly at her hair. She talked to Eamon in their old familiar way, and afterwards an inner peace surrounded her. Returning home, she felt refreshed, her headache gone and her mind clear. There was no doubt that the money would make life easier, but it would not necessarily change her. She wouldn't let it.

After a quick snack, she returned to work and went straight to see Jack. Her new typewriter was sitting on her desk. Smiling, she sat down.

'I hope it wasn't inconvenient this morning, Jack?'

'Of course it wasn't. Is there anything wrong?' He leaned forward on his desk.

'No. Everything is fine. I've heard from my solicitor, you know, about the compensation.' She showed him the letter and confided her feelings about taking the money. 'Can you possibly understand?'

'I think I can.' He sat back in his chair and studied her. 'You're amazing!'

She felt a flush to her cheeks. 'Daft, more likely! It was a shock, you know.'

'You deserve it, every penny of it. In fact, it's not enough for what you've been through. I'm pleased for you both. What will you do now? Or haven't you thought about that yet?'

235

'I don't know. I'd give it away just to know that Vinnie Kelly was out of our lives for good.' She hooked a strand of her hair behind her ear. 'My father suggests paying off my mortgage.'

'Your father's a wise man.'

'Yes, I think so.' She glanced over at him.

'I take it you haven't heard any more from McNally?'

She shook her head.

'You will be careful? I know you're taking every precaution with Sean, but . . . promise me you won't go anywhere alone until *he's* been caught.'

'We're staying at my parents for now.' Smiling, she turned her attention to the pile of invoices on her desk. 'Have we had any new contracts?'

'Well, since you've asked.' His grin made her forget everything except her growing love for him. He got up and, leaning across her desk, kissed her lips before handing her a folder. 'Let me know what you think?'

Opening the folder, she took out the paperwork and studied it closely.

'This is the Guinness contract. That's wonderful, Jack. Mr. Kovac has wanted to get his hands on this for years.' She laughed. 'Well done! This will keep Worldwide Shipping afloat for a long time. Look, you've had no lunch yet, have you? Why don't you nip out and leave me to deal with this?'

She watched him leave, concern clouding his rugged good looks. And she knew that there would be no real happiness for either of them until Vinnie was safely out of their lives.

CHAPTER FORTY-ONE

The news later that night of Vinnie's arrest lifted her spirits. Her father had insisted she remain with them until they knew the outcome. It was the sensible thing to do, although she couldn't wait to return home and get back to normality. Knowing that Jack loved her made her stronger, ready to take on the world if need be to preserve the warm glow she felt inside. Her life was beginning to make sense to her again and she felt more determined than ever to move on.

The next morning was bright and sunny, but when Oona arrived home to her parents' that evening, the blue sky had clouded. Sean was having tea at Connie's and had taken Shep with him. As she turned the key in the lock and the door opened onto a silent room, she remembered her mother had gone out and she was alone.

A sudden movement from behind made her turn. It was him. And before she could call out, he clasped his hand tightly over her mouth. She couldn't breathe.

'I'll take it away if you promise not to scream.'

She nodded.

Keeping his hand in place, he put his other firmly round her waist, and dragged her, kicking out at him, until he got her inside.

He was unshaven and she could smell his stale body odour. Releasing her, he glanced around then reached for the bottle of milk on the table, flicked off the top and slurped it down. Milk ran down his chin.

'What do you want? My father will be back any minute.'

'Do you think I'm stupid? I know what time he'll be back.

And your mother's gone to the picture house with her neighbour.'

Her throat felt dry. My God! He probably knew where Sean was too. He had obviously gone to great lengths to ensure she was alone, but she wasn't going to let him frighten her, not this time.

'Weren't you arrested?'

'Oh, that.' He wiped his mouth with the back of his hand. 'The cops have nothing on me, so you've wasted your time. Some Sergeant questioned me, kept me overnight, but he had to let me go.'

'What? Why?' She couldn't believe it. Rage tore through her body.

'They hadn't enough to hold me.'

'But that's—'

'Never mind that. Where's the boy? It's about time he knew the truth.'

'You can't threaten me any more.'

He looked towards the stairs. 'Call him down.'

'Sean's not here.' Her mind buzzed. If only someone would call. There was always someone calling on her mother, why not tonight?

'I can wait. In the meantime, why can't you be nice to me?' He reached for her.

'Keep away from me.' She edged sideways and picked up her mother's bread knife from the worktop, holding it behind her back. 'You... you can't frighten me anymore. Look at you! You're a mess. I've found happiness with a good man and I'm damned if I'm going to let you spoil it.'

'You don't mean that!' He edged towards her.

She raised the knife. 'Keep away, or I promise you—' She lunged towards him.

He grabbed her wrist, knocking the knife from her grasp. Winding her long hair tightly around his hand, he pulled her head sharply backwards. She screamed. It felt as though her neck was going to snap, but she wasn't going to give him the satisfaction of seeing her cry. When he released her, she eased the back of her neck with her hand. He pushed her ahead of him into the living room where he fingered her mother's ornaments, picking up the most expensive.

'Put that back? It's...' she paused. He cared nothing for sentiment. 'Whatever you're looking for, you're not going to find it here. So why don't you just go?'

'You'd like that, wouldn't you? I'm not going to make it easy for you or the kid.'

Determined to keep her voice steady, she said, 'You're making it impossible for us to be friends for Sean's sake.' She hadn't meant to say that, but she was running out of ideas to keep him from touching her.

'*Friends! Friends*, you say.' He had that wild look in his eyes and the muscles in his face twitched. She tried to think of a way to get him to go. Otherwise, he would be tearing the house apart, searching for drink.

'Well,' he said, with a wicked grin, 'if you want to play games.' Suddenly, he was all over her, his hands everywhere. 'If I can't have *you*, my lovely, I'll have the boy. I'll take him away from you.'

'*Never!* I'll see you in hell first.' Anger strengthened her and she pushed him from her.

He laughed. 'I'm his father. I'll say you've been seen out with your fancy man, leaving the boy alone.' He ran his hand over his stubble. 'Now, are you sure you won't change your mind?'

'Lies, all lies. Where were you for the past thirteen years? You don't love him. You don't even know him,' she said defiantly.

The sudden appearance of Sean and Shep made her gasp. The dog barked loudly. Her eyes rounded and she ran towards her son, placing a protective arm around him.

'What's going on, Mam? Who's that man? I could hear you in the entry.' His eyes flicked suspiciously over Vinnie and back to his mother. 'What's he doing in Granny's?'

'Sean... this is Mr... Mr. Kelly... he's...' She swallowed.

Sean frowned. 'What's he want? Why're you shaking, Mam?'

Vinnie sneered. 'Well, are you going to tell him, or shall I?'

Her heart raced. She couldn't let him do that. She felt dizzy. 'Get out. Go on. Get out now!' she screamed.

'I'm not going anywhere.'

Suddenly Sean ran at him with his fists. The dog barked frantically. 'Get out and leave my mam alone.'

'Slow down, lad, slow down.' But Sean lashed out with a hefty kick to the shin. Vinnie winced and grabbed the boy's wrists.

'Get off him!' Oona rushed to his aid. 'Now, go. Get out.'

Vinnie released Sean, but glared at the frightened, bewildered boy. 'Now then, that's no way to treat your old dad, is it?'

Vinnie's words, so shocking, rendered them all silent. The dog stopped barking and curled up under the table. Oona watched helpless as Sean shifted uncomfortably, a look of disdain on his face. 'My dad's dead.'

***

Having created the damage he intended, Vinnie slunk out of the house, leaving Oona to pick up the pieces. Sadness overwhelmed her as she looked up at her son's confused face.

'What did that man mean?'

Oona, her heart thumping, slumped into a chair and buried her face in her hands.

'Oh, Sean,' she cried. 'He's dangerous and he'll do anything to get revenge.'

'But why?'

Oona sobbed bitterly.

'Shall I go for Uncle Dessie?'

'No! No, love, I'm fine.' It was too late for any more lies. Vinnie had won. Sean deserved to hear the truth from her. But, once she told him, it would be the end of any respect her son had for her. She could see the puzzlement on his young face. Sean sat down next to her, placing his hand on her shoulder, while Shep crept nearer to Sean's feet.

'Mam, are you sure you don't want me to fetch Grandad from work?'

She glanced up at him, her heart bursting with love, and she would have given her life not to have to break his heart in this way. But it was now or never.

'Sean,' she swallowed. 'There's something I have to tell you, something I should have told you a long time ago.' She felt him stiffen. She swallowed again. 'I'm so sorry.' Tears she could no longer control trickled down her face. 'That man... that man... is... is your father.' She reached out to him.

He leapt up from the table, toppling her mother's sugar bowl to the floor. 'You're a liar. A liar!' he shouted. 'I hate you. My father's dead.' She saw tears gather in his eyes. He ran from her and clattered noisily upstairs. When she heard the bedroom door bang, shaking the rafters, it sent a ripple of panic through her.

***

In his room, Sean swiped the schoolbooks from his desk, scattering them to the floor with a loud thud. He put his head in his arm and wept. 'My father's dead,' he blubbed. 'Why's she lying? How can that horrible man be my dad? And why was he threatening her?' He wished with all his heart that his real dad, Eamon, was here to make everything all right. He wiped his tears with his hand. How could he be sure that the woman downstairs was really his mam? And if she was, how could he feel such hatred for her?

241

CHAPTER FORTY-TWO

Sergeant McNally turned towards Oona's father. 'What puzzles me, Mr. O'Hara, is how he knew the whereabouts of each family member?'

'And what puzzles me, Sergeant, is that you had him within your grasp and you let the beggar go. What kind of policing do you call that, when you let a madman back onto the streets?'

'I'm sorry, Mr. O'Hara. We hadn't enough evidence to hold him longer.'

'But that's madness,' Oona said. 'He forced his way into my home, and now my parents' home, threatening me and my son. And that's not enough?' She stood up, wringing her hands.

'Someone like him will trip himself up eventually, Mrs. Quinn.'

'In the meantime, my daughter's at risk and my grandson's confidence is destroyed. It's not good enough, Sergeant. Don't you know where he is now? Where he's living?'

'We picked him up in Baggot Street, of no fixed abode, or so he says.'

'What if he comes back? What about Sean?' Tears of anger welled in Oona's eyes. 'Are you going to protect him?'

The Sergeant ran his finger and thumb round the rim of his hat. 'We don't want to alarm the lad. Besides, I don't think your son is his target, do you?' McNally stood up and walked towards the door. Then he turned. 'Until we find him, don't take any chances, and if you're suspicious about anything at all, please don't hesitate to get in touch. You have my personal number.'

***

Disappointed with police efforts, the family remained supportive of Oona but her mother was furious that her grandson now knew the truth, and Sean refused to speak to his mother. It had been his grandmother who had coaxed him out of his room that night after he'd sobbed openly in her arms.

Oona, shocked at the cruel deliberate way in which Vinnie Kelly had told his son, wished repeatedly that she had been the one to tell him. Now she longed to be the one to hold him and reassure him everything would be all right. She knew the revelation had hurt him deeply. Right now his wounds were fresh and she was the last person he wanted to console him. Would he ever forgive her?

The start of the week was a nightmare, with Oona insisting on walking Sean to school. 'I'm old enough. I don't need you to take me.'

'This man is dangerous, Sean. If he approaches you, you mustn't speak to him.'

'He's my father, isn't he? I'll talk to him if I like.'

The family rearranged their work schedules, and Connie put on hold her appointment with the adoption agency to help chaperone Sean to and from school each day. Although this was of enormous relief to Oona, she couldn't concentrate on anything, continually blaming herself.

A week later, McNally rang with news of Vinnie's arrest. But the family's joy was short lived when he was again released on bail. This time he was due to appear in court the following week and Oona would have to give evidence. At least she could give her side of the story and she didn't care who got to know about it.

'There's no guarantee the courts will convict him either,' her father retorted.

'If he's not sent down, I swear to God, I'll go after him myself and sort the bugger out once and for all,' said Dessie.

Connie glared at her husband. 'You'd end up in prison and you wouldn't be as lucky as Vinnie Kelly. Leave it to McNally.'

No-one realised that Sean had been listening, until Oona heard him clatter back upstairs. She quickly followed. He was about to close the bedroom door, but she held it open with her hand.

'Sean, please listen to me?'

'Why would I want to? You're no better than my so-called father.'

'Because I love you. You mean the world to me.' She tried to stop her voice from shaking.

'How can you, when you've lied to me and hate the man you say is my father?' Then he pushed the door shut with such hostility it made her flinch.

***

Jack's support was a great comfort to Oona and, although she didn't want to involve him, he told her he'd be prepared to give evidence in court should it become necessary. He made her days as pleasant as possible, taking her to lunch when he wasn't out bringing in new business and dealing with queries at the docks.

Brenda was quick to spot Oona's edginess and lack of communication. 'Is there anything wrong? Only you don't look too happy. Have you and Jack had a tiff?'

'No. Everything's fine thanks, Brenda. It's nothing for you to worry about. I'd like that paperwork this morning, please. And can you ask Tim to bring in the Boland's file.' Oona's sharp dismissal sent her scurrying back to her office, a rosy glow colouring her cheeks.

Normally Oona would have smiled and tried to satisfy Brenda's curiosity, but she was not ready to share intimate family information with the teenager.

At the end of the day, she was shrugging into her coat when Jack glanced up. 'I'll take you home, I'm about finished here for tonight.' He stood up and reached for his coat.

'I'll be fine, Jack, really.' She leaned against her desk and glanced up at him. 'Do you think there's any possibility that

Vinnie could take Sean away from me?'

'What, with his record? I'd hardly think so.' He pulled her to him and kissed her gently. 'Believe me, Oona. You've nothing to worry about on that score. But, until he's been to court and convicted, I'm not risking you going home alone.'

They left the building hand-in-hand, Oona deep in thought. And as Jack opened the passenger door, she got in as if she was sleepwalking; as though it was something she did every day. Without commenting, Jack leaned over and clicked her seatbelt in place. As he drove, neither of them spoke. He drove as if he was carrying the finest bone china on the front seat, expecting to be asked to stop the car at any moment once Oona realised what was happening. The fact that she didn't surprised him.

Once they reached Ballsbridge, he gently brought the car to a stop, undid her seatbelt and wrapped her in a huge hug. 'Don't you realise what you've just done?'

She nodded. 'Other things frighten me more, Jack; more than I ever imagined.'

CHAPTER FORTY-THREE

Suitably dressed, Vinnie sat in an upmarket pub close to Dun Laoghaire pier, a glass of whisky in his hand. He missed the old city haunts he once frequented and felt extremely out of place. Downing his drink, he ordered another. So far, he had managed to keep one step ahead of the Gardaí. And, if he was to carry out the final part of his plan, he had to stay that way. If it didn't work, he'd be done for.

He thought about Sean. It was the first time he'd been that close to the boy he'd fathered. A fine lad. Strong. Athletic. Liked football. He had seen his name on the leader board at the boys' club when he went there to make false enquiries. Most young lads, as far as he knew, idolized some footballer. Once he discovered who Sean was cheering for, it would be like nectar to a bee.

Careful planning over the last few days had worked in his favour. Now that he knew the school Sean attended, he would soon have the kid eating out of his hand. First, he would have to gain his trust. He'd noted a sensitive side; knew he was vulnerable. This was a good time to strike. The mother, who supposedly loved him, had lied to him for years. If he was anything like his old man, he'd be feeling lousy and want to get back at her for keeping his real identity from him. That was enough for starters.

On Monday morning, Vinnie sat in his car close to the school, hidden by tall leafy trees that lined the swanky area of Sandycove. He was listening to Gay Byrne on the radio and reading his morning paper. He glanced up as Mr. O'Hara delivered his grandson inside the school gates, surrounded by high green railings. A thick privet hedge had a gap, and a worn patch – where boys took shortcuts – ran down one side of the recreation area.

It was hot and humid for early May and he saw the strained look on the older man's face as he waved goodbye to the boy before returning home. Vinnie remembered with displeasure how Oona's father had hated him; he'd made it clear from the onset that he wasn't good enough for his precious daughter. Well, the boy was his and he had rights.

A loud clanging sound sent the boys scurrying into individual lines that quickly resembled the military. Vinnie watched until they disappeared inside the building and silence again descended on the quiet road. At ten o'clock, the boys were allowed out for a kickabout and a game of marbles.

Just after ten, Sean was one of the first to emerge. Vinnie spotted him straight away. He looked disgruntled. Another kid ran close, bumping shoulders with him. Vinnie couldn't be sure if it was accidental, but Sean bristled angrily, immediately getting into a fight.

Vinnie leapt from his car and ran across the street. Greedy for revenge, he slipped behind the hedge that bordered the school. From his vantage point, he watched the goings-on. In his head he urged his son on, remembering his own school days and how he'd had to fight to protect himself from bullies. A gang of older lads gathered around chanting, fight. Vinnie felt proud of the way Sean handled himself, until one of the Masters ran towards the pack, shouting and wagging his finger. The boys scattered in different directions.

Sean, his shoes scuffed, ran down the playground towards the hedge, where he stood scowling and shuffling his feet. From the way he was glancing round, Vinnie got the impression he was about to bolt through the gap. 'Go for it, boy,' he murmured. It would give him the perfect opportunity.

'Sean! Sean!' he called above the din. 'Over here.'

Sean stiffened, hesitating. With so many boys cluttering the area, it was easy for him to slip through the gap unseen.

'Don't be frightened. I'm not going to hurt you.'

Sean's eyes widened. 'You're... you're that man who came to my grandad's house. What do you want?'

'I'm your father. I told you the truth.'

'I told you... my father's dead.'

'I don't blame you for feeling the way you do, son.'

'I'm not your son. I hate you, and I hate her.'

The harsh sound of the school bell startled them both.

'Look, go back before you get into trouble. I'll be here again tomorrow if you want to talk. If not, I'll go away.'

Sean ran back and lined up with his classmates, and Vinnie's lip curled when he saw him glance over his shoulder more than once before going inside.

'That's my boy.' His plan was working. He slipped away undetected, confident the boy would come looking for him the next day.

***

Over the next few days, Sean appeared brighter, and Oona dared to hope that he might have forgiven her. But she was wrong; his anger towards her showed no signs of abating. His head bent over his school project, he chewed the end of his pencil, a puzzled expression on his face.

'Here, move over. Let me help you with that.' Arithmetic had been Oona's strong subject at school and she had always enjoyed helping him to work out equations in the past. But he refused to move, leaving her in no doubt about his feelings towards her. Sighing, she went back and sat by her dad.

'This is not your mother's fault, Sean.' His grandfather had witnessed his behavior. 'We know you're hurting. None of us wanted you to know your real father. One day you'll understand why we had to protect you.'

'How would you like it, Grandad? I thought it was a sin to lie. How do I know if you're really me grandad?'

'Now you're talking silly, Sean. Of course I'm your grandad.'

248

'If you'd let me explain, love,' Oona said. 'It might help you to understand.'

'I don't want to know.' He jumped up and his books slid to the floor. Not bothering to pick them up, he raced upstairs.

***

Each day, Vinnie waited for Sean. He could see the boy was keen to see him – the way he shuffled his feet, the confusion on his face as he glanced around before sprinting expectantly to the far end of the concrete yard then slipping through the hedge.

'Are you all right, Sean?'

'What do you care?'

'I do. I've never been allowed to tell you. Your mother's made sure of that.'

'What do you mean?'

'It's a long story, son. But... don't ever believe that I didn't care. Now, go back. It wouldn't do for us to be seen together.'

'Why? Why wouldn't it? I want to know why me mam wouldn't let you see me.'

Now that Sean was curious to know more about his elusive father, Vinnie took full advantage, gaining his trust, drip feeding him bit by bit. Finally, chewing his lip, he said, 'Look, I know you must have lots of questions and if you could lose your bodyguards, we could do something after school, like. What do you say?'

Sean dug his hands into his pockets and kicked a stone. 'I've tried already.'

'You see what I mean, son? They've got me all wrong. I'm hardly going to hurt my own flesh and blood now, am I?' Vinnie smiled and, for the first time in days, he saw a hint of a grin brighten the boy's face.

'I could... well... I could find a way to get out early on Friday.'

'You could?' This was better than he'd expected. 'I'll be waiting.' Vinnie spotted a teacher walking down the playground

249

and slipped away unnoticed, a satisfied grin on his face. He murmured to himself, 'Isn't psychology wonderful!'

***

On Friday, fifteen minutes before the school bell, Vinnie saw Sean race outside, oblivious of the rain that lashed the streets. With his tie hanging loose and his blazer trailing on the ground, he slipped through the hedge. He spotted Vinnie and ran towards the car. The door swung open, he jumped in and threw his satchel onto the back seat. There was no-one around to notice anything. No net curtains twitched. People who lived here were out earning the fat salaries that enabled them the lifestyle of living close to the sea.

Apart from beaming a smile, Vinnie didn't speak, but drove off at breakneck speed until he'd covered a safe distance. 'Sorry about that, lad. I can't risk anyone seeing us. You understand, don't you?'

Sean nodded. His wet hair fell limp across his forehead.

'Don't worry. I'll take you home later. You can dry off when we get to the flat.'

'Where is it?'

'Not far. You do realise that we have to trust each other from here on, Sean?'

'What do you mean?'

'Well.' He maneuvered his car into the lock-up garage. 'I'm prepared to let you into my life. That is, if you want to? But, if you were to, say, tell your mother where I was living, she'd have me arrested and you might never see me again.'

'I won't tell her anything, I promise. Is this where you live then?'

'I keep the car here and I live a couple of miles away. Come on, we'll catch the bus before you get soaked.' Vinnie did his best to show he was a caring father by holding his Macintosh over the boy's head as they ran for the bus. Undercover of the bus shelter, Sean made to discard the Mac, but Vinnie pushed his head back underneath. 'Go upstairs, there's less chance of anyone spotting us.'

At the flat, he hurried the boy inside. Sean's eyes wandered aimlessly around him, and he began to fidget nervously. Vinnie poured himself a whisky and a glass of lemonade for Sean. 'No need to get worried. I brought you here so we could talk privately. Get to know each other.' He could hardly believe that he had the boy. 'Here, sit down.' He placed the drinks on the table. 'I'll get you a towel. Can't have you catching cold?'

He could see the boy's face begin to relax. 'You... you have a nice place.'

'Yes, but I can't enjoy it. I'm being hounded like an animal. And all I've done is to try and see my son.' He threw a towel towards Sean.

Sean gave his hair a vigorous rub then placed the towel around his neck.

'Why didn't you get in touch before?'

'Oh, I did, many times,' he lied. 'Your mam was determined not to let me near you. Not only your mam,' he continued. 'The whole family conspired against me.'

Sean drank his lemonade thirstily. 'I thought... you know... me other dad...' He swallowed nervously and shifted uneasily in his chair.

'You mean that guy your mother married after she refused to let me have anything to do with you? The one who died in the car crash?'

Sean nodded.

'Do you miss him?'

'I thought he was my...'

'Well, now you know the truth. But, look, Sean.' Vinnie, who had no time for sentiment, walked to the window. 'It's only fair to tell you. I have to go away.'

Sean's mouth dropped. 'Why'd you bother coming back then?'

'Hang on a minute.' Vinnie placed a hand on the boy's shoulder. 'Do you think I want to lose you again?'

'What?'

'Come with me. After all, we should be together. Once we're out of the country, we can do what we like. How does London strike you?'

Sean's eyes lit up. 'But... but what about..? I don't know.' He lowered his gaze.

'You don't want to, or you want to think about it?'

In the silence that followed, Sean's eyes moved to the clock on the mantel.

'You want me to take you back, is that it? I'm trying to be truthful with you and you want to go back to her. Well,' Vinnie shook his head slowly, 'I've got you all wrong.'

Tears formed in Sean's eyes. 'No. I don't. I hate her. But... I mean... what about the football team? I can't let them down, and I can't leave Shep, Da...'

'It's okay. You can call me Dad, at least it's true, and you might as well get used to it. But, let's get one thing straight, Sean. You can't bring that bloody dog. And, as for your football training, well that can easily be rectified. There's plenty of good clubs in London. Who do you support?'

'Manchester United.'

'We could go to Manchester after London, if that's what you want. Besides, they give free football kits to the fans in England.'

'Really? But, what about... shouldn't we let people know?'

'I don't need permission to take my son on holiday.'

'What about me mam? Shouldn't... shouldn't I ...?'

'Well, if you feel she deserves your loyalty, then go back tonight and tell her.

But I won't be here when you get back.'

'I won't say anything then. Take me with you, please.'

'Can I rely on you?'

'You can... you can, Dad.'

'Okay. Come on. Get your things. I'd best get you home before your mother sets the dogs on me. Come back early Saturday morning, and remember, Sean, not a word about us or you'll never see me again. Oh, and don't bother to pack anything, it'll only arouse suspicion. I'll get you kitted out. And, remember, no dog.'

Later, after he had made a few phone calls, Vinnie lay down on his bed. He'd wondered if Sean was smart enough to hoodwink Oona. Now he couldn't wait to find out. He could see himself in the boy, although he had never been so mollycoddled. Sean lived a charmed life compared to what Vinnie's had been like. The lad had a mother who doted on him. Although he didn't realise any of that now, and by the time he did, it'd be too late.

CHAPTER FORTY-FOUR

With the mortgage fully paid and her outstanding debts cleared, Oona's money worries disappeared. The extra compensation towards Sean's education meant that she would never again have to worry about his school fees. She treated him to some new clothes, mainly football stuff and schoolbooks, which she had previously bought second-hand.

Oona now had a telephone installed and one at her mother's. It was worth every penny, enabling her to return home with the added reassurance that she could call her family at any time of the day or night.

Sean was already running up a bill, phoning one or two of his well-to-do friends. She said nothing, hoping to appease him and get back in his good books, but he continued to keep her at a distance. There was a faraway look in his eyes, and each time she tried to talk to him, he changed the subject, refusing to be drawn into any conversation about his father. Vinnie was due up in court soon and she could hardly wait for the matter to be over and done with.

That evening, when Sean was late back from school, Oona didn't worry. It was her mother's turn to meet him after school, and he was probably sitting in her kitchen right now eating home-made cake and drinking milk, or messing about in the park. When she heard him coming in through the back door, a smile lit her face.

'Are you all right, Sean?'

'I'm fine. Before you start going on at me, I finished school a bit earlier and went to the park. I didn't realise the time.'

'So, you've not seen your granny? She must be worried sick.'

254

'I forgot. I'll go down and apologize.' He threw his bag down. 'Come on, Shep. Come on, boy.' He raced out again, the dog bounding after him, and Uona shook her head. Well, she thought, at least he's talking and behaving normally again. When he got back, she would try again to explain; let him see her justification for having him chaperoned. He needed to know the danger he was in with Vinnie on the loose.

Later, when she went into his room, her eyes widened when she saw Shep lying on his bed. Sean was reading a travel book and stroking the dog at the same time. She glanced down at the floor, strewn with books and discarded clothes, partly covering a plate of half-eaten toast. This wasn't the time to go on about the dog on his bed or the untidy mess, so she swallowed her annoyance, pleased that he seemed a little more content.

'Sean. I'm sorry. I don't want us to fall out.'

He shrugged and lowered the book so she could see his face. 'Why didn't you stay with me... with me dad, me real dad?'

She was surprised that Sean suddenly wanted to talk about Vinnie. She sat on his bed.

Shep glanced up, stretched, climbed down from the bed and curled up on the rug.

'He left me, Sean, straight after you were born, and he never bothered to get in touch again until recently.'

'When did you marry me other dad?'

'When you were two. But never forget that Eamon was a real father to you.

Vinnie Kelly didn't want to know. He hit me, Sean, caused me injury and I lied to protect you. He's a dangerous man and cares for no-one but himself. That's why you mustn't...'

'Stop it... stop it... How... how do you know... you don't know him...'

'Sean, love, listen. Why do you suppose you have to be chaperoned to school?

People like Vinnie can be devious. I don't want him to hurt you the same way he hurt me.'

'I won't listen.' He placed his hands over his ears. 'Go away... leave me alone... you tell lies all the time.'

'Sean!'

He turned his face away and picked up his book, covering his distress.

Sighing, she stood up and, with tears in her eyes, left the room.

***

Vinnie pulled back his living room curtains to a sky that promised sunshine. It was still early but, now that his mind was made up to leave the country, he couldn't wait to get going. He'd told his landlord he'd be away for a few days on business, omitting to tell him that he wouldn't be back.

The car could stay in the lock-up; by the time it was discovered, he and the boy would be long gone. In London, no-one would notice them. Londoners had no time to stop and dally, too busy minding their own business, unlike the nosey Irish.

For all he knew, Sean might suffer from seasickness. He wished now he had asked him to meet him at the bus station – assuming he hadn't changed his mind, or had it changed for him. The kid was more like him than Vinnie had first realised. He was eager to get away; he could see it in his eyes. Taking him away from Oona would do the lad good. She was turning him into a softy. But he'd soon toughen him up. After all, they had the same blood running through their veins.

Sean arrived sooner than Vinnie had expected him to, his face bright, excitement in his eyes.

'Good, you're here. What's the story?'

'Are you sure I can't bring me dog? He won't be any trouble,' Sean asked expectantly.

'We've been over this before. You know the score.'

'Can I still come with you?'

'What's that you've got there?' Vinnie glanced down at the rucksack the boy was holding. 'I told you not to bring anything?'

'It's my kit.'

'Your bloody kit! What do you want that for?'

'Well, if I didn't take it with me, Mam would know I hadn't gone to football.'

Vinnie let out a sigh, ruffling Sean's hair. 'Good lad.' Not as naive as he had first thought. 'I hope you're a good sailor, because we're taking the night ferry to Liverpool and then catching the train to London. What do you say to that then?'

CHAPTER FORTY-FIVE

After a morning's shopping, Oona and Connie were ready for a sit down, and headed for the bistro in Wexford Street. The sun was shining and it was warm for May. They bustled into the restaurant, their bags brushing tables and chairs as they searched for a seat.

'Oh, at last.' Oona flopped down, letting her packages slip to the floor. 'I'm bushed.'

'Me, too! You've spent a lot of money today, our Oona. You'd no need to go buying me that dress, and does Sean really need another pair of football boots?'

'It's time I treated my family. Do you think Mam will like this jumper?' She took it from the bag and held it up. 'I'm still not sure about the colour.'

'Don't be daft. I've seen her in lilac before, she'll be over the moon.'

Connie gave their order. 'No cream cake for me. I'm trying to lose weight.'

'Since when?'

'Almost a week now.' With a smile, she said, 'We may have a ten-year-old boy to look after soon, while his mother recovers from an operation. Dessie and I are quite excited. I'm sure Sean will get on well with him.'

'That's great, Connie. Bring him over to see us. I'll sort out some of Sean's games. I don't know why I keep them really.' She shrugged. 'He never bothers with them.'

'Thanks. That'd be grand. Has he said any more about... you-know-who?'

'Well, he asked me why I'd left Vinnie. Can you believe it?

When I tried to explain, he wouldn't listen, and placed his hands over his ears.'

'How strange.'

Oona shook her head. 'He must be feeling terrible though, Connie, and I don't know what to do to heal the rift between us.'

'It'll come right. Give him time to get his head round it. According to Dessie, he was quite chatty this morning on the way to the football club, although,' she cocked an eyebrow, 'he wanted to go on his own. Don't worry, Dessie wasn't having any of it.'

The server placed their drinks down next to them. 'One cake. Is that right?'

Connie nodded.

Oona smiled and placed the cream bun between them. Then she sliced it in half and pushed it towards her sister.

'No. Really, not for me.'

Oona had never known Connie to refuse cake. 'I'm impressed.'

'Well, I hope that after a few weeks, Dessie will be too.' She leaned her elbow on the table. 'You don't really believe that Vinnie Kelly could get custody of Sean, do you?'

'I wouldn't put it past him to try, and you know how this country favours fathers. But I'm damned if I'll stand by and let that man entice Sean away from me.'

Connie listened, a pained expression on her face. 'Sergeant McNally's a good man. He'll see justice is done.'

'Umm… well, I hope so.' Oona had to admit to her disappointment in McNally, particularly that he hadn't the power to hold Vinnie longer, in spite of him being a convicted conman. 'I'll get a court order, if need be, to keep him away.'

'What about Jack? Are you going to carry on going out with him?'

'Of course. He's been wonderful. And now that he knows about Vinnie, it's a load off my mind.' She sipped her drink and bit into her cake, licking the cream from the side of her mouth.

'I'm glad.' Connie reached across and placed a hand on her sister's arm. 'You deserve some happiness.'

Their coffee break over, they gathered up their belongings. Oona's bags were full of goodies and special foods she planned to cook for Sean. Since losing Jacqueline, she sometimes felt overwhelmed by her love for her son, and she was determined that tonight she would try to set things right between them.

That evening, Oona spent an hour cooking tea. Now that she could afford to buy decent cuts of meat, she had cooked lamb chops with mint sauce, crispy potatoes and baby carrots, and she made bread and butter pudding. She sat down to watch the news while waiting for Sean. She was confident that before the night was over, they would be pals again.

***

'Ah sure, the lad can't be far, Oona.' Her mother was shuffling into her overcoat and hurrying out the door after her daughter. 'He'll be with Dessie or Tommy.'

He wasn't.

'I'll phone Mr. Dunmore.' Dessie ran his finger down the list of names in the phone book. 'We'll see what he has to say.' He dialled the number and waited.

'Where's Connie?' Annie asked. 'Could he be with her?'

Dessie shook his head. 'She's gone to the Alcove to get me some Aspirin for this headache.' There was no reply and he turned towards Oona, her face pale and anxious. 'I'm so sorry I wasn't there to pick him up. When my headache worsened, I lay down on the bed and fell asleep.' He placed his head in his hands. 'If anything's happened to him, I'll never forgive myself.'

Oona looked at him, grief-stricken. 'Oh God, Dessie! Where can he be?'

'You two go back home in case he turns up. I'll go to the club.'

Oona, her breath coming in gasps, ran ahead of her mother and reached the house first, but Sean wasn't there.

'Look, your father will be back shortly. He'll know what to do.'

'I can't wait that long. If Vinnie has taken him, he could be anywhere by now. You stay here, Mam. I'm going to find Sergeant McNally.'

McNally wasn't in his office. Agitated, she paced the room. 'Where is he? I have to speak to him. Will he be back soon?'

'I'm afraid not, Mrs....'

'Quinn. Mrs. Quinn,' she repeated. She had no choice but to give the details to the young Gardá behind the desk.

'What are you going to do? My son is missing, and God only knows where his father's taken him.'

'His father! You know that for sure?' the fresh-faced constable asked.

'No, but it's the only explanation. Look, I need to speak with Sergeant McNally. Can you telephone him? He knows all about it.'

'If the boy's with his father, I'm afraid we can't do anything about that. He's not broken any law.' The lad carried on scribbling in his notebook.

'You don't understand. The man's dangerous. He's been in prison.'

'Have you reported him before?'

'Yes, of course I have. Haven't you been listening?'

'Look, I'll get you a nice cup of tea and we can talk this through.'

'Tea!' She almost exploded. 'Are you mad? Why won't you ring the Sergeant.' Oona wanted to slap his face. Suddenly she remembered the card McNally had given her and rummaged through her handbag. 'I'll phone him myself.' And she made to lift the receiver on the desk.

'I'm afraid you'd be wasting your time. He and his wife are away for the weekend.'

'Oh no. He can't be!' She glared at the constable. It seemed incredible that this young individual wasn't going to help her. 'I told you, the man's not trustworthy. Why don't you believe me?'

'If it'll make you happy, I'll go round and speak to him when my relief arrives.' He licked his finger and turned over a page in his notebook. 'Where does he live?'

'If I knew that, I'd go round there myself. Don't you have it?'

Oona tapped her fingers on the desk impatiently. 'He was picked up and brought in here a week ago.'

'Look, if you don't know where your husband lives, Mrs. Quinn, how can I question him?'

'*Husband!* He's not my husband. If anything happens to my son, your head will roll. I can promise you that.'

Outside, a telephone kiosk stood empty and she hurried inside. With trembling fingers, she dialled Jack's number.

***

There was still no sign of Sean when Jack arrived and by then the family had gathered at Oona's house.

'Oh, Jack… thanks for coming. He's taken him. I'm sure of it. What are we going to do?'

'My poor darling!' He drew her to him, wrapping his arms around her, running his hand down the length of her hair as he kissed the top of her head. 'We'll call back to the police station. See if they've come up with anything.' He took her hand and led her towards the car, helping her into the passenger seat. Only then was he aware of the rest of the family who had followed them to the gate, all tearful and distressed. 'Try not to worry,' he said. 'We'll be back as soon as we have any news.'

At the station, Jack felt as frustrated as Oona. 'Are you telling me that you're not going to investigate this?' Jack addressed the older Gardá now on duty.

'An officer went round to his flat earlier, but there was no-one to let him in. Anything more, we'd need a warrant, and Sergeant McNally's not back until Monday morning.'

'Look,' Jack leaned on the counter. 'Have you any children?'

'Yes, we've got a three-year-old boy and my wife's expecting another.'

'Can you imagine some madman abducting him? Not knowing where he was? Wouldn't you feel like us and want to get the child back safe and unhurt?'

'He's with his *father*.'

As Oona bit back tears, Jack continued, 'You don't know what you're talking about. This man is unstable. He knows nothing about his son. Imagine if this was your child. You'd move heaven and earth to get him back. For God's sake, just give me the address, that's all I'm asking.'

The police officer's face clouded. He picked up his pen. 'According to a neighbour, a Mr. Demspey lives at that flat.' He scribbled down the address and pushed it towards Jack. 'I never gave you that.'

'Good man. Thanks.'

'And no breaking and entering.'

'You won't regret it, I promise you.'

They arrived to find a small block of flats set back from the road in a well-to-do area of Dublin 4, not far from Ballsbridge. Oona wasn't surprised; Vinnie always managed to fall on his feet. Dreading what they might find, her insides churned, her heart beating so fast she thought it would jump from her chest. As they approached, a man was coming out. Jack rushed forward.

'We're looking for a Mr. Dempsey. Is he in?'

'I'm afraid Mr. Dempsey's away. I own these flats. May I enquire who's asking?'

Oona made a sound that came from deep down inside her; a pitying sound which made Jack turn towards her. 'It's all right.' He placed his arm around her shoulder.

'Look, can we come in?'

The man stepped back inside. 'Okay! What's this all about? Are you friends of Mr. Dempsey?'

'We're looking for a young boy whom we believe your Mr. Dempsey may have abducted. Have you seen him with a boy of about thirteen, perhaps looking a little older?'

'Can't say I have. Besides, Mr. Dempsey keeps to himself. Are you sure you've got the right man. I only let to people I feel I can trust. I have a reputation to uphold.'

'Your... your so-called Mr. Dempsey's a crook,' Oona cried. 'He's taken my son. And his name's not Dempsey. Are you sure he didn't have a young boy with him?'

'No child has passed through my premises, I'm sure I'd have known.'

'Can we see his flat?'

'Have you a warrant?'

They lowered their eyes. Sighing, Jack said, 'You can come in with us. After that, we'll leave you in peace.'

The man hesitated.

'Please... we won't take long. Sean could be in there. I have to know. Please.'

'This is highly unusual, but okay. I'll have to fetch my keys.'

The man stood in the doorway while Jack checked the bedroom. The bed hadn't been slept in. The inside was every bit as stylish as Oona had expected. There was a small amount of milk in a glass on the draining board and Oona gasped. She knew how much Sean loved milk and imagined Vinnie filling his head with promises. The thought sickened her. Then she cried out.

'Look! Over here. It's Sean's football kit. Dear God, Jack, he's taken him!'

CHAPTER FORTY-SIX

Vinnie glanced across at the sleeping boy – almost a man – and observed the light downy hair growing on his upper lip. He had to admit to stirrings of pride, although he was less sure he could cope with the responsibility of having him around longer than was necessary. He had achieved his aim, but at times he felt out of his depth. The boy's knowledge of history astounded him; he just couldn't get enough of it. He was clever, quick and alert, probably took after her side of the family, seeing as Vinnie hadn't a clue about his own. Given the chance, the lad could go far but there was something more passionate eating at the boy than his studies. Vinnie had never had any time for this football lark, but if that was what he wanted. Besides, if he was to harp on about his studies it might cause problems; forms to fill in and the like. Sean's schooling was the least of Vinnie's worries. Trying to stay one step ahead of the police was his priority.

Satisfied with the way things had gone, and the smooth way he had managed to persuade the kid to come with him, he sighed. Yes, he had even managed to impress him so much that he was calling him Dad. Vinnie wasn't sure he felt comfortable with that. He had spent a lot of money clothing the boy from head to toe, and he had never known a kid who could eat so much. So far, the boy had only seen his good side, but he wasn't sure he could keep up the charade.

The bed and breakfast in Bayswater was pricey and they were reasonably safe for now. But, after tonight, it was time to move on. He knew of a cheaper lodging house in Dulwich. Decision made, he finished his cigarette and glanced again at his son. Sean muttered and turned in his sleep. Sighing, Vinnie got undressed and lay down in the single bed opposite, his mind too busy to sleep.

***

On Monday, after another sleepless night for Oona and her family, McNally called her father to say he was on his way over. Oona hurried to her parents' house, hoping to hear some positive news. Instead, the Sergeant's questions antagonized her and she stood up pacing the room.

'More questions? I've already told you everything. What are you doing about finding Sean?'

'Oona, love, let's hear what the Sergeant has to say.' Her father tried to calm her.

'I understand your distress, Mrs. Quinn. I've already sent a telex across with details of the boy and his father. It's my feeling they're still in Dublin… As I said before, there's been no sightings of them at the ferry ports.'

'This is getting us nowhere,' Oona said. 'Vinny Kelly's good at covering his tracks. Why would he stay here and risk being caught? You're not making any sense.'

'I'll batter the bastard when I get my hands on him.' Dessie lowered his head into his hands. 'If only I'd been there. All this is my fault.'

'Yes, it is!' Oona's mother wagged her finger accusingly towards Dessie. 'Why in God's name didn't you tell us you couldn't go for Sean? I'd have gone myself.'

'That's not fair, Mam,' Connie placed a hand on her husband's shoulder. 'Dessie feels bad enough, and there's no need to make him feel worse.'

'He should have kept to the arrangement.' Annie sobbed into her handkerchief.

If her mother hadn't said it, Oona would have. She was livid with Dessie and couldn't look him in the eye. Only Connie's grief-stricken face forced her to hold her tongue.

'Come on now, Annie. Everyone's upset.' Her husband

moved closer. 'We have to stick together.'

McNally sighed. 'Recriminations won't help. I wish I had more positive news. Believe me, Mrs. O'Hara, I want to find your grandson as much as you do.'

'Then stop wasting time and do something,' Oona said.

'I need to establish a few more details, Mrs. Quinn. Did you have words with Sean before he left the house that morning?'

'No, no, no!' she screamed. 'He went off happy.' Her mind in turmoil, she sank to her knees. 'Dear God, my little girl, now my son. I can't take any more.'

'Oona, love, don't.' Her father reached out to her, and Connie helped her into a chair. 'They'll find him,' she said, choking back tears.

'I think that'll do for now, Sergeant.' James O'Hara stood up.

'I'm so sorry, Mrs. Quinn.' Then McNally addressed her father. 'We'll get coverage in tonight's newspapers. In the meantime, if anything else comes to mind… anything at all that might help us establish what actually happened to Sean?'

'Look, McNally. I'm inclined to go along with my daughter's theory. If the blackguard's not at his flat, it stands to reason that he's taken Sean to England.'

'If that is the case, Mr. O'Hara, the British police force will be on the lookout for them. I'm afraid if your grandson is happy to stay with his father, there's little they can do. I'll keep you informed.'

∗∗∗

Jack phoned each day and called in on his way home, anxious to be of help. His attempts to relieve Oona of the stress by taking her for a drive were ignored, and at times he felt useless in the midst of such unbearable loss. Desperate to be doing something positive, he had gone himself to the football club and questioned the boys and Mr. Dunmore, only to find that Sean had never arrived. He called on Vinnie's nearby neighbours. No-one had seen Sean that morning.

He hung around Vinnie's flat in the hope of coming face-to-face with him, but it only fuelled his anger and bitterness towards the monster that had plagued Oona and her family for far too long. Jack was doing everything he could to find Sean, until McNally discovered what he was up to and told him not to interfere in police business. Jack had seen his own frustration mirrored in McNally's face and, with police alerted on both sides of the Irish Sea, it seemed incredible that there was still no news.

He considered other ways to help, wondering if his stepfather – a retired police officer living in Liverpool – might be able to help.

At work, he could not concentrate and continually questioned why Oona had been so unlucky as to suffer another tragedy. As each day passed and produced nothing new, it appeared that her resolve grew stronger, but it pained him to see the light gradually fade from her eyes. All he had wanted, from the moment he knew he was falling in love with her, was to make her happy.

He felt sorry for the family who obviously adored the boy. Oona's parents were clearly in shock; two grandchildren snatched away from them. He thought of his own mother, who had yet to experience the joy of having a grandchild, and tried to imagine how she might feel in the same circumstances.

His steely determination matched Oona's and Jack was adamant he wouldn't rest until Sean was home and Vinnie Kelly behind bars. He knew that if he was to have any lasting happiness with Oona, he'd have to find her son and bring him home.

***

From the moment Oona realised Sean was missing, hatred festered inside her for the man who had fathered her son. The nightmare had begun all over again: the media, newspapers, police enquiries, the sleepless nights. Oona swore she would never set foot inside a church again if her prayers for Sean's safe return were not answered. With the dawn of each new day, hope rose then died in her heart. Her longing to see her son's cheeky face looking at her from across the breakfast table, left her feeling bereft.

After a week of heartache that almost sent her over the edge, she was desperate for a glimpse of her boy; her only remaining child. She couldn't bear the thought that anything bad had happened to him; surely Vinnie wouldn't stoop so low as to hurt a child? Alone with her thoughts, she walked dreamlike along the riverbank, unaware she was still in her pink slippers and hadn't washed or combed her hair. The dog glanced up at her and she let him off his lead. Shep was the closest thing she had left of Sean. The collie climbed onto the boy's empty bed most days, refusing to budge.

As she walked further along the riverbank, she regretted every harsh word she had ever spoken to her son. No doubt by now Vinnie would have him hanging on his every word and Sean would be proud to have a father in his life again. Tears stung her eyes. She glanced down at her hands. The fresh hanky she had taken with her was wound tightly, like a piece of string, between her hands. If only she had been able to keep him safe.

Poor Sean when he came to realise, as she had done years ago, that his father was mean and selfish and would always put himself first. What she feared most was Sean's disappointment, humiliation and desolation once his father tired of him; his loneliness and longing for home once Vinnie deserted him. All this she pondered, as her heart crushed into a million pieces.

CHAPTER FORTY-SEVEN

Oona's emotions were all over the place. At home, surrounded by silence, she let rip, crying, screaming and cursing her own misfortune in an outpouring of grief. At her parents' house, she paced the room then moped around until her father persuaded her to return to work.

'If I hear anything at all, I'll phone you.'

Realizing he talked sense and to stop herself from going mad, she forced herself to believe it might help. She put on a bright floral dress and white, low-heeled sandals. She knew she looked terrible, but she couldn't be bothered to put on any make-up.

Brenda came towards her.

'Is there any news of Sean?'

She shook her head slowly. 'Nothing.' People were kind and just wanted to help.

The door to her office was open and Jack stood by the window, his back towards her. At the sound of her voice, he turned.

'Oona! I didn't expect to see you today.' A smile brightened his face as he closed the door behind her, before drawing her close and kissing her. 'You didn't have to come in. It's so good to see you.'

Oona rested her head against his shoulder. His lips brushed the top of her head.

'It's the not knowing... all this time, Jack... It... it feels like a nightmare... a nightmare I'm never going to wake from.' Tears made her eyes sparkle. 'I'm sorry... I've not come in to... I'm here to work. My dad thinks it will help.'

'Are you sure?'

She moved away and slipped off her jacket.

'I'll get you a coffee.'

She nodded. Although Jack had called to see her most evenings, she had barely been aware of his presence. What should have been a happy time for them both was now swamped in sadness. While her son was missing with a man who had no idea how to care for the needs of a child, she couldn't think of anything else. She pictured Sean, his eyes alight with the stories Vinnie would be telling him. She hoped that wherever they were, her son was safe.

Sitting down, she took the cover from her typewriter and began to sift through the mountain of paperwork on her desk.

Jack came back with two mugs of steaming coffee. She cleared a space on her desk and he placed one down next to her. 'I meant to clear that, but with one thing and another...'

'That's okay. You can't do everything. How's Tim been?'

'Yeah, he's learning fast. He and Brenda are making steady progress and working better together. Enough about them. What–' The shrill of the telephone interrupted their conversation and from then on, the morning passed in a blur for Oona. By the time Jack left for the docks that afternoon, she felt shattered. How could she carry on without sleep? The doctor had offered to give her sleeping pills but, after the experience of taking them a year before when she had felt herself turning into an android, she decided against them. All she wanted was for Sean to walk back in through the front door, throw his bags in a heap on the floor, and to hear him clatter up the stairs.

She was rubbing her temples to relieve her aching head, when a tap on her office door made her glance up and Tim wandered in.

'Sorry to trouble you, Oona... especially now. Only, I wondered...'

'It's all right.' She half-smiled. 'What is it?'

'Can I...can I just say . . .' He lowered his eyes and sucked in his cheeks.

'I'm sorry for your trouble and pray that Sean will be home soon.' His lanky arms fell awkwardly by his side.

Nodding, she swallowed. 'Thanks, Tim. Sit down.' She gestured towards a chair. 'What's on your mind?'

'I've had a consignment returned, in spite of it having been sent to the correct address.'

'Have you checked the address in the directory?'

He nodded.

'Could it be the wrong consignment? Check with the shipper and see what they have to say. This kind of thing can happen, and it can take up so much time.' She guessed that Tim already knew this, and she appreciated his concern over Sean.

'Thanks. I'll get on to them first thing,' he said, as Brenda tottered in.

'Is there anything else for the post?'

Oona shook her head. And the girl stood staring until Tim nudged her and they walked back to their own office.

That night, in spite of working hard all day, Oona still couldn't sleep, and sat up most of the night talking with Jack on the phone.

***

By lunchtime the following day, she was struggling to keep her eyes open. Jack swiped his jacket from the back of his chair. 'Come on. I'm taking you for lunch. I want to discuss something with you.'

It was early and Dino's was quiet. Jack joined her in the corner booth, carrying a tray with coffee and lightly cooked cheese omelets. He removed the contents from the tray and pushed the plate of food towards her, then sat down.

'Before I get serious, you must eat something. You've heard the saying, an army marches on its stomach?'

She looked at him, her eyes dark pools of despair. 'If it's about the new contract, Jack, I'm doing my best to concentrate and I'm aware how hard you've been working while I'm languishing.'

He frowned. 'Forget about work.' He reached across and touched her hand. It felt comforting and reassuring. 'Now, eat something.'

She cut into the omelet and placed a forkful into her mouth. It was delicious and she had some more. 'Umm... these are sumptuous, thanks, Jack.' Looking pleased, he began eating his own meal.

'I can't bear to watch you suffering, Oona, and if I could get my hands on that conniving...' he paused. 'I'm sorry. I know he's Sean's father but...'

'No, I'm sorry I ever had anything to do with him.'

'None of this is your fault.' He lowered his head and ran his hands over his face.

'There's something I have to say and I hope it won't sound...'

She glanced up at him. 'What is it?' Her hands rested limply in front of her and he placed his own hands over them.

'I'm looking at a girl who's all ready to give up the fight,' he said. 'This is not the Oona I know.'

Tears of anger slipped down her face onto the strong hands clasping hers. She swallowed. 'How can you say that? I'll never give up; not while there's blood running through my veins.'

'That's more like it.'

'But it just seems so hopeless, Jack. We've exhausted every possibility here, and the police have come up with nothing so far. What can I do?'

'Stay positive and we'll find Sean.'

'How?' she snapped. 'What else can we do?'

'We can go to England. You believe that is where Sean is, and you know him better than anyone. We could go to Liverpool. Tom, my stepfather, is a retired police officer. He can advise us.'

Her eyes sparked to life. 'What about the business?'

'I've been thinking about this for days, Oona. I've spoken to Mr. Mountjoy. He's offered to take over the agency while we're away.'

'Really!' She leaned across and kissed him on the lips. 'McNally will try and stop us.'

'I'd like to see him try.'

CHAPTER FORTY-EIGHT

It amused Vinnie to see Sean's interest in everything. And to keep the boy happy, he took him to Madame Tussauds, where Sean soaked up the history of the English kings and queens, politicians and war heroes. But once outside on the busy streets, Vinnie was anxious to be off.

'Cor blimey, Dad. That was great. I liked the Chamber of Horrors best.'

'It didn't scare you then?'

'Naw!' Sean laughed. 'But I wouldn't like to be in there at night.'

'Pull your hood up until we're away from the crowd,' Vinnie said, hiding his own face with a newspaper. Sean wanted to linger, stopping to glance into shop windows.

'Look, come on, we've got to get away from here, so don't start dawdling. It's easy to get lost. Can you read a map?'

'Sure, I can.'

'Well, come over here and I'll show you where we are.' Vinnie pointed out Marylebone Road, Baker Street and Regent's Park. 'We'll catch the Underground, it'll be quicker.'

'Can't we stay here a bit longer?'

'Do you want us to get caught?'

'Sorry.' Sean lowered his eyes. 'I forgot.'

'I know a bloke in Dulwich who'll put us up. He owes me a favour.' Vinnie had taken a huge risk going to the waxworks and he hoped Sean understood that now. If they got stopped and had to prove the lad was his, Sean would oblige. They had been lucky avoiding the cops so far. But just the same, he wondered how long it would be before the kid started missing the comforts of home.

'How far is it to Wembley? Couldn't we go there?'

'Too far. London's a big place. We're going to Dulwich.'

They arrived at the address, only to discover Vinnie's mate had moved on. After spending the night in a noisy bedsit, they moved to Bradford, Vinnie showing signs of agitation. His money dwindling, he chose a room in a house where drunks were coming and going at all hours of the night and fighting in the hallway. The noise had unnerved the boy and kept them both awake all night. Sean was asleep now, his hair tousled, the vest he was sleeping in showing signs of needing a wash.

Vinnie took a long drag on his cigarette. Having the kid around was cramping his style and he wasn't sure what to do with him. Perhaps taking him along hadn't been such a good idea after all. It had given him enormous satisfaction at first, but not any more. Having to move around was becoming a bit of a bore. Sean appeared to be enjoying the ride so far, although Vinnie had to admit to panicking a bit when the kid wanted to post a card to his friend Tommy and another one to his granny. For God's sake; he had no idea. Afterwards, he'd felt sorry to have shouted at him.

It was on Vinnie's mind to get back to Leicester and lie low for a while, but Roly was still a threat to him and Leicester would be the first place the police would be looking for him. He knew how they worked and how to avoid the trap of being caught.

He glanced over at Sean – sound asleep, his belongings dangling from the bedstead –and muttered a curse. With a growing boy to feed and clothe, he might even have to find a job. He felt his deception of the good father beginning to grate. He stood up and shook Sean awake. 'Come on, kid, get dressed. We can't stay here.'

Sean scowled. Confused, he scrambled from the bed. 'Where are we? Where are we going? What time is it?'

'Time we got out of here.'

***

Oona's case was almost packed and she was anxiously ironing some fresh clothes to take with her for Sean. She had to believe they would find him. Connie called in with Tommy. Shep barked and wagged his tail, and the boy bent down to stroke him.

'You're coming to stay with me, boy, aren't you?'

'Leave the ironing. Come and sit down, Oona. Tommy has something to tell you.'

She immediately stopped what she was doing. 'What is it? Do you know where Sean is, Tommy?'

'No. Honest, Mrs. Quinn. But I saw him two days before he went missing.'

'What did you say?'

'That's when...that's when... when he told me...'

'What? What did he tell you?'

'Go on, Tommy.' Connie smiled to encourage him.

'He'd seen his dad, his real dad, like.' Looking uncomfortable, Tommy dug his hands deep into his pockets and lowered his head. 'I didn't know it was important, Mrs. Quinn.'

'Where? Where did he see him?' Oona wrung her hands impatiently.

'Outside his school.'

Oona gasped. 'Dear God! Did he say anything else, Tommy?'

'He was going to see him again.'

'God, Connie, I knew it.'

'I'm sorry, Mrs. Quinn. I... I didn't think...'

'Why didn't you mention it to Sergeant McNally?'

Tommy's face reddened. 'I was out when he called and he spoke to me ma. As I said, I didn't know it was important until I bumped into Mrs. Flanagan here.' Standing up, he moved closer to the collie. He clipped the lead on the dog's collar and picked up the bag with Shep's food and doggy bowl. 'I'd better be off. I hope Sean comes home soon. If he gets in touch, I'll...'

Oona bit down hard on her lip and Connie said, 'Thanks, Tommy. I'll see you out.'

When she came back, Oona was struggling to contain her emotions.

'Well, that confirms your suspicions.'

She nodded. 'I've never hated anyone in my life, Connie, but God forgive me,' a sob escaped her, 'I hate that man. He'll poison Sean's mind if I don't stop him.'

'Do you think Sean knew where he was going that morning?'

'Most definitely.'

'Shouldn't you let McNally know?'

'Ask Dad to have a word with him after we've gone. I don't want McNally finding any excuse to stop us going.'

Connie gave her a hug and, between them, they finished the packing.

'Sis, you could be on a hiding to nothing and you could be away for ages.'

'I know, but I have to do something. I'm going mad with worry.' Her eyes were red from crying. The circles beneath them darkened with each passing day and her weight had plummeted. 'I can't let him win, Connie, I can't.'

'I know. I know.' Connie choked back a sob. 'At least Mam's stopped blaming Dessie, but he continues to blame himself.'

'I know how much Dessie loves Sean, Connie. Look after them all until we get back. And can you keep doing that Novena to St. Jude?' Tears again formed in her eyes.

'Where are you going to stay?'

'I've no idea. I really don't care. I'll leave that to Jack. All I know is that we're catching the ferry to Liverpool, where Jack's parents live, and driving on to Leicester. Jack's taking his car.'

'How?'

'He left it at the port early today to be crane-loaded on, but we can't board until ten o'clock tonight. He's picking me up about nine.'

'I'll miss you,' Connie sniffed.

'I'll be in touch as soon as I can. Can you tell McNally that

I'll let him know where I'm staying, so he can get in touch when… if?' she sighed. 'And Connie, I'm so sorry you had to cancel your appointment with the adoption woman.'

'Sean's more important.'

'If only this hadn't happened. I should have watched him more closely.'

'You know you did everything you could to protect him.'

'Sometimes I feel the fight draining away from me, Connie. And other times, I feel anger surge through me like I've never known, and I know I won't rest until that madman is behind bars.'

CHAPTER FORTY-NINE

Jack had reserved a cabin for Oona on the night crossing, but sleep was the last thing on her mind. She couldn't relax. Stuck in a cabin by herself would send her crazy, so she graciously declined, preferring to sit it out with Jack for the seven hour journey. An hour out to sea, she couldn't stop her head from lolling, and eventually she fell asleep on Jack's shoulder. When she woke, the ferry was docking in Liverpool and she found herself stretched across the seat, her coat covering her legs, her head resting in Jack's lap. Embarrassed, she got up and straightened her clothes. 'Why didn't you wake me?'

'You needed sleep. Besides, it's only gone six and we have to hang around for the car.'

All around them people were stirring, gathering their belongings, and a haphazard queue was forming in preparation for disembarkation. 'If you want to freshen up, it's that way.' He pointed. 'I'll collect the luggage and meet you back here.'

She joined the queue for the women's toilets. Her head ached badly, and she had a permanent ache in her stomach that intensified with each passing hour. She splashed cold water on her face and glanced up into the mirror. She hardly recognized the woman with red eyes and dejected appearance now staring back. Not bothering to run a comb through her hair, she hurried back to where Jack was waiting.

Finally they were off the ferry and making their way towards the waiting room.

'Will we have to wait long for the car, Jack?'

'Not long, I hope. It depends on what cargo they have to unload first. It's draughty in here. I'll get us some tea; there's not much else.' While Jack waited at the tea counter, she kept getting up and going to the window.

He came back and handed her the hot drink. 'Sip this, Oona. We shouldn't be much longer now.'

Waiting was driving her mad. 'What time is it, Jack?'

'Seven-thirty'

'What? It feels like we've been here ages.'

'Look, you sit here with the cases. I'll go and phone Mum, let her know we've arrived.'

'Sorry, what did you say..?'

'I said... there's a phone over there. I won't be a minute.'

She watched him walk down the room to the telephone and empty loose change from his pocket. She could hear the noise of a train screeching to a stop, and soon the waiting room filled with people she guessed were waiting to board the ferry. She stared into space; everything around her seemed alien. Someone asked if she was all right. She nodded. Her mind was consumed with Sean. If he was in Liverpool, how was he coping in a strange city?

Jack was back at her side. 'That's settled. Mum's making up a bed for you. I thought we could stay the night before driving to Leicester. Is that all right?'

She nodded. 'Is it far?'

'About a mile. Near to the university, in the Kensington area. They're looking forward to meeting you. I told her briefly why we're here.'

'Do you think they will have heard the news about Sean?'

He glanced down at her. She was twisting her hands, one over the other. 'Mum didn't say. Oona, we'll find Sean, even if we have to search the length and breadth of the country.' He clasped her hands in his.

With nothing much to do but wait, she felt drained. And when Jack's car was finally unloaded and they could be on their way, relief washed over her.

Driving away from the dock, in the distance she could see

large cranes swaying back and forth, lifting heavy crates from the ship. Soon they could see the Liver Building towering high in front of them. Glad to be on the move again, Oona was desperate to start searching for Sean. But where would they begin? The city was teeming with people. She glanced up at the Liver's large clock face, her sense of time disoriented.

'That clock is bigger than Big Ben,' Jack said, as a matter of interest, knowing it was Oona's first visit to the city. She made no comment. But Jack kept up a constant chatter, regardless of the fact that her mind was somewhere else and her first glimpse of Liverpool was being seen through a haze of emotional turmoil.

The sun was warm and she felt her blouse sticking to her back. She wondered what Sean was wearing. What he was doing? Was he happy, getting enough to eat or being looked after properly? She remembered what Vinnie could be like; his mood could change at the slightest provocation.

'That boy! Quick, Jack! Stop the car! I've seen Sean.'

Jack almost swerved, before turning down a side street. Oona leaped from the car and ran back through the crowds towards the boy. Jack pursued her. 'Oona, wait?'

She grabbed the boy's arm and swung him round. 'Se..!' The words died on her lips.

'I'm… I'm sorry. I'm so sorry,' she said again, when she saw the frightened look on the young boy's face. She could hear strange concerned voices around her.

Breathless, Jack was at her side. She glanced up. 'Oh, Jack. What's the matter with me?' she cried. 'He looked so like Sean; the same green satchel slung over his shoulder.'

'It's okay, love. It's perfectly natural, given the circumstances. Come on.' He took her arm and they retraced their steps back to the car. 'We'll call at Dale Street Police Station. It's only five minutes away.'

She nodded. She trusted Jack more than she trusted herself. But he wasn't Superman. She swallowed to relieve the tension tightening her stomach.

At the police station, Oona felt uplifted by the treatment they received from the officer they spoke to. 'Ah sure, we've been on the lookout since news of the boy came through from head office, Mrs. Quinn. We've checked the ports this side and found no-one fitting the descriptions. But sure, in a crowd it's always possible to miss someone. It would be grand if you had a photo of the boy, otherwise it's like looking for an ant in a haystack.'

'You're Irish?'

'Ah sure, there's plenty of us in Liverpool. They call it the capital of Ireland.' He chuckled.

She opened her bag and took out a photo of Sean in his football kit. It was her favourite, and tears welled up in her eyes.

'That's grand. We'll have copies made and have it made bigger to stick in shop windows.'

'So, it makes sense that Kelly, or whatever he calls himself, would have come this way?' Jack asked.

'Yes, indeed. If he travelled at night, like. Would he have flown with the boy, do you think?'

'The Irish police checked but came up with nothing,' Jack said.

'He could have smuggled the boy in.'

She knew Vinnie would avoid arrest at all costs. The thought that he may have smuggled Sean over made her feel faint, and she gripped Jack's arm. Noting how pale she had gone, he quickly sat her down by an open window.

'I'm sorry, Mrs. Quinn. I've children myself,' the officer said. 'Eventually someone will spot them and phone in. We will, of course, keep looking. Have you got a number where we can contact you?'

Jack wrote down his mother's number and passed it to the man. 'We're on our way there now. You can contact that number any time.'

Back in the car, Oona felt reassured. 'Are you sure your

mother won't mind? I mean...'

'She'll be pleased to see us.' He reached across and squeezed her hand. 'Don't worry. You'll like Mum, and she'll love you nearly as much as I do.' He started the car and drove up the hill. 'And Dad, well, he might just come up with something we've overlooked.'

'That's wonderful, Jack.' She wondered what his mother would make of it all. Would she think her a bad mother to have allowed such a thing to happen? She felt shattered, so calling on his parents would be a break before driving all the way to Leicester.

They passed the museum and the Mersey Tunnel, and Oona frowned at the grey houses that looked like run-down holiday homes.

'They're called prefabs, emergency housing built during the war,' Jack told her. 'We're almost there.'

Oona began to tidy herself. She took the Alice band from her hair and shook it free. She hadn't put a comb through it since she left Dublin. After several brush strokes, it sprung to life and looked freshly washed. Then she flicked open her compact, powdered her face and coated her lips red.

'You look lovely. How do you feel?'

'Better, thanks. I'm feeling more optimistic, Jack.' She half-smiled.

Tomorrow they would both feel refreshed and she could get her brain into gear for what lay ahead. She wouldn't let herself contemplate the fact that they might not find Sean, but the thought was lurking there, somewhere in the far regions of her mind; somewhere she dare not let herself go.

CHAPTER FIFTY

Jack brought the car to a halt outside a red brick house. The double bay windows had leaded lights, with an extension over the garage. The busy lizzies tumbling from flowerpots on either side of the porch made an eye-catching display. There were two cars parked on the paved driveway.

'Your mother has visitors, Jack, we can hardly intrude.'

'My parents run a guest house.'

'You never said.'

'I never thought.' He turned and looked at her. 'Ready?'

She nodded.

'Come on. Take in what you need for now. I'll bring the rest later.'

Oona picked up her handbag and vanity case, and walked with him to the door. He pushed his key into the lock, almost as though he had only slipped out to buy a newspaper. As the door swung open, she could hear the sound of crockery coming from a room off the hall, like someone setting tables. Then a woman came hurrying to meet them, wiping her hands down the sides of her apron.

'Hello, son.' She reached to kiss Jack. 'And you must be Oona. I'm Gladys.'

She shook Oona's hand warmly.

'It's lovely to meet you, Mrs. Brennan.'

'Oh, give over, will ye, luv? Call me Gladys, everyone does.' She patted her short hair, streaked with grey. Her open face showed her warm personality. 'Jack, take the girl's jacket and hang it up.' Then she turned back to Oona. 'I trust you had a good crossing?'

'Yes, I think so. I can't remember.' She glanced toward Jack and he slipped his fingers through hers. 'I'm so worried about Sean.'

'Not surprising,' she said. 'Any road, is there any news of the boy?'

Oona shook her head.

'Please, go through. I'll put the kettle on.'

As she bustled towards the kitchen, Gladys's full figure put Oona in mind of her own mother and she felt strangely at home. Just then, Jack's stepfather, Tom, appeared in the doorway and followed them into the room. He clapped Jack lightly on the back. 'Aye, it's nice to see you, lad, in spite of the sad circumstances. And this is the young lady we've heard so much about.'

Oona blushed.

'Nice to meet you, lass.' He took her hand in a firm handshake.

They stood in the centre of the large sitting room. 'I'm forgetting me manners, luv. Won't you sit down?'

Oona sat on the settee, Jack next to her. Tom settled into an armchair, keen to know everything about Sean's disappearance.

'Can't be easy for yeh? Ten days now, ye say?' Tom sat forward in his chair. 'My feeling is he's lying low with the boy. But a rat can't stay hidden for long.'

'Have you dealt with cases like this one, Mr. Brennan?'

'Yes, Liverpool's full of missing kids! Some run to get away from their fathers, not the other way round. Most turn up eventually. Try not to worry.'

Tom stopped as Gladys placed a tray with a teapot and bone china cups on the coffee table. Oona knitted her fingers together. She had been hanging on Tom's every word, desperate for something, anything, that would give her renewed hope of finding Sean.

'Go on, Dad,' Jack said.

'From what you've both told me, I reckon Leicester is where

he'd go.' Tom Brennan stood up, straightening his thickset shoulders as though addressing his colleagues at the station. His grey hair stuck up all over his head, like the prickly back of a hedgehog.

'How d'you know that, Dad?'

'Well, for what it's—'

The phone rang. 'Sorry about that, Oona.' Gladys got up to answer it. 'You're never off duty in this business.'

'Of course.' She sat forward, linking and unlinking her fingers.

'What were you saying, Dad?' Jack poured tea and passed each of them a cup.

'In my experience, criminals go back to where they came from.'

'I hope so, Mr. Brennan.' Pleased that her idea hadn't sounded crazy after all, she sipped the hot drink.

'Some criminals, if they're lucky, have mates on the outside, but if this Vinnie chap has crossed one of them, they're sure to grass him up soon as he shows his face.'

'I think we can safely say he'll have made a few enemies,' Oona said.

'As no-one's reported seeing him yet, why don't ye stay here for a while? Get yer strength back. At least you're in the country, should news come through.'

'It's very kind of you, but I can't do that. I have to keep looking.' She placed her teacup back on the saucer and stood up, checking her watch. Was it really only that time? It felt like they'd been here for hours.

'You don't understand, Dad.' Jack placed his hand on her arm and she sat back down.

'I'm sorry, Mr. Brennan. I know you're only trying to help. I just feel restless, I keep feeling I should be doing something.'

'I understand. I didn't mean to upset ye, luv. Sure, you know what they say, once a scuffer...' He sighed. 'That scoundrel sounds as sharp-eyed as a weasel, otherwise he'd have been caught by now.'

Tears stung her eyes. 'You could be right, but I'm just desperate to find Sean.'

'I know,' Tom said. 'Not knowing where he is must be…'

Oona found it almost impossible to keep her emotions in check. All she could think about was Sean in the clutches of Vinnie Kelly, and any light relief she had felt earlier was now spiraling downwards. When Gladys came back into the room, Oona asked, 'Would it be all right to phone my parents?'

'I'll show you where it is, luv.' Gladys went out with her. 'They'll be anxious to know you've arrived safely. I'll rustle up something to eat. I bet you haven't eaten all day.' Smiling, she left her alone.

When she returned, Oona appeared brighter. It had helped to speak to her mam and dad, and she'd managed to reassure them in spite of her own misgivings.

When Gladys called them to the table, the chips, beans and sausages with fresh homemade bread smelt appetizing. Once Oona sat down, she struggled to eat anything. Not wishing to seem ungrateful, she picked up her knife and fork, cut into the sausage and put a small piece into her mouth.

'How is the family?' Tom was asking.

'Sorry?'

'Across the water. Are they coping?'

'Oh, yes. They're trying to stay positive.'

'Well, let's hope you hear something soon, luv. If you like, I'll ask around at the docks. See if anyone's heard a rumble.'

She nodded and pressed her fingertips to her temples; the Anadin she had taken earlier had had no effect on her headache. She felt sick with tiredness, trapped in an all-consuming nightmare. Voices were drifting in and out of her brain. Time dragged. Without Jack to talk to, she did not know how she would get through the night.

'It'll be the change of air,' Jack was saying. 'Why don't you try and get some shut-eye?'

'You must be jaded,' his mother said, getting to her feet. 'I'll show you to your room, Oona.'

She stood up. 'I'm sorry.' She didn't know what she was apologizing for.

'I'll bring you up warm milk,' she heard Jack say. 'It might help.'

Tom added, 'Have a good night, Oona.'

Following Gladys into the hall and up two flights of stairs, she wondered which room was Jack's and how far away he would be. She longed to feel his arms around her, reassuring her. In normal circumstances, she might have felt anxious about meeting his parents for the first time, but this was about as abnormal as it could be.

'I hope you'll find it comfortable,' Gladys said, opening the door for her. 'The students leave early, so you'll have the bathroom to yourself in the morning. Goodnight, luv.'

'Goodnight and thank you.'

Suddenly Jack was behind them. He put the milk down on the bedside table and took her into his arms. She clung to him, looking up with huge, tear-filled eyes. 'I just want you to hold me.'

'I know, sweetheart.' He stroked her hair. 'I'm only across the landing if you need me. And we can get off as early as you like in the morning.' His kisses were urgent, as if he hadn't seen her for a while. 'I'll see you tomorrow, darling.' Squeezing her hand, he left the room. When the door closed behind him, she felt strangely lonely.

***

The following morning, Oona woke, surprised to find that she had slept. A glance at her watch told her it was nearly nine. It was quiet and she wondered where Jack was. At least she didn't have to wait to use the bathroom, and hurried along the landing in her dressing gown and slippers. After showering and washing her hair, she returned to her room feeling refreshed, a towel draped over her head like a nun. She dressed in jeans and a floral summer blouse, pulled on her ankle boots and went downstairs. She could hear the Beatles blasting out Love Me Do on the radio. But she couldn't wait to get to Leicester and start looking for Sean.

She walked into the kitchen, a little embarrassed to be the last one down. Jack's face brightened when he saw her.

'Did you sleep?'

'Yes, I must have.'

His mother pulled out a chair. 'Sit yourself down next to Jack.' She relinquished her seat. Gladys was asking her about a cooked breakfast and porridge, but Oona shook her head. Anxious to get going, she glanced at her watch.

Gladys turned her back and placed some bread in the red toaster. Jack planted a kiss on Oona's lips. 'I love you,' he said. It gave her a warm feeling inside.

'I hope your husband didn't think me ungrateful last night. It's just that...'

'Oh, no, Tom understands, luv, more than most.' Gladys placed the toast in front of her with knobs of butter and a selection of jams. 'He hasn't quite left the Force yet, I'm afraid. He knows how unbearable this must be for you; we both do. And if ye need anything while you're in England, you've only to ask.'

'Thank you, you're very kind.' She nibbled her toast and glanced across at Jack, who was scanning the morning paper.

'So, you say there was nothing in the local newspaper, Mum, but just a mention on the radio. Is that right?'

'That's right, son. But God is good. Many a child goes missing, only to turn up unharmed.' She began placing dishes into the sink.

'I hope to God you're right, Mum.' Jack folded the paper. 'Where's Dad? We must be off. It's a fair drive to Leicester.'

The front door clicked. 'Oh, here he is now,' Gladys said. 'He had to go to the suppliers this morning. He'd have been upset to have missed you.'

Jack ran upstairs and carried the cases down to the car.

'Keep in touch, son.' There was a tear in Gladys's eyes.

'I'll call you from Leicester.'

Tom added, 'And I'll be in touch if I get wind of anything.'

'Thanks, Dad.'

Hugging them in turn, Gladys said. 'Until Sean is found, you'll be in our thoughts.'

'And anything I can do or advise on, I'm here,' Tom said, before waving them off. As they drove away, she noticed the concern etched on both their faces.

CHAPTER FIFTY-ONE

Vinnie sat in a pub in a run-down district of Huddersfield. He had left Sean sulking in an airless room not far from the railway station, after another row about going to Manchester. Anyone would think he was on permanent holiday. The room had a television set as temperamental as the boy, so he could watch that until Vinnie got back.

Long days of keeping a low profile with a kid in tow were beginning to do his head in. Harping on and on about going to Manchester. He was sick of his chatter. He talked non-stop; at first about football, and then it was Tommy this, and Tommy that. Now he was beginning to irritate him by talking about Oona and wanting to get in touch with her. And he'd heard him cry out in his sleep. *Soft lad.*

At first, he'd been as keen as Vinnie to keep their whereabouts secret, but boredom was setting in and he could tell the boy was missing home. He'd even stopped calling him Dad. But what did he care? He didn't want to be a father anyway. That's why he'd had to get out of the stuffy room. He needed to think without the boy in his face all the time. He had no more use for the kid, and his plan was to get him back to Dublin by smuggling him on board a boat back in Liverpool, then getting off himself before they cast off. That way he'd be free again. He wasn't going down again, not for anyone.

Oona would be out of her mind with worry by now. Serves her right! If she'd only agreed to go with him – once would have been enough to prove his point – he'd have left her alone. But she'd chosen the hard way.

God, how he missed having a woman, and he'd have had no

trouble bringing a Scouse tart back. From what he had observed, they seemed friendly and affordable, but he hadn't been able to risk it with a kid.

The pub was hot, even with the back door slung open. He swallowed the last of his drink before slipping away unnoticed.

Quickening his pace, he hurried back to tell Sean his plan. When he unlocked the door and let himself in, Sean was thumping the television set with his fists. He was naked from the waist up, and greasy marks stained his long grey trousers. He turned and glared at Vinnie.

'Why'd you bring me to this *dump*?' Sweat, mingled with tears, trickled down his hot face. 'There's no air. I could die in here. I'm going to smash a window pane.' He took up his shoe and aimed at the window.

Vinnie grabbed his arm and, lifting him bodily, threw him to the floor. 'Do you want to draw attention?'

'Don't care. You're an *eejit*! You promised we'd go to Manchester.'

'Shush now. Someone will hear you.'

'So? You're a liar, just like me mam.' He got to his feet and gave the television another thump, then – his energy spent – he slumped down onto the stained mattress.

'Look, if you can't hack it, boy, I'll get you back to Dublin tonight. You'd like that, wouldn't you? See your mother? She must be worried.'

'She won't want me back now.' Sean sniffed, wiping his tears with the back of his hand. 'Why can't we go to Manchester?'

'I can't risk it. By now the coppers will be swarming all over the place.'

'Give me some money then and I'll find my own way.'

A train rumbled past and Sean rushed to the grimy window, watching until it was out of sight. Vinnie could almost read his mind. The boy was desperate to get outside, and he couldn't keep him hidden much longer. Vinnie drummed his fingers on the table. The kid had some pluck after all. He'd chosen

Manchester over Oona. He was a clever little git; he knew how to get his own way.

'Okay! I'll take you to Manchester.' Anything to stop him whining. Besides, it was in the right direction to get him back on that ferry.

Sean swirled round and looked at him. 'When? When can we go?'

'In the morning! Pack your stuff tonight.'

***

Vinnie purchased two one-way bus tickets and handed one to Sean. The boy had already been schooled on getting around without being spotted.

'Remember, Sean. Keep that hood up at all times, don't sit too close to me, and keep your mouth shut. That Dublin accent's a real giveaway.' He glanced at Sean. His hair needed clippers to it and he looked more like a street urchin. 'Where's the blue t-shirt I bought you?'

'I washed it under the tap outside. It's still wet.'

'It'll have to dry on you then. That red one smells.' He wasn't going to spend another penny on him; not if he could help it. They boarded the bus separately, keeping a discreet distance, and Vinnie arranged to meet him in the central library in Manchester.

Although Sean had begged for some money, his father had refused, saying he needed money for a room. Once off the bus, Vinnie walked in front of him in the direction of the library, where they parted company. Sean didn't care if he never saw him again, apart from the fact that he had no money. The library was busy and no-one took any notice of him as he roamed around, picking up book after book. The library in Ballsbridge was small, and sometimes he went to the big library in Dublin to get what he wanted. He could have stayed here all day, except that his stomach ached.

Outside, he could see a phone box, and longed to phone his mam. If only his dad would give him some money. He had money for drink, so he wasn't skint.

Delighted at the prospect of taking books away with him, Sean was in the corner thumbing through a book about dogs and thinking about Shep, when Vinnie joined him. But once he realised Sean's intention, he quickly doused his enthusiasm. 'Are you stupid, boy?' he muttered.

Sean narrowed his eyes. 'I soon will be, if I don't do some reading.'

He felt his father's tight grip on his arm. 'What have I told you? You can't join a library or take books out. Do you want us to get caught?'

'Don't care. I've done nothing wrong.'

'Shut up! Put the books back, Sean,' Vinnie gritted his teeth. In a day or two he could do what he bloody well liked and there would be no come-back, because he would be miles away. When Sean reluctantly obeyed, Vinnie dug him in the back 'Come on. Let's get out of here.'

***

They ate in a nearby cafe mostly frequented by transport men. Vinnie paid for the food then forced Sean to sit separately. The man behind the counter gave Vinnie an odd look and nodded towards Sean, asking if he was okay. Sean shook his head, but turned his nose up when the man put a plate of greasy food in front of him

Later, they walked the short distance to the rented room that Vinnie had secured earlier. It was no better than the one they had left behind, except it had two single beds, no sheets, and just a pillow and a dog-eared grey blanket on each. Vinnie threw down his bags.

Sean looked around their new abode. 'This place stinks.'

'Well, you can clean it up. Give you something to do, you fussy little beggar.'

Vinnie threw off his jacket and stripped to his vest. He slipped a beer from his bag and slurped it down, wiping his mouth with the back of his hand. The springs went ping as he slumped into the old armchair.

'When can we go to Old Trafford?'

'Tomorrow. Now shut up, will you, and let me be?'

'I'm bored. Why can't we go now?

'Stop belly aching, will you? You're doing me head in.' He jumped up and, curling his fists, struck Sean hard across the head. The boy fell backwards onto the mattress. Crying out, he held the side of his head, immediately recalling his mother's bruised face.

Rolling up into a ball, he sobbed himself to sleep. While he slept, Vinnie got dressed and went out.

The following morning, over a makeshift breakfast of tea and bread, Sean was quiet. 'Look, lad. About last night... I didn't mean to strike you. I'm overwrought and I'm nearly broke, like. I'm seeing this guy about work later this morning. After that, I'll take you to the football ground.' He scraped back his chair and stood up.

Scowling, Sean placed his elbows on the table. Then he picked up the milk and drank from the bottle.

'The way you drink milk, I'd better get some more.'

'Can't I come?'

Vinnie glared at him then snatched his jacket from the back of the chair. A two-shilling piece fell out and rolled underneath the bed. Sean shifted in his chair, about to retrieve it, but quickly changed his mind when he realised Vinnie hadn't noticed. 'Stay here and keep quiet and I'll bring you back a couple of comics.'

***

When he'd left, Sean scrambled underneath the bed. It was filthy; littered with empty beer bottles and cigarette packets. He felt around until he had a tight grip on the money. The door was unlocked, which meant his father wouldn't be long. Peering along the landing, he ran down the stairs. A sour smell of urine wafted upwards, and rubbish of every description had blown in through the open door. He couldn't wait to be outside.

296

Not caring who might see him, he raced towards the phone box, taking in gulps of fresh air. It was the most exercise he had had in days. Fearful of his father returning and catching him, he hurried inside. Would two shillings be enough to phone Ireland? He had no idea. Tears pricking his eyes, his hand shook as he lifted the receiver. Once he heard the friendly voice of the operator, he began to relax and reeled off his mother's phone number.

'You'll need two shillings and sixpence. Please have your money ready,' the operator said.

Sean glanced down at the money in his hand. 'But, I haven't got enough.'

'I'm sorry, you'll have to try again later,' the voice said.

The phone went dead. Sean dropped the receiver, letting it swing, and kicked the door of the phone box until his toe hurt and he cried out in pain.

Tears of rage and frustration streaming down his face, he limped back to the room to wait for his dad. This wasn't the adventure he had first thought it would be, and if Vinnie was his real dad, he didn't much care for him. He was nothing like Eamon.

Sean wasn't sure what the truth was any more. His mother had lied to him, the whole family had, even his grandad. He hated grown-ups. This dad made promises he couldn't keep. Sean wiped his tears with the back of his hand and fingered the two-shilling piece in his pocket. Was it enough to get him to Old Trafford? He didn't know how far it was. But he'd find it, even if he had to walk. He wasn't going to play his dad's silly game of hiding from the police any more.

Hot and sticky, he longed for a soak in a bath, but his dad said they'd have to pay for one at the baths somewhere. He used the toilet on the landing, had a strip wash in the cracked sink, and splashed cold water on his face. There was still no sign of his dad. The last time he had gone out, he had been away for most of the day. Sean lay on his bed clutching his stomach, hoping the hunger pains would go away. He thought about his mam, wished he had brought Shep with him, and cried softly to himself.

By morning, when Vinnie hadn't returned, Sean searched through their bags and threw everything out onto the bed, but there was no money. Then he packed his own bag, left the room and made his way to the bus station.

CHAPTER FIFTY-TWO

The journey to Leicester proved to be an arduous one, resulting in Jack's car overheating. Determined to get there, Oona pushed the car for all she was worth, her feet slipping from under her. She was hot and her clothes stuck to her back. They had just managed to get the car onto the grass verge, when the heel of her shoe snapped. Flushed and frustrated, she kicked off her other shoe and flung them both into a hedge.

'I'm sorry, Oona,' Jack called breathlessly over his shoulder.

Her legs ached, but when she stood by the roadside, Jack's arm around her, looking helpless in her stocking feet, a passing motorist stopped and helped push the car to the nearest garage. Once the hood was lifted, the smell of burnt oil and hot steam filled the air.

'You're lucky you didn't blow the gasket,' the mechanic said, his head underneath the bonnet. 'Are you planning to take her much further?'

'Are we far from Leicester?' Oona asked.

'Another twenty miles, me duck.'

'Twenty miles!' Oona looked crestfallen. She had hoped to be there by now, combing the streets for Sean. As her mind jumped from one crazy idea to another, she looked helplessly towards Jack. He was undoing the cuffs of his blue shirt, and rolling back his sleeves.

'Don't worry,' he said, giving her a reassuring smile before peering over the mechanic's shoulder. 'Can you fix it?'

Oona crossed her fingers.

'Once it's cooled down, yes,' the man said. 'You might need to take some water with you in case the level drops again. You don't want a cracked radiator.'

The kindly mechanic made them tea while they waited and, after taking his advice, Jack filled a couple of empty lemonade bottles from the boot, and they were on their way again.

'Sorry about your shoes, Oona. Have you another pair you can wear in the meantime?'

'Don't worry, Jack. Shoes are the least of my worries.'

Neither of them had been to Leicester before and by the time they arrived, it was getting dark. With no idea what part of the city they were in, Jack pulled in next to a neon sign that read B&B. 'We're both bushed, love. I think we'll chance staying here for tonight. What do you think?'

She nodded, overcome by tiredness, yet knowing she wouldn't sleep. Jack took charge, just as he had from the moment they'd left Dublin. She wondered how she would have managed without him. He looked tired. She wanted to tell him how much she loved him and appreciated him coming with her. She said nothing, hoping that he knew.

The woman who ran the B&B, introduced herself as Ann. She was a sharp-faced woman with a gaunt expression, wearing too much rouge.

'You'll find this very convenient,' she said. 'Quite close to the city centre.' She placed the book on the counter for them to sign as Jack carried in their bags. 'Have you come far?' She looked pointedly at Oona's shoeless feet.

'Dublin.'

'Well, there's plenty of work for women in Leicester but...' she glanced at Jack, 'you might find it a tad harder.' Then she smiled. 'Unless, that is, you're in the hosiery or knitwear business.'

'We're not looking for work,' Jack said. 'We're here to find a young boy missing from home.'

The welcome smile slipped from the woman's face.

'I don't want any trouble here,' she said tersely.

'We're not offering any.' Jack looked her in the eye. 'Right now, Ann, we'd be very grateful for a room each for the night.'

'Of course, follow me. Separate rooms, is it? Only it's been busy.' She eyed them in a strange way and Oona, for the first time since leaving home, realised that not everyone would be sympathetic to her cause. 'I'll show the young lady up first, then I'll see what I've got downstairs for you, sir.'

***

After a restless night, Oona drew back the curtains. With a heavy heart, she glanced out at the busy traffic, wondering where Sean was. She had spent most of the night running over their last conversation, their last words, the last time she'd touched him, joked and laughed with him, until sobs had racked her body.

Turning back into the room, she pulled her case from underneath the bed. The chest of drawers smelt of mothballs and she had decided against using it. Pulling her nightdress over her head, she pressed the plug into the sink in the corner of the room and filled it with warm water. She pulled open her washbag and took out her pink flannel and Lux toilet soap. Undoing the wrapper, she pressed it to her nose, inhaling the sweet fragrance before swishing it round and round in the water until it resembled a milky substance.

In a listless mood, she ran the soap up and down her arms and over the rest of her body, then dried herself. From her case she picked the first thing that came to hand – a white blouse, a floral patterned dirndl skirt – and got dressed, slipping her bare feet into flat white shoes. She'd rinsed her stockings out before going to bed, leaving them to dry overnight, and she wasn't surprised to find them laddered.

A light tap on her bedroom door made her jump.

'Oona, it's me. Are you decent? May I come in?'

The urgency of his words made her rush to open it. Holding the morning paper in his hand, he hurried inside and closed the door. 'Take a look at this!' He sat down on her bed and pulled open the pages of a national newspaper.

301

'Oh, Jack. At last they're taking it seriously.' Tears formed in her eyes. She took in the picture of Sean smiling proudly in his football kit, his foot firmly placed on top of the ball. Underneath the picture, the caption read: *Have you seen this boy? Any information please, to the Irish police on this number, or to any UK police station.*

Jack stood up, took her in his arms and kissed her. 'Come on, this is a good start. I've found out where the police station is.' Taking hold of her hand, he pulled her behind him. 'It's not far. We'll have breakfast later.'

Outside, traffic was still heavy; mostly buses. It was a normal working day for most, and if anyone did notice the attractive couple hurrying along hand-in-hand past the railway station, they would have thought they were on holiday, enjoying the late May sunshine.

When they walked into Charles Street police station, the young bobby behind the desk glanced up. 'How can I help?'

Jack unfolded his newspaper and placed it down on the desk. 'This young boy is my girlfriend's son…'

'Take a seat while I phone S.E.U.' He disappeared through the door at the back.

Jack pursed his lips, and picked up the newspaper.

'What does he mean, Jack? Do you think they know something?'

'Let's wait and see.'

Within minutes, a woman police officer from their Special Enquiry Unit was directing them into the interview room. 'I'm PC Moran,' she said, shaking their hands. 'Please, sit down.'

'Is there any news?'

'Am I to assume that you are the boy's mother, Mrs…?'

'Quinn, Mrs. Quinn. And this is Jack Walsh.'

'This is the youngster who ran away from his home in Ireland?'

Oona glared at her and Jack sat forward in his seat. 'Sean

didn't run away. He was enticed away by his no-good father. He could be in serious danger.' Jack opened the newspaper and placed it in front of the policewoman.

'Look, I know this is upsetting, especially for you, Mrs. Quinn. I could show you a list as long as my arm of children who went missing this year alone.'

'But this is different!' she cried. 'His father is Vinnie Kelly, a known criminal.'

'I'm so sorry. But the fact still remains that the boy is with his father,' PC Moran explained.

Oona gripped Jack's hand. 'Haven't you heard what I've said? He's abducted my son.' She was beginning to despair.

'Dublin has circulated details of the boy and his father, and we are on the lookout. Mrs. Quinn, I understand how distressed you must be; any mother would be, under such circumstances. Do you have any proof that your son is in Leicester?'

'No. No proof, but Vinnie Kelly spent a lot of time in Leicester. And I can't believe you haven't come across him before now.'

'Look, I'm here to offer support in any way I can. We will, of course, assist the Irish police in finding the boy, Mrs. Quinn. If you feel the need to talk, you can get me on this number.' She passed it to Oona, but she appeared not to notice, so Jack took the card and helped Oona to her feet. He pulled a small card from his inside pocket. 'This is where we're staying at present. If you do hear anything in response to the newspaper photo...'

'Of course, we'll be in touch.' She shook their hands. 'You could try asking the Leicester Mercury to mention something about Sean. Lots of people read it,' she offered.

Oona nodded, but felt she'd been hit by a thunderbolt. 'What... what are the chances of finding my son?' She had to ask.

'There's every chance that Sean will come home of his

own volition, Mrs. Quinn. Keep that in mind.'

***

Outside, the sun made her squint, and she wished she'd brought her sunglasses, not just to block out the bright sunshine but to hide her heartache. They walked a few steps in silence and Jack placed a protective arm around her shoulder.

'Don't get discouraged, my love.'

'The police woman was reluctant to talk about Vinnie Kelly. Why was that?'

'They won't discuss his criminal record with us, Oona. Besides, I don't think they know where he is.'

She choked back a sob. 'Jack, I can't endure another day without seeing Sean, not knowing where he is, what might have happened to him. I can't...' Tears overwhelmed her, and Jack paused to wrap his arms around her.

A few people walked past. One or two gave them a cursory glance before walking on.

'Honey, no-one should have to go through this, especially not you. Sean's photo is great progress. Don't you agree? It will jog people's memories.'

'Yes, you're right. I'm sorry.' She forced a smile. Then, holding hands, they crossed the street towards the shops. They were outside Lewis's department store, and she glanced toward the clock tower. How relaxing this city was. She couldn't help noticing so many people from Indian and Asian backgrounds. Men walked upright in long white gowns, some with turbans and bushy beards. The women walked a pace behind, in brightly coloured saris that reached their sandaled feet. Customs of another world, she thought. What a contrast to Dublin, where most people were Irish, and a glimpse of a Chinese student going into Trinity College was a rare sight.

They paused inside the doorway of Lewis's and, after a quick glance at the noticeboard, Jack said, 'We can get

304

something to eat here. There's a restaurant upstairs.' He led her towards the escalator.

Sean's photo in the newspaper was progress, and commonsense told her if she wanted to continue searching for her son she had to keep her strength up.

CHAPTER FIFTY-THREE

Later that evening, Jack went to the Leicester Mercury to appeal for more coverage while Oona phoned home.

'McNally's working around the clock and we're more hopeful after seeing Sean's picture in the national newspaper,' Connie told her.

'Has he had any response yet?'

'Nothing of worth! Stay focused, Oona! The police will find him.'

'The Leicester police have been kind, and are doing all they can to help us find Sean. Look, I'm running out of change. Phone me here if you hear anything.'

'We miss you, Oona. Everyone sends their love.'

She couldn't let Connie know how she really felt, how her heart ached, how every day without Sean was like a life sentence. She sat on the brown leather sofa in the lounge at the B&B and waited for Jack to return. Since arriving, she had hardly noticed her surroundings; she hardly knew what day it was.

To stop herself from dwelling on what could be happening to Sean, she glanced around the room, at the pink floral wallpaper. The dark heavy furniture was old-fashioned, and green velvet drapes curtained the windows, keeping the room cool. Her body ached as if she had run a marathon and she willed the phone to ring with good news.

A couple who had been sitting by the window got up and left, giving her a cursory smile as they passed. Easing back onto the sofa, she wondered how Jack was getting on. She still felt guilty to have taken him away from the business. Every time she was left alone for a short time, doubts began to crowd her mind. Had she been deluding herself? If McNally and the English police had not managed to find Sean, what made her think that she and Jack could? Her energy draining, she closed her eyes.

When Jack returned, he came over and sat next to her. She glanced up anxiously. 'There's been no call from the policewoman, Jack. I can't believe nobody's seen them.'

'She'll ring when she's got something positive to tell us.' Jack guessed Sean was being kept hidden, but he did not intend to add to Oona's misery.

'How did you get on?'

'If they've got space, they'll give it a mention in tomorrow night's Mercury,' Jack said flatly.

'Thanks anyway, Jack.' She sighed. 'I'm grateful for all you've done.'

'We're not done yet. How are things at home?'

'No change. McNally hasn't any new leads either.' She swallowed. 'I can't expect you to stay away from the business any longer, Jack. It's not fair.'

Turning to face her, he took both her hands in his. 'What are you saying, Oona?' He searched her eyes. 'We're here to find Sean. The business is fine. Mr. Mountjoy has assured me, so there's no need to worry on that score.' He drew her close. 'We're not giving up.' He spoke softly into her ear.

Jack was her strength; she was painfully aware how much she needed his constant reassurance. Without warning, she covered her face with her hands and wept.

He gently wiped her tears. 'Everything you feel is perfectly normal after what you've been through.' He tilted her chin. 'You are the bravest person I've ever known.' He kissed the tip of her nose. 'You're the star in my life and I love you very much.'

'Don't. You'll start me off again.' She took a deep breath. How could she help loving Jack, who showed her his love in so many ways? She wanted to comfort him, tell him she felt the same way. Reaching up, she put her arms around his neck and kissed him.

Drawing her closer, he responded, their kisses growing more passionate. She felt an overwhelming desire, as powerful sensations swirled through her. Aroused by feelings she hadn't experienced in a long time, she drew back.

Jack said, 'I'm sorry. I shouldn't have... I mean, forgive me.'

She stroked his cheek. 'There's nothing to forgive, Jack.'

'Are you saying you feel the same way?'

'Yes, I do, but...' She looked away. It never occurred to her that someone might come in and see them. All she knew was that her feelings would have to wait until she had satisfied her desperate need to find her son.

'I understand.' He appeared to read her mind. 'Let's go down town and have dinner.'

That night, Oona lay in bed staring up at the ceiling. Her feelings for Jack had briefly released her from her tormented mind. The night was warm and the weatherman had forecast rain tomorrow. The busy road outside was quiet, apart from the sound of taxis that ran to and from the railway station. 'Where are you, Sean?' she whispered into the dark. 'Wherever you are, I'm thinking of you.'

When sleep came, it was as unexpected as her dream. Sean called out to her. His cry was one of desperation. He looked cold and hungry. She ran towards him, her arms outstretched.

Oona woke in a panic, her heart thumping, and reached for the bedside lamp. It was only 3am. It took a few minutes for her to calm down. Propping up her pillows, she sat upright, recounting the dream in her head, trying to recall every detail of his troubled face and the bleak surroundings.

She tried to picture where he was; it wasn't somewhere she recognized. It had only been a dream, but it had overwhelmed her.

There was a knock on her door. Thinking it was the landlady, who was strict about lights being left on, she switched off her lamp and slid down beneath the eiderdown. Then she heard it again.

'Who is it?'

'It's me, Jack.'

Struggling into her dressing gown, she pulled open the door. Jack, in his Paisley dressing gown and slippers, smiled down at her.

Surprised to see him, she swept her dark hair from her face.

'I saw your lamp on through the skylight.' His eyes shot upwards to the glass panel above the door. 'I can't sleep either.' Leaning in closer, he whispered, 'What do you say we go down and I'll make us a warm drink?'

Oona didn't need coaxing. Slipping her feet into her slippers, she crept along the landing after Jack.

They were seated in the guests' sitting room, Oona sipping her drink, her legs tucked up underneath her on the leather sofa and Jack in the armchair opposite. She told him about her dream.

'Dreams can be disturbing, Oona, but my old granny believed them to be significant.' He sat forward, his hands clasped in front of him. 'Try and put it out of your mind for now.'

'Oh, Jack! He looked ill.' She stared into her cup then placed it on the coffee table. 'He's in terrible trouble. I can feel it.'

'After that dream, I'm not surprised you feel like that.' He glanced at his watch then moved to sit next to her, kissing her gently on the forehead. She closed her eyes, resting her head on his shoulder. She could feel his warm gaze upon her, the concern in his eyes as he stroked her hair. Just the touch of his hand felt wonderful. There were times when she wanted to stay in his arms all night. The more she thought about it, it seemed like the most natural thing in the world. If it had not been for her anxiety over Sean, she might have broken her resolve and slept with him.

Reluctantly she got to her feet, pulling Jack to his. 'I'd better get back to my room before Ann comes down and labels me a scarlet woman.'

CHAPTER FIFTY-FOUR

Vinnie Kelly felt only a slight pang of guilt at leaving the boy. What the hell! He reckoned he had done the lad a favour by giving him his freedom. A strong boy like that wouldn't be long in finding work. Besides, hadn't he offered to put him on the ferry? Sean's choice had surprised him. The kid wasn't that keen to get back to Oona after all.

Seeing Sean's picture staring up at him from the newspaper meant the coppers were getting close and Vinnie's only concern was to save his own skin. He checked his current identity card, tucked inside his wallet, as he stepped from the train at Liverpool. Still in the navy striped t-shirt he'd slipped on the previous morning, he could feel the perspiration running down the insides of his arms. The blast of a ship's horn penetrated his brain and he quickened his pace, passing warehouses on his way towards the docks. He hoped to get work on one of the cargo liners – to Canada, if possible.

Two young men in caps walked out of the shipping office.

'Anything going, lads?'

'Aye, we're on the Isle of Man. But yeh better get your skates on, matey. She sails in half an hour.' Laughing, they made haste along the dockside. Glancing over his shoulder, Vinnie hurried inside. He'd worked on the docks before. It was where he'd met Roly – a man never known to forget an old score. Vinnie was taking a risk working on the boats, but he'd no choice.

The clerk behind the tall mahogany counter looked up as he walked in. 'Sorry, mister. If you're looking for work, I've enough hands this trip.'

'I'll work for free. Please! I have to get home.' He conjured up a sad expression, forcing a quiver into his voice. 'Me… me mother's dying.'

The clerk eyed him suspiciously, while glancing at his identity card. 'Have you worked on ships before?'

'Sure have,' he lied.

'Okay! I suppose I could use one more deckhand. You'll have to be prepared to leave now. It's hard work mind, heavy containers like.' He looked down. 'Any road, where's your kit?'

'When I heard about me ma, I panicked. You see, there's no-one else. I must get there… before . . . You understand?'

The clerk nodded. 'Well you'd better sign here, O'Leary.' He pointed. 'She's berthed in dock four. You've got ten minutes.'

As Vinnie ran towards the ship, he cursed. Bloody Isle of Man. Just my luck! He could hardly lose himself there. He made his way down the steps to the gangplank of the floating dock and had just stepped on board when the roar went up to cast off.

***

Sean found his way to the football ground with only coppers to spare and a rumbling tummy. It was almost lunchtime and the area around the stadium was quiet. A Ford Anglia was parked nearby.

Sean stood and stared. He couldn't believe he was outside Old Trafford, the place he had dreamt about for so long. He'd never seen anything to match its size before. It had been a magical moment the time he and his team had played at Croke Park in Dublin, but this place was something else. Drawing his lips together, he whistled his approval.

In spite of his hunger pangs, he couldn't resist walking around all four sides of the stadium. It took him ages. The entrances to the turnstiles were closed. He rattled the door, disappointed when he found it locked. If only he could find somewhere to tidy up first before asking for work. He looked down at his dirty, sticky hands. They'd think he was a beggar

312

off the streets. His mother would kill him if she could see the state of him.

The memory of how she had lied still upset him, but maybe what she'd said about his real dad was true after all. If he had enough money he'd phone her; tell her he didn't mean the things he'd said. But, with only two pennies in his pocket... Perhaps when he got back, his dad would give him the money to phone her.

Confused and hungry, he turned to leave when the sudden rattle of keys and the creaking of a door opening sent him darting for cover. He watched a man walk a few yards to his car. The door swung open behind him and, without thinking, Sean slipped inside unnoticed. He heard the man return then the door was locked behind him. Not sure whether to panic or feel relief, he decided that inside the grounds of Old Trafford was better than sleeping in a stuffy room with his dad.

Once he found his bearings, he went through and stood on the terraces. The pitch was perfect. He smiled properly for the first time since leaving Liverpool. Standing on the most famous pitch in the world, he raised his arms as though he'd just scored a goal. He imagined the crowd on Saturdays, could hear the roar of the supporters, feel the atmosphere. Excitement giving him energy, he ran around the pitch as if he was one of the players. He'd be in trouble when the man came back, but he didn't care. Afterwards, he felt weak and exhausted, bent over, his hands resting on his knees.

Inside, pictures of footballers adorned the walls. The door to the office was locked, but he found the dressing rooms and wondered which locker belonged to George Best. Stripping off, he found a shower and washed his hair, then dried himself on one of his t-shirts and got dressed again. He hadn't felt this clean since they left London. Vinnie had been generous then, but he'd changed and Sean didn't like him much, even if he was his father. He didn't want to be like him, either. Once he found work, he'd make his mum proud.

Feeling faint, his stomach made loud rumbling noises before he came across a room he guessed was where the players made tea and ate their food. The milk had gone off and the cheese had little bits of green mould, but he ate it anyway. The bowl of fruit looked fresh. He grabbed a green apple, eating the core as well. Then he peeled a brown-skinned banana that was dry, and ate it. Still hungry, he found a comfortable chair and curled up. Darkness fell, leaving him cold and lonely with no idea what to do next.

He must have slept, for when he woke with a pain in his neck, it was light. Remembering where he was, he jumped up, gathered up his belongings and stuffed them into his bag. He went through to the showers, used the lavatory and splashed water on his face. On his way back, he was about to snatch another piece of fruit when the sound of men's voices made his heart race. Holding his breath, he hid behind the door and watched three men walk towards the office, unlock the door and go inside. Sean made a run for the door and, once outside, blew out his lips.

The weather had turned cooler, the heat of the sun nothing like the previous day and it looked like it was about to rain again. He pulled the hood of his jacket up over his head. He wasn't going back to the dingy room without first trying for work. If Vinnie wasn't back, he'd have no money to make another journey. He sat outside near the doorway, his knees pulled up to his chin, feeling miserable. A man got out of his car and approached the club.

'If yeh want tickets, laddie, you'll have to come back when the ticket office opens.'

'I want to... can I...' He stood holding his shoulders back. 'I want to see Mr. Busby, please.'

'Aye. Darrafact?' Shaking his head, the man smiled. 'What's yer name, kid?'

'Sean. Sean Quinn, sir.'

'And what would you like to see Mr. Busby about, like?'

'I need work. I'll do anything?'

'Sixteen, are yeh?'

Sean nodded. If lying got him a job, so be it.

'Well, my name's Jimmy Murphy, I'm the assistant manager of the club.'

Anticipation widened Sean's eyes.

'I'm afraid we have no jobs on offer at the moment, but if yeh care to come back in a few months…'

'Oh no, please… Mr. Murphy. I need work now.'

'I'm sorry, sonny. There's plenty of other places yeh can try. Now, if you'll excuse me.' And he went into the club and the door closed behind him.

Disappointed, Sean hung his head and walked away, kicking the dust before him.

Light rain fell, wetting his head and shoulders, turning his fair hair dark. He drew the zip of his jacket up to his chin and walked faster. In need of energy, he spent the last of his money on sweets, and by the time he reached the bedsit he was soggy, tired and his stomach ached. Would his father be back? Sean wasn't sure he even cared.

The room was just as he'd left it the previous day. He flopped down on his bed and cried. Then, pulling himself together, he began to think of ways to survive. He had learned a few tricks in the Boy Scouts and he knew how to work as a team, but this was different. He was in a hopeless situation. If he had a pen and paper, he could write to his mam, then he cursed himself for spending his last pennies at the sweet shop; he could have bought a stamp.

He felt a raging hatred towards Vinnie Kelly, and a longing to see his mother and his family. But would they want to see him, after the things he'd said? He cried again and kicked the wall.

He awoke to heavy footsteps on the landing. His dad must be back! He jumped from the bed, flung open the door, and found himself face to face with a man he didn't know, an ugly-looking man with rough skin and a strawberry nose. Frightened, he tried to close the door.

'Hang on a minute, you young whipper snapper,' the man yelled, pushing the door. 'I want me rent.'

'But… me… me dad's not in.'

'I've been paid for two nights, that's all.' He banged his fist on the door. 'So in that case, yeh can clear off. Do you hear me?'

Sean nodded, too frightened to speak. He went back inside, in no doubt that the man meant business. His father was wicked and Sean didn't care if he never saw him again. He tried to think in a grown-up way. He'd seen his mother making lists when she couldn't decide what best to do. He could stay in Manchester and starve, or he could go begging or even steal some food. He'd seen children as young as ten begging on the streets in Dublin. Sometimes their containers were full of money.

He rummaged through his father's bag, dumping everything out onto the floor just in case he'd missed something the first time, but there was nothing worth selling. The *mean bugger!* He cried and kicked the bag across the room. He thought of asking the property owner for money, but quickly changed his mind. Sniffing back tears, he shoved all he owned into his rucksack, left the key on the table and walked out onto the streets as the rain beat down on him.

CHAPTER FIFTY-FIVE

Sean walked blindly on, with no idea where he was going or what he should do. By now, the rain had soaked through his jacket and was dripping down his legs into his shoes. Being out at night in a strange place frightened him. He passed no-one and the further he walked, the more frightened he became. He wished he was at home with his family instead of wandering the streets of Manchester with no money and an empty stomach. His mouth felt dry and he ran his tongue around his cracked lips.

Confused, he slowed down to get his bearings. Was he on the right road to Old Trafford? He couldn't be sure. It was growing dark and the streets were desolate. He glanced furtively over his shoulder, jumping nervously when he heard a dog bark. One or two cars sloshed past, and a half-empty bus. The shops were shut and, with nowhere to shelter, he feared he wouldn't make it.

He missed Tommy and the company of his school pals. Dripping from the rain, he took cover underneath a railway bridge and crouched down, holding his stomach. He decided to stay there for the night. At least he would be out of the rain. Holding his head, he cried. Suddenly a noise echoed. He jerked upright and caught his breath. It was a mournful sound, like someone or something in pain. Frightened, he jumped to his feet, peering through the darkness. When he heard it again, he gulped nervously. Clinging to the wall, he edged along until he stumbled over a slight figure propped up against the side of the bridge. Sean squatted down close.

'Are you hurt?' he asked tentatively.

Another moan.

He knelt down next to the youth, surprised at how small

and thin he was. Sean guessed he was around eleven years old. He was bleeding from his head and nose. If Sean felt grubby, he looked well dressed in comparison. The boy's frayed coat swung open, revealing a red football shirt and, underneath the grime, Sean could just make out the oval club crest with Liverbird inscribed for Liverpool Football Club.

'I'll get someone.' Sean stood up.

The boy caught his leg and pulled him off his feet.

'Hey! What'd you do that for?' Sean was beginning to wish he hadn't offered to help, when the boy wagged his finger and shook his head. 'No... no help,' he said, his voice weak. 'Ge' me up and... and I'll show ye where to tek me.'

'What happened to you?'

'Are ye going te help me, or what?'

Sean placed his arm around the skeletal figure, and the boy moaned as he got to his feet. There was a smell of unwashed clothes and tobacco and, as he hobbled, he cried out. The boy's leg appeared to be sprained or broken, Sean wasn't sure. As they left the shelter of the bridge, the rain eased to a drizzle. 'I'm Sean, what's your name?'

'Dead posh, aren't ye?'

'No!' Sean stopped and gripped his stomach. 'I'm from Dublin, that's all; not posh!'

'Ye can call me Duffy. That ain't me real name, mind.' Pain made the boy wince with every step until they reached some old warehouses, where he instructed Sean to leave him. 'I take it you've somewhere better to lay your head?'

'No, no, I haven't.' Sean was staring in disbelief at Duffy's shelter, made up of two large sheets of corrugated roofing leaning up against a wall. An old grey blanket, full of holes, hung down one side. Inside was a dry concrete slab, but nothing else.

'Ye can stay here if ye want.' Duffy crawled in underneath, dragging his leg and moaning. 'Been on the streets long, have ye?'

Sean shook his head, fighting back tears. 'Me dad's walked out on me. What about you?'

Duffy laughed. 'I ran away from the kids' 'ome when I was eleven. That was five years ago, mate.'

'You're sixteen?' Sean, unable to stand up much longer, slid down onto a wet patch against the wall. 'Got any food?'

'No. You?'

Sean shook his head, feeling as though his stomach was about to drop out.

'Ye don't look hungry.'

'I am.'

'The Sally Army comes round with soup.'

'When? I'm starving!'

Duffy shrugged. 'Don't know. Lost track o' time. Anyroad, ye'll know when. The 'omeless gather round here at night. Loads o' kids, some older guys, but I like to keep to meself.' He sniffed.

'Do you know of any jobs around here?'

Duffy sniggered. 'When ye've been round here long enough, you'll change your tune.'

'What do you mean?'

'Are ye t'ick as well as posh?' He pulled a small grey blanket out from underneath a red and white cone, and wrapped it around his injured leg. Then he took a bottle of beer from his inside pocket and slurped it down. Sean's stomach cramps grew worse and he wrapped his arms across his stomach. 'Here.' Duffy handed him a Mars bar. 'Ye look like ye need it more than me.'

'Thanks.' Sean's face lifted. He tore at the wrapper and chomped into the thick chocolate bar, savouring every morsel. When he turned back, Duffy was fast asleep.

Sean felt vulnerable and frightened. Thoughts of walking any further in the dark made him weak. Lonelier than he'd ever felt in his entire life, he crawled in closer to the older boy. If only this was a nightmare and his mam would soon be calling him to get up for school. But this was too raw, too painful not to be real, and he swallowed hard.

He stayed awake, listening for footsteps, scared by the noisy brawls that went on up and down the street. The soup women arrived and a portion was doled out to everyone except Duffy, who slept on as if in a comatose state fuelled by drink and pain. The soup only took the edge off Sean's hunger. Cold and shivery, he snuggled up to Duffy as fights and arguments broke out well into the night.

Too frightened to sleep, his stomach pains worsened, and he couldn't help remembering his granny's dinners; the plate piled so high he could hardly finish. He wondered what his mam was doing and if she was thinking of him. 'I miss you, Mam,' he murmured.

He woke feeling damp and cold. Duffy was nowhere to be seen. Sean realised that if he hadn't met the boy, he could have died of starvation or been mugged, as Duffy must have been. He wondered where he'd gone. He could hardly walk last night and his leg was hurting real bad. Had he gone for more drink, or perhaps to rob food? That was something he'd be doing himself before long, if he was to survive.

Sean wanted to see Duffy before making his way back to Old Trafford. In daylight, it would be easier to find his way. He crossed his fingers he'd be lucky this time. If nothing turned up, he'd have no choice but to come back and ask Duffy if he could sleep here for another night. At least he knew he'd get soup when those kind ladies came round again. He yawned, ran his hands over his face and dragged his fingers through his tousled hair. Pulling his hood closely around his head, he got stiffly to his feet. It was then that he realised his rucksack had disappeared.

Duffy had warned him about things getting nicked on the streets. There hadn't been much in his bag, but everything he was wearing was damp. Now he had to get a job, or else he'd find himself back here again, cold and hungry. As he walked away, he could hear shouting as arguments began to brew again. Frightened, he quickened his step.

By the time he reached United's football ground, his stomach ached and he felt faint. He had no idea what time it was, and he wasn't sure what day it was. He huddled in the doorway, willing someone to turn up. In spite of the hazy sunshine, he felt cold and shivery and, without his rucksack, he didn't have another jumper.

After what seemed like hours, the Assistant Manager, Jimmy Murphy turned up. He didn't look pleased to see Sean waiting for him.

'*Not you again!*' he said in a dispirited voice. 'Have you no home to go to, kid?'

Sean stood up and stuffed his hands into his empty pockets. He was shivering.

'Please, Mr. Murphy. I need work. I'm starving… I'll do…' The next thing his legs buckled and he couldn't stop himself falling to the ground.

CHAPTER FIFTY-SIX

McNally sighed when the phone rang. 'If this is more shenanigans,' he said aloud. 'I swear to God, I'll–' Snatching up the receiver, he pressed it against his ear while working on the report in front of him. 'Yes! Who is this?' As he listened, his shoulders straightened. His bored expression now animated, he reached for his notebook and fountain pen. Listening more intently, he scribbled something down.

'Are you sure? How long ago?' He scribbled some more. 'Have you seen the boy? Is he hurt?' He shook his head. 'Any news of the father's whereabouts? I see… yes… well… of course. Thanks for your assistance, Sergeant Smith. Much appreciated. I'll contact the family and we'll take it from there.' The phone clicked off.

'God be praised!' This was indeed good news; better than he had dared to hope. Solace at last for a mother who had already lost so much. He closed his eyes briefly as the image of the little girl flashed before him. Then he dialled the operator and asked her to put him through to a Leicester phone number. As he waited to be connected, he tapped his fingers impatiently. He cleared his throat. 'Thank you. Hello, look, my name is Sergeant McNally. I believe you have a Mrs. Oona Quinn stopping with you. *Sergeant McNally.* Irish Police. *Yes, yes.* I need to speak to Mrs. Quinn urgently, please. Yes, I'll hang on.'

It seemed to take forever. If she wasn't in, he'd have no choice but to phone Mr. O'Hara with the news, but he felt the mother had the right to be told first. Sighing, he changed the phone to his other ear. Then he heard Mrs. Quinn, heard the quiver in her voice, the heartbreaking uncertainty. 'Is… is it bad news?'

'Mrs. Quinn. Your son's been found! I'm sorry it's taken us so long.'

'You've found Sean! Oh my God! Is he all right?'

'Your son is doing fine, Mrs. Quinn. He's on the children's ward in Manchester General. He collapsed outside Old Trafford football ground. Rest assured that he is being well cared for. Sean was alone when he was found, so I'm sure the police will want to question him about his father.' He imagined her brain struggling to make sense of what he'd just told her and it brought a lump to his throat. 'You can go there as soon as you like and be reunited with him.'

He could hear the excitement at the other end as the phone was passed to Jack Walsh. 'This is great news, McNally. Do you know how Sean is?'

'I can't say what injuries the boy has, if any, Mr. Walsh, but he's in good hands. I'm assuming you will want to go there straight away. Drive carefully now,' he said. 'I'll let the rest of the family know.'

McNally replaced the receiver, allowing himself to smile. Then he pushed back his chair and stood up. 'I'll nail that bastard Kelly if it's the last thing I do,' he muttered.

Outside in reception, an officer glanced up. 'Off out, Sergeant?'

'When the Duty Sergeant arrives, tell him we've found the Quinn boy.'

***

On the way to the hospital, Oona was overwhelmed with thoughts of how Sean would look when she finally got to see him. The journey to Manchester seemed endless and she couldn't get there soon enough. Sean was alive, McNally had reassured her, and the hospital said he was comfortable. Yet she needed to see for herself; to find out why he had collapsed?

It was three o'clock when they finally arrived in Manchester.

Jack pulled up outside the hospital and Oona bit her bottom lip to stem her emotions.

'All right, love?' Jack patted her knee. She nodded, and hand-in-hand they hurried inside. After a word with the receptionist, they ran upstairs and along the passage towards the children's ward. Her heels clicked on the hard floor and there was the smell of surgical spirits.

Jack hesitated at the end of the long passage, and Oona turned towards him.

'Go ahead, honey. I won't be far away.' It was obvious he wanted to give her time alone with Sean, and she felt grateful. Once she glimpsed sight of Sean, she wouldn't be able to stop herself from breaking down.

Her heart pounding, she walked into the ward. He was at the far end of the room, his face turned to the wall. The nurse at the desk smiled and nodded. As Oona got closer, she saw he was wearing a hospital gown. Her throat tightened but she ran towards him.

'Mam!' he cried. 'I didn't think you'd come! How'd you get here so fast?'

'Are you hurt?' She sat on the bed, shaking with relief. She touched his face, his hair. He shook his head. 'Thank God we found you. Where in the name of heaven have you been? I've been out of my mind with worry.'

'I'm sorry, Mam.'

'It's so good to see you, love.' She choked back a sob.

'I thought I'd never see you again,' he cried. And, as they clung each to the other, Oona couldn't speak.

'I'll draw the curtain,' the young nurse smiled. 'It'll give you a bit more privacy.'

'Thank you.' Oona whipped out her handkerchief and blew her nose. 'Let me look at you.' Her once-healthy boy looked pale and drawn, thinner too, like someone who'd been cooped up for a month. Now she just wanted to get him home.

'Come here.' She threw her arms around him again, stroking

his hair, taking in every inch of his face as if she could hardly believe he was here in front of her. He looked different, wiser somehow. 'I did my best to keep him away from you. We all did.'

'I... I'm sorry I went away with him.'

'He's evil! How are you feeling?'

'I'm grand, but can... can I come home, Mam?' His eyes filled and he bit his lip. 'My dog! Who's looking after Shep?'

'He's fine. Tommy's taking good care of him.'

He wiped a tear with the back of his hand. 'I tried to phone you but I didn't have enough money and he... he ran out on me, left me with nothing. He said if I went to the police, they'd treat me like a runaway! I didn't know what to do!'

'Shush, darling... I'm here now and you'll be coming home with us.'

He frowned. 'Is Uncle Dessie with you?' He glanced down the ward.

'No, he stayed at home in case... well, Sergeant McNally wasn't convinced he'd taken you to England. I'm here with Jack. You remember my boss, Jack Walsh. We've been in England for days searching for you. We've just driven from Leicester where Vin... your father used to live.'

'He's not my father! I don't want to see him ever again. I hate him, Mam! He was really nice at first, then... then he changed. He left me with no food. I was starving.' Tears sprung into his eyes.

'Oh, Sean, love.' She tightened her arms around him and felt his body tremble. 'He'll never hurt you again, I promise.' She swallowed. 'Do you have any idea where he might have gone? The police are doing their best to catch him.'

He shook his head. 'I know they are.'

'They've questioned you?'

'Yes, and I've told the police everything, but I don't know where he went. I hope he never comes back.'

Oona rocked him in her arms. This whole episode had

affected him badly and she could only hope that he'd be able to put it all behind him.

'He said he'd take me to Old Trafford to meet George Best, but he never kept his promise. He lied to me all the time.' He lowered his eyes. 'You did too.'

'Only to protect you, love. Eamon wanted to tell you before he... well, afterwards, we were both too upset. I should have told you the first time Vinnie came back and threatened me, but I didn't want you to know he was your father, and neither did Grandma! I'm sorry, Sean.'

'I think I understand now. Now I know what is good and what is bad. You're the best.' He threw his arms around her and they both cried. All the pent-up feelings of the past weeks evaporated in that moment.

Stretching her shoulders, she stood up and drew back the curtain. 'I'm going to see the Sister about taking you home.'

'Mam.' He looked up at her, dark shadows under his eyes. Somehow he looked older than twelve. 'Can we..? I need to see someone before we leave.'

'Who? Who do you mean, Sean?'

'Duffy! I want to see Duffy!'

CHAPTER FIFTY-SEVEN

Oona was shocked to hear of Sean's ordeal, but wanted to find Duffy and see where her son had spent the night. His short stay in hospital had revived him and the doctors agreed that he was fit to leave with his mother and Jack.

Once Sean was out of bed, he got dressed in the fresh clothes Oona had brought with her, and together they thanked the hospital staff and bid them farewell. As they walked slowly towards the car, Jack asked, 'Sean, do you think you can remember where you met Duffy?'

'I think so. It was near some warehouses. I don't know where he goes during the day, but he comes back early; otherwise someone will pinch his spot.'

'How sad!' Oona shook her head and offered a silent prayer of thanks. If Vinnie had decided to take Sean abroad, she might never have seen him again.

'In that case,' Jack said, 'he won't show for a couple of hours yet, so I suggest we have something to eat.'

'Will we have time to shop?' Oona looked down at Sean's scuffed shoes with the toes almost coming through.

'I've already rung the B&I office and they've agreed for me to book the car in tonight, later than scheduled. I doubt we'd get it on tomorrow night's sailing as it's the weekend,' Jack said kindly.

'That's grand.'

'Can we get something for Duffy?'

'How old is he, Sean?' Jack asked.

'Sixteen.'

'I think, as we don't know his size, it might be better to give him a few pounds.'

Sean nodded. 'Yeah, but he has nothing to sleep on.'

'We could buy him a sleeping bag! What do you think, Oona?'

'That would be useful. He can roll it up and take it with him. He might manage to keep it for a while.'

'I know where there's a camping shop in the city,' Jack said.

***

Later, Jack drove around the streets of Manchester, following directions from Sean. After many wrong turns, Sean said, 'It's got to be around here somewhere.'

'It might be further on down,' Jack offered.

'Stop! I remember those warehouses. This is definitely it. Yes, there it is, look!' Sean pointed towards open wasteland resembling a redundant building site. Broken bottles and discarded newspapers were strewn across the patchy grass. Two men of unkempt appearance had their hands inside dustbins, spilling the contents onto the ground.

Oona stared in disbelief. 'How can anyone sleep there, Sean?'

'I slept over there by that wall with Duffy.'

'These poor beggars aren't fussed.'

'Dear God. Anything could have happened.' She gave Jack a meaningful glance. She wasn't at all surprised that Vinnie had left Sean to face such danger. It had been her biggest fear from the moment she discovered he'd taken him, and now she wouldn't rest until he got his come-uppance.

'This is certainly no place for an adult at night, let alone a child.' Jack stopped the car on the corner and turned off the engine. 'You must have been frightened.'

'Yeah... I was really scared until I bumped into Duffy. Someone had hurt him real bad, but he wouldn't talk about it. He told me how to stay safe, but even so, someone made off with my rucksack.'

'At least you had the good sense to make your way back to Old Trafford.'

'Thank God someone there remembered seeing your picture in the newspaper,' Oona added.

One of the tramps ambled towards the car and Jack waved him away. Half an hour later, with still no sign of Duffy, Jack stretched his shoulders and glanced at his watch.

'Don't go yet, please… he should be here soon.'

'It's all right, Sean. We'll stay as long as we possibly can.'

'What about the ferry?' Oona asked.

'Let me worry about that!'

Finally, a thin waif of a boy limped round the corner in the direction of his makeshift home.

'That's him!' Sean cried.

Oona gasped and was about to step from the car until Sean placed his hand on her arm. 'No, Mam! I want to talk to him on me own. He might run if he sees grown-ups.'

'Be careful.'

Jack passed over the bags and Sean got out and walked towards him. 'Duffy! Duffy! It's me, Sean. Wait up, will you!'

Oona looked at Jack. He was biting down on his lower lip. She could see that the sight of Duffy moved him too. She reached for his hand, thankful to have found Sean before he ended up like Duffy. They watched in silence.

Duffy looked over his shoulder, taking in the car and its occupants. 'What'd ye want, kid? You haven't snitched on me, have ye? Who's that in the car? If they're from the kids' home, I'm not—'

'No, Duffy. It's only me mam and her boss. We've brought you some food and a sleeping bag.' Sean placed the parcel and the food down next to him.

Duffy glanced quickly around him before rummaging through the food bag.

'What's the catch?'

'There's none, honest. Where'd you go the other night?'

'I told ye, no questions. It's too risky.'

'How's the leg?'

He shrugged.

'Look, we have to go now. We're catching the ferry to Dublin. If you ever… I mean if you want to come and see me. Here's my home phone number.'

'Ta, kid. I might just do that.' The hint of a smile puckered his lips.

'Good. See ye then.' Sean raised his arm in a hesitant wave, before turning away and sprinting back to the safety of Jack's car. They stayed long enough to see Duffy tear into the crusty bread and shake out his new sleeping bag.

After his chat with Duffy, Sean was subdued in the back of the car. Oona could well imagine how he was feeling. 'It seems terrible to just leave him there, Jack.'

'Not much else we can do, Oona! There are a hundred more just like him all over the city. If they kip in shop doorways, the police wake them up and move them on. It'd break your heart if we stayed around here much longer.' He sighed. 'If we're going to make the ferry, we'll have to go now.'

As they drove away from the derelict site, Oona pulled her cardigan closer around her. Just thinking about her son sleeping rough on the streets of Manchester sent a shiver through her body.

***

With Sean asleep on the back seat of the car, Oona closed her eyes and dozed off. Jack glanced across at her lovely face, her head to one side and a slight smile on her lips. They had hoped to call in on Jack's parents, but instead had to make do with a hurried phone call to his mother. She was disappointed at not seeing them but, at the risk of them missing the ferry, she understood and asked Jack to bring Oona and Sean over for a holiday in the autumn.

Now that Sean was safe and on his way home, Jack wanted to ask Oona to marry him. He couldn't do a proper job without an engagement ring but if he asked her on the ship, he would at least be sure of how she felt, one way or the other.

As they neared the port, the sound of the ship's horn brought them awake. Sean was still subdued. 'Aren't you excited to be going home?' his mother asked.

He moved forward in his seat until he was wedged between them both. 'Yes, but... Do you..? Will Granny and Grandad be cross with me when I get home?'

'Of course not! They'll be so happy to see you.'

Jack swung his car into the port and it was quickly taken away to be crane-lifted on board while they hurried up the gangplank onto the ship. 'I'm sure you'd like to do a bit of exploring, Sean. I gather you didn't see much of it on the journey over?'

'He told me to stay in the cabin all the time. It was boring.'

Oona looked at Jack and shook her head.

'Not much fun then,' Jack said.

Once the sailing was underway, the three went on deck and gazed back at the twinkling lights of Liverpool. 'We must come over and visit your parents again, Jack, very soon,' she said.

As they went back inside, Sean asked, 'Can I go around the ship on me own?'

'The boat's packed... will you..?'

'He'll be fine,' Jack reassured her.

She smiled. Of course he would. Everything was coming right, and she felt overjoyed to be taking her son home. While Sean explored, Oona and Jack walked on deck. The wind blew wildly, tossing her hair over her face. Jack let go of her hand to remove strands of her hair from her face. Smiling, she lifted her face to meet his gaze.

'Are you happy, Oona?'

She nodded. 'I never expected to reach this level of happiness again.'

'Then, marry me.'

'What!' Her eyes widened. Although it was what she had hoped for, it was still a shock to hear him say it. To be proposed to on a ship was, she thought, the most romantic of places.

'Is it too soon?'

She wanted to marry him more than anything and, after all they'd been through, it wasn't a moment too soon. But what about Sean? She hoped he liked Jack, but how would he feel about having another dad?

'Sean will be fine, you'll see.' It was as if he had read her thoughts.

'Do you really think so?'

He nodded. 'Yes. I do.' Then he kissed her lightly on the lips.

As the ferry moved into deeper waters and waves lapped the sides, Oona felt the fine spray wet her face and she could taste the salt on her lips. Jack took her hand and moved to a sheltered spot. He drew her close. 'Now, as I was saying. After the past few days, I'm sure we can cope with anything, don't you? So, what do you say? It needn't be straight away, just when you feel you're ready.'

Unable to contain her excitement, she threw her arms around his neck. 'Yes. Yes, I'll marry you.'

Their eyes met and, lifting her off her feet, he swung her round until, laughing, she called for him to put her down. Regardless of the passengers moving around them, he held her in his arms and buried his face in her hair. This time his kiss was long and passionate, leaving her breathless. When they drew apart, he said, 'Shall we go and find Sean, and maybe a bottle of something to celebrate?'

'I'm not sure if he's up to hearing something like this yet, Jack.'

'Oh.' He sounded disappointed. 'If you'd rather wait...' He pursed his lips.

'I'd like to tell my parents and Connie first.' She beamed him a smile.

They found Sean hanging over the ship's rails. Immediately concerned, Oona rushed towards him. 'Are you all right, Sean? Are you seasick?'

Raising his head, he laughed. 'No. I'm just looking at the waves. Do you think there's sharks in there?'

'Yes, Sean. There are Basking Sharks and others besides, and grey seals nearer the coastline.'

'Oh, let's go back inside,' Oona shivered. The idea of sharks swimming around so close to them made her uneasy. Suddenly the ship began to list, and Oona, unable to keep upright, reached for Jack. Sean loved every minute of it, his movements resembling someone who had had too much to drink.

'It'll soon pass,' Jack said. 'In the meantime, let's see if we can find something to eat.'

'Not for me.' Oona, feeling a bit queasy, wished she had eaten something earlier. 'I'm going for a lie down until the sea calms.' Making her excuses, she made her way towards the cabins, leaving Sean and Jack to look after each other.

CHAPTER FIFTY-EIGHT

After the past five exhausting days, Oona could hardly contain her joy to be home, with Sean looking none the worse for his ordeal. 'Isn't it just wonderful?'

'I can't wait to see everyone,' he said. They were hanging around in the draughty waiting room, drinking tea before Jack's car was off-loaded.

'It won't be long now, Sean.' She couldn't wait to see her family either; to see her mother's eyes light up once she saw her grandson again. Something else was giving Oona butterflies and she longed to share her good news with everyone. She hoped they would all be happy for her.

Before long, Jack was pulling up outside her parents' house. The door flew open and everyone rushed out, all except her mother who watched from the window, misty-eyed.

'Welcome home,' Connie said, tears in her eyes. She glanced lovingly at Sean, her arms outstretched. 'Come here, you.'

'You look... you look different, Connie.' Oona hugged her sister. 'What have you done to yourself?'

'Nothing.' She brushed off the remark with a smile. 'Just a new hairdo. We've all had sleepless nights here.'

Amid tears and hugs, Sean was hoisted up and carried inside by his grandad and Uncle Dessie to appetizing smells of fried sausages, eggs, rashers and fried bread. Annie was standing in the kitchen doorway, a look of sheer joy on her face.

Clambering down from his elevated position, Sean rushed into her arms. 'Thanks be t' God!' She hugged her grandson tight. 'Are you all right? That... that man didn't hurt you, did he?'

Sean shook his head. His grandmother clung to him as she shed more tears. When she released him, she turned her attentions to Jack 'We can't thank you enough for what you've done, Mr. Walsh.'

'Please, call me Jack. I was glad to help.'

'Please come through,' she said, walking ahead of them into the room where the dining table was set for breakfast. She placed Jack at the head of the table, as her husband took his place at the other end.

'Where's Shep?' Sean asked. The back door burst open and the dog, wagging its tail furiously, ran in, followed by Tommy. They all sat down to eat and enjoy being together again as a family. Suddenly the noise around the table grew to a crescendo, as one question followed another. Sean at times laughed then cried, as he retold his harrowing tale, bringing a tear to everyone's eyes. They were so engrossed that no-one heard the knock on the front door, until Sergeant McNally popped his head round the door.

'I hope you don't mind, but the door was on the catch.'

'Not at all, Sergeant. Come in and join us. Sit yourself down.' James O'Hara pulled over another chair. Annie poured tea and handed him a cup.

'What a joy to see a happy family again,' he said. 'I'm delighted that the boy is home safe and sound. So here's another bit of good news.' Everyone looked up. Oona stopped laughing and glanced towards Sean; he was hunkered down, stroking Shep.

'The police in the Isle of Man have arrested Vinnie Kelly, alias O'Leary, Dempsey, Cockran, and who knows how many other assumed names the man had. They got him on desertion of a minor while the child was in his care. He was working on the docks and some guy – one of his old cronies, probably, with a score to settle – informed the police. I can assure you that justice will be done.'

'Will he have to appear in the Dublin court?' A concerned

frown wrinkled Jack's face.

'No. Not necessarily, Mr. Walsh. I think the English police will deal with him appropriately. You're hardly likely to see him again.'

The smile slipped from Sean's face and silence descended the room. 'Why was my dad so bad, Grandad?'

James slipped his arm around the boy's shoulders. 'Well, he didn't have the love of a good mother and he couldn't integrate into family life, so I guess it made him bitter. But you've no need to worry about him any more.'

'I'm all right now, Grandad. I'm home with my family. And I'm never going away again, not until I'm at least sixteen.'

Smiling, Oona shook her head. 'Oh, not long then.' They all laughed.

'How about a game of footie?' Tommy suggested.

Shep barked and Sean did not need asking twice. The two boys disappeared, leaving the adults smiling. The news of Vinnie's arrest was the icing on the cake for Oona and her family and, for the first time in ages, she felt relaxed about Sean.

'Well, thanks for the tea, Mrs. O'Hara.' McNally got to his feet and turned towards Oona, who was pouring another cup for Jack. 'You know, I'm so pleased that things turned out the way they did, Mrs. Quinn. I'm sorry I didn't trust your instincts, but I did everything that I could with what I had.'

'Yes, I realise that, Sergeant.'

'You are an amazing young woman. You deserve to be happy and I wish you no less in the future.'

'Thanks for coming with that news, Sergeant. It's most reassuring.'

Nodding in agreement, James O'Hara stood up and went with the policeman to the door.

After he left, they continued to discuss Sean's father, until Jack glanced at his watch. 'Well, I'd better be getting off too. I've things to do. And you two,' he glanced towards Connie,

'I'm sure, will have lots of catching up to do.' As he reached over and squeezed Oona's hand, the gesture didn't go unnoticed.

'Before you go, Jack,' Oona held onto his hand. 'Mam, Dad, Jack has asked me to marry him and I've said yes.'

Connie screamed and rushed to her side, hugging them both. Everyone offered their congratulations. 'This seems to be a day for celebrations all round,' her mother said, smiling and glancing at Connie.

'Come on, our Connie,' her father chuckled. 'Your sister will be as pleased as punch to hear your news, now she's got Sean back.'

Placing her hands on her tummy, Connie said, 'I'm going to have a baby.' She bit back tears of joy. 'I've been dying to tell you.'

Oona's eyes widened and her mouth dropped open. Dessie came and stood next to his wife. 'It's true, Oona. We don't need to adopt after all.'

'Oh, Connie, this is wonderful news. The best homecoming ever,' Oona cried. She could not have been happier for her sister. What a perfect ending to the grief-stricken weeks of frustration and worry. Jumping to her feet, she threw her arms around Connie. 'When did you find out?'

'The day Sean went missing. I couldn't tell you then, we were all too upset. I still can't believe it.'

'Hold on,' Jack said. 'This calls for a real celebration.' He rushed outside to his car and carried in the rest of Oona's luggage, as well as a bottle of Italian red wine.

When Jack eventually left, saying that he would see her later, Oona found herself counting the hours.

Back in her own house, she was sorting out the washing when Sean dashed in, followed by Shep. 'Where's Jack?'

'Why, he's gone home, love. I'm sure he has things to do.' She smiled lovingly at her son. 'How are you feeling?'

'I'm fine. I can't wait to get back to school.'

Oona sat down at the table. 'That's great. Sean… I'd like… well, I have something to ask you! And I'm… I'm not sure how you'll feel about it.'

'What is it?' He slumped down into a chair. 'I don't want to talk about, you know, me dad. I don't want to think about him. He hurt you and he hurt me.'

'No, love.' She moved her chair closer. 'It's about Jack. Do you like him?'

'Yeah. He's okay.'

Oona bit her lip. Okay was a start, she supposed. At least it wasn't no, and it gave her confidence to continue. 'He's asked me to marry him, and I've said yes.' She paused, waiting for his reply, wondering what she would do if he got upset.

'I know.'

'You do? But how come?'

'Jack told me when you went for a lie down on the ferry. I said it was okay if it's what you wanted, but I told him I didn't want another dad.'

'Oh, love, really? And you don't mind?'

'I want you to be happy, Mam.'

Was this really Sean, concerned for her happiness, and with a grown-up attitude to life? 'Oh, Sean. That's just wonderful.' She swallowed to relieve a lump in her throat. 'And I want nothing less for you. It doesn't mean I'll ever forget Eamon. He'll always be your father.'

And when she hugged him, her son reciprocated, staying in her arms longer than she expected.

Then he said, 'It's nice to be home, Mam. Do you think Aunty Connie will have a baby boy?'

Smiling, Oona shook her head. 'We'll have to wait and see, son.'

CHAPTER FIFTY-NINE

Jack drove back to his flat, situated across the road from the sea front; he hoped it would fetch a good price once he put it on the market. He threw his travel bag onto the bed and got himself washed and shaved then changed into his best suit. There was something important he had to do after he had spoken to Mr. Mountjoy at Worldwide Shipping.

Brenda picked up the phone and, on hearing his voice, she whooped and hollered, 'It's Jack! They're back.'

Making the call her own, she bombarded him with questions. Jack did his best to placate her, knowing she had been anxious to hear news of Sean.

'Yes, grand thanks, Brenda. And yes, Sean is home safe and well,' he told her. 'How is Tim? I hope he is still settling in okay.'

He had expected a few complaints but was surprised when she praised Tim more than once.

'That's good. I'm pleased to hear it. I'll see you soon, but now, would you kindly put me through to Mr. Mountjoy?'

'Good man, Jack,' the man was clearly delighted to hear they were back. 'That's great news. Have the papers got wind of the boy's safe return yet?'

'We've not said anything, besides, the Irish press made nothing of it when Sean went missing in the first place. I've a feeling Oona won't want to make a fuss now that the lad's safe and well.'

'Too right! I'll see you next week, so.'

Smiling, Jack replaced the receiver.

Outside, he walked along the sea front, one hand inside his

trouser pocket, the fresh breeze blowing at his hair. He thought about Oona, recalling how brave she had been in England, especially when it had appeared at times that their search was hopeless. How she kept going in the face of such adversity, he'd never know! A rush of love engulfed him. He missed her already and hoped she was missing him too. He had never expected to find anyone like her, so strong and yet at times so vulnerable. Now he could not contemplate life without her.

He arrived outside the jeweller's shop, the one where he had bought his watch that hadn't lost a minute in two years. He glanced in the window, but the ring he had set his heart on buying for Oona was missing. The doorbell jangled as he stepped inside, and an elderly man in a grey pinstriped suit came out from behind a dark blue curtain at the back of the shop. 'How can I help you, sir?'

'A few weeks ago, you had an unusual engagement ring in the window. I'd never seen anything like it. It doesn't appear to be there now. Have you sold it?'

'Let me see.' He drew his fingers through his thinning hair and frowned, as if trying to remember. 'Can you describe it, sir?'

'Well. It was an emerald; a solitaire.'

'Oh, yes. I know just the one you mean, sir. It's one of our finest range and most expensive. You have, of course, seen the price; the reason I lock it in the safe at night.' The man paused to put on his spectacles. 'Would you like to see it?'

'Yes, please. I'd like to buy it, if it's the same ring.'

'Give me a moment. I'll fetch it for you.'

Jack stood patiently, rubbing his hands together. He knew Oona well enough now to know that she would love it. He had already made secret plans and now he could hardly wait to place the ring on her finger. It was some time since she had worn her late husband's engagement ring – a pretty cluster – although she continued to wear her wedding ring.

The man returned behind the polished mahogany counter.

He was holding a cushion with the emerald on top. 'Is this the ring you mean?' He laid it down in front of Jack.

'Yes, that's the one.'

'Do you have the young lady's finger measurement?'

'No, but it looks small enough. I'll take it anyhow.' If anything, it might be too big for Oona's small hands and slim fingers. But, without the ring, his plan would not work.

'I can see how much you want the ring, sir. I hope the young lady enjoys wearing it,' he said, reaching underneath the counter. Producing a cream, heart-shaped box, the elderly man placed the emerald inside. 'Of course, please bring it back if you have any problems.'

Jack handed over the cash and picked up his receipt. With the ring safe inside his pocket, he thanked the man and headed back to his flat, taking in the sea breeze as he walked.

There was one more important thing to do before tonight. Once in his car, he drove towards Dublin. He wondered what Oona was doing, if she was still at her mother's house chatting about Connie's pregnancy. He smiled to himself. Things had worked out well. Finding Sean and bringing him home safely had been nothing short of a miracle, especially when he recalled the kind of man Vinnie Kelly was. At least Sean now had a chance to continue growing up without his influence. Even so, he would not rest easy until the man was behind bars.

Sean appeared to have matured a little, perhaps as a result of his ordeal, and had so far shown no signs of disliking Jack. After what the lad had been through, Jack expected his trust would come gradually. Nevertheless, he felt confident that he would be able to create a happy family life for all three of them.

CHAPTER SIXTY

It was a balmy June evening. Oona ran her hand along the clothes hanging in her wardrobe. Although she had bought a few new outfits since receiving her compensation, she just could not make up her mind what to wear – the pink chiffon dress, or the sleeveless, peacock blue with a full skirt and sweeping white collar that buttoned to the waist. Once she tried it on, she decided on the latter, notching the white belt around her slim waist. With no idea where Jack was taking her – only that he was picking her up at seven-thirty – she hoped she was suitably dressed. She was so looking forward to seeing him again, to have a relaxing meal and share a bottle of wine to celebrate Sean's safe return. Her mother had gone to a Novena in thanksgiving, and Sean was with Connie and Dessie.

Her hair fell across her shoulders as she checked her make-up, adding a touch of mascara to her long lashes. She hardly recognized the girl looking back at her from the mirror. The worry that had weighed her down for so long had completely disappeared. She felt wonderfully happy, with nothing to occupy her except plans for their wedding day and their life together. Satisfied with her appearance, she picked up her white cardigan with the sparkly brooch her mother had bought her for her last birthday, and sat on the stairs waiting for the sound of Jack's car.

She was in love; something she never thought would happen to her again. In spite of the love she felt for Jack, there would always be a special place in her heart for Eamon. Now that she was moving on, she recalled what a devoted husband and father he had been. And her eyes glazed over when she thought of her darling daughter, Jacqueline, her baby girl. She would never forget them and knew that Jack would not want her to.

Tonight she was looking to the future and happier times. She checked her watch. It was just gone seven-thirty, so unlike Jack to be late, and she hoped he had not fallen asleep after all the driving he had done. Sean had surprised her by the way he had taken to Jack, and she was delighted at the way they were getting on.

The sound of a car horn alerted her and she hurried outside. She slid onto the seat next to Jack, who leaned across and kissed her. 'Where are we going?'

'It's a surprise.'

They cruised past fine houses with long pebbled driveways, until Jack pulled up outside what looked like a coaching house, with a courtyard and stables built alongside. It looked busy, with cars some parked on the pavement. Oona had passed Beaufield Mews before and had thought it to be a riding school, so when Jack turned off the engine, she looked towards him. 'Why have we stopped here? I'm hardly dressed for a riding lesson,' she giggled.

'You look absolutely gorgeous. I'll be the envy of every man in the room tonight.' Smiling, he stepped from the car and hurried round to open the door for her.

Intrigued, she gave him a quizzical look. 'What is this place?'

'Let's go inside and you'll see.'

Her eyes widened in anticipation. Taking her hand, he drew her towards the entrance. The doors gave the impression of opening onto a large barn, but instead she walked into the cozy ambiance of a restaurant, her feet sinking into rich red carpet.

'Well, I'd never have believed it,' Oona said, as a friendly waiter showed them to a table for two in a corner of the

Cathy Mansell

room. The bare stone walls were whitewashed and covered in a black trellis; it was unique, unlike anything she had ever seen before. With the restaurant so busy, she wondered how Jack had managed to book a table at such short notice, and then she remembered how persuasive he could be.

'This is charming, Jack. What a lovely surprise.'

'I hoped you'd like it.' He relaxed back into his chair, enjoying Oona's reaction as she gazed across at the marble bar then upwards to the wooden beams and the crystal chandeliers which gave the restaurant its old-fashioned atmosphere.

Their table was next to a small barn window, dressed with red checked curtains. Oona leaned across and whispered. 'Why has everything got a price tag?'

The waiter crossed the room and passed them each a menu.

'The young lady was wondering,' Jack said, glancing down the menu, 'why everything appears to be for sale?'

'We sell antiques, madam. Everything is for sale, from the table you dine on to the crockery you eat off. You'll find a price tag underneath.'

'How amazing!' She lifted the water jug to look, as Jack ordered her a Dubonnet and a Martini with ice for himself. As they sipped their drinks, their starters arrived. Oona had prawn cocktail and Jack the paté maison with smoked salmon. They both followed with the fresh trout and vegetables. Later, the waiter wheeled a dessert trolley from table to table.

'That was scrumptious, Jack. I don't know when I enjoyed food so much. Can we afford to pay for it?'

'I wouldn't worry, love,' he said, laughing. 'They can always put a price tag on us.'

She placed her crumpled napkin on the table. 'I can't remember the last time I felt so relaxed.'

He reached for her hand. 'Oona, I know how much

344

you've lost, both you and Sean, but I'll always be there for you both. Sean's a spirited boy and that's not a bad thing. If he thinks of me as a good friend, someone he can talk to, I'll settle for that.'

'Thank you, Jack. It means so much to hear you say that.' They kissed, oblivious to anyone who might have noticed.

'You're adorable. Do you know how much I love you?'

'Yes, I think I do.' They were holding hands across the table when Jack turned and nodded towards the waiter. He carried over a bottle of champagne in an ice bucket and began to pour them each a glass.

'Champagne!' Raising the glass, Oona felt the bubbles tickle her nose. 'What shall we drink to, Jack? So much has happened.'

'Tonight, my darling, we are celebrating our engagement and forthcoming wedding.' A second waiter handed Jack a small walnut box with Mother of Pearl inserts. 'This is for you, darling. I bought it as a keepsake to remind you of tonight.'

'Why, it's lovely.' She ran her finger over the raised Mother of Pearl. 'Is it an antique?'

'I believe so.' Jack slid the key across the veneer cherry table.

She felt a flush to her face and her heart race as she turned the key in the small lock. Inside, on a red velvet cushion, sat a stunning emerald engagement ring, surrounded by tiny diamonds. Her hand flew to her mouth. She was speechless.

'I know you've already agreed to marry me,' Jack was saying, 'but just so I believe it's real, I'd like to propose again. Properly, this time.' He got down on one knee.

Her eyes widened and couples, previously caught up in their own intimate chatter, stopped to glance their way. 'I love you, Oona, and I can't live without you in my life.' He took the ring from its cushion. 'Will you honour me by becoming my wife, and accept this ring as a token of my love?'

Her eyes pooled as she looked down at Jack. 'I love you, too, and I'd be proud to be your wife.' As he slipped the sparkling ring onto her finger, it fitted perfectly.

'Oh, Jack! What a stunning ring. It's so beautiful.' She reached down and their lips touched.

There were gasps and smiles of delight as everyone, including the waiters, clapped and wished them many years of happy married life. Oona looked into the eyes of the man who loved her and she knew that their love, grown out of mutual respect, would endure. Nothing would break the bond between them.

ABOUT CATHY MANSELL

Cathy Mansell writes romantic fiction. Her recently written family sagas are set in her home country of Ireland. One of these sagas closely explores her affinities with Dublin and Leicester. Her children's stories are frequently broadcast on local radio and she also writes newspaper and magazine articles. Cathy has lived in Leicester for fifty years. She belongs to Leicester Writers' Club and edited an Arts Council-funded anthology of work by Lutterworth Writers, of which she is president.

GET IN TOUCH WITH CATHY MANSELL

Cathy Mansell
(http://cathymansell.com)

Facebook
(http://www.facebook.com/cathy.mansell4)

Twitter
(https://twitter.com/ashbymagna)

Tirgearr Publishing
(http://www.tirpub.com/cmansell)

Thank you for reading Shadow Across the Liffey

Please log into Tirgearr Publishing
(www.tirgearrpublishing.com)
and Cathy Mansell's website for upcoming releases.

Cover Art: Amanda Stephanie
Editor: Christine McPherson
Proofreader: Kemberlee Shortland

More From Cathy Mansell

Her Father's Daughter

Set in 1950s Ireland, twenty-year-old Sarah Nolan leaves her Dublin home after a series of arguments. She's taken a job in Cork City with The Gazette, a move her parents strongly oppose. With her limited budget, she is forced to take unsavoury accommodations where the landlord can't be trusted. Soon after she settles in, Sarah befriends sixteen-year-old Lucy who has been left abandoned and pregnant.

Dan Madden is a charming and flirtatious journalist who wins Sarah's heart. He promises to end his engagement with Ruth, but can Sarah trust him to keep his word?

It's when her employer asks to see her birth certificate that Sarah discovers some long-hidden secrets. Her parents' behaviour continue to baffle her and her problems with Dan and Lucy multiply.

Will Dan stand by Sarah in her time of need? Will Sarah be able to help Lucy keep her baby? Or will the secrets destroy Sarah and everything she dreams of for her future?